# Coffins

# Coffins

Rodman Philbrick

FORGE®

A Tom Doherty Associates Book
New York

COFFINS

Copyright © 2002 by Rodman Philbrick

This book is printed on acid-free paper.

Design by Jane Adele Regina

A Forge Book
Published by Tom Doherty Associates, LLC
175 Fifth Avenue
New York, NY 10010

www.tor.com

Forge® is a registered trademark of Tom Doherty Associates, LLC.

ISBN 0-312-87273-9

First Edition: February 2002

Printed in the United States of America

0  9  8  7  6  5  4  3  2  1

For the Friday night transcendental billiard boys:
Dennis, Julian, Ronan, Steve, Sol, and Tim,
whose conversations helped steer this book to port—
and a fine smooth port it was, too!

# EDITOR'S NOTE

The following manuscript was assembled from the contents of four notebooks and a ship's log recovered from the effects of Davis A. Bentwood, a battlefield surgeon with the 20th Maine, under the command of Joshua Chamberlain at Gettysburg. The personal notebooks were bound in calfskin and imprinted with the author's name and rank, and are generally in a good state of preservation. The ship's log is partially water-damaged, and bears stains of what was recently determined to be human blood. Although not authored by Dr. Bentwood, the ship's log was firmly bound to his own notebooks with a stout black ribbon, of the type used for armband mourning displays in the nineteenth century. The material was found among the thousands of other objects of Civil War memorabilia collected by Mr. Denton Wattle, late of York, Maine.

It was Mr. Wattle's heir, Miriam Coffin Wattle, who first brought the Bentwood material to my attention. Indeed she may have been the first person to actually read Dr. Bentwood's strange narrative, after locating the notebooks and the attached ship's log in the false bottom of the surgeon's monogrammed medical valise, which had been part of the immense and impressive Wattle Collection for at least fifty years.

I have been able to determine that a Davis A. Bentwood did indeed enlist with Chamberlain's famous fighting corps, at the rank of captain, which was typical for a medical officer. An examination of the archives of Harvard Medical School prove beyond a doubt the narrative was written in Bentwood's very distinctive hand. Other than that, I cannot vouch for the veracity of what he wrote, as the events he describes in such chilling detail were never mentioned in any contemporary newspaper or journal.

Read it and judge for yourself.

*Rodman Philbrick*
*Kittery, Maine*

# Coffins

# I

# MANIFESTATIONS

*The vanished gods to me appear;*
*And one to me are shame and fear.*

RALPH WALDO EMERSON

## March 4, 1861
### White Harbor, Maine

We were playing pinochle in the parlor, cousin Lucy and I, when the screaming began.

The parlor was the darkest of the many rooms in the Coffin mansion, and my right hand was wrapped protectively around a glass of whiskey, not my first. You should know that I am not a drinking man, not usually, but this was an unusual evening, all things considered, and the draught of fine Kentucky sour mash had a calming affect upon my shattered nerves. It enabled me to deal the cards without trembling much, and if beautiful dark-haired Lucy—Lucy of the startlingly pale, icicle-blue eyes—if Lucy noticed my discomfort she did not comment upon it. She was aware of what had happened in the tower earlier that day, and since the Coffins did not speak of madness in the family, and in particular of the Captain's white-eyed, pistol-waving madness, we spoke instead of trifling things. The scandalous price of the sperm oil that barely illuminated the gloomy room. The fair weather that seemed to promise a mild winter. Jeb's new hat. Barky's remarkable cooking.

Meanwhile I concentrated on the turn of the cards, and Lucy's trill of laughter when she won, which was most of the time.

"Does your friend Emerson play at cards?" she wanted to know as she lay down yet another triumphant hand.

"I assume he does," I said. "Though as you know Mr. Emerson is not exactly my friend."

"Not exactly?" said Lucy with a teasing smile. "What is he to you then, the great man?"

"More a mentor than a friend. His writing guides me, and his sermons."

"Then you're what, a transcendentalist? Do I say the word correctly?"

"Exactly so," I said, shuffling the cards together.

"So tell me, Dr. Bentwood, does a transcendentalist believe in God?"

The question was not unfamiliar, and I answered it as I usually do, with the reasoned equanimity of a modern man of science. "What is God? If God is an eye hovering over the wilderness, an eye whose light gives us life, and meaning, then yes, I believe in God."

My companion smirked prettily. "God as a floating eyeball? How very strange, Dr. Bentwood."

"Please," I asked, "call me Davis."

"Davis," Lucy said, as if savoring the word, or tasting the name, which put a delicious shiver through me. "Tell me, Davis, does this floating God of yours believe in you?"

I was searching for a witty remark, something wise and amusing, something to impress this ravishing young woman, whose dark beauty seemed strangely suited to her modest, and very plain, black mourning attire, when the first scream came echoing through the empty rooms of the great house.

Lucy stood at once, as did I.

"No," she whispered, as if to herself. "Not again."

*Not again.* And yet this was, so far as I knew, the first such scream, although not, as it happened, the last. Far from the last.

"The nursery," cried Lucy. "Sarah!"

Sarah was her cousin Nathaniel's wife, and mother of a

newly christened infant. Sarah had impressed me as a quiet, sober, intelligent sort of woman, and the thought of her crying out from the nursery made my blood run as cold as the currents in the harbor that lay a thousand yards from us, full of ships snug at their winter moorings.

I held the lamp but let my companion guide us, for in the last few days I'd more than once gotten lost in the maze of rooms and intersecting hallways. Lucy, however, was surefooted, and rushed ahead, a rustle of black crinoline vanishing into the darkness. I followed the sound of her running feet as much as the vague shape of her, but she was soon lost in the shadows. Leaving me alone with the house all around me.

The first spate of screaming had settled into an awful keening, and it was that mournful quality that cleared my head of whiskey. Something terrible had happened, and the thrill of that now familiar fear—an unspeakable fear that had first manifested itself that morning in a visit to the family crypt, and continued unabated through my terrifying experience in the tower—made me want to race for the front porch and down the steps, and away from this awful house.

I did no such thing, of course, being a gentleman and a friend of the family. Instead I steeled myself against the keening and attempted to follow that wretched, heartrending sound through the dark hallways.

"Are you there?" I called out, affecting a calmness I did not feel. "Am I near?"

Another scream echoed. Not Sarah, this time, but cousin Lucy. A scream distinct and vibrant, and yet for the life of me I could not place the direction. Something about the way sound carried within the cavernous house was strangely disorienting. The keening echoed weirdly, and at times seemed to emanate from the very walls, as if the house itself gave voice to a terrifying despair.

Finally I stopped and set the lamp upon the floor, and

attempted to somehow get my bearings. There. The sound was definitely coming from behind. I picked up the lamp, retraced my steps, and with my empty hand found a break in the wall, an intersection with yet another hallway. In the distance— how far I could not tell—a light glowed faintly. Making my way toward the light, I came upon the nursery at last, and the source of the horrible keening.

Inside the nursery an oak fire blazed in the hearth. My first impression upon stumbling into the small, low-ceilinged room was that the place was stifling, the air close and fragrant with the mingled scents of perfumed powder and something that might have been milk. Baby smells, and something else—the sweat of fear.

Two women were embraced near the hearth, as if poised for a sentimental silhouette. Lucy, her arms enfolded around the sobbing, keening Sarah, whose face was buried in her cousin's shoulder. Lucy looked at me beseechingly, willing me to take charge of the situation, as custom and friendship demanded.

Nathaniel Coffin, Sarah's husband, stood by the crib, his broad-shouldered, six-foot frame stooped with grief. I went to him, still holding the lamp, but he was at first oblivious to my presence.

"Casey," his broken voice whispered. "Poor little Casey."

"Let me see," I said gently. "Maybe I can be of help."

But the baby lay unmoving in the center of the crib, with an utter stillness that meant there was nothing to be done. Tangled around his tiny feet was the soft lamb's-wool blanket he'd evidently kicked away; and no wonder, for the room was as warm as a summer day. Then, holding the lamp aloft, I noticed that the infant's skin had taken on a strange blue hue. Blue and glistening.

"He's froze up hard," Nathaniel murmured, his big hands

gripping the sides of the crib so firmly that his knuckles had gone as white as his face.

*Froze up hard.* Was this some local expression for the death that so frequently came to newborn babies, snuffing them in their cradles? I reached out to touch little Casey, and my hand encountered not the soft, lifeless flesh I'd expected, but a hard and icy coldness. A cold so intense it instantly numbed my fingers.

"My God!"

The baby was not simply dead, it was frozen solid.

# 1. A Stern Angel

It all began, I suppose, the day I first saw the abolitionist dwarf waddling across Harvard Yard. This was in the year 1857, in Cambridge, Massachusetts, where I was completing medical school and contemplating a life of well-disciplined leisure. I'd recently inherited a small but tidy fortune that would enable me to live quite comfortably without having to enter practice, or apprentice with a surgeon, options that lately had begun to seem more and more unsuitable to my nature. My ambition, if you can call it that, was to be an amateur scientist, in the tradition of America's great lightning bug, Benjamin Franklin, save that I would trap transcendentalism in a jar, and make it charge the battery of the mind.

My name is Davis Arthur Bentwood, distant but sole-surviving relation to the owners of the now-defunct Bentwood Mills, and the dwarf (the one in the Yard, the abolitionist) went by the name of Jeb, alias Jebediah Coffin, of the famous, seafaring Coffins of White Harbor, Maine. The strange little gnome of a man was famous for his fanatical attachment to the cause of ending slavery, violently if need be. Violently because young Coffin had, despite his diminutive size, beaten a student of contrary opinion with a knobbed cane and been brought up on charges, dismissed when an amused magistrate saw what was before him.

"That one so small holds opinions so large is bound to cause trouble," the magistrate had said, looking down from the bench to where Jeb stood, his largish head no higher than the desk behind which his lawyers cowered. "I admonish you to relinquish the cane, if not the cause."

The defendant surrendered the weapon and promptly acquired an exact duplicate. Or so it was reported in *The Liberator*, an abolitionist broadside. But then abolitionists have been known to bend the truth if it serves their purpose, and for all I know the entire scene was improved upon. Suffice to say it made Jebediah Coffin an object of even more curiosity, including certain salacious comments overheard from the painted, gin-scented mouth of a not-too-particular female who made her living granting amorous interludes to some of the more depraved undergraduates.

"You want the scale of the thing," she had cackled, "look to that big head of his, not to his hands, no bigger'n a child's hands them are. But the thing of him, I swear, larger than the usual by the length of my thumb, ha!"

Oh, yes, there was much speculation about the odd little man, most of it unkind. For in the company of his fellow students he would not play the clown, as was expected of a man with his affliction. An observer sensed this instantly, by the way he held his head—handsome and noble enough to be inscribed on a coin—and by the will with which he forced his small, twisted body into an aspect of proper, gentlemanly posture, with his short little back held straight as a ramrod. I have described his walk as a waddle, and it is true it had something in the way of a waddle; it must have, given the shortness of his legs. But there was an element of strutting, too, the restrained but nevertheless confident strut of one who has hitched his wagon to a star, and knows it.

Emerson again, for when my mind seeks a way through the complexities of recollection, I hitch myself to the sage of Concord, and try to see things as he might see them. What would the great thinker make of Jebediah Coffin, whose tem-

perament was as foreign to reasoned philosophical contemplation as China is to Arkansas? Jeb who cared little for Nature,
and less for Religion? Jeb whose wrath was not the wrath of a
vengeful God, not John Brown's righteous fury, but the
rational anger of a human being who sees a great injustice and
cannot rest until it has been expunged from the earth?

I understood or sensed only the smallest part of this, of
him, that first day in the Yard, where I witnessed an incident of
casual, thoughtless cruelty. A mob of street boys had followed
the dapper little man in from the Square and made him the
target of their mockery. Taunting him with "There's the freak,
where's the sideshow?" and the like. Nothing very imaginative,
just what you might expect from a pack of idlers who had
endured, no doubt, much cruelty themselves. The boys pecked
at him as pigeons will do when one of their number shows
deformity, and oh, how they suffered for it. The boys, I mean,
not the pigeons.

I witnessed the incident from a short distance away, while
exiting a lecture hall, and was about to intercede when something about the small man's demeanor gave me pause. From
my vantage his great and noble head was in profile. The skull
was strong and well molded, with a powerful, slightly hooked
nose and a fine curl to his lips. Beneath his tall black stovepipe
hat, hair the color of raw honey fell in thick waves to his
shoulders, and seemed to surround his head in a nimbus of
light, as if he were a stern angel painted on some popish altar.
But it was the set of his jaw that paused me, for he had the
fore-thrust, deeply cleft chin of a man who would brook no
interference, and quite possibly curse the fool who dared to
offer.

This, then, was the man the gang of youths taunted, pranc-
ing about in crude imitation of his reduced stature, and his distinct, upright manner of walking. At first the little man did not
react, continuing on his way as if they did not exist, serene and

dignified in his exquisitely tailored black frock coat and his gleaming patent leather boots. Serene and oblivious until the tallest of the n'er-do-wells blocked his path and knocked the tall hat from his head.

"Looky here, boys! It ain't got horns, but it might've sawed 'em off, like they do with cattle. Is that what happened, after them demon horns ripped out yer mama's belly? Sawed 'em off did you? Any stumps left, eh? Here, let me touch 'em for luck."

The boy, the biggest of the gang, made the mistake of reaching out to brush the dwarf's hair away, as if looking for evidence of the "demon horns," which surely he did not believe existed except as a means of tormenting a victim half his size. The boy's mistake being that his victim, though small, was far from defenseless.

In a flash the cane was rammed into the youth's lean belly with such force that it looked at first to be a fatal blow, and might well have proved so, had it not been the blunt end of the cane.

Dumbstruck by the unexpected turn of events, the other boys hesitated before reacting, but then gathered up their courage and swarmed forward, intent upon rescuing their leader. But the dwarf stood over the groaning bully and waved his cane like a scythe, holding his ground. "Back, or I'll slit his throat with my fingernail! Demon nails are sharp as razors!" he roared, making a claw of his small and harmless-looking hand.

The gang of toughs hesitated, and he saw he had their measure.

"Yes, I've lost my demon horns," said the dwarf, fastening his eyes upon them with an intensity that made the boys quiver. "But still I can see the future. Your future. You!" he said, indicating a particular boy, a youth with skin like coddled milk. "You shall die a coward's death, running away from battle, and be shot in the gut by your own officers. You shall live in agony for three days and die with your mouth and eyes open. Flies will enter your throat and breed maggots in your eyes before your death. And you!" he said, picking another youth, "you will have your legs sawed off by a man who stinks of whiskey, and gangrene will eat the stumps and then the stumps will be sawed off, and when eventually you return to this place you'll be shorter than me, and you shall remember this day, and rue it, and end your wretched life by drinking lye."

Boys of all types are a superstitious lot, and these shrank from the dwarf, in the belief that he could, as he claimed, foresee their deaths. Death which had, I suppose, never been imagined until that moment, or certainly not in such horrific detail. For if they had seen a drowned body or two bobbing in the Charles, as any street boy might, or a man crushed by a horse, as had happened only last week, right in the Square, and no doubt innumerable relatives laid out and waked, never had they looked at death and seen themselves.

All of the foreseen deaths were the result of war, a notion the dwarf clearly relished. "You'll try to hide behind the cannon mounts," he told one pale-faced youth, "shitting your drawers in terror. But when the shell strikes it blows the rampart to hell, and you with it, a splinter of oak through your shriveled heart."

At that moment the prostrate gang leader revived enough to grab the dwarf's cane, catching him by surprise. The bloody-mouthed youth was attempting to force the smaller man to the ground and beat him with his own cane when I finally intervened.

Normally a gang of street boys wouldn't turn tail and run at the sight of a single adversary, even a full-grown specimen as sturdily built as myself. But they'd been shaken by the visions of destruction visited upon them by the dwarf—who, for all they knew, really did have the powers of prophesy—and so they fled, dragging their leader with them, and left me to hand the little man his tall silk hat. A very expensive item, with the label of an exclusive Boston haberdashery, and it was, I noted, somewhat larger in size than my own.

"Thank you, sir," he said, rather gruffly.

"Not at all," I responded. "You had them well in hand. Or maybe I should say 'well in mind,' for you got inside their thick skulls and gave 'em the fright they so richly deserved."

"You think so?" he said, studying me, unsure of my intentions.

"Davis Bentwood," I said, offering my hand. "I'd be most pleased if you'd join me for a brandy. You'll notice my hand trembling, even if yours is not."

Looking up at me were a pair of eyes as bright and filled with light as a wave about to crest in a clear blue sea. Truth-seeking eyes, and they found enough truth in my good intentions to agree that yes, a brandy might be just the thing.

And so we repaired to my rooms, uncorked a bottle, and raised our glasses eagerly, for by then we both knew, without having to speak of it, that we were well on our way to becoming friends. "I have only one request," I said before drinking. "Don't, please, say how or when I will die."

Jeb's face—remarkably well formed, if out of proportion to his body—creased with a smile that made me feel the sun was out, and heaven had come upon the earth.

"There's nothing whatever to say upon the subject," he said. "Because you're going to live forever."

That was but the first of many lies that would be told by my dear friend Jebediah Coffin. Who drew me into a horror he could not comprehend, though in some ways he was the unwitting cause of it. For no man is truly innocent, that much I have learned, even if he lives on the side of angels.

## 2. Collectors of the Heavenly Spark

Had I all the time in the world, now would begin a lengthy recollection of how my friendship with Jebediah Coffin shaped itself over the years. How, exactly, our contrasting natures formed a bond, as if two opposite elements, once combined, made an unbreakable mortar, binding flint to granite. Jeb being the flint, of course, and myself the boring, unsparkable granite.

But as to time—there is none. My hand races ahead of the bullet that will soon make an end of me, and so I must trust the reader to imagine that such a friendship does indeed exist. That is, between a stolid, scientifically trained, philosophically inclined dilettante (myself), a contemplator of Science and Nature and Self (and his own navel, as Jeb would say), and a curiously crippled, intensely focused man of action, who thought little enough about himself, and nothing whatever about the nature of Thought.

In any event, three years later, on the last day of February 1861, I placed myself upon a train leaving Boston for Portland, Maine, having been summoned by an urgent telegram.

TWO COFFINS BURIED THIS DAY. THE CAPTAIN INSENSIBLE WITH GRIEF. YOU ARE NEEDED, PLEASE COME AT ONCE.

JEBEDIAH, WHITE HARBOR

"Two Coffins buried" must, I assumed, mean that two of his family had recently passed away. The Captain had to be his father, revered by Jeb and invariably referred to by his mariner's title. The Captain said this, the Captain did that, always in a tone implying the highest kind of filial devotion. So if I parsed it right, the patriarch of the Coffin family was insensible with the tragedy, and Jeb, in his distress, had need of a friend.

Naturally I could not refuse. Indeed, I packed up clothing suitable for mourning and boarded the train eagerly. I am ashamed to say the darker part of my nature was glad of the excuse to leave the smoke and stink of the city for an excursion into what I envisioned to be a kind of salty paradise. I pictured slumbering mountains sloping gently to a pine-treed shore. White sails luffing in a still and perfect harbor. A church steeple poised to pierce clouds of cotton bunting. For my image of White Harbor was derived entirely from a painted postcard that I carried in my breast pocket as a reminder of destination, to be consulted frequently, if not mooned over.

White Harbor, Maine. Surely, despite the expected lamentations, and the orderly rituals of grief (with which I was all too familiar, having buried the sum total of my blood relations), the change of scenery would be most welcome. My work, if it could be called work, had not been going well. To be truthful, it had not been "going" at all.

Each day at noon, having wasted as much of the morning as possible over a late breakfast, I would finally, gingerly, sit down at my desk and take up my pen—and then stare for hours at the blank page before me. My book had a lofty title, *The Transcendental Journey, Reflections on the Teachings of Ralph Waldo Emerson*. Oh, yes, a lofty title and little else, for I'd torn up a number of false starts and at present my "book" was comprised of a few scribbled notes and an outline that had been revised so many times it no longer made sense to the would-be author.

I'd not much to show after nearly a year of labor. You think me lazy, but there's nothing more exhausting than attempting to force that which will not come. Say to yourself "I shall write a fine poem, as good as any by Byron or Tennyson." Now take up your pen and begin. What's the problem—can't think of a first line? A first word? No? Try starting with the letter "A," as in "A fool attempts to mimic his betters."

So I left my unfinished book behind, spurned like a reluctant lover, and hurried off to the wilds of Maine with barely a twinge of regret.

Jebediah I had not seen for some months. He'd given up his rooms in Cambridge and had been accompanying various fanatical abolitionists to rallies and lectures throughout the Northern states. Though he never himself took the stage, my little friend was the force behind many an impassioned speech, and acted as a financial backer, paying expenses for the speakers, who invariably had vast appetites. Lately, with the prospect of war more and more likely, the abolitionist cause seemed to be at one with the idea of battle, and the true believers spoke of the necessity of spilling blood. At the time I was of two minds regarding this unfortunate situation; opposed to slavery, and equally opposed to war, for what can be settled by cacophonous battle, when the true freedom of man is held within?

I was soon to find out, in a way unimaginable.

The Boston & Maine Railroad crosses into Maine through the sleepy hamlet of Dover, New Hampshire. From there it is a little more than two hours to Portland, the primary port and by far the largest city in the state. The industrious nature of the Portland waterfront rivals that of Boston, and is in some ways more hectic, with ships and schooners and lighters plying what seemed every square yard of the bay. Hundreds of vessels were lashed or moored to all available docking space, often rafted five or six deep, making the air bristle with a forest of spars and masts. The citizens liked to say that a man could walk from one end of Casco Bay to the other without getting his feet wet, simply by trodding upon boats. They're exaggerating, but not by much.

A hackney coach conveyed me from the train station to the main wharves, where a ferry service would, I was told, provide a more direct route to White Harbor than could be had by land. My destination lay a little less than twenty miles east by sea, whereas the overland route was nearer forty, due to the curvaceous nature of the coastline. There were certain villages in these parts separated by no more than a few miles of water, whose remove by the shoreline route exceeded a hundred miles.

All of this information, possibly quite dubious, was had from the loquacious hack driver as we bumped over the cobbles of Exchange Street, avoiding clumps of snow and ice. The Downeaster of legend may be taciturn, but the real item is far from it. The locals have, it is true, developed a slower manner of speech than is common in Boston, but they make up for it with a dry wit, and a tendency to constantly amend and improve their answers with amusing anecdotes. So it was with the hack, who, upon hearing where I was headed, assured me that my destination was home to more master mariners than in any other place on earth.

"Near a hundred ship captains sail out of White Harbor, in every kind of vessel, from whalers bound for the frozen oceans to coasters that never lose sight of Portland Light. 'Tis a breeding ground for mariners, and captains in particular," he drawled, as if delighted to have a subject on which to converse, and show off his expertise. "The cows there drink straight from the salt marsh, and everyone knows that salty milk is what makes boys take to the water. White Harbor babies are toothed on hardtack biscuits and rum, and sleep in sailor hammocks. Every house is built like a copper-bottomed ship and stinks of tar, and their privies of bilge water. The captains stand watch at home, just as they would at sea, and sail their proud little village through the universe. As to the Coffins, aye, course I've heard of 'em, everyone has. They're the best of the lot, and the boss of them all is Cassius Coffin, what's called Cash, for the very reason that he's the richer than Croesus."

Cash Coffin. It was the first time I'd heard him called that. To Jeb he was always "the Captain" or, more rarely, "my dear father." As to more specific information about the family, or any recent deaths therein, the hack had none, or if he did was not willing to share it.

Curiously, though I'd spent many an hour in deep conversation with my diminutive friend, I had only the vaguest sort of impression about his family. A tribe of seafarers, I knew that much, of course, and that Jeb was the youngest of six brothers. But our impassioned talks had more to do with issues than with the personal, and now that I was about to invade his home territory, I felt the need to gird myself with whatever information I could gather, and so behave accordingly, with less risk of offense.

The friendly hack left me at the ferry landing with a bit of droll advice. "If you feel the need to puke, seek the rail away from the wind."

A surprise awaited me in the ferry building, when a suspicious-looking fellow waylaid me, placing his gnarled hand upon my shoulder.

"Be you Dr. Davis Bentwood?" he muttered, in a voice that sounded like something shaken from a bag of broken glass.

Startled, I confessed my identity. Before me was one who might have modeled for an illustration entitled "Old Tar." He had bandy legs and a sailor's pigtail jutting from under a knit wool cap. As well he was dressed in a worn pea jacket of dark blue wool, knee-high boots, and a black eye patch. In his face were etched the lines of a hundred voyages, and the scars, no doubt, of more than a few battles and waterfront skirmishes.

"We wuz sent by Jebediah," the Old Tar hissed, fixing his claw upon my elbow and attempting to guide me, none too gently.

My first impulse was to resist, for I find the touch of a stranger a loathsome intrusion. But before I could react, another salty character—slightly younger, but no less shop-worn—grabbed hold of my bags and began to stalk off.

When the Old Tar saw my eyes flash, he attempted to explain. "I beg you take no offense, Dr. Bentwood," said he. "But only Jebediah is in a great hurry to have you home. We've brought a fast schooner for that purpose, but the ebb is almost gone and you'll have to shake a leg or miss the tide."

"And who might you be?" I demanded, attempting to maintain some dignity as I was being hurried along the docks.

"Black Jack Sweeney at your service," rumbled the Old Tar, grasping me by the hand. "And as you're a friend to Jeb, I take you to my bosom, for we all love the boy."

"All?" I sputtered. "Who, might I ask, is 'all'?"

"Why, the Captain's crew," he said, as if it was the most obvious of answers, and would allay my fears. "Hurry now, son! Step along right quick and we'll be on our way!"

Our little ship was the sleekest of schooners, with a long delicate bowsprit, steeply raked masts, and a low, beautifully shaped hull that bore little or no resemblance to the tubby coasters used for the ferry trade. The hull itself was painted black, with a tasteful gold filigree below the rail, and the letters "RAVEN" carved upon the stern and filled with glittering gold leaf.

"You'll naught find a faster ship for her length," said the tar who called himself Black Jack. "Ninety feet from stem to stern, and flies like a bird, I swear, a lovely swift seabird, and not the raven she's named for. But wait, you'll see for yourself soon enough. Aboard, and quickly! Boys, let go the lines! There and there! Jump and pull, you buggers, jump!"

Four of his men leaped into a small narrow launch and by the use of long oars and strong backs pulled *Raven*'s bow away from the wharf. Black Jack roared orders, causing the sails to be run up. "Heave up, lads, heave up! For your lives, heave up!" As the bowsprit came by the wind, the canvas filled with what sounded very like a rumble of thunder, and suddenly the schooner came alive, as a thoroughbred might to the crack of a whip, and it was all the oarsmen could do to get back aboard and stow their little boat before we were under way.

Moments later, under a full press of sail, *Raven* flew through the crowded harbor, drawing looks of astonishment from those employed on the many moored vessels we so narrowly missed. More than once we came near enough to reach out and touch the rail of another ship as we cut and dodged and came about. And yet I never once felt we were in danger of actual collision, for it was immediately obvious that with old, one-eyed Jack at the wheel, the schooner was under a master's hand. Of those who watched us pass, many would have agreed, for I saw in their startled eyes an admiration for so lively a vessel, so handsomely managed.

In no time at all we cleared Portland Light and veered east from the shores of Cape Elizabeth, where a grove of maple trees raised bare branches to the sky, as if wanting to scratch the clouds from the sky. It was a glorious winter day, bright and clean, and the air was so fresh and bracing that I felt my heart bloom in a way I hadn't experienced while confined to the city. Something to do with the ever-changing, ever-forming white-caps, or the salty spray, or the glorious hum of the wind in the rigging—whatever it was, my wild ride in *Raven* made me alive to myself, sensitive to the heavenly spark within. Thoreau can have his pond: give me a fast ship, the sparkled sea, and the coast of Maine!

With Portland Light dwindling in our wake, our one-eyed master stopped shouting orders and stood by the great spoked wheel, steering with supreme confidence as he puffed on a long clay pipe. "Ain't she a beauty?" he asked me, squinting up at what seemed a mile or two of canvas spread above us.

I agreed there was never a vessel more beautiful, and this prompted a small lecture on the various features of this particular and unique design, most of which went over my head. But my willingness to listen, and to prompt further details, pleased my host, and he looked on me with such a friendly (if still slightly frightening) visage I felt free to ask how he'd come by his name.

"Aye, the Black Jack of me," he said, puffing contentedly on his pipe. "Because for a time I was held captive in Senegal, in Africa, and lived among the wretched slaves in their barracoons."

"Indeed?" I said, astonished. "And when was this?"

But something like a cloud passed over one-eyed Jack's expression, and he would speak no more of it, but steered our conversation to a discussion of the ship. So intimate was he with the behavior of sailing vessels that he was able to communicate a sense of what he knew, even to so ignorant a lubber as myself. He told me *Raven*'s lines were drawn by a naval architect in Baltimore—hence the raked masts—but that she'd been built of stout Maine oak in a yard in Waldoboro. "Every board-foot from the Captain's own wood lots," he added with a grunt of satisfaction, "and the cabins paneled in white cedar, so the whole ship smells like a lady's wardrobe, fresh as a new-cut shaving. The spars, well, there's the exception, for they were carried down from New Hampshire, though cut by Maine men, straight and true."

I expected him to mention what Coffins, exactly, had just been recently buried, but despite my broad hints he affected not to get my meaning, save only to mention, as an aside, that it was bad luck to name the dead while aboard a ship.

"Have a cigar, Dr. Bentwood," he advised, handing me a prime Havana robusto from his waistcoat pocket. "Rest easy and we'll make port before you finish your smoke."

And so we raced east on a broad reach, sails taut, our slim hull cutting through the seas like a surgeon's knife, and for a time my worries were left in the wake that boiled behind us. I remember every detail of that glorious passage, and how my heart lifted with each surge of the bowsprit. I somehow managed to convince myself that whatever troubles might lie ahead, they were no more than the usual human trifles and tribulations.

This was the plan I embraced in all my insufferable ignorance: I would comfort a friend, take strength from the vigor of Nature, and then return to the plodding business of writing my book. A brief relief from citified drudgery, nothing more, then back to work, where, like my hero Emerson, I would attempt to collect the heavenly spark and discharge it upon my readers.

Blame it on the folly of youth, or the wind in my face, but I knew no better, and was all the happier for it.

# 3. Men As Bolts of Lightning

The postcard did not lie. If anything, White Harbor was even more serene and beautiful than the painted image fixed in my mind. The mountains to the north sloped gently down to a shoreline stiff with tall pine trees, dark green boughs lightly dusted with the fluffiest and whitest snow. Within the village proper stood a great number of white clapboard houses with cedar shingled roofs. The largest of them was set upon a hill, and equipped with a central tower no less high than the church steeple. The harbor itself, protected from the prevailing winds by a low, rocky promontory, was as calm and pristine as anyone could wish. Most of the vessels—and there were more than could be counted, of all types and sizes—were neatly moored fore-and-aft. The impression was of order and precision, in contrast to the frantic confusion of Portland.

Surely this was the perfect landfall, I decided, while our one-eyed master sailed *Raven* through the rows of watercraft and brought the proud little ship up to her mooring. The man was as good as his promise, for the cigar stub was still hot in my fingers as the stern swung round and the sails were dropped and folded.

"Take Dr. Bentwood ashore, smartly now!" came the order, and without quite knowing how it came to pass I found myself in the launch, being rowed by two energetic sailors who bared their tobacco-stained teeth in silent if somewhat ferocious smiles.

Upon the village wharf was a small figure, dressed entirely in black, from great coat to boots. The figure paced energetically, now and then waving his arms, as if exhorting the launch to move faster, which was scarcely possible. As we approached, my little friend raised his tall, stovepipe hat and hailed me, his distinctive voice booming over the water.

"Davis Bentwood!" he shouted. "Friend to Man and friend of mine!"

The launch was deftly positioned beneath a ladder, and soon I was clambering up, lent a hand by Jeb, who seemed loath to relinquish it. "At last," he said, heaving a great sigh. "You'll put things right. You're a medical man, not prone to superstition. You'll talk sense to him, make him see reason."

He rambled on, not making a great deal of sense, but I decided not to press him, not so soon after my arrival. It was instantly obvious that Jebediah was suffering a terrible distress that affected even his posture. His back was hunched, his waddle more pronounced, and as he led me to a waiting carriage he moved as if he carried some great mass upon his small shoulders.

The carriage was set in motion by a man whose primary occupation had obviously been that of a seaman, but he handled the horse as well as Black Jack Sweeney had handled *Raven*. I was pleased to see that we were heading for the largest of the clapboard houses, the towered one on the hill, for it was, as I'd surmised, home to the Coffins.

"Dear, dear Davis, it was good of you to come," said Jeb. He sighed again and looked up at me with doleful eyes. "We lost the twins, and now my poor father seems to have lost his mind."

"Oh, Jeb, I'm so sorry."

As it happened "the twins"—two of his nearest brothers— were the only other members of his family I'd actually met. More than a year ago they'd come into Boston on business (something to do with the shipping trade) and Jeb had invited me to join them for a pleasant luncheon at the Long Wharf

Tavern. I recalled a pair of tall, powerful men whose mutual resemblance was uncanny, save that one had a slightly more luxuriant beard. The greatest impression I took away from the meal was how much they were devoted to their youngest brother, treating him with warm affection and respect, clearly vying for his approval. Among them it was as if his affliction did not exist; as if his man-sized head was, like their own, mounted upon a six-foot body. These two, being closest in age to Jeb—although a full ten years his senior—had in youth been his primary defenders, and I could well imagine that in White Harbor, at least, no one had dared taunt the village dwarf for fear of facing the bare-knuckle wrath of Samuel and Ezekiel Coffin. Called "Sam'n'Zeke," as if theirs was one name divided between two men. Magnificent examples of man-hood, they were, in the prime of their lives, and it was difficult to imagine that anything could have felled them.

As if sensing my disbelief, Jeb explained that Sam'n'Zeke had been killed in a gruesome milling accident—cut to pieces, both of them—while overseeing the construction of a coastal schooner for the Coffin fleet, and that their father had been there when it happened, and considered himself somehow at fault. "Of course he had nothing whatever to do with it," Jeb added. "There were a dozen witnesses who testified that he was in no way to blame, but still he's in a fearful torment, and without peace. He scarcely sleeps. Sometimes he rages like a madman, although I'm not convinced he's truly mad, but only somehow unhinged by what happened to the twins. You'll set him right," he added, patting me briskly on the knee. "He'll listen to you, Davis. He's a great admirer of your friend Emerson. You'll speak to him of reason and enlightenment. It will ease his mind. It's a great comfort to have you here. Indeed, indeed."

Then, staring straight ahead, my friend suddenly wept silently, and copiously, until the tears dripped from the cleft of his chin and stained the stiffly starched collar of his black suit of mourning.

I did not have the heart to tell him that mere conversation with a rational stranger was unlikely to set his father's mind at ease, and there was at present no effective medical treatment for sudden fits of madness. Only time could bring that sort of release, or death. Nevertheless it was my duty to honor his request, and I silently vowed to do so without complaint or equivocation.

Besides, I thought, what harm could it do, spouting on about Emerson and enlightenment, if it pleased my friend?

There is no such thing as a typical sea captain's house. As a class of men, mariners favor a wide range of eccentric designs, and Cassius Coffin was apparently no exception in that regard. A fashionable "shell drive," composed of crushed and whitened oyster shells, crunched pleasantly under our carriage wheels as we approached. At close hand the house was even larger than it had first appeared, seen from a distance. The main building faced toward the harbor below, and was enclosed by a wide porch that curved to a point in the center, suggesting the prow of a ship. On this "prow," neatly arranged, was a row of wicker rocking chairs, apparently left out even in the depths of winter. To one side, where our carriage delivered us, was a handsome portico supported by Greek columns, and under it a formal entrance that would have been worthy of a Virginia mansion. I could see that at some point a wing had been added to the original construction, in effect doubling the size of the structure, which, if the plethora of windows and chimneys was any indication, must contain thirty rooms or more.

Inside, the entire house had the look and feel of a well-constructed vessel, and indeed the entire structure had been built by ships' carpenters. The doorways were gently rounded

over the top, like hatchways. The white oak floors were fastened and bunged like the deck of a yacht, and honed, as I would later discover, with holystones. Everything was neat and shipshape, with none of the usual clutter of small possessions, as if the occupants were prepared to stow the contents at a moment's notice, should the seas get rough. The only decoration, save for a few framed paintings and mementos hung on the walls, was the black crepe draped from the mantelpieces. Compared to the Boston homes I was used to visiting, this was an empty place, filled not with furniture but with shadow and light—and more shadow than light, come to think of it.

Promising a tour somewhat later, Jeb led me directly to the kitchen or galley, as he called it. A warm meal awaited us, served up by a pigtailed cook whose massive forearms were decorated with elaborate tattoos; a souvenir, Jeb explained, of the South Pacific. Wrapped around his left biceps was a black mourning band, another reminder of the recent tragedy.

"Brisket, taters, 'n' gravy," the massive fellow announced in a squeaky voice that startled me, for it was as high as that of a girl.

"This is Mr. Barkham," Jeb explained, looking fondly upon the cook. "Barky had his throat crushed by a shackle."

" 'Twas a fall of block 'n' tackle," Barky gently squeaked. "I was stone drunk at the time."

"Never mind," said Jeb amiably, "He's the best cook that ever primed a stove."

We took seats at a wide, pine-board table, sitting side by side, as Barky ladled out the food. The fellow was, as Jeb had promised, an exemplary cook. His brisket, lightly seasoned with pepper and gratings of horse radish, was delicious, melting in the mouth. A generous side dish of boiled vegetables still tasted of the garden. Honey-flavored biscuits, hot from the oven, were a kind of buttered ambrosia. With a sea-sharpened

appetite, I stuffed my gullet while the cook beamed with pleasure, standing ready to keep the plates heaped full.

"Why, it's the first proper meal master Jeb has eaten in
days," Barky squeaked.

My diminutive friend nodded solemnly. "I am greatly
relieved by Dr. Bentwood's presence," he explained, "and that
has eased my digestion. Has the Captain taken food today?"

"Only enough for the cat," said Barky in his strangely small
voice. "I left ship rations outside his door, thinking he might
respond to the old ways, but it was not to be."

"Ah," said Jeb, "we must keep trying."

When I attempted to tactfully suggest that his poor father
needed not the services of a physician, particularly an unli-
censed scamp like myself, but those of a minister, Jeb dismissed the suggestion out of hand. "The Captain cannot abide
men of either persuasion," he explained. "Since my mother's
death—my birthday, as it happened—he has never been seen
by a doctor, nor set foot inside a church." Seeing my reaction,
he added, "Talk to him, Davis. That's all I ask. He'll not speak
reasonably with any of the family, but he'll listen to you. He
must."

"Am I to see your father now?"

He shook his head. "We must pick a moment when he's
amenable to conversation. I can't say when that will be
exactly, but within the next few days, certainly."

I thought it strange that having got me here in great
haste, he now seemed in no particular rush to use me, but I
would not insult him by saying so. "Whenever you think
right," I told him.

"Excellent fellow! In the meantime, you shall treat this
home as your own and have the run of White Harbor. I hope
you approve of our little village."

"Indeed!" I exclaimed. "From what I have seen, I could not
like it better."

At that moment a few more Coffins appeared, lured by the odors emanating from Barky's kitchen. Jeb introduced Nathaniel and Benjamin, two of his siblings, employed in the coastal trade but now grounded for a period of mourning. Both were large, strongly built men in their forties, instantly recognizable as mariners from their rolling gaits to their whiskered, weathered faces and sun-squinted eyes. Nathaniel, the second son, was affable, even gregarious, and seemed to know a great deal about the various adventures his youngest brother and I had shared in college. The eldest son Benjamin, on the other hand, parted with words reluctantly and, after mumbling his good-byes, hurried from the kitchen with a generous pail of brisket and biscuits in hand.

"Poor Ben has taken it hard," Nathaniel explained after his brother had gone. "He particularly depended on Sam'n'Zeke. And it was he who ordered the building of another schooner."

"Surely he doesn't blame himself," I said.

Nathaniel was seated opposite, and contented himself with a single biscuit and a glass of milk. "I fear he does," he said. "Blames himself for the twins, and for father's trouble, too. If he hadn't fancied another ship, none of this would have happened, is how he sees it. He won't be shed of the notion. Believe me, I've tried."

"Perhaps in time. . . ." I began, and then to my embarrassment, couldn't find a way to finish the thought.

"Maybe," said Nathaniel, sounding doubtful, but clearly understanding my unexpressed intentions. "Ben always takes things deep, ever since he was a tyke. Once he broke my finger, accidental-like, by slamming it in a trunk lid. Oh, how he suffered! He wept and he prayed for forgiveness, which I readily supplied, but it was weeks before he could see me without a tear coming to his eye."

Despite the vividness of his descriptions, it was hard to imagine that either of the men had ever been children. I could easily picture them pacing a deck or braving a storm, but it was difficult to conjure up an image of a Coffin in nappies, or engaged in the frivolity of childhood. Surely the whole clan had sprung full blown from their father's brow, like the offspring of Zeus. Men as bolts of lightning, yes, but children, never.

"Do you play pinochle, sir?" Nathaniel suddenly inquired.

"Passably," I admitted. "If the stakes are small."

"I imagine the stakes would be matchsticks or the like," he said with a grin. Turning to Jeb he added. "I was thinking of our cousin, Miss Lucy Wattle, who has come to stay with us since her father passed. You know how she loves her cards, Jeb, and we're all quite hopeless."

"That would depend on Davis," Jeb responded, then looked at me with eyebrows raised. "Our cousin is something of a suffragist, but very well mannered, despite that. Doesn't bite, or rarely."

"I have, um, no particular objection to women's suffrage," I said, somewhat gallantly.

"Do you not?" He grinned amiably. "I can think of many objections. Are you an enthusiast, then? I hadn't noticed. Somehow I can't quite picture you marching for the cause, sir."

It was said in such a wry way that it was intended to make me laugh, and did. "You may count on me for a hand of cards," I said, "if not for radical political opinions."

"Splendid, we can ask no more. The house has been very dour, as you might imagine, and our cousin will, I'm sure, appreciate the diversion. Perhaps tomorrow evening, if you would be so kind?"

"Done."

"Speaking of diversions," Jeb continued, "we will soon have the honor of welcoming that great advocate of freedom, Frederick Douglass. He and some of his people will arrive within the fortnight."

It was not the first I'd heard of Mr. Douglass, far from it. At Jeb's insistence, I had accompanied him to an abolitionist rally in Boston, and had been astonished by the famous Negro's mastery of rhetoric. That the great man had once been a lowly slave seemed inconceivable, given his obvious education and eloquence. Having expressed this sentiment to Jeb, he'd flown into high dudgeon, exhorting me to purge such prejudicial thoughts from my mind, for did I not know that any Negro taken from the field and given the opportunity might equal the example of Douglass? Did I not? he had demanded, banging his cane.

What then transpired was a collegial battle of wits that soon degenerated into the lowest form of argument, although we never actually came to blows. Jeb simply could not abide my own strongly held opinion that great men of any complexion were rare specimens. Example: how many gentlemen of means had been educated in Cambridge or New Haven, and how few of them had developed into Hawthornes or Emersons? Was it any more likely that mere education would turn every field hand into a Frederick Douglass? Not likely, I thought, and still think, but Jeb had taken my position to mean that I opposed the education of the Negro, and prefer he remained unlettered.

Now, it seemed, the great man was soon to be among us, sheltering in this very house. Quite suddenly a lantern lit itself within my mind, illuminating yet another possible motivation for my having been summoned to White Harbor: to serve as a foil for the Captain's recent madness, a kind of metaphysician whose special task was to soothe a troubled mind. It's one thing to keep a mad relation chained in the attic (many a New England home has just such a closet, well padded to muffle the screams), but quite another to be seen as arranging treatment for an unfortunate nervous affliction in one you hold dear. And with the family physician and minister both forbidden, what other option remained but to send for your friend the amateur philosopher?

If this was true—and Jebediah was more than capable of such subtleties—then on one level at least I was present simply as a demonstration of filial concern. You think me unkind, impugning such base motivations to a dear friend, but be assured I was not the least offended by the possibility. Indeed, the notion was a relief, for this was a role I could play, so long as I wasn't expected to effect an actual cure.

Like the black crepe hanging from the mantles, I would assume a decorous role. Davis Bentwood, Consulting Metaphysician. All the better because his specialty, transcendentalism, was in vogue, proclaimed as the only sensible spiritual guide for the thoroughly modern man. How else might a troubled mind transcend the inadequacies of the empirical and scientific realities, and by sheer intuition sense the Supreme Mind, the god that exists within ourselves?

"Frederick Douglass," Jeb was saying, his eyes aglow with admiration. "In an ideal world he'd be elected to the highest office. A Negro as president of the United States! Do you doubt him capable of such service?" he demanded.

"I have not one scintilla of doubt," I responded. "Mr. Douglass would make an exemplary president. Of course, such a thing would never happen. Not in this century, or the next."

"How can you be so sure?" said my friend, as if amused by my obdurate ignorance.

"Look around you, Jeb. Talk to the blacksmith, the farmer, the clerk. Such folk may be willing to support the idea of a United States—may even be willing to die for it—but while many of them despise the institution of slavery, they will not fight for Negro suffrage, any more than they will fight for female suffrage. It is too alien a thing to be embraced by the masses. Men such as you and I have the run of the country, and it will ever be so, because we will not easily relinquish what we believe to be our right by birth."

"Piffle and nonsense!" Jeb exclaimed. "Fixed notions can be changed. It was a fixed notion that the colonies were sovereign to the Crown. A fixed notion that kings ruled by divine right. I put it to you that only white men may be elected to high office is likewise a fixed notion, and therefore subject to change."

And so we debated the issue until well after the twilight had dissipated, with neither of us yielding an inch and both, I think, relishing the battle of wits. The others in the house, which included Nathaniel's wife Sarah and their newborn baby, and the as-yet-unseen-by-me cousin Lucy, apparently avoided entering whatever room Jeb and I occupied (for we moved around, it being an ambulatory sort of argument) and left us to unfurl our passions without interruption.

Then, having pleasantly exhausted ourselves, we took hot toddies of Jamaican rum and retired for a while to the main salon, where Jeb, stirring the fire with a poker, remarked that the fading embers looked like the souls of doomed men.

"Shall we debate the point?" said I.

This drew, as I knew it must, a warm smile from my small friend. "Another time. For now, let me show you to your chamber, and you can debate the subject of sleep with your pillow. I've no doubt you can win *that* argument, if no other."

And so my first day in White Harbor ended pleasantly, and I went to bed a little woozy from the rum, and did not awaken until the beast began to wail.

# 4. The Wailing of the Beast

Some hours later the squalling of a cat roused me from a deep slumber. Sitting up in the dark, stupefied by sleep, I knocked over the sperm-oil lantern. So it was that several minutes passed before I could shed my oil-soaked nightshirt, somehow dress myself in the dark—collar and cuffs nowhere to be found, and therefore done without. I then made a fumbling search for the box of sulfur matches and, finally, put light to a candle.

By then the noise was beginning to sound human. As if it was not a cat at all, but a man reduced to some terrible animal distress. Candle in hand, I ventured out into the hallway. Try as I might I could not pinpoint the origin of the squalling noise. The anguished sound seemed to echo over the cool oak floorboards from various directions. As if the animal—if it was an animal—was trapped somewhere within the walls, and moving around.

Using my hand as a shield so the candle would not gutter, I had to proceed with caution. The weakness of the flame rendered me nearly blind in a house whose layout was barely known to me. At times the awful wail had the timbre of a human infant, and then, abruptly, a mewling quality that could be naught but a cat; it was the uncanny changes that kept me going, as much as the wailing itself. Whatever the origin, the cry bespoke a desperate fear.

Moving cautiously through the darkness, I knew there had to be a rational explanation for the awful noise. Despite the nightmarish quality of the experience, this was no dream or troubled sleepwalk. Something alive was obviously terrified, and had succeeded in frightening me.

Suddenly I was struck in the forehead, as if by a stony fist. But my opponent, on closer inspection, turned out to be a door standing open into the hallway. I must have cursed, because a nearby voice admonished me with a curt, "Sir!"

It was a woman's voice, and before my heart had slowed she appeared out of the gloom, holding up a sperm-oil lantern, twin to the one I'd spilled. "Oh," she said, examining the welt on my forehead. "Sorry. It was I who left the door open."

"Cousin Lucy?" I asked. Draped in a sheer cotton night-dress, she looked, in the lantern glow, like a spectral succubus, perhaps, with long dark hair loose upon her shoulders. Hers was radiant, porcelain beauty of the type that makes men into stumbling fools. Even in the dim light her eyes had a peculiar stimulating effect, for they were large almond-shaped eyes set slightly farther apart than is the norm, and of a pale, icicle-blue color that seemed to dazzle the lantern flame, rather than the reverse.

"I am Lucy Wattle," she said, sounding amused to be rec-ognized. "Captain Coffin's poor relation. His niece, to be exact. And you must be Jebediah's friend."

At that moment the wail rose up a pitch or two, and then was cut short by what could only be a pistol shot.

"Oh!" exclaimed Lucy, losing her grip on the lantern.

The glass shattered on the oaken floor, and the blue glow of flame spread around her. Instantly I dropped to my knees and smothered the fire with my sleeve, and could see nothing but Lucy's slim, elegant, and quite naked feet dance lithely away.

When the flames were finally extinguished, we were left once again in absolute darkness, for my own candle had flick-ered out.

"Oh, dear," came Lucy's voice, sounding very close. "I feel so silly. Was that a pistol?"

"Yes, I think so."

"There must a thousand explanations for why a pistol might be fired in the night," she mused. "Maybe that horrible screaming was a rabid animal, and it had to be put down."

"Possibly," I agreed. "I caution you—don't move. There is broken glass scattered all around your feet."

"Stupid of me to drop the lantern. I keep thinking my eyes will adjust to the dark. So far I can't see a thing. Are you standing right next to me, by any chance?"

A hand fumbled along my arm and came to rest on my wrist, which was instantly warmed by her touch. I confess that my mind, which should have been concentrating on the pistol shot, was addled with all sorts of erotic phantasms, for there is nothing quite so stimulating as to be touched by a beautiful woman under condition of absolute darkness. It was as if her slim hand had a life of its own, though she touched only my wrist, and that quite chastely.

"What shall we do?" she asked, her voice soft and whimsical. "We can't stand here until dawn. Or can we?"

Her hand tightened on my wrist. Could she feel my pulse? Did she know my heart was pounding like a steam thresher? What, I wondered, would be her reaction if I offered to carry her away from the broken glass and back to her chamber? It was the prospect of her laughter—being the object of a young woman's scornful amusement—that prevented my making the suggestion. And just as well I refrained, for a minute or so later another light appeared in the hallway, carried by none other than Benjamin Coffin.

"No cause for alarm," he said, but even in the soft glow of his lantern, I could see that he was hesitant to meet our eyes. And not just out of natural shyness, of which he had an abundance, but because he was discomforted by speaking less than the truth.

"But we heard a pistol shot!" Lucy exclaimed, letting go of my wrist.

Benjamin gave the distinct impression he was hiding behind his beard. I noted that he was fully dressed in a way that suggested he'd never been to bed, right down to his black frock coat, and that a large, sturdy key ring peeked from his waistcoat pocket. Keys that he fingered nervously as he hastened to guide us back to our rooms. "Nothing to worry about," he said of the pistol shot. "An accidental kind of thing. Please put it from your mind."

As a guest it was not my place to question him. Even Lucy, his blood relation, evidently did not feel comfortable pressing the matter. When he'd got us back to her door she thanked him, and nodding at me said, in a voice that seemed to promise more, "Tomorrow we shall be properly introduced, Dr. Bentwood. Until then, sleep well."

It was a sweet sentiment, but sleep was impossible. After the dour Benjamin left me, I went to lock my door and discovered there was no locking mechanism, not even a latch or bolt. After propping a chair against the door, I lay upon the bed, staring up into the darkness, as my brain burned with two feverish trains of thought. The first concerned Lucy, beautiful raven-haired Lucy, and the other the peculiarity of the wailing and the shot in the night. Had it been a rabid animal, would not Benjamin have said so? What did he have to lie about, this man who quite obviously loathed prevarication? And what message had his cousin meant to impart, by touching her supple hands upon my wrist? Had she been amused by my charm, or by my failings? Did the hideous wailing emanate from the tower, is that what made it strangely echo throughout the house? What was Lucy doing now, at this very moment? Was she lying there in her gauzy nightdress, staring into the darkness and thinking of me?

I slept a little, and suffered dreams that cannot be written, else they burn the page.

The next morning at breakfast, something of the mystery was solved. Jeb entered the dining room in company with Nathaniel's pretty, plump, red-haired wife Sarah, who carried a six-week-old infant in her arms. A boy, she said, christened Cassius in honor of his grandfather. "I expect we'll call him Casey," she said, giving me the distinct impression that the intended nickname was the result of compromise with the child's father. She took her place at the table with a great swish of her crinolined black skirt.

"I'm sorry you were disturbed by all that fuss last night," were Jeb's first words to me. "Father had a bad spell," he added vaguely.

"Your father?"

He nodded. "And his cat."

My friend did not intend to make a further explanation, that much was clear. There was no mention of a pistol shot, and from his foreboding expression, I knew better than to inquire. Maybe he would satisfy my curiosity later, when his sister-in-law was no longer present.

Jeb climbed awkwardly into a chair whose seat had been raised several inches higher than the others, bringing his head almost to normal level above the table. There were dark circles under his clouded blue eyes, and a haggard look about him— more evidence of his father's "bad spell," whatever that might mean. "Nate and Ben have taken *Raven* down to Falmouth on pressing business," he said, attempting conversation as Barky brought out platters of eggs, sausage, and currant muffins. "If the wind cooperates, we can expect them back by evening."

Sarah, who had quite a pleasant face, spoiled it with a dark scowl. Clearly she did not approve of her husband's absence. "Tonight for certain. He promised," she said, casting a sidelong glance at Jeb.

"Nothing to worry about, dear," said Jeb, but his own brow furrowed with concern, as if the very thought of his brothers' business in Falmouth was troubling. "Tell me, Davis, is the coffee here as bitter as it is in Boston?"

"By no means," I answered, raising my cup. "Your cook is a treasure. I'll leave here a fat man, and the happier for it."

Jeb was quite obviously relieved that I'd let him steer the conversation into safer waters, and he chatted amiably enough. By an effort of will he brought a smile to his face and began to discuss the attractions of White Harbor. It seemed my Portland hack driver was not far off in his estimations. Almost a hundred sea captains did indeed make their homes in the village, or nearby, though only a score were in residence at any one time, waiting to ship out. Some were gone for years at a stretch, while others plied more local waters for the thriving coastal trade. It had long been a White Harbor tradition that every able-bodied boy was destined for a life at sea, and many of the master tickets were passed from father to son. It had been so for generations.

"The only place to touch it is Nantucket, where the trade is pretty much confined to whaling," Jeb said. "The Coffins there are as likely to be innkeepers as mariners, and are no relation to us, at least so far as we can determine."

I had read a rather odd book on the whaling industry by Hawthorne's friend Melville, but truthfully had not been able to make head nor tails of it, so loaded down was the story with heavy-handed symbolism. I was no Ishmael when it came to tales of the sea, but preferred the clear prose of Richard Henry Dana, who made his voyaging seem more an adventure, and less a quest for strained metaphor.

"The White Harbor Coffins are related to none but the

White Harbor Coffins," Sarah stated, as if she expected an argument. She got none, however, and was left to butter her muffins and care for the infant Casey, who fussed quietly at her bosom.

"I promise a tour," Jeb said to me. "On foot, I think, so you can observe the exquisite smallness of the place. Then, once we've seen the living, we'll stop by the cemetery and pay our respects to the departed."

"A most excellent idea," I responded, rising from the table.

And so we went out to the village of White Harbor, and saw what there was of it. Or as much as was not hidden from outsiders like myself.

# 5. Intruders in the Crypt

Jebediah strode purposefully along with his peculiar, saunter-
ing gait, the result of forcing his extremely short legs to keep
pace with me. The top of his high silk hat came nearly up to
my chin and his cane rat-tatted along the cobblestones, as if
keeping count. I got the impression he'd resurrected his good
spirits by sheer force of will.

"You see this small hill?" he asked, indicating the rise upon
which the Coffin mansion loomed over the village. "For me, as
a boy, it was a great mountain of a place, and to this day I associate it with gleeful joy. Sam'n'Zeke, clever lads, built me a little wagon fitted out to look like a boat. They 'sailed' me down
this hill many a time. Oh, those were grand days! I was all of
five years old," he added wistfully, "and hadn't yet realized that
I'd already reached the height God intended. All things still
seemed possible then."

Although none of the merchant homes we passed were as
large or imposing as that of the Coffins', many were very fine
indeed, rivaling any to be found in Marblehead, Newburyport,
or Portsmouth. One needn't have the eye of an architect or
builder to note how the houses of White Harbor had been
improved upon over time, adding filigrees of trim here and
there, and fine entrances framed with classical columns. No
doubt the increasing prosperity of the village was reflected in
such numerous additions and adornments. The majority of the
cedar-shingled rooftops were interrupted by sun-sparkled
cupolas, and by the curious, fenced-in roof structures known
as "widow's walks." Jeb explained that by means of a hatch cut

into the attic, a mariner's wife could stand almost upon the peak of her own roof and scan the horizon for sails, for ships, for the promise of a husband's safe return.

"A dangerous life, the sea," I said.

"Indeed. Though far more dangerous for, say, the Gloucester fisherman than the White Harbor mariner. So many of those poor Gloucester lads who venture out in codfish boats never return. A single storm may drown them by the dozen. Whereas our village can sometimes go almost an entire year without losing a man. And never, to my certain knowledge, has a Coffin failed to return from a voyage."

"Extraordinary," I said.

Jeb thumped the brim of his tall hat with the knob of his cane. "Like all men we must die, of course, but apparently not at sea. I speak not from hubris, but from simple statement of fact. 'Fear the sea, and it shall fear you.' My father's refrain. His prayer, one might say."

I waited, expecting this to lead into the delicate subject of the Captain's condition, but Jeb lapsed into thoughtful silence for a time, and we walked amiably, if quietly, through the narrower streets of White Harbor, traversing an area where the houses were built close upon the cobbled roadway, with little space between. Many a doorpost advertised for boarders, and it became clear that while a few score of Harborites might be wealthy sea captains, another class of lesser beings dwelled in the shadows below the great merchant homes, living upon scraps left by the wealthy.

Soon enough the street widened on a rise above the harbor, and here the shops and commercial enterprises flourished. Many of the shops had been fixed up "fancy" and made to look as "rich" as the finer shops of Boston; indeed the sizable business district reeked of a prosperity rare in a small, coastal village town of barely three thousand souls. Evidently all the gold was not in California, but was to be found at sea, and extracted by ships and the men who sailed them.

"There are not just one, as you might expect, but two tailor shops catering exclusively to the trade," Jeb informed me. "No ship's master would dream of departing this harbor without proper attire. Merchant sailors may not be uniformed like navy officers, and yet there is a kind of uniform, I assure you, and it does not come cheap."

The "uniform" of a White Harbor shipmaster was not confined to dark blue wool, double-breasted jackets and pea coats, or brass buttons, or sturdy knee-high leather boots. He would be expected to drive a fine coach, supplied by Chase & Sons Livery, and dine upon silver plate, and drink from crystal goblets, and light his home with the finest lanterns and the most fragrant oils. I remarked that this was the kind of expectation our British brothers had of the royal class, and Jebediah agreed, although he made a joke of it. "Can you doubt that I was raised as a little prince, a tyrant to the servants?"

"I doubt it not. Except that you had not only the servants and merchants waiting upon you, but all of your brothers as well." The remark, intended lightly, brought a clenched look to my friend's face, and I instantly attempted to apologize.

"No, no," he said, his breath steaming in the chilly air. "You have it exactly right. What a fortunate boy I was! Lacking a mother, I had so many brothers willing to mother me. Five brothers," he repeated softly. "Five of the best!"

It seemed that any reference to family brought him up sharp against the recent tragedy, for the six had been reduced to four, and that unfortunate pair were those two he had held in the closest affection. Sam'n'Zeke had been as much like male nursemaids as elder brothers, having raised and nurtured him deep within the protective Coffin bosom. To make matters worse, and extend the period of mourning, another of the

Coffin brothers was yet at sea, returning from the Orient, unaware of the tragedy.

"Lucky Tom," he said, speaking of the absent brother. "I so envy him his ignorance."

Attempting to distract him from these sad ruminations, I pointed out an inn upon whose dining-room windows was etched a promise of "The Finest Coffees & Teas." Jeb agreed, but insisted upon first purchasing a handful of Portland news-papers to, as he said, "soak up the java beans" as we drank.

It was well before noon but long after breakfast, so we had the dining room to ourselves, with the steaming beverage—*the best Brazilian beans!*—served by the proprietor himself, who bowed and scraped as if Jebediah really was of the aristocracy we'd joked about. "You'll give my best wishes to the Captain?" the innkeeper asked, rather plaintively, as he pulled nervously at the ends of his rat-brown mustache, and then attempted to put right his unbuttoned and none-too-clean collar.

"Yes, of course, I shall mention you to my father," Jeb responded, cracking open a newspaper, effectively dismissing the poor man, who did not seem the least bit offended.

"Look here," Jeb said, indicating a dispatch on the front page. "That humbug Lincoln has found his backbone at last. He's persuaded Buchanan to send a cutter to Charleston with orders to protect the customs revenue."

The comment brought a smile to my lips, for scarcely three months before, Jeb had been a great enthusiast for the Republican candidate, believing that the man from Illinois embraced the abolitionist cause with a fervor similar to his own. Now, only a few months after he'd been elected, Lincoln was a "humbug" for not pledging to dispatch troops to the slave states, with orders to enforce all federal laws. Having stated that a nation half slave-owning, half free was a house divided against itself, and could not stand, Mr. Lincoln was now busy contemplating the prickly realities of a presidency he would not formally assume for another few days. The slave states had vowed to ratify their own confederacy if an abolitionist was elected, and the populace, knowing this, had nevertheless voted for one; but now, having done so, the whole nation seemed gripped with a kind of nervous hesitation, as if slowly awakening to the full meaning of their convictions. Several states had already passed formal resolutions of secession. Meanwhile Senator Douglas, whose loathing of Lincoln seemed palpable, had failed to forge yet another compromise that might somehow appeal to the anti-slavery faction and still keep the South from abandoning the ship of state. The South Carolina legislature had been the first to vote for secession, and many of the other slave states had followed, but what legal import did those votes have, in light of the Constitution, which made no provision for dissolving the union? At the moment it was only pique and hot air, and hostilities might still be avoided.

Knowing that an excess of coffee tended to stimulate my small friend, I did not rise to the "humbug" bait, but diverted his attention to a dispatch regarding shipment of arms to the South.

" 'As for the armament of the South,' " I read aloud, " 'it is intended to defend the whites against a servile insurrection. There has been so much said about the abolitionism of Lincoln and Hamlin, that the Negroes have become indoctrinated with the idea that they will be free on the fourth of March, when the new president takes the oath of office. It is to guard against a 'rising' that Sharpe rifles and Colt revolvers, and Ame cutlasses, are being sent southward. These weapons have to be paid for in good funds, and the Yankees who take them receive kind treatment.' "

This brought me an owlish look from my companion. "I'm confident a man of your intelligence doesn't believe such poppycock," he said.

I affected surprise. "You mean arms are not being shipped southward by greedy Yankees?"

"I mean nothing of the kind! We Yankees are known for our greed, and we're proud if it. But I have my own 'dispatches' from the South, and they tell me there is, unfortunately, little to fear of a slave insurrection. The Southerners know this very well, having beaten and tortured the Negroes into submission for many generations. At the first sign of spirit or independence in a male Negro, he is whipped. At the second sign, he is castrated or hung. If the spirited Negro happens to be female, her children are taken and then she is sold to an even harsher master. No, the spirited Negro does not rise up if he wishes to live, he flees north! And it is to stop this fleeing, and to repel federal troops, that the South is arming itself. They have refused to allow any of the federal forts to be relieved. Soldiers at Pickens and Sumter cannot leave, for fear of being attacked by the populace."

"But they have not been attacked, that's my point. So far it is nothing but Southern bluster."

"Hardly. I'll give the Southerners this much: they know there must be war to settle the question, even if you—and your like—do not."

"My like?" I said, somewhat disingenuously.

"All you Free Democrats," he said dismissively, with an impatient wave of his hand. "Am I wrong to lump you in with them?"

He was not wrong. Fearing Lincoln's obstinacy, I had cast my vote for Senator Douglas, the Free Democrat candidate. Full-throated abolitionists like Jebediah believed that Free Democrats were somehow worse than the Pro-Slavery Democrats, for being opposed to slavery but lacking the will to abolish it by bloody means if necessary.

"Just because I voted for Douglas doesn't mean I'm in favor of slavery. You know I abhor the very idea. What I *am* in favor of is preserving the Union. And if Congress fails to find compromise, the South will carry through on its threats, which will leave us either divided or at war, or both."

"Exactly my point," was Jeb's happy reply. "War is inevitable."

I could not contain a sigh of frustration. In the several years of our acquaintance, never once could it be said that I had prevailed in argument. My friend's belief in the cause was absolute, like the faith another might have in God, and he could not be "reasoned" out of it.

"Look here," he said, giving his broadsheet another sharp snap. "A new gun has been invented by a Mr. L. Thomas, and is represented to be better than either the Armstrong or the Whitworth piece. It has a range of nearly six miles, with a shot of 170 pounds. Incredible! Mr. Lincoln may never have to leave Washington. He can make war from his front yard!"

Jebediah's expression was gleeful—the first I had seen since my visit—and I could not bring myself to puncture this most welcome elevation of mood. If gloating about the imminence of civil strife made him happy, so be it. I drank my coffee and tried to agree with everything he said, no matter how extreme. Therefore I found myself agreeing that all slave owners were, in effect, traitors, and should be dealt with as such. And that non-slave owners in slave states were complicit in the crime and subject to the same penalty. That after the situation had been "resolved," as he put it, a Negro State should be founded, possibly several Negro States, and certainly a Negro Territory or two, and that any blacks wishing to be repatriated to Africa would be carried there as guests of the United States Navy, and given such implements as they required to farm the land.

In my compliancy I agreed that we must invade Cuba and force the end of slavery there, too, as the conditions on that island were even more abominable than those in the South. I may even have agreed to lead such an expedition, single-handed if necessary.

My reward was a hearty laugh from Jeb, and a slap on the back with the knob of his cane.

"Done!" he cried. "Admiral Bentwood you shall be, Liberator of Cuba and the World!"

Not long after leaving the inn we found ourselves treading uphill, on a course to intercept the soaring, sunlit spire that dominated the center of the village. Jeb grew more and more quiet with every step. We came to the Episcopal church. It was a neat, clapboard affair, white as a May cloud, but we did not enter. Through the open doors I saw rows of white benches dappled with light from the high-peaked windows, and beyond that, a tall lectern partially obscured by shadows.

"The Captain cannot abide Father Whipple," Jeb explained, breaking the silence. "It's no fault of Whipple's, he's a decent fellow. But his predecessor, a certain Cornelius Remick, had unkind things to say about the family, in the form of a sermon shortly after that my mother passed away. My father connects the two events in his mind."

"Ah," said I, expecting my friend to reveal the topic of the offensive sermon, but he did not, and we continued on, taking a neatly bricked path into the adjacent cemetery.

Here, built as a miniature of the church, but without the spire, was the family mausoleum, made of finely pebbled granite. Because graves are difficult to excavate in the winter-months, there were many such aboveground crypts, inscribed with local names like Drake and Locke and Kilburn and Griswold, although none were so large or neatly appointed as this. Below the family name "COFFIN," in smaller letters, was a second inscription, "SEAFARERS," and the chiseled relief of a three-masted schooner under full sail. Beneath the schooner, the final inscription, in the old style: "To Heaven If The Wind Be Fair."

In the center of the crypt was a plain, black-iron door, of a size that would require a man of my height to stoop, were I inclined to enter. Strangely enough, the door was partly open, revealing a shadowed interior as black and cold as the iron itself.

Although I am not inclined to superstition or morbidity, a chill came into my bones, and with it a kind of dread that could not be explained by a mere unlocked door. Perhaps it was the smell, for there was the hint of it even then, some yards away. Not the smell of corruption, I hasten to add, but something much more foul.

Beside me Jeb seemed to freeze in place, his eyes gone large and owlish, as if he could not believe what he was seeing. "The vault was shut as of yesterday. I locked the hasp myself."

"One of your brothers, perhaps?"

To which he snapped a curt, "No, impossible."

He stepped forward, braced his cane against the iron door, and pushed it all the way open. Daylight did not seem to relieve the shadows, but the stench was suddenly overpowering, and brought a flood of tears to my eyes. Coughing into his handkerchief, Jeb cursed and then muttered, "Light. We need a light."

I volunteered to fetch a lantern from the church. "But you must promise not to enter until I return," I added, quite firmly.

"A promise easily kept," was Jeb's weak reply. He retreated from the open doorway and, catching another whiff of the horrible stench, uttered, "What can it be?" in such a way it was obvious he didn't expect me to answer. Instead I hurried into the vestry of the church, found an old candle lantern with an inch or two of beeswax left to burn, and hastily returned to the family crypt.

Jebediah was nowhere to be seen.

Fearing that he had entered alone, into that foul darkness,

I cried out his name, only to have him step out from behind a stout oak tree. His face was ashen and his hands, as he reached for the lantern, trembled.

"Allow me," I insisted, lighting the candle with a sulfur match. I was determined to enter the crypt first, and try to save my friend from the distress of whatever was causing the ungodly stench.

Holding the lantern out, I held my breath, stooped, and entered the pall of darkness.

At first I could see nothing, the light from the small candle was so faint. It seemed impossible that daylight did not penetrate, at least a little, but the sun was more or less directly overhead, which must have accounted for the unnatural darkness. The only sound was my own boots scratching crablike upon the stone. Turning very slowly, I was barely able to make out the walls and the low ceiling—as if the darkness had a kind of substance that absorbed the candlelight. It did not help that the noxious fumes made my eyes water.

Behind me, his small silhouette sharply defined in the doorway, Jeb called out, "Hullo!"

"There's no one here," I said, without much confidence.

"No one alive," Jeb replied softly. "My brothers lie in their caskets, do you see?"

Eventually I did see, when I had gone far enough into the interior to bump up against something solid. That "something" was revealed to be a stone tier. A kind of low platform meant to keep a casket above water should the crypt be flooded by the spring rains. It wasn't the local practice to inter the remains within the mausoleum itself; once spring had come, and the frost had safely dissipated from the ground, a waiting casket was buried beneath the grass close by, and marked with a modest stone.

A disruption had somehow occurred. The two fresh caskets were not upon the tier, but lay toppled on the floor. I was greatly relieved to see that the casket lids remained fastened in place, but one pass of the candle revealed the source of the horrible stench.

Both caskets had been fouled with excrement.

It was as if some large animal had forced entry into the crypt, shoved the wooden boxes from the tier, and then squatted over them to do its business. I say a large animal, because the excrement was copious—much more than, say, a dog or even a bear could have supplied. And then came a thought nearly as odious as the stench: that this was the action of human agents. Vandals who had forced their way into the Coffin tomb and purposefully debased it in as wretched a way as possible.

"What do you find?" Jeb asked, calling in a clenched voice from the open door.

And so I returned to the light of day and guided him some distance away, so we could both breathe a bit of fresh air. Jeb waited for my reply, anticipating the worst, and in this he was not disappointed. There was nothing for it but to describe, in plain words, what I had discovered.

"Vandals?" he said doubtfully. "And you say they used it as a privy? But that isn't human shit, I know that smell."

He was right, not even the foulest privy smelled so rank. "Then they collected the filth and brought it with them for that purpose," I suggested.

"But who would do such a thing?" my friend asked plaintively.

There was only one possible answer. Someone consumed with righteous loathing for the deceased, and for the living who shared their name. Someone who hated Coffins, alive or dead.

# 6. The Creature with Yellow Eyes

On the way back home Jeb swore me to secrecy. "No one in the family must know. It will only add to their distress."

"Let me be your agent in this matter," I said. "The church sexton will know someone willing to clean up the mess, and be quiet about it, if the price is right."

"I'll pay, of course."

I stopped my friend with a hand upon his shoulder, and turned him to face me. "You will do nothing of the kind. You will leave everything to me, and you will banish this whole affair from your mind, exactly as if it had never happened." There must have been something in my manner that prevented further argument, because Jebediah acquiesced with a kind of shrug, his eyes downcast.

When home was at last in sight he stopped and took off his stovepipe hat. "I must ask another favor of you," he began, and then faltered. Finally he blurted out, "Will you see the Captain now?"

"Of course," I responded without hesitation. "Though I doubt it will do much good, if he's as disturbed as you describe."

Jeb's smile was grim. "My dear Davis, you underestimate your powers of persuasion, and the comfort of your rational mind. But I hasten to add, this is no small favor. The Captain, my father, he's . . . he's quite reasonable much of the time. But there have been spells—that is, he's suffered from spells of . . . some sort of brain fever or dementia. A kind of madness that comes and goes, although it never leaves him entirely.

While in this, ah, 'feverish' state he can be quite dangerous. He's an old man, but still fearsomely strong. So you must exercise caution. Whatever you do, don't tell him you're a doctor."

When we reached the house, Jeb asked me to wait in the parlor while he made sure the old man was "amenable to visitors," as if I was about to undertake a social call. I wasn't sure the word "amenable" applied to an apparently dangerous madman, but kept my reservations to myself. Poor Jebediah was having a terrible time trying to cope with the ravages of death and madness in his family, and it was understandable that he hadn't yet fully accepted his father's condition, even as he warned me against him.

The parlor had the feel of a ship's salon, long and narrow and dark with mahogany. Heavy black velvet mourning drapes made it dim, despite the hour. No fire had been lit, and the air was cool and sea-damp. I sat upon a hard-bottomed chair in the gloom, awaiting my summons, and could not help but doubt the situation. My friend was convinced that I could, by mere conversation, ferret out the cause of his father's illness, but the whole enterprise seemed doomed to failure.

After a few minutes I looked up, startled, as a shadow entered the parlor.

"So you are still here," said a familiar voice.

"Miss Wattle! Yes, well, so I am," I stammered, rising, as the young cousin glided close enough so that her exquisite face was visible, pale and perfect over the satiny blackness of her mourning attire. "Why—why would I not be here?"

She laughed softly before sitting primly upon a chair a few yards from me, spreading out her full black skirt, her pale hands folded upon her lap. Her lustrous hair, I could not help noticing, was held in place with a black ribbon, and her porcelain complexion required no powder to achieve an exquisite paleness. "I thought perhaps the events of last night might have driven you from our company," she said. "You were dis-

turbed, were you not? I certainly was. That horrible screaming, and the pistol shot. I'm obliged to stay—indeed, I have
nowhere else to go—but you are not."

"But I am," I said resolutely, settling back into the chair.
"Jebediah is my friend."

"Ah," she said. "Your friend. And in the name of friendship
you're willing to brave the fiends of the night?"

"Fiends of the night? Surely you're joking!" I exclaimed.

But she relieved my anxiety with the warmth of her
laughter. "A bad habit of mine, making jokes at a time like
this."

"Not at all."

She shook her head. "You're being polite. I'm well aware of
my deficiencies."

No deficiency was visible. Hers was a lovely head, with a
long neck, large expressive eyes set wide, full lips, that flawless
complexion, and fine thick hair. A delicately crocheted black
shawl covered her shoulders, and served to accent the startling
blue paleness of her eyes. A black satin dress, tightly corseted,
showed off a slim waist, and the skirts were full and of a length
to conceal her ankles and even her shoes. Her crinoline, which
in fashionable belles can make the width of the skirt a full six
feet, was much more modest. Boston is known for its jeweled
beauties—it is the Hub of society, after all—but I'd seen none
there to rival this young woman. Not that she wore jewelry, of
course—to do so while in mourning would have been inap-
propriate.

I knew little about her, beyond her connection to the
Coffins, and the vague and possibly erroneous suggestion that
she was a suffragist. If so, she was an uncommonly lovely suffragist, but then Jeb and Nathaniel could have been pulling
my leg in that regard. That matter aside, I had gotten the
impression she was something of a poor relation, or anyhow
had need of shelter, being alone and unmarried, and I longed

to be better informed, but could not think of a way to ask without sounding presumptuous.

"You and Jeb were college chums, do I have that right?" she asked brightly. "No doubt like most college boys you frequented gambling halls, and dens of iniquity, and the like."

"I do not gamble," I replied, rather stiffly. "To my knowledge, neither does Jebediah."

Lucy's eyes sparkled with amusement. "What a shame! All that naughty fun in the big city, and you didn't partake. I suppose that means you're a serious young man. Were you at the divinity school, then?"

I understood that she was teasing me, and did my best to respond in kind. "The Reverend Bentwood at your service," I said, effecting a seated curtsy. "But no, I'm sorry to disappoint you. My interest was more science than religion. I've a conceit that Emerson's teachings about the mind and spirit can somehow be tied to modern medicine. So far I've failed to find the connection."

That brought another kind of smile to her face. "Emerson, yes, yes. The Sage of Concord, isn't that what he calls himself?"

"Others do. Emerson himself is a modest man, despite his genius."

"I know him as a friend to the cause of women's suffrage, and of course as a poet."

"And?" I prompted.

"And what?"

"What do you think of his poetry?" I asked, wanting to steer clear of the whole delicate matter of women's suffrage, as it was not an easy topic for first meetings.

Lucy sighed. "Poetry. Ah. No doubt Mr. Emerson is, as you say, a genius of some kind. But I find him rather dry. I'm more partial to the English poets. Byron, Shelley, Keats. Though I don't care a fig for that man Tennyson," she added.

I was not startled to discover she was a woman of strongly held opinions—her confident poise suggested as much, and her mention of suffrage had indicated a certain fervor for the cause—but to dismiss Tennyson with a slight wave of her hand, it was somehow breathtaking, and made me admire her all the more, though I myself held Tennyson in high esteem. "Did you not appreciate 'The Princess'?" I asked tentatively.

"Why? Because it speaks of women's emancipation? Do you fancy me an emancipator, Dr. Bentwood? One of those modern harridans? The keening suffragist?"

There it was, the subject I'd thought best avoided, until we were more thoroughly acquainted. And clearly she expected a reaction from me. "I would describe you as a modern sort of woman," I said tactfully. "Never a harridan. And if you are a suffragist, you do not keen."

She liked that, and rewarded me with a smile. "If I admitted to a previous interest in suffrage, Dr. Bentwood, would you flee the room?"

"Certainly not. But why do you say a 'previous' interest?"

She shrugged prettily. "Before my father's illness I did support the cause. Since that sad event I've retired from it, although still believing that I and all my sisters should have the vote."

"And so you would, were it mine to give," I offered gallantly, but without the slightest confidence that such a thing would ever truly come to pass.

"I think you are jesting with me, Dr. Bentwood."

"Oh? I didn't mean to offend." I was glad of the gloom, or she might have noticed the blush upon my face. To cover my embarrassment I decided to change the subject from suffragists and poets to something more prosaic.

"I understand you have a fondness for pinochle."

That earned me a lift of her lovely eyebrows. "Apparently my reputation precedes me," she said. "Which leaves us with the question, does a 'modern woman' play pinochle? For all I know, emancipation and games of chance may be mutually exclusive."

"Surely pinochle involves skill."

"Not much. It's all in the cards, as they say. Are you suggesting we play a hand? And what stakes do you have in mind, if you're not, as you claim, a gambling man?"

I was trying to think of a witty reply, something worthy of this intoxicating young woman, when Jebediah returned with the news that the Captain was "amenable."

"Ah!" I turned to make my apologies and could not help but notice the look that passed between Jebediah and his cousin, as if they were both privy to a discomforting secret that could not be revealed in my presence.

Before I could do more than bid her a hasty farewell, Jeb was hurrying me along a dark hallway deep within the interior of the great house. "He seems to be himself today," he said. "And of course he's greatly relieved that Charley survived."

"Charley?" I asked, racking my brains to think if there was a brother by that name.

"You'll see," Jeb said mysteriously. "Father is eager to meet you by the way. I told him you were a friend of Emerson's."

"Hardly that!" I exclaimed. "Would that I were. But really, Jeb, you know better. Emerson and I are barely acquainted. I doubt he'd remember me."

"Nonsense. You're too modest. And if I exaggerate slightly, it is because the Captain holds Emerson in such high regard."

"As a poet?"

Jeb shook his head. "As an abolitionist. I doubt my father has ever read the great man's poetry. Or any poetry, for that matter, beyond sea chantey doggerel."

"I see."

Jeb turned and studied me directly. "Do you? No matter."

We had come to a door somewhere in the center of the

house. My friend took a key from his waistcoat, unlocked the door, and opened it. "All the way to the top," he said, gesturing at the steep stairs within the door.

"You won't accompany me?"

He shook his head firmly. "Two of us would likely confuse the issue. I'll wait below—if there's a problem, you have only to shout."

I mounted the stairs with more than a little trepidation. It was a long ways up—three landings—but the way was lighted by a series of round windows, very like portholes, and a spectacular view of the harbor gradually came into view. This pretty picture lightened my mood. What, after all, was there to fear from an old man uneasy in his mind? If the meeting did not go well, all I had to do, as Jeb suggested, was call for assistance.

My destination was at the top of the tower, which rose like a lighthouse over all of White Harbor. With each turn of the stairs another portion of the village appeared and I could not help but linger for a few moments at each of the portholes, one higher than the next, until I felt like a bird hovering above the world. From here I had a clear view of the wharf where I had arrived, of *Raven* at her mooring, and the protected harbor, the rocky promontory, and the sea beyond, which seemed to melt into the wintery blueness of the sky without a sharply defined horizon.

At the top of the stairway I came upon a stout door of unpainted oak. There was no knocker. For that matter it lacked a handle, though a pattern of screw holes indicated there had once been a handle, and that it had been removed.

I was poised to knock my fist upon the oak when an inside bolt was drawn and the door swung open a few inches.

"State your name," came a muffled voice from behind the door.

"Davis Arthur Bentwood."

A glittering eye surveyed me through the hinge gap, and then blinked furiously. "Remove your jacket!" the voice ordered.

"Captain Coffin? Good day, sir. I'm a friend of Jebediah's, I believe he mentioned—"

"REMOVE YOUR JACKET!" he bellowed from behind the door.

This was a voice capable of "starting" a sailor as efficiently as the strike of a lash, and my arms hastened to shed my black frock jacket before my mind had given the order.

"Waistcoat, shirt, collar, cuffs, pantaloons. Step lively now!"

"I'm not armed, sir. There's no need to—"

"I *AM* ARMED, DAMN YOUR SOUL! NOW STRIP OFF YOUR GEAR OR I'LL PUT A BLOWHOLE IN YOUR BELLY!"

Was it true? Had the family allowed the madman to arm himself? Recalling the pistol shot of the previous evening, I hurried to obey his command.

It is amazing how fast a man can strip when he believes his life may be at stake. In less time than it takes to recite one of the shorter psalms I whipped off my waistcoat, unclipped my starched shirt collar, unbuttoned and removed my cuffs, shed my boiled shirt, dropped my pants, kicked off my boots, and stood before that glittering eye in only the long, one-piece woolen underwear that concealed my nakedness from neck to ankle.

"Turn around! Right! Go on inside then! Sit yourself on the stool and keep your hands on your knees!"

The tower room was no more than a dozen paces on a side, with windows all around. Other than a small ship's stove with a tin chimney, the only furnishings were an upholstered sofa, a Turkey rug, a seaman's trunk, a cedar bucket, and a three-legged stool. The stool was short, the room was cold—

no heat radiating from the little stove—and as I took my place every inch of exposed flesh seemed a welter of goose bumps.

A sudden *bang!* made me jump inside my skin, but it was only the heavy oak door slamming shut.

"There now," said Cassius Coffin in a conversational tone. "So you're the famous abolitionist. I've always wanted to meet you, sir."

Standing before me was a man who at first glance did not give the impression of madness. To my physician's eye his complexion was perhaps a little too ruddy, indicating a choleric humor and a bilious temperament (which he had already demonstrated) but high choler is hardly a mental deficiency. Nor did his confident poise or upright posture betray any of the muscular twitching or spasmatic indications of insanity. Unlike his taller sons he was of medium height, although broad-shouldered and unusually robust for a man of his years. A full white beard fit him like a bib, or the rays of light emanating from the visage of the sun found in certain archaic illustrations. His hair, white and thinning, curled in oily tendrils from a widow's peak upon his deeply furrowed brow, and looked as if it hadn't been properly trimmed in quite some time. He had the prominent, hooked nose characteristic of all the Coffins, and the familiar deep-set eyes, which seemed to glitter now with curiosity, not the mad gleam I'd thought to perceive from behind the crack in the door.

The old sea captain wore the dark blue, tightly woven uniform of his trade, with a double-breasted jacket and enough brass buttons to please an admiral. His fully bloused trouser legs were tucked into knee-high, badly scuffed boots. He had the look of a man who could live within a single change of clothes for months, if necessary. Indeed he had about him the distinct pong of one who hadn't bathed recently; a thin, not entirely unpleasant scent of tar, tobacco, sawdust, and sweat.

There was, as promised, a rather large flintlock pistol suspended from a wide leather belt, of an ancient type unfamiliar to me, but deadly in appearance nonetheless.

"I've heard tell of you, Mr. Emerson. How came you to be in these parts?"

It was obvious he'd somehow confabulated Jeb's explanation of my identity as Emerson's friend, and confused me with the man himself. I opened my mouth to correct him, saw his blunt hands nervously stroking the barrel of the pistol, and reconsidered. He might not be drooling mad—a sure sign— but there was something "off" about the old man, and if it eased his mind to think his visitor was a famous philosopher and abolitionist, so be it. Under the circumstances I could play along without dishonoring myself, as one might humor the witless or infirm.

"I am acquainted with your son Jebediah," said I, my mind racing as it searched for a credible explanation, given my new "identity." "Your son has, um, devoted himself to the cause and I, ah, I wished to converse with him upon the subject."

"We agree, all of us, that slavery is a great evil," replied the old man. Suddenly he looked fearfully around the small room, as if suspecting that we were being overheard. "My Jebediah has the soul of a giant," he hissed. "Do you agree?"

"I do," I replied without hesitation.

That seemed to please him. Muttering to himself, the old man took a seat on the narrow horsehair sofa, which I gathered also served as his bed, and placed the heavy pistol within easy reach.

"Come, Charley," he called out.

It was all I could do not to leap up from my stool when something brushed against my leg. Gliding quietly along the floor like a puff of condensed smoke was the largest cat I'd ever seen. A ringed tail, thick as my hand, trailed above it like a fat exclamation point. With a small mew—small for an animal so large—it raised its forepaws and labored to mount the sofa. Labored because a white bandage encased most of one haunch—a fresh bandage, from the look of it.

Presently the cat settled upon the old man's lap and regarded me solemnly with a pair of exquisitely beautiful green and yellow-flecked eyes. "My Charley, poor lad," the old man said by way of introduction.

"What manner of cat is that?" I asked.

"Called a 'coon' in these parts," he said, stroking under the beast's ample chin. Soon the thing was purring, or possibly growling, and its startling eyes never left mine. "On account of the ringed tail, I suppose. They're particular animals, but pretty fair sailors. Charley here has been full ways round the world more than once, and he never complained so long as he got his vittles."

"And how was Charley injured?" I asked, innocently enough, wanting to express concern for an animal so much in his favor.

"I shot him," said the old man.

The simplicity of the statement left me speechless. At once I guessed that this remarkable creature had been the source of the horrible squalling from the previous night, and the pistol shot had obviously found its mark upon the cat's haunch.

"Had to shoot him," the old man explained with a weary shrug. "He was taken hold of."

"Taken hold of?" I stammered. "By whom?"

"Him that cursed me," he said, as if that explained everything. "Never mind my troubles, lad. Tell me how you and Jebediah aim to put an end to slavery, that's what I've a mind to hear."

I pried my tongue form the roof of my mouth and tried to form an answer. "Well, you see . . . the problem is . . ." I began, and then trailed off as my mind went blank.

"Ha!" he said, chuckling beneath his beard. "Sinking a long-established evil ain't so easy, is it?"

"No," I agreed, feeling grateful for the lead. "Not easy at all."

The old man nodded eagerly, his eyes as bright and moist as chips of melting ice. "Work of a lifetime!" he said. "That's what I been telling Jebediah. As he's made it, and as he progresses. Seeking the end of an institution older than Moses. But fair work, and noble good. It pleases me the boy has aimed his sights so high."

"Oh, indeed, very high."

"And you're lending a hand, is that it?" His fingers strayed from the cat's chin to the pistol.

"Oh, yes, lending a hand," I said eagerly.

He resumed stroking the green-eyed beast sprawled in his lap. There was silence between us that was beginning to feel almost comfortable when suddenly the old man said, in a conspiratorial tone, "You heard what happened to my twins? My precious book-end boys?"

There was something about his manner that suggested the question was a trick, and that I must answer correctly.

"I heard," I said carefully. "Please accept my condolences."

"Wasn't no accident," he told me fiercely. "They was murdered."

"Oh?"

"Murdered by him that cursed me! Him that stuck them to the log and would not let move until they was sawed to pieces before my eyes!"

"Him?" I asked.

The glittering madness had returned to his eyes. "Don't trifle with me, lad, you know who I'm talking about!" he bellowed. And then, softly, "The same who took hold of Charley, that's who. The same who'll take hold of you, if it pleases him." He picked up the pistol and aimed it at my heart. "Don't think I won't shoot."

"Please don't," I pleaded.

"Hands on your knees, Mr. Emerson. If that be your name. Is it?"

"No," I said, feeling an urgent need to speak the truth. As if truth might blunt the bullet. "My true name is Davis Arthur Bentwood." The pistol did not waver, prompting me to babble rather desperately. "I, ah, studied with Emerson, or rather I studied *him*, you see. I'm writing a book. Not much of a book, but it follows the lamp of Emerson. Jeb and I were friends at Harvard. Splendid fellow, your son Jebediah. As you say, the soul of a giant. Asked me to visit with you, chat about Emerson and abolition and so on. Happy to oblige."

"Bentwood," he mused. "I recollect that name. Bentwoods round about Lowell and Boston. You one of them?"

"I am," I said eagerly. "That's me, last of the Bentwoods."

That seemed to please him. "The last?" he asked, his eyes narrowing. "Was you cursed?"

"Not that I know of."

"You'd know a thing like that. The cursing, that would be enough to make a man change his name, I guess," as if that explained the misunderstanding. He returned the pistol to the sofa and resumed petting the cat.

I remained perched on the stool, trying to stem the shivers, hands grasping my knees. Not wanting to disabuse him of the notion that I, too, was cursed. That we had it in common, which ought to prevent my being shot by that dreadful weapon.

For a time the old man occupied himself muttering to the cat, stroking it softly and fussing with the bandage. But soon enough he took note of me again, and I was relieved to see that his expression had softened. "I've enjoyed yarning with you, Mr. Emerson. You'd best leave now, before he takes hold of you and I'm obliged to shoot."

Hastily I backed away from the stool and picked up my pile of clothing where it lay by the door.

"If he does take hold, tell him he can't have Cash Coffin. I know his ways. I can see him coming. I'll kill him before he kills me, just as I did before. Only this time he'll stay dead!" he thundered, again brandishing the pistol, though not taking aim. "You tell him that, Mr. Emerson. Cash Coffin can't be had! Not in this world he can't!"

With that I fled, and did not stop trembling until I was dressed and safe away, with an oak door and three flights of stairs behind me, and a glass of whiskey in my shaking hands.

# 7. The Frozen Baby

As the reader has no doubt surmised from the title given to this chapter, we've come round at last to where we began, to the mystery of the infant dead in his cradle. A poor, ten-week-old child somehow frozen solid in a room as stifling warm as an Indian sweat lodge. My recollection is somewhat confused by the emotional state of all concerned, not the least myself, and I do not recall precisely how we managed to remove Sarah from the nursery, or how I was able to pry Nathaniel's hands from the bar of the cradle. By then Benjamin Coffin had entered along with Jebediah, and eventually Barky the cook, who had been roused from his hammock nearby the kitchen, and whose stoic presence helped to calm us all somewhat.

" 'Twas an unfortunate draft," he muttered in his peculiar, high-pitched voice. "All the heat was sucked up the chimney with the blaze of the fire, and drew the cold up through the floorboards. Something like that. Must have been. Just a misfortunate accident, and there's nothing to be done about it. Poor child, he never felt a thing. He's in heaven now, missus, never doubt it," and so on, seeking to ease the shock of the cruelly bereaved mother.

It was Benjamin who insisted that we all remove to the parlor and await the arrival of the family doctor, who had already been summoned. Nathaniel at first resisted, as if he expected his little son to somehow return to life from an icy nightmare, but stern Benjamin prevailed and we soon found ourselves—the men, at least—sitting around the card table that had been hastily abandoned when the screaming began. Quite numbed and speechless, all of us, for what was there to say?

Sarah lay insensible upon the appropriately named fainting couch, attended by cousin Lucy. I quickly procured smelling salts from the family medicine chest, and she revived somewhat, although her pulse was rapid and erratic. Still, she was a sturdy woman, if cruelly shocked, and would soon recover, or so I thought at the time.

"Would you fetch a cool compress, and place it upon her forehead?" I asked Lucy, who readily complied.

Jebediah had the look of a man possessed by some terrible and unbearable knowledge. He seized the nearly empty glass of whiskey I'd abandoned and downed the meager contents like a man dying of thirst. "Impossible," he said at last, keeping his voice low and conspiratorial, excluding the women. "Never mind what Barky said, there was no draft in that room. None that I could feel."

"God took him," Nathaniel said, burying his face in his hands. "God takes what he likes, don't he? The mighty bastard!"

"You mustn't speak that way," Benjamin hissed. "Think of your wife and mind what you say."

Insensible to his brother's admonition, Nathaniel looked up through a blur of tears and said, to no one in particular, "If it wasn't God took him, who was it then?"

I spoke not a word—it wasn't my place—but my mind was in a fever, searching for a rational explanation. Had someone snatched the baby, exposed his frail little body to the cold night air, and then returned it frozen to the nursery? But according to Sarah, or what we could make out of her keening, she'd never left the room. She'd nursed the baby, laid him down in his crib, adjusted the lamb's-wool blanket, and then proceeded to knit by the fire. When she checked to see if he'd fallen asleep, she found him in the state we'd all seen. As cold and hard to the touch as a block of January pond ice.

Was it possible that she'd nodded off by that roaring fire—lulled by the heat—and not been aware that her baby had somehow been removed and then returned, all without waking her? Possible, perhaps, but there was another factor, that being the actual weather conditions outside. It had been temperate these last few days, and though the winter frost had seeped into the ground, a skim of ice had just barely begun to form on the puddles left behind by the melting snow. An infant might well perish from such exposure, but it could scarcely be frozen solid in so short a time. Which brought me back to the cook's theory, that a curious, icy draft had been caused by the heat roaring up the chimney. A blast of frozen air sucked up through the floorboards from some deeper, colder area beneath the house. Was it possible?

Soon enough the family physician arrived. A certain Dr. Griswold, whose most notable feature was a pair of protuberant, bulging eyes, magnified by the lenses of a pince-nez. Apparently Griswold had heard a bit of the circumstances from the sailor who'd gone to fetch him. With barely a glance at Sarah, prostrate upon the couch, or Nathaniel hunched in paroxysm of grief at the card table, he turned his attention to Jebediah.

"Take me to the nursery," he demanded. "At once."

As there was nothing for me to do in the parlor, I felt it my duty to accompany Jeb and the stolid doctor. Dreading what undoubtedly awaited us, I was at the same time half convinced we would find the baby dead in his cradle, but otherwise normal. The blueness, the numbing cold of his tiny body, surely we'd all imagined it, mistaking the commonplace of death for something even more terrible.

But there had been no mistake. The nursery was still warm to the point of stifling, and little Casey Coffin was as we'd left him: a block of blue ice, cold enough to burn the doctor's fingers.

"Good Lord!" Griswold cried out, snatching his hand away. So startled that the pince-nez fell from his eye and dangled violently upon its ribbon. "What mischief is this? Jebediah, how did this happen?"

Jeb regarded the tiny body somberly, indeed mournfully, but without the distress he'd first expressed. "There is no explanation, none that you would believe," he finally responded.

"No explanation?" said the incredulous doctor. "You show me this . . . this *thing*, and you say there's no explanation?"

Death seemed to have made him angry, though at first the anger wasn't focused upon us in particular, but at a world where babies died in their cribs, in warm rooms with loving mothers in attendance. Dr. Griswold was a middle-aged, small-boned man of less than medium height, somewhat swelled by the necessary overconfidence of his profession, but the anger had shrunk him small again, and when he'd digested what Jeb had said he focused a pop-eyed, glowering look in my direction. "What do you have to say for yourself, young man? Were you a witness to this event? Is that why you're skulking around?"

"Griswold!" Jebediah barked in a warning tone. "This is my good friend Davis Bentwood. He's a graduate of Harvard Medical School, and a guest in this house, and must be treated with respect."

"You're a doctor?" he responded with surprise and irritation. "Then why have I been called?"

"I received my degree, but I've never actually practiced medicine. And in any case I know little or nothing about babies."

The doctor nodded stiffly, but continued to look on me with suspicion.

It was only later, as the recollection burned itself into my mind, that I had occasion to reflect how strange was this scene. Three men surround a crib. The object of their interest is a dead baby. One of the men is a dwarf and he's clearly in charge, a commanding presence all out of proportion to his stature. Shadows flicker, low flames cast spiky glows upon the low ceiling, and all three men are sweating profusely as they contemplate that which has no explanation.

"There must be an inquest," Griswold finally said, as if trying to convince himself that an inquest would put things right.

"I leave that to you," said Jeb, moderating his tone. "Will you take it with you," he added, "out of this house?"

"It?" asked the doctor helplessly.

"The baby, sir. I'm concerned for the mother. She mustn't see it again, not in this state."

The strangeness of the "state" he referred to was not just the original icy condition, eerie enough, but that after an hour in a hot room the little body hadn't yet begun to thaw. It remained as hard as marble, and so cold that the good doctor—and he was, I think, a good man, despite his reflexive distrust of a stranger—the good doctor had to wrap the remains in several layers of blankets to prevent his own hands being frostbitten by contact.

When at last he was ready to leave, bearing the tiny, swaddled corpse, he looked to Jebediah with a glance that was stern enough to curdle cream. "The body will be taken to Caswell's," he announced, naming the village funeral parlor. "I will examine the cadaver in the light of day, and make my report for the inquest. Burial can be anytime after, say, noon tomorrow. I will not attend, is that clear? I will have nothing more to do with this hideous affair. If the mother requires treatment for nervous prostration—and I assume she must—and if your Boston doctor doesn't feel competent to attend her you are to call on Dr. Shattuck. Do I make myself clear?"

"Very clear, sir."

And with hollow eyes he left us, clutching his sad cargo and convinced, I'm certain, that someone in the house, and possibly all of us, had played a ghastly, damnable prank resulting in the death of an innocent child.

There was, as you might imagine, no chance of sleep that night. Jeb and Benjamin and I sat in the kitchen—or galley, as the Coffins called it—in the glow of a well-tended stove, drinking strong coffee and trying to make some sense of what had happened. And yet the more we talked the clearer it became that there was no rational or scientific explanation that made any sense. There were old wives tales about "cold spots," of course, and we'd all had the experience of detecting a chill in an otherwise warm room, but we all agreed that nothing less than exposure in a nor'east blizzard would so quickly turn a body to ice. And yet it had happened, there was no denying that, and if it happened then it must, ipso facto, be possible.

It was only, I told Benjamin, our ignorance that prevented an understanding of what, exactly, had occurred.

"Ignorance?" he said groggily, and for an instant a dangerous look flickered in his eyes, as if he was resisting an urge to strike me with his powerful fist. "I suppose I am ignorant, never having been educated like you and Jebediah. But I went to my own school, the school of hardtack and salt beef, and I guess I know when a cursed thing has happened, and this is a cursed thing, in the same way Sam'n'Zeke getting sawed to bits was a cursed thing. Sailors know about cursed things. They know there's nothing you can do but pray, and that's what I aim to do, if God will hear me. I'm going to pray hard, as hard as I've ever driven a ship in beastly weather. I'm going to pray until my knees hurt, see if I don't."

With that he got up from the trestle table and stalked from the kitchen, his leonine head dipping as he passed through the door.

"Poor Ben," Jebediah said when he was gone. "This has riled him something awful. They say as a boy he prayed most devoutly, but never, I think, since Mother died. Since I was born," he added, and then turned to me with a curious look. "Do you think it might work? Prayer? What does Mr. Emerson say about prayer?"

"He would never, I think, underestimate the importance of prayer," I responded, somewhat diplomatically. My mentor had, of course, resigned from his ministry over a matter of theology, but that had not affected his spiritual nature. What I did not add, given the circumstances, was that Emerson's transformative ideas about communing with the God-within-us-all would not likely meet with the approval of, say, the local Methodists or Lutherans. Indeed, in an earlier age they might well have burned him at the stake.

The sun having fully risen, I suggested that we take a turn around the grounds and fill our lungs with fresh air. Although I could not say so without risking offense, the house itself had a morbid grip on me, and I was eager to get away, if only briefly.

"You go, Davis," Jeb said wearily. "I must see to things here."

"Then I shall stay," I said instantly.

Jebediah shook his head and sighed. "I insist that you walk as far as the harbor and stretch your legs. Stretch your mind, too, because we have another problem to solve. It is this: how do we bury a frozen baby? Under normal circumstances the body would lie in the crypt until spring. But I won't risk exposing that poor child to the ravages we found there."

He looked so hopeless, so woeful, that my first instinct was to take his hands in mine. "My dear Jebediah. Please do not torment yourself about these matters. The crypt is being cleaned even as we speak, and once it has been returned to a presentable state the vault door will be sealed in a way that prevents any further defilement. Certainly little Casey will not have to enter the place, nor will you or anyone from the family. Let me take care of the arrangements for the poor child. May I do so without being presumptuous, or causing offense?"

In reply Jebediah gripped my hands, bowed his great head, and wept.

# 8. Ice to Ice

A ten-dollar gold piece bought the services of three strong men recommended by the church sexton. My excuse that only an immediate burial would relieve the mother's mind was accepted without comment, as all eyes focused upon the gold piece. Using sharply honed pickaxes the laborers managed to chip out a grave deep enough for the purpose, and later that day, after a final and useless examination by Dr. Griswold, little Casey was placed in a tiny coffin and laid to rest. The brief ceremony was attended only by immediate members of the family, along with Father Whipple (a severe though calming presence) and myself.

The Captain, informed of his grandson's death, raged for hours in his tower, but could not be persuaded to leave the place, which I thought was just as well, considering his strange and sometimes violent behavior. Not to mention his aversion to the Episcopal priest, whose presence was more or less demanded by Benjamin. The elder brother seemed to have recovered the fervency of religion he'd lost as a boy. He had, as he vowed, prayed excessively, and the effort had evidently appeased his grief at the inexplicable loss of his infant nephew. God's will, he informed us, and he had become convinced, like Barky, that the baby had been carried off to heaven.

Whatever Jebediah's opinion on the subject, he kept it to himself. Indeed, a strange and uncharacteristic silence had descended upon my friend, and he scarcely spoke until the tiny casket was below ground and covered with frozen earth.

"Ashes to ashes," he muttered as we walked away from the snow-dusted cemetery, his cane skidding on the cobblestones. "They might as well have added, ice to ice," was all he had to say on the subject.

On reflection, Dr. Griswold had changed his mind about the necessity of the inquest. Perhaps because even many hours after the event the small corpse remained inexplicably frozen, despite the warmth of the examination room, and with no explanation in hand he despaired of making a reasonable and defensible conclusion as to the cause of death.

"He still vows not to set foot in the house, ever again," Jebediah complained to me the day after the burial, as he began to emerge from his cocoon of silence. "As if it is the house itself, and not the inhabitants, that has offended him."

Clearly my friend expected a response, although I was as yet unclear as to what he craved, agreement or argument. My reaction was in no way irreverent, for the Jebediah I knew thrived on argument, preferring it to what he called the "pap" of polite consensus. Still, he was in some way diminished by recent events, and the last thing I wanted to do was add to his distress by speaking insensitively on the subject. "The man took an oath," I reminded him. "I feel certain that despite what Griswold says, if summoned he will respond."

Jeb turned to me with his darkest look. "The weasel has one thing right. He'll never set foot in this house again, so long as I live. There's another sawbones in the village—he'll be glad enough for our business."

"Quite right," I said. And then gathered up my courage and prepared to raise a related subject, one that had been preying on my mind. "As to the house. Griswold may be, as you say, more weasel than man. But I don't think he's entirely wrong about the effect of the house itself."

"Oh?"

"It is well known that a place may become infected with

gloom. Have you not noticed this, Jeb? How a certain room or landscape may affect your mood, for good or for ill?"

"What are you saying?" he responded suspiciously.

I decided to abandon my carefully measured arguments and simply tell him the truth. "This is my prescription: take leave of this house for the time being, at least for the long, melancholy months of winter. Come back to Boston with me. I know a house on Beacon Street that can be had quite reasonable. A cheerful, sunny place, with no taint of bad memories. Surely a change of scene will lift your spirits. And you've friends and associates in the city—they'd be delighted to have you back, right in the thick of the action. Why there's hardly a week goes by without a rally!"

Jeb's expression was cool enough to chill. "And what of my brothers? Lucy? My father?"

"By all means, bring them along! Plenty of room for everybody! A change of scene, Jeb, sometimes that's the best thing in the world."

My old friend stared at me for a long time, as if taking my measure, and then shook his head. "The Captain won't leave. Even if he was entirely himself he'd never abandon ship. We Coffins are born in these parts, and we die here. We travel the world but always return. We're of this place, Davis, and we can't be shut of it, or it of us." After a deep sigh he continued. "I do, however, understand that you yourself are anxious to leave. You may go without prejudice. I've imposed on you long enough. We all have. And you've done us good service. I shall always be grateful."

His speech stunned me into silence, to think that my intentions had been so completely misunderstood. When I finally found my tongue I attempted to make it clear that my misgivings about the house had nothing whatsoever to do with any desire to abandon my friend in his hour of need.

"I meant only what I said and nothing more," I said with

a kind of furious urgency to be understood. "It is my belief that the atmosphere of this place, and memories associated with it, may contribute to your father's illness. I believe that you, too, have been affected. But if you disagree, if you choose to remain, so shall I. Assuming that you want me to remain, that is."

I saw that my small friend was weeping again, and that he was unashamed as the tears ran down his face. "My dear Davis," he said thickly. "I don't know what I should do without you. You are the rock we've clung to, these last few days. These last few terrible days. It was wrong for me to take offense at your kind suggestion. Please forgive me."

Although I was greatly touched by my friend's apology, I made a dismissive motion, saying, "There's nothing to forgive," and then went on in as light a tone as possible, to demonstrate my willingness to remain, and assist him to the best of my abilities. "What must be done? Shall we summon this other sawbones, and have him attend to Sarah? She may require a sleeping powder, or some other concoction for her nerves. Or, if you wish, I shall see to her, as best I can." I went on, until at last the light returned to Jebediah's eyes, and he looked about him like a man under siege, but no longer defeated.

That very afternoon a telegram was delivered, containing the welcome news that another of Jebediah's brothers, Thomas Coffin, had at last arrived in New York Harbor aboard the clipper *Rapunzel*, and was returning to Portland immediately by train. I was made to understand that *Rapunzel* was owned by a consortium of investors, of whom the Coffins were the majority holders, and that the voyage to the Orient had been spectacularly successful, her sleek hull fully laden with pre-mium teas, exotic herbs and medical ointments, and bales of silk and cotton from India.

Alas, poor Tom hadn't even a pause to celebrate his suc-

cess before the shipping agents informed him of the events at
home, casting a shadow over his last few weeks at sea, when
he had sailed on unaware of the recent tragedies.

The last leg of his homeward journey was, like mine,
aboard the swift *Raven*, and this time Jebediah and cousin
Lucy and I were waiting at the wharf when the schooner
sliced into the placid little harbor under full sail. It was a cold,
clear day, and the horizon seemed to be half a world away.
Squint and you could almost see the towers of Toledo, or
China's great wall. *Raven* leaped toward us as if from a great
distance, sails an incandescent white against the glittering
black waters. Once again all I could do was marvel at the mas-
terful handling as one-eyed Black Jack and his crew made
*Raven* turn and dash about like a thoroughbred in the able
hands of an experienced rider.

Lucy, of course, continued to wear full mourning attire out
of respect for her departed cousins, and her black dress that
morning included a full-length hooded cape and a dark veil.
Her mood, previously irreverent and infectious despite the
tragedy of Sam'n'Zeke's demise, had been unrelievedly
somber since the baby's passing. She had, she confided, not
seen her cousin Tom since she was thirteen and he already a
ship's master. "You can scarcely comprehend the impression of
a handsome young captain on a girl of that delicate age. I
nearly swooned when he deigned to kiss my hand! Of course
he was only joking, but how was I to know at the time? I
remember running to my mother, God rest her soul, and
demanding to know if Tom was a 'kissing cousin.' "

"And what did your mother say?" I asked, eyes on the
approaching launch.

"Such a look! 'There will be none of that in *this* family,' or
words to that effect. My mother was sister to his mother,
never forget. No Wattle could marry a Coffin. First cousins

might marry in the hills of Tennessee, but not here. Whereupon I suggested we all move to Tennessee."

"You were willful even then."

Her expression was unreadable behind the dark veil. "You disapprove of willful girls?"

"Not in the least," I said. "Or willful women, for that matter."

When the man in question stepped onto the wharf, his expression seemed equal parts joy and grief. The first thing he did was drop to his knees and rest his head on Jebediah's shoulder. This was, I thought, an extraordinary gesture. From what I'd witnessed, the Coffins were not a family given to open displays of affection. For instance, I'd seen Jeb greet Nathaniel with nothing more than a brief, cool handshake. And when the moment came, that was exactly how Tom greeted Lucy, though she was clearly poised to receive his full embrace, having thrown back her hood and lifted her veil.

Perhaps sensing her disappointment, he attempted to make amends by praising her.

"Lucy! My word, you've turned into a ravishing beauty. Breaking hearts from Boston to Bar Harbor, I reckon. And how is your dear father?"

"Dead six months," said Lucy with a dip of her head.

Tom, having been so long at sea, had not heard of her father's passing, and apologized for his ignorance. "We mariners can't help but sail out of the past, for even with the telegraph, very little reaches us at sea. I am only now catching up, and part of me wishes I had never docked, but sailed on unaware."

Lucy was instantly solicitous of his feelings. "Forgive me, Tom. My dear old father's passing was in some ways a blessed thing, an end to a long, painful illness, although it has left me alone in the world, and nearly penniless, and reliant upon my dear and generous cousins. Whereas, poor Sam'n'Zeke—it must have been a terrible shock to hear what happened."

"I still can't believe they're gone," he admitted, with a nervous stroke of his thick brown mustache. Unlike most of his brothers, he kept his chin clean-shaven and his face went pink with a blush not of shame, I fancied, but of grief.

As was revealed on the way home—his sailing trunk and a matched pair of large canvas bags stowed in the carriage—he'd also not been aware of baby Casey's existence, for that happy event occurred some months after his departure for New York, and thence to the Orient. "What a cruel thing!" he exclaimed. "So many children die at that age, I wonder how parents can stand it. Poor Sarah and Nate have endured a hard blow. Are they as well as can be expected?"

Jebediah cut me a look that said *he knows nothing of the circumstances, let him remain ignorant for now*, and I readily complied, while Lucy kindly distracted him from the unhappy subject by chatting brightly and ironically about her "season" in Portland. The bustling city was a mere village compared to Boston, but still there was a kind of social register, and Lucy had been presented in the proper fashion a few months before her father had lapsed into his final illness, and when, unbeknownst to her, he had spent the last of his fortune "bringing her out." At some length she described the gala affair, the elaborate ball gown she had worn, the problem with the punch that made lips pucker, and the orchestra that featured, of all things, an Irish fiddler, considered scandalous by the more conservative guests—although not, obviously, by Lucy herself.

"And how many suitors did you spurn?" Tom wanted to know, more out of kindness, I think, than any real curiosity. He was making an effort to be cordial, although clearly his mind dwelled on more somber events than a debutante ball.

"All of them," Lucy replied primly. "They were not suitors so much as codfish men and lobster boys. I decided then and there that I shall be a spinster and haunt a house in my old age."

That wrung a grin from Tom, and for a moment put a sparkle in his fine sea-green eyes. For the briefest moment a hint of his youth shone through, and then, just like that, he was a man of nearly forty years, creased and shaped by the life he'd lived.

As the carriage approached the great house upon the hill, with its austere tower glinting in the sunlight, the attempts at conversation floundered, and we drew up to the portico as silent as the mourners who follow a funeral cortege. Tom climbed down with a sigh that made me wonder how much he knew, or guessed, of what awaited him. He turned to offer Lucy his hand, but she was already down, and heading resolutely to the open door where Barky, smelling of freshly baked bread, waited to greet us.

"Master Tom," he squeaked. "Home at last."

## 9. Links in the Chain

The invisible baby began to cry shortly after midnight, but by then the evening was long ruined.

Earlier there had been a brief respite from the gloom. Despite everything, the Coffins rose to the occasion of Tom's homecoming, and made him feel welcome. Even Sarah, who had taken to her bed, emerged for long enough to attend an intimate gathering held in his honor. It was Benjamin who presided over the candlelit dinner, summoning various succulent dishes from Barky's kitchen, and then, after the cake was served, he urged the retelling of amusing anecdotes touching upon Tom's childhood.

"Jebediah, tell the time you put the toad under Tom's pillow," elicited a tale that brought tears to my eyes, for the oft-told story was in equal parts hilarious and affectionate.

As Jeb launched into his recitation, I formed a picture of a much-younger brother desperately trying to attract the attention of a full-grown man who was something of a hero to the boy. More telling, the offending toad was a kind of metaphor for how young Jebediah saw himself at the time: ugly and stunted. Tom evidently understood this, and lavished such affection upon the "noble toad," and in so doing upon Jeb himself, that it somehow helped the boy make the difficult transition to manhood. Of course my friend made the point without so baldly stating it, and with great warmth, but the impression to a stranger like me was indelible. The Coffins were all links in the same chain, forged together by blood and circumstance, and nothing, not even death, could diminish the strength they took from each other. Having been raised an only child by elderly, if kindly spinster aunts, I could not but be impressed, and more than a little envious of such intimate connections.

Benjamin, who was a year older than handsome Tom, then launched into a tale whose main point seemed to be how the Captain had always favored his third and "prettiest" son, lavishing him with presents that included, on his tenth birthday, an exquisite sloop done up in the finest "Bristol" style. "It was built by Hiram Lowell himself," Ben said, his eyes twinkling, "of the best white cedar. Frames of oak, and trimmed out with scads of varnished Honduran mahogany. I believe the tiller was carved from the jawbone of a whale, was it not?"

"Right enough," Nathaniel agreed. "Father brought it back from New Bedford when he sold *Sandpiper*, to be converted into a whaler. I remember that ship, a stout three-master—and I remember the whalebone tiller on Tom's little sloop. A man in New Bedford made a specialty of items like that. Very stylish in those days. Everybody had to have a whalebone tiller."

"Do you remember how bad it leaked, Tom's little sloop?"

"Oh," said Nathaniel with a chuckle. "Indeed. What terrible boys we were, Ben, to do a thing like that. And Tom such a good sport about it, despite our cruelty."

Their "cruelty," it seemed, was opening up the seams of the birthday present that had made them so envious, causing it to sink at its mooring. Fortunately the little boat was kept in shallow water, and at low tide most of the mast was exposed, and the three elder brothers were eventually able to raise the sunken boat and effect the necessary repairs. In the course of which they came not only to regret their prank, but arrived at an understanding of why their father held young Tom in such high regard. A regard that his brothers shared from that moment on.

For himself, Tom seemed a bit embarrassed by all the kind

words. "It was only a boat you sunk, not me," he said. "And if I didn't run tattling to the Captain, it was only because he'd have boxed my ears. Really, I was a horrid little scab, like most boys."

The subject of their father having entered the discussion, Benjamin evidently felt compelled to say something about the old man's condition. "I think we all understand why the Captain wasn't able to join us this evening. He's been hit hard. Stove in, you might say. As we all have," he added, with a glance at Sarah, who wept silently, comforted by her husband. "Sometimes things happen that are so terrible the mind can't rightly comprehend why God has struck us so cruel and hard. In our sorrow, we might even rail against the Lord, and hold him accountable for his mysterious ways. There's only one thing to do when that happens, and that's to pray for the aggrieved. So I ask you all to join hands. Let us bow our heads in prayer, and ask God to relieve the Captain of his terrible burden, and put his mind right."

We all did as he requested, and I found my right hand linked to Jeb's, and my left to Lucy's supple palm. As I glanced down, I fancied there was a light blush upon her neck, and then like the others I closed my eyes and listened as Benjamin Coffin spoke to his God.

"Our Lord in heaven, look down upon us, and hear us. You have lately taken three of our family to your bosom, and in our weakness we grieve exceedingly. We ask that you relieve our sorrow, and give us a sign of your benevolence."

Ben took a deep breath and was about to go on when he was interrupted by the startling sound of a glass breaking. My eyes snapped open and I saw Nathaniel glance about with a puzzled expression, trying to locate what glass had tumbled.

Suddenly the whole table began to shake, and more crockery toppled and was smashed upon the floor. A strange gargling noise came from Ben's throat. His eyes had rolled white and his whole body shook, but not so hard that he released the hands in his grasp.

"O Lord!" he cried. "O God, be with us!"

A gust of wind came into the room and the candles guttered and went out, leaving us in the dark, save for the glow of the hearth. And then the hearth fire itself was extinguished and the table ceased to rumble, and all was silent.

Out of the silence came Sarah's voice, thick with rage. "Damn you!" she cried. "Damn every last one of you!"

A chair tipped over, and as the flames flickered back up from the candles, I saw her flee the room, flinging her hands at her husband, who followed most desperately.

When the soft glow light returned to the room. Jebediah stared at the disorder on the long dining table, the floor littered with broken bits of china, and said. "Yes, I suppose we are damned. Every last one of us."

Beside me Lucy wept quietly into her handkerchief.

Having secured some medicinal brandy from the family stores, I had retired to my room shortly after the disaster in the dining room. But rather than soothing my palsied nerves, the brandy seemed to intensify my sensation of dread. A dread caused not by the quaking table, which might have Sarah shaking it in rage, or the guttered candles—a puff of wind let in by Barky, perhaps—but by the mournful pronouncement of my friend Jebediah.

*Damned, every last one of us.*

Said in such a way that I could not doubt he believed it to be true. It is an intolerable burden, to believe oneself doomed. The soul itself seems to go numb, and one so afflicted sleepwalks through life, having already resigned himself to his fate. There are many such victims on the battlefield—whole armies of sleepwalking men—and they do not wake until the bullet strikes.

This I know now, for lately I myself have become a kind of doomed sleepwalker—one who longs for the final awakening—but that night in White Harbor I had no experience with the cursed or the damned, or for that matter the chaos of war, and I searched in vain for a way to bring comfort to my friend. Was there nothing in Emerson that applied? Feverishly I leafed through the sermons and essays, most of which I knew by heart, but the words seemed to blur upon the page. I was struck by the realization that there were situations that could not be rectified by the application of written wisdom or the reading of books.

You think me a fool, no doubt, but until that night—really, until the dead baby cried—it was my firm belief that there was a solution for every problem, if one only knew where to look, who to consult, what to do. Emerson knew, and if not Emerson, Thoreau. If not Thoreau, then Hawthorne. Or the answer lay somewhere in the works of Rousseau, Carlyle, Kant, Hegel, Schelling, Fichte, or Goethe. Failing the Moderns, there was always Plato and Plotinus. Wiser men than I had puzzled out the answers, had seen the world in a drop of dew, understood the transcendent nature of the Universal Soul and the primitive fears that prey upon the individual mind. If we are all part of the same mechanism, if every man is divine unto himself, then that dreary, Calvinist idea of inescapable Fate ceases to exist, and no man can be cursed or doomed except within his own mind. That is what I had read, studied, memorized. That is what I believed.

Until the dead baby cried.

It began so distantly, so quietly, that it seemed to originate in my imagination. The ghost of an echo of a sound. A kind of pang or reminder of what had transpired, no doubt stimulated by my concern for Jebediah. But rather than dissipate into memory, the sound grew steadily stronger, louder.

It was not my imagination. Somewhere in the house a

baby was crying. This time there was no confusion about it being a cat or some other animal. This was, undeniably, an infant human wailing in distress.

My first thought was that to console his wife, Nathaniel had somehow gotten hold of another baby. Taken from some local orphanage, perhaps, where they were glad of a willing parent.

At that moment someone rattled the door to my chamber.

"Davis!" Jebediah hissed. "Come along!"

I hastily drew the sash around my robe, put on my slippers, and opened the door. There was Tom, fully dressed, and beside him, face pinched and eyes like embers, the much smaller form of Jebediah, attired in his cotton sleeping gown.

"The nursery," said Tom in a quavering voice. "Who can it be? Is there another child in the house?"

"Poor Sarah," said Jeb.

And at that moment we heard her shriek from a nearby chamber.

"Nate will see to her," said Tom, sounding not at all convinced, as the three of us made our way more or less resolutely toward the nursery.

My second impression, hurrying toward the unsettling noise, was that some enemy of the family had contrived another horrible prank, different from the defilement of the crypt, but no less repulsive. Someone mean-spirited enough to bring a baby into the house and induce it to cry, as a means of further tormenting the mother.

The mere thought of such miserable behavior made me wish I'd brought along a firearm. Not to murder but to wound, as we had been wounded, as poor Sarah had been wounded.

The impulse gave me pause, actually stopped me in my tracks. Was there really some dark part of me that wanted to stifle that pitiful sound? I had little experience of infants, being an only child, but my instinctive response, in the presence of a baby, had always been to coo and smile. Surely I would not harm this particular infant, who could not be held to blame for the cruel intrusion?

As if in answer, an image came into my mind, sharp as an engraving: myself with pistol in hand, my face distorted by an expression of cold and furious anger.

My hands shook so that it made the lantern cast wild shadows upon the wall. *Dear God*, I thought. *This cannot be me.*

"Davis, are you all right?" asked Jeb, looking up at me with distracted concern.

"Yes," I lied. "It was nothing."

We arrived to find the nursery shut up. Behind a locked door the baby wailed, louder and louder. To my horror I saw that Jeb held a pistol at his side, partially obscured by the folds of his sleeping gown. Much like the pistol I'd possessed in my imagination. Possibly I'd caught a glimpse of it, and incorporated it into my thoughts without realizing the source.

"What is your intention?" I demanded, indicating the weapon.

"Never mind my intention," he replied. "Open the door."

Tom searched a ring of keys, and as he did so the baby's crying rose to a higher pitch. "Oh, God," Tom said, fumbling at the lock.

"God has nothing to do with this," said Jeb, sounding both terrified and furious.

I believe he was preparing to shoot away the lock when Tom finally managed to find the right key. Hastily he opened the door, and at that exact moment the baby ceased crying.

"Hold high the lanterns," Jeb ordered, and it was done.

In less than a minute we ascertained that the nursery was empty. The crib had been taken away—by Nathaniel, as we later determined—and the room itself was cool and dark, no fire having been lit.

"I d-don't understand," Tom stammered. "Where can it be?"

A moment later the baby began crying again, from some other, more distant place in the house.

For what seemed an eternity we followed the sound of the crying baby. From room to room we searched, lighting candles as we went, but the pitiful wailing kept moving from chamber to chamber, always just ahead of us. Sometimes it would stop, only to resume at a more desperate pitch. It was all I could do not to stop up my ears with some of the candle wax, for the crying seemed to resonate within my own breast, producing a kind of insufferable anguish, and pains upon the heart.

Finally we came to the kitchen, where we found Barky the cook sound asleep in his hammock, evidently insensible to the din. At my prodding he slowly snorted himself to full wakefulness, and sought to aid us in our search of the premises.

The wailing baby sounded close enough to reach out and touch, but we found nothing. Not in the cupboards, the closets, the pantry, or under the tables, no matter how frantically we searched. Nothing. And yet the crying continued, if anything louder and more distinct.

It was there that Sarah found us. She rushed in with her gown flying, eyes as big as tea saucers.

Tom went to her but she would not be calmed.

"Make it stop!" she screamed when she found her voice. "Make it stop!" and then collapsed to the cold floor in a fit of sobbing that seemed to take her breath away.

When poor Nathaniel finally reached us it was clear that Sarah had raked his face with her fingernails, although he was scarcely aware of the wounds, or the blood that seeped into his beard.

I shouted to make myself heard. "Get her out of the house! Do it! Now, man, now!" He looked at me with an expression of horrified confusion, but slowly seemed to understand, and finally he scooped his wife up in his strong arms and carried her into the night.

He was barely out the door when the crying turned into a wild peal of laughter. Hideous, vengeful. Laughter triumphant.

"Oh, Jeb, no," said Tom, sounding small and helpless, and much younger than his years.

It was only then I noticed that my friend Jebediah Coffin was holding the pistol to his own head, and that his finger was squeezing hard upon the trigger.

# II

# THE ABOLITIONIST

*Men do not love those who remind them of their sins.*

FREDERICK DOUGLASS

# 1. Thou Seek a Mighty Blade

I will end this now," Jeb whispered, gazing at the floor. "I can make it stop."

Handsome Tom seemed frozen, wanting to seize the pistol from his brother's hand, but afraid to do so. He looked at me, pleading with bewildered, frantic eyes, *Do something!*

Jeb remained exactly as he was when he'd surprised us in the galley, with the heavy pistol held against his temple. "Look at me," he said, indicating his small, distorted body. "Is it not obvious? Was I not an abomination from birth? Cursed in my spine, cursed in my ridiculous legs?"

"Jeb, please."

"Listen! The voice cries for my death. I'm inclined to oblige."

By then Barky the cook had become fully aware of the danger Jebediah posed to himself. Moving with a silent grace unusual for a man his size, he took me gently but firmly aside. "It ain't poor Jeb that's at fault," he squeaked in confidence. "Persuade him to live, won't you?"

The Jebediah I knew had little enough interest in religion, let alone the more commonly held superstitions, but apparently the recent deaths and the strange, inexplicable phenomena of home and crypt had inflamed the nervous fibers of his mind. My little friend had come to believe that some sort of curse had settled upon the family, and that he was the living embodiment of it. Nothing in either my medical or philosophical training had prepared me for dealing with the irrational state, or the self-destructive impulse. The best I could venture was, "You are mistaken, Jeb. No one can be cursed. It's an old wives' tale. A superstition. And you're the least superstitious man I know. Now please, put down the pistol." Feeble, but it was enough to make his trigger finger relax somewhat.

In the end it was the cook who knew exactly what to say. "Hear that, Master Jeb?" Barky said, cocking an ear. "The ghosty cryin' stopped. Take it as a sign."

Finally he lowered the weapon and I was able to pry it from his grasp.

"Sorry, sorry," he muttered, weeping openly.

Tom then picked him up bodily and ever so gently carried him to a narrow couch in the parlor, where he lay convulsed, covering his own face in shame as he wept like a child. I could do nothing but make some small noises of comfort, which he did not seem to hear. Never had I felt so helpless, so ignorant of human behavior.

"Oh, the poor lad," said Tom, wiping his eyes with his sleeve. "You mustn't think to leave us, Jeb. What would we do without you? Hey? Couldn't cope without our Jebediah, hey?"

Barky, good man that he was, prepared a tot of brandy to "thin his blood," which sounded very sensible. Jeb accepted the glass and drank from it gratefully. "I am s-so ashamed," he stammered, unable to meet our eyes. "I hadn't the courage to pull the trigger. I'm a c-coward."

"Nonsense," I said. "You're the bravest man I know. It was courage that made you stop."

At which Tom placed his hand on Jebediah's brow and added, "Whatever might be cursed in this place, it can't be you, little brother."

Our collective imprecations were awkward but eventually effectual. Jeb finally smiled sadly and said, "Dear friends, I fear you are wrong. But I give you my pledge that I will not shoot myself, whatever happens."

That was how it stood when dawn finally came. With

Nathaniel and his poor, grief-addled wife gone from the house, and Jebediah lapsed into a brandy-induced sleep, and Benjamin praying with both hands, the weird "ghosty" crying was heard no more that night.

Having returned to my chamber, I drew the heavy drapes and tried to sleep, but my mind raced with a thousand anxious concerns. What of poor Sarah, poor Jeb? Would they soon recover their senses, or were the wounds too deep? Who had defiled the family crypt? Could such an enemy have somehow contrived to murder an infant? And what if the mad Captain came storming down from his tower and confused me with some imaginary foe? Unlike the odd and loyal cat, I had no lives to spare.

It was the vision of Cash Coffin blazing away with his antique miniballs that finally roused me from my fitful slumber, and to a rational decision: if there were no sensible answers to be had in this house, I must journey to the shipyard where the tragedy began, and there demonstrate to my own satisfaction that the deaths of the twins, Samuel and Ezekial Coffin, had been merely accidental. Having done so, I might persuade Jebediah that his "curse" was but a tragic coincidence. Difficult to bear, horrible to contemplate, but nothing of the supernatural. This was my thesis, soon to be proved: tragedy sometimes came by the cartload, without the help of vengeful spirits.

From the amply appointed stable I was given a small, lightly sprung chaise and a sturdy, high-stepping bay to pull it. The path was more or less direct, I was told, by a narrow, hard-packed road that veered from the shoreline for some six miles. Stick to the road, pay heed to the fingerboards pointing the way, and I couldn't put myself wrong. The horse, the stable boy assured me, knew the way if I did not, and so I set out with confidence, eager to be away.

The morning was chilly but glorious. A blue-streaked sky

raced with high-blown clouds, and within a few minutes of leaving the Coffin estate I felt a great weight lift from my mind. As if the house itself had unfisted my heart and set me free.

The horse, too, seemed eager enough to be gone, and drew the chaise through the miles without apparent effort, snorting happily whenever a cool shift of breeze brought the sea to our noses. There was but one serious hill on the Waldoboro road, and once over that a gentle incline led to a broad, shallow bay lapping against a pine-treed shore. From there the road curved—down into the crowded inner harbor, where a number of ramshackle yards had ships on the ways in various stages of completion. I say ramshackle because the building sheds appeared to have been thrown together haphazardly, in contrast to the precisely assembled schooners that swarmed with furious activity.

A query shouted up into the staging caused a workman to lower his shaping adz and solemnly point me toward the largest of the building sheds. There I found Mr. Gunther Buchen, whose yard it was, and whose name was painted in man-high letters on the side of the shed, which I'd somehow overlooked.

Herr Buchen oversaw his laborers from a small perch in the eaves. He summoned me up the ladder with a jerk of his thumb.

I soon discovered that the shipbuilder, being both German and Quaker, was a doubly serious man, a full-bearded, black-eyed smoker of long-stemmed clay pipes who did not suffer fools, or visitors, gladly.

"Does thee have business here?" he demanded, pointing the pipe stem at me as if it were a rifle barrel and me the squirrel.

Such was the din of adzes, hammers, caulking mauls, and oaths that I had difficulty making myself understood, but when the shipbuilder heard the name "Coffin" his expression grew if anything more serious. Beckoning with that same curi-

ously stiffened thumb, he bade me follow him along the cat-
walks until we reached a three-sided alcove where the
cacophony was somewhat diminished.

"Did thou say Cassius sent thee? It's said the Captain has
taken ill."

"Very ill," I said. "I'm his, um, physician and, er, a friend of
the family."

"Oh?" Buchen said suspiciously. "If that be true, why don't
I know thee?"

I explained, as best I could, my relation to the youngest
Coffin. Though I dared not break confidence by describing the
Captain's actual symptoms of madness, I was able to leave
Herr Buchen with the impression that Cash Coffin was prostrate with grief, and blamed himself for the accident that had
taken his twin sons. This was not strictly true, but was as much
as the shipbuilder needed to know, nor did he press for further
details of the Captain's condition, as if he already knew something of the actual situation. Having heard me out, he sighed
deeply, loaded and lighted his next pipe (he smoked a half
dozen of the clay pipes in careful sequence, so as not to over-
heat the stems), and announced that accidents were common
enough in shipyards, hadn't he lost a hand himself?

He held up the stiffened thumb, which startled me, as I
had not realized his "hand" was carved from wood, and clev-
erly painted to look like flesh. "Mine got crushed when some
timber shifted, and then festered so it had to be cut off. Thee
truly didn't notice?"

"I assumed the hand was injured, but that it was real
enough."

This pleased Herr Buchen, and from then on he warmed
to my presence, or at least to our conversation. It seemed that
unlike any of the other owners who contracted to have ships
made in Gunther Buchen's yard, the Coffins were actively
involved in the actual building process.

"The brothers, Sam'n'Zeke, they oversee many a schooner, from carving of the model to the building of the whole ship, until she floats free of the cradle. Only one man in all these yards knows more than the Coffin boys about the making of a true-found schooner. And that be Gunther Buchen!" he crowed, tapping himself in the chest with his pipe stem. "Smart boys, them Coffins, and fine gentlemen. Always 'thee'd and thou'd' me. Like they were my own two sons. Acch! Terrible thing! Terrible thing!"

We left his little hidden alcove and emerged once more into the din. I followed the spry fellow down another ladder—the wooden hand seemed no bane to agility—to the hard-packed earth of the main shed, an area he called the "lofting floor." Herr Buchen indicated that I should sit on an empty hogshead while he leaned against a workbench. The bench was neatly arrayed with a number of the hand-carved, model-sized hulls that ship designers call "half models." I had seen such things displayed before, but never in the workplace where they were put to use, and my curiosity drew me closer. One of the models had been disassembled—cut lengthwise like the layers of a cake—and its component curves carefully traced upon a sheet of paper. These curves were then precisely expanded, Herr Buchen explained, and traced out on the lofting floor—"lofting" being the term used for the process of expansion from carved-hull model to full-sized ship.

Above the bench, beautifully rendered in ink on parchment, was the detailed profile of a four-masted schooner.

"*Rebecca*," the shipbuilder said wistfully. "Named for Cash's late wife."

"Beautiful," I said, commenting quite truthfully, although the ship was not as ravishing, I thought, as the sleek *Raven*, which had been built for speed rather than cargo.

"Oh, yes, very beautiful. And now it is the first ship of mine that sinks before it leaves the shed. Terrible! Terrible!"

"How did it happen?" I asked. "If I can see it for myself, maybe I can help put the Captain's mind at rest."

The shipbuilder studied me as if I were a knotty piece of oak, one he wasn't quite sure how to shape or fasten. "You come," he said and from the lofting floor led me out of the shed. There, on a long, gently sloped incline that led down to the bay, three massive ships were under construction, aswarm with workers bending long planks to the giant, curved frames that gave shape to the characteristic Waldoboro schooner. Carriers of coastal freight, each was of a length to require four masts, and from my keel-eyed vantage at the very bottom, they seemed immense arks, ready to weather the Flood that might soon sweep clean our nation.

I followed Herr Buchen to the last of his shipways, where a bare oak keel had been partially laid on a set of inclining blocks and wedges. This was all that existed of *Rebecca*, which would have been the largest of the Coffin schooners, one of the rare five-masters, intended for the coastal coal trade.

The shipbuilder produced his next pipe in the sequence, ignited the clay bowl, and crouched with his wooden hand touching the wooden keel. "If thou will know what happened to the Coffin boys, thee must understand the laying of the keel. If the keel is true and straight and properly fastened, so will the ship be true. Coffin boys know this. See how they skarf?" he said, raising his grizzled eyebrows to see if I understood.

"Skarf?" I asked, for I knew little or no shipbuilding or sailor talk.

He indicated a long, neatly executed joint in the length of the keel. "Skarf," he grunted. "Keel is made of many pieces. Forty-foot lengths joined together with skarf joints. Cut the skarf true, it locks each piece to the other. Coffin boys cut each skarf. My men very good jointers, but Coffin boys are best." He showed me the last skarf joint, which lay open, yet to be covered with the final length of keel oak. "Boys working on this piece," he said. "Want to get it right. Must be exactly so. Does thee understand?"

"Is this where it happened?" I asked. "Is this where they died?"

Buchen shook his head. "Happen inside," he said.

Inside we crossed the lofting floor, and then down to a lower level, a kind of trough within the shed building, where a steam-driven sawmill squatted like a gleaming war machine. The boiler was cold, however, as the great milling blade hadn't been used since the accident, having been abandoned by the crew of French Canadian sawyers who had helped maintain it.

"Sawmill is new, less than one year, but my Canucks, they run away, back to Quebec! It is good saw, best in all the schooner yards. Blade is six foot, tall as a big man, and see this? Teeth, eight inches! See this? Counterweights! Keep balance always smooth, cut-cut-cut, always smooth. Ha! Cuts through oak like butter! Best saw! Best money can buy!"

The sawmill was a complex piece of machinery, with many leather belts and pulleys, and levers that controlled steam power to the drive shafts and to the trundling device that pulled timber into the voracious teeth of the giant blade. The trundle carriage ran on rails, drawn by chain, and it was there the accident had happened.

"Coffin boys standing here by the lever, see? One on this side, other on that side. Old man, Cash, he's over there, in charge of carriage. This is lever that starts and stops the carriage," he said, pointing out a waist-high lever that stuck up from the trundle bed. "You pull, carriage goes along track like little railroad car. Forty-foot length of keel, rough cut from

tree. Coffin boys want to square it up true. The old man, he
wants to help them. They don't need help, but he is their
father and so they let him help. Sam has one side of keel,
Zeke has other. They make sure it stays in line. Sam, he says,
'Now, Father!' and the Captain squeezes this handle, see!
That releases the brake. Then he pulls back on the lever.
Chain is engaged—here—and carriage goes that way, into the
blade."

"It goes very fast?" I asked, trying to imagine what went
wrong. How, exactly, the twins got in the way of the blade.

Herr Buchen shook his head. "No, no, not fast. Walking
speed. See, like this?" He walked along the trundle track at a
stately pace. "Only this speed. Terrible, terrible."

It finally dawned on me that his "terrible, terrible" referred
as much to the speed as the accident itself. For the whole thing
had happened very slowly, at a walking pace. It seemed that
Sam'n'Zeke, having taken hold of the keel timber, found themselves somehow stuck to the massive timber as it entered the
whirling saw blade. "Like this," he said, pretending to place his
hands where the keel would have been upon the trundle car.

Cash Coffin, having engaged the lever, struggled to disengage it, but failed to do so.

"Nothing wrong now," Herr Buchen told me, working the
lever back and forth. "But then, something wrong. Stuck. Coffin boys are stuck to keel. The grain of the oak open up, and
then shut tight, trapping their hands."

"How is that possible?" I asked.

"Don't ask me how, I do not know. I know only what happen next. The boys are stuck to keel and keel is stuck to carriage, and carriage will not stop. My Canucks, they hear
Captain scream. They right away stop steam engine. But big
saw, you see, the counterweights keep it spinning."

Yes, I could see it now. The terrible spinning blade with its
eight-inch teeth. The trundle inexorably drawn by the

whirling counterweights. Two men cut in two, twins divided, their blood gushing in high, blade-strewn spatters as their father screams and throws his whole weight against the lever, unable to disengage the chain.

"You say their hands were trapped in the grain of the wood. You mean like a fissure that opened and then closed?"

"I don't know what is 'fissure.' "

"Could it have been splinters that snagged them somehow?"

"No splinters. A man can pull loose from splinters, if he sees that he will die. Their hands were pinned, so," he said, demonstrating.

"You were here? Saw the whole thing?"

The shipbuilder nodded and pointed up to his perch above the loft floor. So he'd been up there in the eaves, a shipbuilder god looking down upon his saw-dusty angels. "Nothing I could do. Nothing anyone could do. And now my beautiful new sawmill is finished, kaput."

The actual mechanism had not been damaged, he explained, but his men refused to work the great, steam-driven saw. "I say it is only a machine, I say accidents happen, they do not believe me. They are superstitious people, these French Canucks. They think a devil lives inside," he said, tapping the boiler.

I shook my head, confused. "Why do they think that?"

"Because it laughed. After the Coffin boys die, my Canucks say the devil laughed and spoke his name. From inside the boiler."

"My God!"

"Not God," the shipbuilder corrected, sucking on his pipe, studying me. "The devil. And his name, they say, his name is Monbasu."

"Monbasu?"

He shrugged. "I suppose it is their name for devil."

"I see."

"Do you?" Herr Buchen stared hard at me, as hard as a hammer setting nails. "What do you see? Tell me please, so I can see it, too."

# 2. The Dark Gibraltar

Daylight was already dimming by the time I drew within sight of White Harbor, but the feeling of dread I'd been anticipating did not return. By then I'd had sufficient time to digest the shipbuilder's description of the terrible accident, and in a strange way the grim facts had assembled themselves into something that made sense. There was no doubt in my mind that the seeds of superstition—the whole idea of a "curse"—had been planted by Gunther Buchen's French-speaking workmen. Confronted with an inexplicable horror, they heard the echo of their own fears in the last dying hiss of the steam boiler, and gave it a name. Their curious Canadian word for devil: Monbasu. As mankind has, for centuries, named the source of countless inexplicable tragedies. Flood, famine, plague; who but the devil himself could be blamed for such calamities? Certainly not the God who inhabits our white churches, and who appeals to our better angels. Better a curse on someone else than to face the even more terrifying prospect of an accident that could take any one of them, on any given day, in a trade where sharply honed edges, killing edges, shaped not only the ships they built, but their very destinies.

And what of the Coffin brothers, hewn by the insentient, uncaring blade? Why had they been unable to free themselves in time? We would probably never know—how could we?—but I was satisfied that despite what Herr Buchen thought he saw from the eaves, it could have been something as simple, and mortally dangerous, as unseen splinters of oak, snagging at their sleeves.

Killed by splinters? Why not? Kingdoms had been lost for less.

At noon of the following day, a telegram came from Portland, announcing that a "Great Man" would soon embark for White Harbor. The "Great Man" could be none other than Frederick Douglass himself, and in his case the description was hardly an exaggeration. No other figure from the Negro race had made such an impression upon the white race, with his books and his speeches and his impregnable dignity. He was the dark Gibraltar upon which the cruel and violent sea of slavery crashed, wave upon wave, and yet he could not be eroded. The circumstances of his life, so powerfully recounted in his autobiography, were themselves a perfectly articulated argument against the institution of slavery. I had heard the man speak only once, and that from a distance, and yet his carefully reasoned rhetoric, made vivid by his impassioned recollections of life under the lash, had been forever burned into my mind. Whatever my differences with Jebediah about the necessity of civil war, Mr. Douglass had left me with no doubt that slavery was an abomination, and that it must be eradicated. I was therefore eager to make his acquaintance, even in the present strained circumstances.

Despite the inclement weather, Mr. Douglass and his party made use of that favorite mode of Coffin transportation, namely the swift schooner *Raven*. While many travelers might have chosen the Eastern Railroad as a safer and drier alternative, Mr. Douglass by his own reckoning did not have that option, for he had long ago refused to take passage in what was commonly known as the "Jim Crow" car, the fetid box at the back of the train where Negroes were obliged to ride.

Jebediah, roused from his melancholy languor by the much anticipated arrival, recounted for me the incident that had precipitated Douglass's famous "Jim Crow" refusal. "Frederick always sends someone ahead to buy his ticket, to avoid prohibition if he can. In this case he had purchased a first-class ticket and took his seat," Jeb said, his eyes warming in recollection. "One of the other passengers objected and ordered him to proceed to the 'nigger car.' Fred said nothing, but refused to give up his seat. The enforcers were sent for. You know how roughly railroad enforcers handle customers, given the opportunity? Well, four of those brutes took hold of Fred, and Fred took hold of his seat. I need not remind you how immensely strong he is, in body as well as mind. They could not pry loose his fingers—four men!—and when they finally did 'loosen' him, that first-class seat came with him!"

I knew the story well, but Jeb's enthusiasm made it worth hearing again. "The Eastern Railroad has since done away with the 'Jim Crow' car," he went on, rubbing his hands together in a kind of anticipatory glee, "but they still discourage Negroes in the first-class compartment, so Frederick comes to us by *Raven* wings, first class all the way!"

First class, perhaps, but in the teeth of a winter squall that turned the harbor into a raging froth of spume and spray. Jeb not yet feeling well enough to leave the house, I went at the appointed time with the carriage driver, and it was all the horses could do to pull us into the wind. Wind that screeched and moaned through the pristine village, setting my teeth on edge, and rain driven so hard the shingled buildings seemed to be coated with glass as the rain froze on contact. The very wharf shuddered with the force of the gale, and so much salt water flew through the air I couldn't make out the first line of moorings, let alone the mouth of the harbor.

It didn't seem possible that even so fine and seaworthy a craft as *Raven* could prevail in such a squall, but barely had we gained the wharf when suddenly the storm eased and the spray dropped enough for me to catch a glimpse of the schooner entering the harbor under heavily reefed sails. She glided easily enough, betraying only a slight shudder at the peak of each wave, as if to shake off the remnants of the driving rain. It gladdened my heart to see the little ship prevail, and I was reminded that what may seem terrifying to a landsman is often but a "spot of weather" to the mariner.

In less than a half hour we had Mr. Douglass and his party safely aboard the carriage with their trunks stowed. I was surprised to find the famous abolitionist soaked through to his light, coffee-colored, skin, but grinning as if he'd just enjoyed a great joke. "What exhilaration!" he exclaimed. "I've always loved a ship, even when I was obliged to take passage on the open deck, but I never quite realized how much I loved a storm. All it wanted was a lightning bolt or two, to make things perfect, hey, Ottie?"

Mr. Douglass had addressed himself to a thoroughly bedraggled creature who was, I soon learned, Miss Ottilie Assing, a native of Germany who assisted Mr. Douglass in the publication of his newspapers and pamphlets, and who had translated his autobiography into the German language. Miss Assing obviously did not share the great abolitionist's enthusiasm for stormy weather. Her eyes had the look of someone who has seen, in all too vivid detail, the approaching scythe of the Grim Reaper. However, she soon recovered, and with the help of a dry towel made herself presentable. I should say more than merely presentable, for Miss Assing or "Ottie" had a kind of physical intensity that transcended mere beauty. Taken at a glance or seen in a crowd, she might have been dismissed as ordinary, but I was soon to learn that there was nothing ordinary about her.

In addition to Miss Assing, Mr. Douglass was accompanied by two gentlemen who were active in abolitionist societies,

Mr. Hugh Clinton, of Portland, and Mr. Benton Chivers, of Boston. Clinton, at thirty years of age the younger by a decade, had affected a pair of side-whiskers so large they made him look faintly ridiculous. Nothing he was to do or say in the next few days would alter that first impression. Chivers was, in contrast, a man of substantial intellect, although something of a prude, for he was not only an abolitionist, but a fervent advocate of temperance, and a Methodist. It was he who rolled his eyes and told me that at the height of the storm Mr. Douglass had clung to the forward mast and insisted on reciting "The Rime of the Ancient Mariner" in a very loud voice.

"Why did you protest?" Mr. Douglass asked with obvious amusement. "Is it not a fine poem? You know how I love Coleridge."

"And what if you'd been swept overboard?" Chivers retorted primly. "What then? Would you have us lose you for a whim?"

Mr. Douglass shrugged his broad shoulders. "I was in no such danger," he said, but seemed very satisfied to have disturbed his fellow travelers, and beamed at them with a sunny expression that contained an element of ferocity, as if daring them to disagree. Although about forty years of age, with more than a few streaks of gray woven into his dense shock of frizzled hair, Mr. Douglass retained a youthful vigor that seemed to warm whatever space he occupied. His face was very nearly as striking as his voice, an intoxicating mixture of the races, wherein the high, broad cheekbones of Africa balanced the prominent nose and thin-lipped mouth of the white man who had fathered him by committing a savage act. He was, then, the very embodiment of slave and slaveholder, physical proof of black bondage and white depravity. That such a combination should be also strikingly handsome made him all the more disconcerting, and he seemed to know it, and to revel in it, and at the same time to always be offering an unspoken apology for the audacity of his very existence.

It was Miss Assing who first remembered to inquire about Jebediah. "Is the little man not well?" she asked. I explained that the tragic circumstances of the past week had incapacitated our host, but that he seemed on the mend, and that the excitement of their visit could be nothing but a positive stimulation.

"Two brothers, you say, and a baby?" Mr. Douglass blinked his startlingly large eyes, which had lost their challenging frivolity. "The poor fellow. I know something of what he must be feeling."

Miss Assing patted the great man's hand and looked to me with a somber expression. "Frederick lost his dear Annie less than a year ago."

Annie, I was made to understand, was Mr. Douglass's eleven-year-old daughter, whose death had caused him to leave England and return home despite an outstanding warrant for his arrest in connection with the John Brown conspiracy. That he had tried to dissuade Brown from his doomed assault upon Harper's Ferry was conveniently overlooked by his enemies, who doubtless wished to see Mr. Douglass's body "moldering in the grave" as well that of the late and song-lamented John Brown.

Having brought the subject of death into the carriage, I attempted to lighten the mood by describing the rainswept village and its seafaring inhabitants as we passed through it. Later, after learning that this was by no means Mr. Douglass's first visit to White Harbor, I could only appreciate his politeness at listening to my rather ignorant travelogue. But then an exquisite sense of politeness was but one of the great man's many facets.

Clinton, the fellow with the ridiculous side-whiskers,

stared pop-eyed as we approached our destination. "Why the house has a face!" he cried. "A terrible face!"

I peered through the blurred rain and at first saw nothing but the now-familiar building. Porch, portico, wings, and tower. But then my eyes were drawn to a pair of illuminated windows on the second floor, and to the storm lanterns that had been set in a row along the porch. Clinton might be a fool, but he was not without imagination. The effect was that of a jack-o'-lantern: two glowing eyes and a row of glowing teeth below.

It was not those glowing "eyes" that put a sparkle of ice in my blood. It was the reaction of Frederick Douglass.

"My God," he said in a badly shaken voice. "It's the head of Death, and it's looking right at me."

## 3. That a Broken Hand Might Play So Well

The spell was soon broken when the carriage creaked to a stop under the portico. By then Mr. Douglass was shaking his head in self-admonition. "How silly," he exclaimed, "to fear a few ordinary lanterns. What was I thinking?" To lighten the mood, and relieve our anxiety, he proceeded to recount an anecdote about a superstition on his old plantation. I overheard it only in part, as I attended to the luggage.

The famed abolitionist was saying something like, "Kind old Sandy handed me that root and swore it would keep me safe from beatings, if only I carried it on my right side. Well, I did so, and wouldn't you know? I was never beaten again! At least not on that particular farm. Now the Baltimore waterfront, that's another thing entirely."

By then the driver and I had got the trunks inside without them being further soaked, and Jebediah was calling from the salon: "Fred! Are you there! Is that you, Fred? Come quick! If I have to wait another minute, I promise to explode!"

Mr. Douglass and his party strode dripping into the Coffin house, as bold as an invading army, but more certain of their welcome. Tom Coffin waited just inside the door, eager to shake the famous man's hand, and pious Benjamin bowed from the waist, as if admitting a king, and cousin Lucy kissed Ottilie Assing upon the cheek, although they had never in life met before. Even Barky stood ready with a tray of steaming hot chocolate, and followed us all into the salon, where Jebediah had been made comfortable on a fainting couch upholstered in maroon velvet.

"Friends! Romans! Countrymen!" Jeb exclaimed, his face alive with welcome.

"We shan't be lending you our ears," Mr. Douglass joked as he grasped Jeb's outstretched hands. "Our ears are wet and full of the sea."

"Was it a terrible storm?"

"Most terrible. I enjoyed every minute of it," crowed Mr. Douglass, seating himself on the foot of the fainting couch. And then, in a more sober tone: "I'll tell you all, dear fellow, but first let me offer you my condolences."

"You're most kind," said Jeb with a dismissive wave of the hand, "but let us put aside the convention of mourning while you are in residence. I can't bear to think of sad things when I feel such joy. Is that dear Ottie? Why you look more enchanting than ever!"

Miss Assing beamed at the compliment and murmured her thanks. Mr. Clinton and Mr. Chivers were then brought forward for introductions—yes, Jeb did recall meeting both men at the abolitionist convention in New York two years previous, what a long time ago that was—and we all took cups of Barky's chocolate concoction and drew chairs around Mr. Douglass, as if he were the magnet and we so many iron filings.

"And did the cargo arrive safely, by the way?" Jeb asked mysteriously.

After glancing at me, Mr. Douglass nodded, and no more was said of this mysterious cargo. By the look Jeb gave me—amused and pleased with his little secret—I was confident of an explanation, eventually, but it was clear the subject would be discussed no further in the present circumstance, which soon became entirely social.

"Do you have a Miss Wattle in residence?" Douglass wanted to know. When Lucy presented herself with a formal curtsy, the abolitionist took her hand and said, "Your friend

Mrs. Stanton wishes to be remembered to you. We shared the speaker's podium in Portland, and when she heard my destination, she asked that I convey her regards."

Lucy blushed to the roots of her slim neck and seemed, for a moment, struck speechless. But after a pause—a very genial pause warmed by Mr. Douglass's kindly smile—she recovered her composure and responded. "I am honored that Elizabeth Cady Stanton considers me a friend. In truth, I was only her secretary for a time, before my father's illness. I'm astonished that she remembers me at all."

"She spoke very warmly of you, Miss Wattle. Your assistance has not been forgotten, I'm sure."

I was myself somewhat distressed to know that Lucy had never seen fit to confide that she had acted as secretary to the great suffragist. Did she have the impression that I was not sympathetic to the cause of women's suffrage? Was she concerned that potential suitors might object to her radical beliefs? Was I, then, a potential suitor?

I didn't have the time nor the occasion to raise the delicate subject, as we directly went into supper, and ate sumptuously. Soon enough the concern slipped my mind entirely, as we were regaled by many a tale from Mr. Douglass, who seemed to have an inexhaustible supply of fascinating anecdotes. He managed to put himself at the center of every story in the most charming way, as if he were the bemused observer of a life he'd never imagined possible. I found him to be quite the most likable and natural companion, despite his elevated stature, for he had the ability to place his listeners on equal footing with himself. As if we too might easily have been the toast of England, speaking to cheering thousands, showered with invitations, hobnobbing with famous aristocrats. It was like being in the presence of an enormous, soul-warming fire, as if we were all small chunks of coal eagerly seeking his spark. No, more like small planets orbiting his gigantic sun. All of us drawn by his warmth, his gravity, his physical beauty, and the radiance of his intelligence. None more than Jebediah, whose condition seemed to improve by the minute.

"Shall there be war at last?" Jeb asked him, with all the eagerness of a child anticipating Christmas.

The big man shrugged, and his expression became somber. "I have given up attempting to divine the mind of Mr. Lincoln," he said. "Certainly the Southern states will continue to secede, as they are doing this very moment. But the new government may well continue to seek compromise. Lincoln could yet decide to let his famous house be divided into two houses, rather than let it fall. I think not even Mr. Lincoln knows his own mind on the subject, and won't until he feels the flow of power, and where the currents of state may take him."

"So the office makes the man?" Jeb teased.

Mr. Douglass considered the question gravely. "Yes," he decided, "on balance I think it does. Or amend that to 'changes the man.' One day I am hopeful, regarding Mr. Lincoln's intention, the next I am consumed by despair. Even if war is declared, it will be up to the new president to rouse the people. The Southern militias are well armed and eager for battle. And the North?" Mr. Douglass cupped a hand to his ear and pretended to listen. "I hear neither drum nor fife."

"You will hear it," Jeb promised. "The people will rise up, once blood has been spilled. But for now, might we hear a sweet fiddle, dear Fred? You know how I love a sweet fiddle."

Mr. Douglass obliged and had his instrument brought to the salon. In truth it required no great powers of persuasion, as the great abolitionist loved to play upon his violin, and did so with considerable skill. Accompanied by Miss Assing on the piano, Douglass entertained us with a selection of the simple country tunes he'd learned as a child, as well as pieces from the European composers. He had a particular fondness for

Mozart. His technique was somewhat peculiar because of a prior injury to his hand, which had been broken by a cruel overseer, but he played with such intensity of feeling that his audience was often moved to tears. That a broken hand might play so well! Indeed, cousin Lucy wept openly, and stood to applaud when the piece jogged to an end.

Upon seeing her, Mr. Hugh Clinton rose to join her in applauding. He gave the impression of doing so more for Lucy's approval than for any love of the music, and that hardened my heart to the fellow. Did he not know he was an interloper here? But the unkind thought only served to remind me that I, too, was an interloper, at least in regard to my admiration of Jeb's beautiful young cousin.

"Bravo!" Clinton barked. "Bravo!"

Mr. Douglass bowed, gesturing in appreciation to Miss Assing at the piano. "You are too kind," he said to his audience, but clearly he was pleased by the emotional effect of his music. After putting away his instrument he returned to the foot of the fainting couch and laid his hand upon the knitted comforter that warmed Jebediah's stunted legs. "And now, my friend, what can we do for you? You ask that we put aside tragedy, but I cannot. Shall we pray for your dead, and for the living who endure so much pain? When my Annie passed I prayed and it seemed to help."

"My brother Ben has prayers enough for all of us," Jeb said. "But tell me, Fred, does this mean you and the church have been reconciled?"

It was obvious the thrust of the question made Mr. Douglass uncomfortable. His differences with several of the more popular denominations had been frequent, and public, since while the majority of pastors had been persuaded to agree that slavery was an abomination, and that Negroes were to be considered as human beings, still these same pastors were loath to allow dark skin to soil their white pews. In their minds God had divided the races for good reason, and the proximity of a dark-skinned person was naturally repulsive to a white-skinned person. It wasn't only pastors or their parishioners; many of the more fervent white abolitionists actually agreed with this thesis, and behaved accordingly, in church and out. The general opinion in the North was that while Negroes might be human, and therefore not to be sold as chattel property, they were an inferior and degraded race, deemed so by God, and not fit for cohabitation with the white race. Worse, many of the popular Northern congregations, Methodists and so on, continued to preach that slaves were legal property, in the same way that white-skinned indentured servants owed labor to their masters, and could therefore be pursued into the free states, captured by bounty hunters, and returned to their rightful owners.

So Frederick Douglass, who as a young man had secretly ministered the gospel to his fellow slaves, and who knew the Bible as well as any man, had over the years put considerable distance between himself and organized religion, as a matter of principle.

"A man can pray outside of church," he said gently. "Indeed, is it not encouraged?"

"What do you hear from Garrison?" Jeb said, deflecting the question of prayer. "Are you reconciled?"

"I hear from him," Mr. Douglass admitted, "but no, we are not reconciled. How can we be?"

It was obvious that the split with his mentor, William Lloyd Garrison, troubled him even more than his divisions with the church. It was Garrison who had first discovered and promoted young Fred Douglass as a speaker for the cause, a luminous example of the Negro's equality of intelligence, but the two men had fallen out when, with his fame increased, Mr. Douglass decided to publish his own newspaper, *The North Star*, in competition with Garrison's *The Liberator*. More serious was their public disagreement about the very idea of secession. Garrison and many of his fellow abolitionists had for decades believed that the Constitution was fatally flawed and that the free states must therefore separate themselves from the slave states and form a new abolitionist government. Out of loyalty to Garrison, Mr. Douglass had originally adhered to this view, but over the years had changed his mind. It was not the Constitution that was flawed, he decided, but the men who interpreted it. Secession of the free states was no answer, because it did nothing to address Mr. Douglass's fundamental concern—the slaves themselves, who would remain in chains, secession or no. And now, lately, the Southern states had themselves embraced the idea of secession, exactly as Mr. Douglass had predicted they would, further embarrassing Mr. Garrison.

Garrison's response had been to encourage rumors about the impropriety of Mr. Douglass's apparently intimate relationship with Miss Assing, while alluding to the fact that Anna Douglass, his wife, was illiterate, unable to read the books her famous husband had written. Indeed, that Douglass had hired tutors to remedy the embarrassing situation, but Anna refused them. This reference to his wife's illiteracy and willful ignorance seemed to rile Douglass more than any hint of impropriety with Miss Assing.

"Never mind my little concerns," Mr. Douglass said to Jeb, admonishing him gently. "What of your concerns? I know of the terrible tragedies, and I understand if you do not wish to speak of them, but tell me, please, what has made you so ill you couldn't rise and dance to my fiddle? Is it grief, or something worse?"

"Worse," Jeb admitted. "I am doomed."

"Doomed?" Mr. Douglass asked, incredulous.

Jeb gave us all a sickly sort of smile and then shrugged. "We are all doomed, are we not? Never mind. You are here,

Fred, and for as long as you are in this house, doom must wait! Now tell us, dear Ottie, of the latest books," he said resolutely, closing the subject of his recent distress.

And so the conversation touched on the latest translations of the great man's autobiography, and his various essays and speeches, until all of us began to yawn. We made our excuses and retired, each of us, to our own private chambers, and passed the night in blessed silence.

Almost.

# 4. Strange Cargo

Strangely enough, the screams did not awaken me. I slept as soundly as if I were dead, drifting in a limbo of gray, shapeless dreams, until Lucy came into my chamber and, finding me insensible, finally managed to rouse me by tugging firmly upon my left ear.

"Wake up!" she hissed. "You are needed!"

With lantern in hand she seemed but another phantasm, although more radiant, and infinitely more beautiful. What? I thought, struggling to wake. Who needed me? Could it be this lovely creature before me, her face pinched with concern?

If I was sluggish upon being roused, the echo of a dying moan soon brought me fully conscious. Instantly I understood that this time it was not a baby crying, but an adult woman experiencing intolerable pain. You will not forget such a sound if ever you have walked the night wards. Never had I felt so helpless, and so unable to help others, as in those wards, during the last year of medical school. Night rounds, and the dire emergencies that seem to occur only then—the experience had so unnerved me that I soon relinquished any thought of a residency or apprenticeship to a surgeon. And now in the cold December night, the moaning seemed to have followed me all the way from Boston City Hospital.

"Gather your things," Lucy said, urging me with the lantern.

"My things? What things?"

"Your doctoring tools."

"But I don't have any," I protested, rather weakly.

"Then gather yourself, and follow," she retorted with an air
of disgust.

What could I do but obey?

In an alcove by the kitchen we were met by Mr. Douglass and
Miss Assing, both in their nightclothes, as well as by a worried-
looking Jebediah. Worried, I noted, but not frightened. There
was never any question in my mind but that this nocturnal
outburst was corporeal, and human. Unlike the eerie, maddening wails of the crying infant, the moaning did not move from
room to room. It originated from a particular location beneath
the house, somewhere in the cellars, the inside entrance to
which we found, within the alcove.

It was Frederick Douglass himself who led us below, holding high the lantern and admonishing the taller of us to mind
our heads. Before we got to the bottom step, even before I
could see the glistening dark faces illuminated in the glow of
the lantern, I understood that we had here, in the subter-
ranean shelter of the Coffin house, a group of runaway slaves.

It made sense, considering Jebediah's fanatical abolitionism, that he would make his own home a stop on the so-called
underground railway. And these poor frightened creatures—
no, these poor human beings—were quite literally underground, having been transported, I was soon made aware, from
the harbor at Gloucester, via the swift *Raven*, which was often
secretly utilized for that purpose.

"Black Jack Sweeney is one of our most trusted 'conduc-
tors,' " Mr. Douglass confided, referring to *Raven*'s one-eyed
master. "More than a thousand former slaves owe their freedom to that pretty little ship. When the weather improves this
group is bound for Yarmouth, Nova Scotia, to join the com-
munity we've established there. But meantime their numbers
are about to increase by one. Provided you can help with a difficult birthing."

Such was the source of the frantic moaning. A terrified young woman, no more than twenty, was being attended by the other females in the group, the men having placed themselves in the far end of the cellar, where they crouched and stared worriedly at the moving lanterns. Truthfully, I wanted to join them, for my entire experience of the birth process had been strictly as an observer, in the charity wards, when some poor unfortunate happened to find herself there at the crucial moment, rather than safe at home where babies are more properly, and more safely, delivered. I had but once assisted (stood by in horror is more like it) while a whiskey-scented surgeon—a charming fellow with intelligent, kindly eyes— attempted a cesarean and botched it badly, murdering the mother in the process. Thus had I finally been cured of any desire, however faint, to take up the actual practice of medicine, because by necessity a physician's hands are stained with the blood of his patients, called by some his victims.

So you will understand my anxiety upon being summoned to this scene, which was even more hopeless than the situation preceding the fatal cesarean. The group of women helping the young mother turned to me so beseechingly that at the very least I must give my opinion, and I'm afraid my opinion was very grave: the baby was breached in the birth canal and as it continued its feeble struggle the umbilical cord was wrapping ever tighter around its tiny neck. There was no reason to suppose the baby could live, and every passing minute made it less likely that the young, terrified mother would survive the ordeal.

Had beautiful, alluring cousin Lucy not been there, it is likely I would have refused to intervene in a natural process whose culmination could only be death. As it was, I hadn't the courage to reveal the truth: that the esteemed Dr. Bentwood was a physician in title only, highly educated but virtually inexperienced. In other words, as capable of worsening the situation as of improving it. But being unwilling to shame myself in the presence of a woman who I wished to think well of me, I bade one of the frightened female slaves hold the lantern while I interfered with the struggling mother.

"You there, grip her ankles," I ordered, affecting an authority I did not feel. "Someone else get a cold compress for her forehead. And you, put something between her teeth, if you please. And, madam," I said, addressing the poor young female who writhed in pain, "please try to relax between contractions. There's no point in pushing until we get this little fellow pointed in the right direction."

"Good man!" Mr. Douglass exclaimed, keeping his distance. "Do not despair," he announced to the male runaways, who continued to avert their eyes from female mysteries. "We've a fine Boston doctor attending. All that can be done, will be done."

If only you knew! I thought. Crouched between the woman's trembling legs, I frantically tried to remember what the textbooks had to say on the subject of breached births. I vaguely recalled that forceps were recommended, and possibly speculums, but I had neither, and all I could do was prod at the tiny little being who was trapped, as it were, between two worlds. Its heart was still beating—beating very rapidly—but that could not long continue. Truthfully, I was merely waiting for its life to ebb away, with some vague idea that I might then pry it loose and save the mother, when something grasped my bloody finger.

A hand it was, not much larger than my knuckle. And yet the tiny fingers grasped my own with desperate strength. A reflex, I thought—the poor child is in the throes of death. And yet it did not die. Instead, with no real assistance from me, the infant suddenly shifted position. First the elbow slid into view, and then a round glistening object that thrummed with the pulse of life.

"The head!" I cried. "I see the head!"

The mother gasped with hope, then groaned heavily, thrust her hips, and tensed every muscle in her slender body.

"Keep pushing!" I cried. Quite suddenly, and almost easily, the slick, blood-smeared baby slid into my open hands. The umbilical cord was loosely wrapped around its neck and under one tiny shoulder, and once that was free the boy—yes, it was a boy, no doubt about that—the boy opened his gasping little mouth, coughed up a knot of phlegm, and then cried quite loudly, as if to say, I live, I live.

I left the women to tidy up the afterbirth and fled, as if from the scene of a crime.

An hour later, having thrown away my ruined nightgown, and washed up with the heated water and soap supplied by a grinning Barky, I made a more dignified entrance into the dining room, where Mr. Douglass and his party were breakfasting.

Upon seeing me the big man threw down his napkin, rose from the table, and eagerly wrung my hands. "We thought the poor girl was doomed and you saved her! You saved them both!"

Lucy smiled at me as she had never smiled before, as if I had surpassed her rather meager expectations. That this fine woman might admire me was a pleasant prospect, but I couldn't let the lie stand, not and live with myself.

"I did nothing," I confessed to all. "It was a miracle."

Mr. Douglass studied me with bemusement. "A miracle? Oh, I'm sure God helped, but you, sir, are the miracle. That you were here. That you had the skill. That's miracle enough."

"You don't understand," I said. "The baby grabbed my hand."

"Yes?"

"A newborn can't grasp like that," I explained. "It hasn't the strength or the ability."

Mr. Douglass's fine dark eyes crinkled as he smiled. "Good sir, didn't I just grasp your hand in gratitude? Boston did the same, and for the same reason."

"Boston?" I asked.

"The boy's name. In your honor."

"Here! Here! Hail the conquering hero!" Jebediah clapped his hands and led a rousing huzzah. Lucy joined him, beaming approval.

What could I do but sit down to breakfast?

## 5. The Face in the Tower Window

The great abolitionist left in three days time, bound for rallies in Springfield and Hartford, and thence back home to New York for a spell, where he would await the decision of the new president and the new Congress, as to the ongoing secession of the slave states. The band of twenty-eight fugitives remained hidden away in the cellars of the Coffin house, for the wind was fierce and contrary, and *Raven* lay double-anchored in White Harbor, her ice-coated shrouds moaning *eeeeh . . . ahhh, eeeeh . . . ahhh,* like a seabird grounded in a frozen nest.

Her master, Black Jack Sweeney, had taken ill and been brought ashore suffering from chills, catarrh, muscle tremors, and a troubling congestion of the lungs. The esteemed Dr. Bentwood, having supposedly saved two lives, was expected to work a similar miracle with the ailing mariner. Bowing to expectations, I began, for the first time, to assume the responsibilities of a general practitioner or country doctor, in so far as family and friends of the family were concerned. An eager young druggist helped me put together a rudimentary bag of medicines, and I worked up courage sufficient to approach the crusty, foul-mouthed (and now foul-tempered) old coot.

"Leave me be, young fool!" he roared when I tried to spoon a calomel purgative into his pipe-stained mouth. "If I survived the cholera I can survive a winter ague. Take your stinkin' poison away! Be gone!"

The calomel was poisonous only in larger doses, but I was willing enough to leave his sick-smelling chamber. Other, more sympathetic patients required attention. There was

Jebediah with his lingering melancholy, which returned the moment Mr. Douglass departed. For Jeb I prescribed a small dose of jalap, followed by a brisk walk, and it seemed to help a little, although he continued to complain about the fatalistic gloom that weighed so heavily upon his small, stunted shoulders. He was doomed, his family was doomed, the nation was doomed, humanity was doomed, and so on, as if he were trapped in a dark pit and couldn't raise himself high enough to see over the edge, to the daylight beyond.

Then there was poor Sarah, who remained virtually insensible with grief. Her devoted husband Nathaniel had arranged temporary rooms in the village, since Sarah appeared to believe that the Coffin house itself—or something in it—had killed little Casey. According to his brother Benjamin, who made frequent visits to pray over them, Nathaniel was beside himself with fear that in her delirium Sarah would take her own life. Would the esteemed doctor do what he could? Of course. And so I prescribed various sleeping powders, then a nerve tonic, and finally an elixir to stimulate appetite. Lastly, at Nathaniel's insistence, I bled the woman. Nothing seemed to have any positive effect. I shared Nathaniel's concern about his wife's will to live, but there was naught to be done but pray, and hope that time eventually eased her grief.

As to the original patient, and my reason for being summoned to White Harbor, little enough was heard. There had been no further outbursts from the tower, no pistol shots or raving, and Barky the cook reported that the Captain was eating again. Nor had there been any more inexplicable phenomenon. It was as if the famous abolitionist's whirlwind visit had swept the old house free of vengeful spirits, or vengeful neighbors, or whatever it was that had so cruelly tormented the family.

Having established myself, however fraudulently, as an

effective physician, I should have taken my leave before the truth of my actual incompetence inevitably made itself known. Two things held me: concern for Jebediah, and my growing interest in his beautiful cousin, Lucy. Day by day, minute by minute, I became more intrigued by her radiant presence. I was particularly fascinated by the way she seemed to study everyone she came in contact with, peering at them from all sides, ceaselessly questioning, as if seeking some sort of revelation, an answer to all the mysteries of life. The most fundamental mystery came down to this: was she as intrigued by me as I with her? And if true, how deeply felt was the attraction? Was I shaping up as a prospective lover, or was she weighing my potential as a husband, or both?

Even if I'd had the courage to inquire of her feelings, the present circumstances made it impossible. The house was in triple mourning, hardly a propitious time for courtship. The best I could do was use every excuse to be in her company. To this she was amenable. We dined together, played cards, and each morning discussed the dispatches from the numerous journals, weekly broadsides, and inflammatory pamphlets delivered to the house at Jebediah's request. Each day brought news of yet another Southern state voting to join South Carolina, and it seemed clear that secessionists would soon band together in what they were calling a "confederacy" of the slave states.

"Item from Richmond," I read aloud, after clearing my throat. " 'It is rumored that former United States Senator Jefferson Davis, who has assumed the presidency of the new confederacy, has been in communication with General Robert E. Lee. Would the general consider resigning from the Army of the United States and throw his support to the Confederacy? General Lee is thus far undecided, even if the secessionists are not.' "

Erect in her straight-backed chair, pale as new snow in the faint winter light of midafternoon, Lucy shook her head and frowned prettily. "That would be treason, would it not?"

"Not if he resigns first."

"Is General Lee so important to their wretched 'cause'?"

"He's very well respected. It would be a great blow if he goes over to the other side."

"Then let him go. Surely there are plenty of generals at West Point?"

"Few so highly regarded. The question, as I see it, isn't what general will command the secessionist militias, but what President Lincoln will do about it."

"What can he do?" Lucy said. "At this moment the so-called Confederacy has no army, no money—or not much—and no duly elected authority. All it has is hot air by the acre. What would you have the president do about a rebellion that so far is no more than a bad idea?"

"The nation looks to him for guidance. We wish to know his intentions. Will it be compromise or war?"

"Is there no other alternative?" she asked slyly. "Can we not remain as we are?"

"Is that what you wish? To remain as we are?" I asked, taking the opportunity to nudge my chair an inch closer to hers.

"Cousin Jebediah says blood must be shed," she said, parrying the question. "It is the only way to cleanse the nation of our sins."

I nodded. "Yes. Jeb wants to see the slaveholders punished as cruelly as the slaves themselves have been tormented."

"And you do not?"

"I wish to see slavery abolished. I also wish to see the nation preserved without the necessity of taking up arms."

Lucy leaned forward. Her ivory fingers lightly touched my wrist, and it was all I could do to disguise a shudder of pleasure. "And how do you reconcile those two positions?" she asked. "Can an army make war without firing a shot? Will Jeff Davis surrender before the battle begins? What could persuade such a man to give up everything he believes in?" Her hand squeezed my wrist and then withdrew. "No, my dear, there must be war. Some trifling thing will set it off."

"No," said I.

"Yes," she insisted. "The age of compromise ended with Lincoln's election, and war was certain the day he took office. If you don't believe in fate then you must at least believe in math."

"Math?" I asked with a laugh. "What has math to do with war?"

"Why everything," she said, affecting surprise. "As new states are added, and new senators, the mathematical balance in Congress must shift. With compromise no longer possible, slavery will be outlawed within the next few years. Rather than free their slaves, who they fear—having beaten the men and ravished the women—rather than free such people for retribution, the so-called gentlemen of the South will fight. 'States' rights!' they shout, but the only 'right' they're really interested in is the right to own slaves. The 'right' to bed, beat, torture, and murder them as they see fit. There is no other 'right' in dispute."

"Murdering a slave is a crime in every state," I reminded her. "Even the slave states."

Lucy's eyes flashed and her voice became more forceful— but attractively, passionately so. "Has a white man ever been arrested for such a crime? No, he has not. Never in the history of our nation. And yet many slaves are murdered each year. Thousands, perhaps. Murdered or worked to death. Murdered for whims, or because the overseer was drunk, or because the slave had 'dangerous ideas.' And those that are not actually killed, beaten, or raped are slow-tortured by the withholding of food. Even as we idle here, digesting a luncheon that would feed an enslaved family for a week, there are tens of thousands of men, women, and children already hard at work with empty bellies. What causes this, a famine? No. There is no lack of food in the South. Slaves are starved as a means of keeping them compliant."

Her passion stirred me, if not the subject itself. "I read Mr. Douglass's essay on that very subject," I said.

"And did you not believe him?"

"Of course I believed him!"

Lucy eyed me doubtfully, then rattled another broadside newspaper, pointing to a particularly offensive paragraph. "States' rights! Even the wretched Free Democrats echo the lie. But here is the truth of it, in cold ink. Here is Jefferson Davis himself on the subject of states' rights: 'What is the reason we are compelled to assert our rights? That the labor of our African slaves would be taken away by the federal government.' Oh, and listen to Alexander Stevens, the Confederacy's vice president. This is what the good Mr. Stevens has to say about states' rights: 'The immediate cause of our present revolution is the threat to the institution of slavery. Our new government is founded upon the great truth that the Negro is not equal to the white man, that slavery, subordination to the superior race, is his natural and moral condition.' " Lucy snapped the newspaper sharply upon her knees. "The words come from their own mouths. These men will never give up slavery so long as they live. Jebediah has it right. Blood must be shed. And if the federal forces don't shed it first, the South will. They are sick with the suspense, and so if Lincoln won't pick the fight, they will do it for him."

A small sigh escaped me, and Lucy did not miss it. "I suppose it must be especially difficult for one who was trained to be a doctor," she said. "I mean, for such a man to contemplate the taking of lives."

"What?" I said, aghast. "Let me assure you, my dear, I do not contemplate taking lives."

"You must pardon me, 'my dear,'" she said, giving the phrase a wry twist as she sent it back to me. "Of course you will not take lives. What was I thinking. You are a physician and so will save lives for a greater purpose. Surgeons are not employed to fire bullets or wield bayonets. Surgeons are employed to lop off ruined limbs and sew up wounds and send the soldiers back into battle."

"Lucy!" I cried, aghast.

"Oh? Are you offended by my language? Have I said something that isn't true?"

"No, but . . . I mean to say, we are not yet at war and I am not yet a surgeon, nor will I ever be."

"But you have such fine, clever hands," she said, tracing her fingertips across the back of my hands. "What a shame it would be to waste them."

Blood pounded behind my eyes and for a moment the room was tinted pink. Fantastic images came to mind, and fantastic, lascivious desires. Mere proximity to this vibrant woman was suddenly intolerable. I leaped to my feet and paced the sitting room. Lucy thought she had offended me and attempted to apologize. "No, no!" I protested. "Nothing you could do or say could ever be offensive! I'm simply, ah, overstimulated by all this talk of war and bloodshed. Ha! The air is close, do you not find it close?"

I was babbling like a schoolboy caught in full blush of adolescent craving, and like a schoolboy I ran away.

Outside, the noon-high sun melted snow from the eaves, and it tinkled merrily, mocking my embarrassment. What an ass! How could the touch of a female hand so inflame a full-grown man? But then, recalling the uncanny and irresistible electricity of that contact, how could it not?

I told myself that something was wrong. It was as if there was some stifling effect within the great house that caused normal human desire to fester like a lingering wound, until desire itself became diseased. There was no other explanation for the feverish, repellent thoughts that coursed through my mind, images of ravishment and violent ecstasies of the flesh that were alien to my nature. Images so vile that if Lucy were to share my mind for the merest moment, she would flee from my presence.

Determined to stop these hideous thoughts, I plunged my hands into an icy puddle and splashed myself in the face. The shock of the cold brought me back to my senses, and after several deep, shuddering breaths I was able to return to the house in a more sensible state.

My distraction was such that I did not at first see the face in the window. The face in the tower window. The white-bearded face of Cassius Coffin, who stared down at me from the heights of his lunacy with the ancient mocking eyes of an insane prophet. The force of his gaze was such that I stopped in my tracks, as if I were a lost ship suddenly illuminated by a lighthouse beacon. A mad, blue-eyed beacon.

Suddenly the old sea captain threw upon the window, and pointing down to where I stood in slack-jawed astonishment, launched a word that pierced my heart like a poisoned arrow.

"Beware the alchemy!" he bellowed. "Monbasu lives!"

# 6. Bounty Men

It may be that any words shouted by a madman have the power to invoke fear. "Beware the alchemy," yes, surely, but what alchemy? As to "monbasu," certainly I was aware that the old sea captain must have heard the French-Canadian sawyers muttering about "monbasu" at the shipyard where his sons were killed. And yet the word itself produced an instantaneous physical effect within me, as if the icy water of the snowmelt had leached into my bones. Before the echo of his scream died my teeth were chattering and my whole body began to shake uncontrollably. It was all I could do to lurch to the portico and gain entrance by the side door, which deposited me in Barky's kitchen.

"Oh, deary," the cook squeaked in his high-choked voice. "Dr. Bentwood has taken himself a chill."

I was shivering so hard I couldn't make myself understood, and in any case there was no point in arguing. "Chill" was a weak description of whatever had overcome me, but it would have to do. It was as if the heat of my unseemly desire for Lucy was being punished by an extreme reversal of bodily temperature, in some strange way triggered by the Captain's outburst. Before I quite knew what was happening, the cook had swathed me in woolen blankets and pressed a hot mug of coffee into my trembling hands. Gradually the violent fit of shivering passed, and I was at last able to speak, and to thank this kindly, charitable gentleman.

"Best dose yourself with your own medicine," was his

reply. "But just for now we'll rely on Barky's cure. See can you choke this down."

There was no need to "choke down" the generous slice of hot, fresh from-the-oven bread soaked with dark, pungent honey. It was as if the fit of shivering had somehow famished me, and I devoured Barky's "cure" like a starving man. When I was able to express my thanks I did so, and then without really considering it beforehand, asked if he was familiar with the term "monbasu."

"What's that then," he responded in all innocence, "a kind of stew?"

"I think it is a kind of curse word," I told him. "Peculiar to French Canada."

Barky chuckled as he loaded kindling into his huge kitchen stove. "Like any has been to sea, I know many a cuss," he said. "English cuss words. American cuss words. Schooner cusses, whaler cusses, and navy cusses. There's Portagee cusses'll make your ears hurt, and French, Italian, and Greek that leave smoke in the air. And then there's a couple of choice cusses I learnt from a New Quineaman that claimed to be a cannibal. But I never heard 'mon bassoon.' "

"Monbasu," I corrected.

"That neither."

"You never heard the Captain use it, when you delivered his meals?"

The gentle cook bridled. "What? Cuss when I bring him his vittles? Never!"

I hastened to apologize, explaining that I meant no connection to his cooking, but that he'd often been in the Captain's proximity, more so than anyone else in the house.

"Any but the cat," Barky agreed. "I heard himself cuss, of course, him being a seafaring sort of man, but always the usual variants. 'G' words and 'F' words and the like."

"Thank you, Barky. Please take no insult."

"No insult taken, sir," he squeaked amiably. "Have some more coffee, and there's pie on the way."

That evening Jebediah came to me in a state of agitation. For a moment I feared that his eyes glowed with the same lunacy that afflicted his father. Like his father he had a kind of brightness in his gaze that seemed to look beyond this world, into the next. But I soon learned that his agitation was not a result of madness or melancholy, but of a very real threat to the refugees he was harboring.

"Word has come!" he announced. "Bounty hunters have found us!"

"Bounty hunters? Surely not!"

It was absurd to think that, with the nation on the brink of war, slave owners would still be offering rewards for runaway slaves. But as Jeb quickly explained, nothing had yet changed in that regard. The slave owner still had the law on his side, and retained the absolute right to retrieve his property anywhere within the United States and its territories. If anything the prospect of a split with the federal government had increased the foul activity of that seedy brotherhood of bounty hunters, whose efforts had become more violent and unseemly than ever before. And although care had been taken to bring the runaways to the Coffin house under cover of darkness, and keep them all confined and out of sight, somehow word had passed to the bounty men, who were already en route from Falmouth, and expected by daybreak, which was their favorite hour for striking. At one hundred in gold "per woolly head" (as the return posters exclaimed) a fortune was hidden in the Coffin cellars, waiting to be mined by the fiendish, soulless beasts who roamed the countryside, returning men to shackles, and women to the masters who had ravished them.

There was nothing for it but to hastily put the runaways back aboard *Raven* and flee the harbor.

"The wind has subsided even if the seas have not," Jeb explained as he waddled anxiously about the room, gesturing with his stunted arms. "Any chance you can cure Captain Sweeney within the hour?"

"None whatsoever," I said. "He has an inflammation of the bronchial tubes that could develop into pneumonia. He's a tough old bird, but exposure to cold sea air would likely prove fatal."

Tom Coffin, who had been ashore but briefly following his recent voyage to the Orient, volunteered to take charge of *Raven*. As master of a giant clipper ship with a sky full of sails, he was possibly overqualified to command a small coastal schooner for the relatively short passage to Nova Scotia, which lay a mere hundred and fifty miles or so to the east. Rather than condescend to the favor, his enthusiasm for the idea was such that Jebediah leaped into a nearby chair and embraced the young sea captain until he was quite red in the face.

"You are a most excellent man!" Jeb exclaimed, and then, turning to me, "My dear Davis, will you be good enough to help?"

Although I hadn't previously paid more than lip service to the underground railroad, the actual proximity of brutal bounty hunters was so despicable that I found myself quite willing to break the law, and vowed to assist the desperate refugees in any way possible.

"Excellent! Perhaps you could drive one of the wagons. We must get them to the harbor all in one go." Jeb turned back to his handsome, seafaring brother, who seemed to glow with the prospect of action. "Tom, good Tom! Let us be quick. Quicker than the eye of God, or they'll have us all in jail!"

# 7. Dark Passage

There was never a sky so dark, so oppressively dismal, as the starless, moonless sky that enclosed White Harbor like a great black fist. There is nothing inherently "supernatural" about an overcast sky, not in winter on the coast of Maine, and yet the clouds themselves were invisible, and therefore somehow dreadful. As if the familiar, reassuring starlight had been forever extinguished by a sepulchral darkness rising up from the frozen nothing of hell itself.

Jebediah had forbidden the use of lanterns, fearing that the bounty hunters might have sent scouts ahead, and so our hurried procession to the wharf, and from there to the waiting *Raven*, was a floundering parade of the blind and frightened. The black refugees, roused from uneasy sleep, were obviously terrified, but maintained a communal silence that was violated only by the softly muffled mewling of the newborn baby. They were, as a group, well acquainted with the necessity for silence, and for furtive movement in the darkest hours. And yet I sensed, along with their understandable anxiety, a sense of keen anticipation, for they were all aware that if this last transfer was successful, the next time they touched land, freedom would be theirs. And yet, considering the bleakness of the night, and the ferocity of the sea, I could not but think that theirs was the hooded hope of a condemned man who expects to enter paradise when the trap beneath his feet has finally been sprung.

*Raven*'s crew met us at the wharf and began the dangerous business of transferring passengers out to the schooner. I say "dangerous" because although the ferocious northeast wind had abated somewhat, huge ocean waves still surged over the promontory, sending steep, rolling swells throughout the harbor. *Raven* heaved and yanked on her double mooring like a maddened horse, as if determined to free herself from the anchorage. At times the swell lifted the approaching whaleboat well above the deck of the plunging schooner. Bringing the lightly built whaleboat alongside was treacherous indeed, but the crewmen went about their task with great aplomb, as if this was nothing to what they'd accomplished in other, even more wretched circumstances. Given the number of passengers, it would take, at minimum, four round-trips to get them all aboard. Four chances to capsize or be cracked like an egg against *Raven*'s unforgiving hull.

"Looks worse than it is," Tom Coffin confided jauntily as we waited our turn on the wharf.

I could barely make him out in the darkness, but his brimming confidence was reassuring. "It will be a miracle if no one drowns," I said, keeping my voice low, so as not to impart even more fear to the refugees who huddled along the wharf, awaiting the return of the whaleboat.

"There's one thing we've got in our favor," he replied with a droll turn of the tongue.

"What's that?"

"I'm the luckiest captain that ever steered a ship!" he said, clapping me on the back.

"Sir! You astonish me! Is it not tempting ill fortune to say so, given what has happened to your brothers?"

"What? Oh, I see. Please don't misunderstand. I speak of my seafaring fortunes, not the awful luck we've had ashore. At sea, I assure you, my luck does hold."

"Surely you are referring to your skills as a mariner," I said, scuttling away from the edge as a giant swell spewed up against the wharf timbers, showering us with icy spray. "What has luck or good fortune to do with skill?" I sputtered, clearing the salty cold water from my mouth. "You do not give yourself credit for skill."

Tom laughed easily and then stood closer, so that I might make out the merry twinkle in his eyes. "The skills of a mariner are enough to get him to the place where his ship sinks, or goes aground. It is luck, and only luck, that saves him from that fate. We Coffins have always had great luck at sea. My father sailed for thirty years and never lost a ship. Of our coastal fleet, none has ever been lost with a Coffin aboard. A little nor'east swell won't trouble my luck this evening, Dr. Bentwood, I promise you that."

As to my accompanying the party, there was never any question about that. My duty as friend compelled me to stand by Jebediah in this particular hour of need. It was, on reflection, a way for me to demonstrate that despite our differences regarding the prospect of war, on this one issue we were agreed: slavery was such an abomination that the laws enforcing it could and must be disregarded, and disobeyed when necessary, by all men of conscience. There was also the necessity of providing medical attention to the refugees themselves, a number of whom were neither young nor sturdy. As for Captain Sweeney, I was reasonably sure he would improve in my absence, and if necessary he could be better attended by Dr. Griswold, who no doubt had a thousand times more experience treating respiratory ailments than did I.

As it happened, Jeb and I were ferried out to *Raven* together, after the last of the refugees was safely aboard. There had been no sign of our pursuers, the night was fine, if over dark, and my little friend was greatly relieved.

"We are embarked on a great voyage!" he exclaimed as we all clung to the sides of the heaving whaleboat.

I had no words to reply, as my stomach had been left upon the wharf. Our small, fragile boat plunged down the face of an impossibly steep swell and I shut my eyes rather than see us overturned. And yet such was the skill of the oarsmen that we did not capsize, and aside from being thoroughly soaked by the bitterly cold mist rising off the waves, we were delivered to the schooner without further incident.

At first it appeared we had merely been transferred from one small heaving deck to another, larger heaving deck, which was scarcely an improvement. But a strange and wonderful thing happened when Tom Coffin caused the storm-shortened sails to be raised. All at once *Raven* ceased her violent movements. The force of her canvas seemed to have a steadying effect, and as she slipped away from her moorings and gathered speed, the little ship came alive in a way that gave me confidence in her new master's promise that his luck would hold.

On deck were the grizzled crew who had manned *Raven* when it had taken me from Portland to White Harbor. They went about their business, scarce needing a word of command from Tom Coffin, who had assumed the role of helmsman, as well as that of sailing master. It was reassuring to see his steady hands upon the great wheel, and the ready smile that was visible in the light from the binnacle. Surely with this man in charge, no harm could come to us.

I found a suitable cubbyhole on deck and watched in fear, and soon enough in a kind of excited, seasick wonder as the towering waves rose up behind the stern of the schooner, rolling and breaking quite harmlessly in our wake. For, as Tom Coffin explained, the wind had shifted round to the south, in our favor, and under these conditions *Raven* could outrun the following sea, heading downwind for Yarmouth.

"A fair summer kind of wind!" he cried from the wheel. "And here we are in the teeth of winter!"

The majority of the refugees had taken shelter below, the women and infant in the cabin salon, while the men huddled together in the cargo hold, warming themselves under damp woolen blankets. A few, however, chose to remain on deck, believing the open air less conducive to seasickness. I soon found myself in conversation with one Richard Daws, a Baltimore Negro who was accompanying his young wife. It was she, he confided, who had recently given birth, and he was obviously grateful for any small help I'd provided.

"I did little enough," I confided. "The child was determined to be born. Just as, I suppose, you are determined to be free."

Mr. Daws tightened his woolen blanket and turned so that I might see his face, which was not so dark as many of the others. I could make out very little of him, other than that his eyes bulged alarmingly, but he had a fine, melodious baritone that carried over the creaking of the masts and the mournful hum of the rigging. "I was already free," he informed me. "My master, who was also my father, he made me a freedman on his death, and give me papers to prove it. I been free since I was eight years old."

"Extraordinary," I said. "If you are already free, then why are you leaving the country?"

"My wife," he explained. "She was trained a seamstress, owned by Mrs. Purley, who is sister-in-law to my old master. We grew up neighborly, you see, my wife and me. Then I went off to Baltimore, to 'prentice a cooper. And come her sixteenth birthday, my Addie was hired out in the city, to sew for Mrs. Purley. Everything she made but ten cent a week, that went to Mrs. Purley, you see, and it vexed her. Vexed us both. So my Addie ran off to another 'stablishment in Baltimore, where she could keep what she earned, even though it was but half the reg'lar rate, on account of her situation, and Mrs. Purley sent a man to catch her. Man beat her, took her back to the Purley place, beat her some mo', then they locked her in a cupboard without no food and only 'nuff water as to keep her alive. They aim to keep her in that cupboard, too, 'til they broke her. Anyhow, one of Addie's sisters got word to me."

"My God, man, what did you do?"

"I went down there and stole her out and we been on the run ever since. We finally made New York and got us church-married by a Negro preacher, but the bounty men, they got on to Addie, and the preacher man put us on to the Douglass rail-way. My little Addie, she first thought that meant we'd go by train like the white folk do, but mostly we traveled by foot, all the way up to Rhode Island. I'd a fixed to stay in Rhode Island, but the coopers there took a vote and decided they won't abide a freedman in their guild. Even a freedman light as me. They swore they'd break my niggerish hands if I bent a stave, so it's all the way to Canada for us, and hopes we find work there."

Daws had recounted his travails with very little emotional inflection, as if commenting upon the weather, but his story took my breath away. How had we come to this state of affairs in our nation, when a free Negro tradesman was compelled by circumstance to leave the country of his birth? I attempted to express my outrage, but Mr. Daws calmly shook his head and said, "Don't you trouble yourself on my 'count, sir. We's mighty grateful the way you helped my Addie."

With that he took his leave and rejoined the other few Negroes who remained on deck, sheltered in the lee of the fore cabin. Something in me wanted to follow him, this pro-foundly decent and brave man, and apologize for the injustices he and his young wife had suffered. But it wasn't my wish to humble him in any way, as if I had the right to beg forgiveness for the cruelty of my fellows, and so I kept my silence, for bet-ter or worse, and comforted myself with the notion that he would find a better life.

Meantime Tom Coffin stood boldly at the helm, both hands upon the spokes of the great wheel, steering *Raven* down the steep seas. Now and again he issued cryptic orders to the schooner's crewmen, causing lines to be shortened or lengthened, sails adjusted and so on. I knew nothing of their business, but the result was an ever-increasing speed. At times the hull seemed to lift out of the water, as if wanting to skim upon the very surface. The whole effect was at once exhilarating and terrifying, as if we were perpetually on the verge of losing our balance, only to keep recovering by flying ever faster before the wind.

"Nothing to worry about!" our handsome captain bellowed, sensing my concern, if not my palpable fear. "She steers like a dream, this one!"

Like a dream, yes, thus far perhaps, but just lately my dreams had a way of warping into nightmare, and flying headlong into the black of night, blind but for the compass, did nothing to relieve my anxiety.

Soon thereafter Jebediah returned from below, where he'd been overseeing the production of enough hot potato stew to warm the innards of the entire company. Handing me a two-handled tin of the stuff, he conferred briefly with his brother Tom at the helm. With a knit woolen cap pulled over his ears, Jeb looked the runt of a sailor man, a comical figure whose awkward, waddling gait seemed almost a purposeful attempt at humor. But when he returned to engage me in conversation he remained upright, with his back braced to the cabin, which put us at the same level. Observing him that way, in profile with his chin thrust out, I noted, not for the first time, that were we of the same height, his would be the more imposing figure.

"Tom says we'll be there by midday, if the wind holds on this heading," he said, quite satisfied. "We're making ten knots, which is quite an excellent speed, if you didn't know."

"I didn't. Thank you for the stew. I was expecting hardtack, whatever that is."

Jeb chuckled affectionately. "You don't want to know, not if you value your teeth."

"I just heard the most remarkable story," I said, and told him of my conversation with Mr. Daws.

Much to my surprise, Jeb seemed strangely unmoved by the account. "They all have stories like that," he said matter-of-factly. "Most of them worse. Daws was lucky his wife was only beaten and locked away. The time-honored method of 'breaking' a rebellious female slave is to get her with child, preferably one of your own. But enough," he said, interrupting himself with an abrupt and violent gesture of his clenched fist, "we are sailing these poor folks away from a wretched past, into an uncertain future."

"Uncertain, yes, but free," I reminded him.

Jeb snorted at my ignorance. "Oh, yes, free. Free to live in poverty and be loathed by their fellow citizens."

"Jebediah!"

"What? You find me cynical? I assure you, I do not exaggerate. The British may have outlawed slavery, but no one can outlaw hatred, particularly that form of hatred based on skin color. We will be allowed to land these folk on British soil because British law holds that we must. But believe me, free Negroes are no more welcome in Halifax than in Richmond."

"Then why risk it?" I asked, with an involuntary glance at the enormous seas piling up behind us.

My small friend shrugged. "What else can I do? If I were a full-made man I'd be a general. I'd raise an army, invade the slave states, and send the oppressors to hell. I'd do so gladly and without hesitation—doubt me not! But even if the righteous win the coming war, and we must, I fear that race hatred will prevail."

I did not doubt that were it possible, Jebediah would indeed become a smaller Napoleon laying waste to the land of cotton. But his despair for the future of these particular

refugees, and of all the colored race, was something I'd never heard before, for all his ranting upon the subject. This was a new darkness within, born of the family disaster, and in the belief that his very existence was a curse upon his kin.

I found this new Jebediah disturbing, and longed for the return of my jolly, if excitable, old friend. Was he still there beneath the shadows, or had tragedy altered him irrevocably?

Events would soon render the answer moot, for we were both about to be changed forever, and led into a darkness that made the starless sky above seem cheery by comparison.

# 8. When Lightning Speaks

As it happened, *Raven* made the small port of Yarmouth in fourteen hours, a run never before achieved by the schooner in the full depth of winter, according to its crew. Not a shroud parted, nor was any sail torn, and the bilge remained as dry as an autumn leaf, as if some power of Providence had puffed the favorable winds and kept us safe.

We were met at a certain wharf by agents of the local abolitionist society, who had arranged transportation and shelter for the refugees. Although, as one Abner Simms confided, they hadn't anticipated the arrival of quite so many of the black souls. "Our little Nigger Town has become somewhat overcrowded," he told me. "Not so many as we'd hoped have elected to depart for Africa."

"You call the encampment Nigger Town?" I asked him pointedly.

"No possible offense intended," the glum little man assured me. "That's the local name, it has no other, being a temporary accommodation." His none-too-clean fingers thrummed upon his wet blubberous lips, and he seemed intent upon studying his own dung-stained boots rather than the faces of the refugees, who were being helped into crude, horse-drawn wagons.

"And what is this about sailing for Africa?" I demanded.

"Liberia, of course. The slave colony. I should say the colony founded by former slaves, with the help of enlightened white men. We had assumed, those of us who sacrificed so much to welcome the poor nigger folk, that most if not all would continue on to Liberia, where they might be more naturally comfortable."

I was appalled by this statement. The idea of returning former slaves to the pestilence and anarchy of the African colony was a cruel phantasm lately supported by the slave owners themselves, who feared an ever-increasing population of free Negroes circulating among those who were still bound by chattel laws. The New England abolitionists understood this ruse perfectly well, but the intelligence had not penetrated the thick, self-satisfied skull of Mr. Abner Simms, of Yarmouth, Nova Scotia, and nothing I could say or do made any impression upon the man. His small mind had all the dexterity of a tidewater mussel, clinging to his original purpose, and he would not be shed.

Jebediah, seeing my temper rise, cautioned me not to offend Mr. Simms, or his other more well-intentioned minions, who believed themselves to be doing God's work, and therefore deserving of God's praise. "We leave this place within the hour," he reminded me. "These others must stay, and they must get along with Simms and his ilk."

Thus chastened, I returned to *Raven* and spoke no more with the charitable white gentleman who condescended to aid runaway slaves. In hopes, apparently, they would keep running until they vanished from the earth. But my original conviction had been etched more deeply by the experience: if slavery had a solution its name was not Africa. Consider: none of the refugees I'd spoken to had any firsthand knowledge of that troubled continent. All were native to America, born on her soil, and all too often bled for her soil. Their proper home was therefore no more Africa than mine was England.

And so *Raven* departed Yarmouth lighter by twenty-eight souls. As we passed out of the harbor, the winter sun slipped wanly below the horizon, leaving the seas dark and glassy, but open before us, and not nearly so steep. By then the wind had shifted to its more common bearing, fitful and cold from the northeast, which would serve us well for the passage to White Harbor. With things so unsettled at home, the Coffin brothers were both anxious to return, and Tom cracked on as much canvas as he judged the masts could stand. Then, exhausted from his long watch at the helm, the young captain turned the wheel over to this first mate and retired below, leaving orders that he be roused if anything should go wrong.

"Not that it will," he assured us gruffly, his icicle-blue eyes puffy from lack of sleep. "This little ship practically sails herself, that's how sweet she is."

Sleep, what a splendid idea. With the passengers departed *Raven* had room to spare, and I found myself a narrow, empty bunk that smelled not too strongly of its previous inhabitant (a sailor by the tar-touched scent of him) and "racked out." I slipped away almost instantly, and dreamed of a cargo hold full of dark faces, all of them beseeching me to do something, I knew not what. Scurrying about a nightmare ship that seemed confused with the Coffin house, I searched frantically for some object, I knew not what exactly, only that I would recognize it when I found it. Gradually I became aware of an evil presence in the house/ship, an invisible something that seeped into the atmosphere, draining away what little light there was, until I was completely blind. At which point a cold hand touched my face and I sat up screaming, and bumped my head on the slats of the bunk above.

"Calm yourself, Davis!"

"What? What?"

"I thought you should know," said Jebediah. "We are becalmed. Tom has set out the whaleboat."

My little friend sounded worried, but it seemed to me that while an excess of wind might be dangerous, the reverse was simply inconvenient, for it would delay our return to White

Harbor. Upon reaching the deck I discovered that my landlub-
berly assumption was mistaken.

"We have a hundred fathoms under our keel," Tom Coffin
explained. He was standing in the bows of the schooner,
directing the oarsmen in the whaleboat, who were attempting
to tow *Raven* by strength of oar. "Hundred fathom is too deep
to anchor—we haven't the rode. And yet a tidal current is setting us north. A very strong current. Too damned strong!
Never seen the like in these parts." He cupped his hands to his
mouth. "Ahoy the whaleboat! Put your backs into it, men! Pull
for your life! Pull! Pull!"

While his brother was busy exhorting the oarsmen, and
setting canvas for whatever breath of wind he might find, Jeb
explained that an unusually strong tidal current was carrying
the schooner directly toward a notoriously dangerous reef. By
last reckoning the reef was somewhat less than a mile distant,
and with the strange tide sweeping *Raven* northward at something like three knots, we would be upon the rocks in less than
an hour. Fortunately the oarsmen were making progress. The
idea was not so much to fight the powerful current—quite
impossible—but to veer on a heading that would clear the
rocks.

"I believe we shall just clear it," Tom declared, staring
hopefully up at the slack sails. "My luck will hold," he said
with a fierce promise. "It must hold, even if the anchors will
not."

My own sense was that misfortune had been brought
upon us by all this talk of the seafaring good fortune peculiar
to the Coffins. If there ever had been such a thing, surely it
had been dissolved by the fog. A dense, nose-wetting fog had
arisen during the night, shrinking our world to a circumfer-
ence that barely extended as far as the whaleboat, whose ever-
thrusting bow threatened to dissolve in the heavy mist. Unlike

the rogue current, there was nothing strange about pea soup fog in the Gulf of Maine. But even a novice like me understood that dense fog made accurate navigation difficult if not impossible—no stars, fixed points, or landmarks to reference—and Tom's calculations had to be made by what he called "dead reckoning," which seemed an unfortunate phrase, considering our situation.

I offered my services as an oarsman, but Tom politely declined. "These boys have rowed together for years. A new apple would upset the cart."

"I see," I said. "Is there anything at all I can do?"

"All that can be done, is being done," the young captain said resolutely. "Wind! Bring me some wind, dammit!"

At that very moment—*crack!*—a sharp explosion of thunder made us all jump, and then laugh nervously at the coincidence. But though thunder began to rumble, and the pale fog pulsed weakly with the flash of distant lightning, the wind would not stir. We remained becalmed, in thrall to the ravenous current.

"Wind!" cried Tom Coffin, shaking his fist into the damp, still air. "Damn the lightning, give me wind! Wind from any point of the compass and I'll take my chances!"

But the wind would not rise, and we continued to be drawn inexorably toward the reef, which Jeb described to me as a series of small, unpopulated stone islands connected by a veritable tooth line of jutting rocks and perilous ledges. It was a hazard well known to all mariners, and the course we'd set from Yarmouth should have cleared it by fifty miles. And yet while the captain slept an unanticipated current had arisen, an invisible force undetected because the stars had been obscured.

"There is only one possible explanation," Jeb said hoarsely. "Some evil force is at work upon us."

In the light of the storm lantern his eyes had a flat, unfocused sheen and his flesh was bloodless and pale. Rather than try to argue some sense into him—it being no rare thing that a ship encounter peril at sea—I bade him lie down so that I might count his pulse. A touch told me all I needed to know—his blood pounded like a steam hammer. "You are overstimulated," I cautioned him. "This is perfectly understandable, given our situation, but you must calm yourself or I can't answer for your heart."

Jebediah stared at me, unheeding. Or really it seemed as if he stared through me, to another person or place. "Would that I might die," he whispered. "Be a true friend, Davis, and kill me."

"Hush. You're talking nonsense. Brother Tom is as skilled a mariner as ever sailed the seas. Trust in him, he will save us. If worst comes to worst, we'll abandon ship and take to the whaleboat."

Indeed, that very course of action had been suggested by Tom Coffin himself, should *Raven* ground upon the reef. We were, he said, no more than thirty miles from the coast and the whaleboat was sound enough to carry all of us safely to shore, if it came to that.

Until then he would do everything within his power to save the schooner. With all sails slack and the oarsmen making little or no headway, he ordered the anchors let go, and all of the rode played out. The hope was that one or more of the anchors would snag bottom before the ship did, but it was a desperate attempt, and it failed. With the current dragging us so fast, the anchors were unable to reach bottom, or skipped along if they did, shivering the ship timbers but failing to slow our inevitable collision.

"Wind!" Tom Coffin roared in frustration. "Give me wind!"

"Too late," Jebediah muttered, from where he'd slumped on the deck. "Whatever will be was long ago ordained."

"Stuff and nonsense," I said, affecting a cheerfulness I did not feel. "There is no such thing as Fate. Fate is a Calvinist conceit. Remember what our friend Emerson has taught us. We make our own way, dear Jeb, and your brother will save us yet, even if he fails to save the ship."

In the end our progress toward destruction was curiously slow. Three knots is no faster than a brisk stroll. But let a man stroll briskly into a brick wall and he won't come away unbroken. As we closed upon the reef, oily swells rose through the fog, rocking *Raven* and making her slack halyards shudder and her spars creak and moan most piteously. Tom Coffin ordered the oarsmen to leave off towing—it was quite useless—and stand by for collision. At the first touch of keel on rock we were to all fling ourselves over the side and be recovered by the whaleboat, which could be rowed to safety even if it couldn't save the ship.

That was the plan. It was not to be. Before the keel touched at our placid, strolling pace, the lightning spoke.

*Raven* was, in that moment before it happened, alive with electricity. My hair rose high above my head. The shrouds and halyards seemed to be coated with a luminous green moss that sparkled and pulsated like something alive. I saw my own fingernails glowing eerily. No doubt my own face was as cadaverous as Jebediah's, as if the flesh had become translucent, revealing the skull within.

"Look! In the shrouds!" one of the crewmen screamed, his voice breaking in panic.

A strange luminescent form had taken shape at the crosstree spar of the main mast, forty feet above the deck. The glow became recognizable: a translucent man-shape made of cold fire, writhing in the shrouds, as if alive. Alive or dying.

"God help us," someone moaned. "That's a hung man, look at 'im kick. A hung man in the throes of death!"

It was true, the glowing, crackling thing seemed to shudder and kick the way a hanged man kicks. My rational mind assured that it was not a man, or the shape of a man, but some weird electrical or atmospheric effect grounded between mast and shrouds. A variant, perhaps, of the Saint Elmo's fire that had been terrifying ignorant sailors for centuries. That's what my rational mind said. But all my human instincts told me to shrink in horror from the palpable evil that charged the very air with the stink of ozone—or was it sulfur?

At that moment, at the very instant when I had almost convinced myself not to be afraid, the wind suddenly piped up and spoke through the vibrating shrouds. It was not as if we heard recognizable words resonating from the shrouds. No, not words as we could understand words. It was enough to hear the sudden wind transformed into the amplified moan of someone in great distress or incandescent rage. Then the wind increased and it became not one moan, but many. A great moaning of humanity amplified and alive in the way a sounding board makes piano strings resonate more loudly.

*"Mmmmooooooaaaannnnnaaaaaaaaahhhhhhhhooooooooh!"*

My knees trembled so violently that I lost balance and tumbled to the deck not far from where Jebediah lay, his face bathed in the ghastly light. My friend looked more than merely cadaverous, he had the look of a man who had just been condemned to spend eternity in hell.

"There is no need to kill me," Jeb croaked, "for I am already dead."

Suddenly the air itself became more dense, as if we had all been cast in dark amber or molten glass. I knew what must happen but could not move to save myself.

"Cover!" Tom Coffin screamed from where he stood, legs braced at the helm, hands on the wheel. "Take cover! Save yourselves!"

Then it struck. First a blinding flash, then the *CRRRRAAAAAAAK!* of the smoking foremast crashing to the deck as a bolt of lightning exploded in the shrouds. A

moment later the vast expanse of sails caught the full brunt of
the sudden gale of wind and the ship was knocked down. We
careened heavily to one side—was it port? starboard?—I knew
not where I was facing, and had room for only one thought,
striking like a small bell in my mind: we are doomed, doomed,
doomed.

And yet the noble little ship, though knocked flat into the
still placid waters, did not completely capsize. *Raven*'s spars
were immersed as the top of the remaining mast touched
water and then, slowly, as if inhaling very painfully, the mast
lifted away from the seas and *Raven* began to rise.

Through all of this I clung to the deck and to Jebediah,
who did nothing to save himself. At last the schooner righted
herself. The seas she'd taken aboard roared back through the
scuppers. We bobbed and shook like a dog ridding himself of
water as the deck rose. *Raven* still lived.

The first thing I noticed, aside from my own tangled proximity to the damaged rail (another inch or two and Jeb and I
would have been flung overboard), was that the wind had
dropped as fast as it had risen.

We were once more becalmed and in thrall to the relentless current.

"Cap'n Tom!" a frightened voice cried out. "Where's Cap'n
Tom?"

I looked back to the helm and saw that the wheel had
been smashed away by a fallen spar. There was no sign of Tom
Coffin, who had been handling the great spoked wheel when
disaster struck.

Untangling myself from Jebediah, I ran to the rail at the
stern of the ship, searching the dark waters. Barrels and parts
of shattered spars bobbed nearby, turning and whirling in the
current, but I could see no sign of the young captain. Could he
swim? I wondered. If so he might save himself. Or even if he

couldn't swim he might be clinging to a piece of debris in that icy water.

The medical man in me was calculating how long poor Tom might last in the frigid waters before his blood thickened, when suddenly *Raven* caught something beneath her keel and began to rise, her hull groaning. There was a series of small, muffled explosions as her ribs cracked and her planks sprang open.

Our collision with the reef was not so violent as I had feared it would be. It was as if the seas had grown tired of us and simply handed the ship up onto the rocks without further ceremony. When *Raven* settled, the decks were actually almost level, and I saw that the schooner had been pinched between two enormous, barely submerged boulders.

The broken hull sighed as seas began to circulate through the newly rent openings below the water line. It was obvious that although *Raven* had been fatally damaged it could not actually sink any farther. Thus we had all the time in the world to gather our things and board the waiting whaleboat, which was miraculously unscathed by either the lightning or the sudden squall that followed.

I was attempting to help Jebediah to his feet—he was muttering strangely and seemed disoriented—when a hollow voice cried out from the bow of the dead ship.

"There! Look there! It's our Tom!"

I ran forward, my heart curiously light with the hope that our young captain had been found alive, floating unharmed.

It was my last true moment of hope, for what I found turned my heart to stone and my blood to ash. Had I a soul it must in that horrible moment have shriveled like meat on a spit, and departed myself forever.

For there, impaled on the shattered bowsprit, hands and feet still writhing as life ebbed from his body, was our brave

Tom Coffin. The great splinter of oak had passed through the center of his abdomen and protruded a yard beyond. In the throes of death his neck arched and his handsome head was thrown back. His mouth worked silently, piteously, as if he wanted desperately to say something. But it was impossible, for the spar that passed through him had taken the last breath from his lungs. Still he would not die, but struggled like a bug on a pin.

I had never before wished for a man's death, but his final agony was such that I prayed for his heart to stop.

Eventually, of course, it did.

# III

## MONBASU

*The slave trade has been the ruling principle of my people. It is the source of their glory and wealth. . . .*

GEZO, KING OF DAHOMEY

# 1. The Cask and the Kiss

Our return to White Harbor was a kind of long and ponderously slow funeral cortege. We proceeded first by paddle-steamer, then locomotive, and finally by horse-drawn carriage, and in the whole of the journey my dear friend Jebediah spoke scarcely a word. There was nothing insensible about his grief—he was perfectly aware of his surroundings and his companions—it was as if he could not bring himself to speak. Such was the depth of his sorrow and dread that no words could express the loss of his cherished brother, or the inexplicable tragedy that had stalked his entire family.

I left my little friend to his enormous silence, and took it upon myself to arrange our transportation, and to notify the surviving Coffins of the latest catastrophe. By the cold, inhuman pulse of the telegraph they were informed that the schooner *Raven* had been destroyed, that Thomas Coffin was no more, that Jebediah and the rest of the crew had survived, and that we had been taken from the wreck by a passing paddle-steamer, which had sighted our unhappy party soon after the fog lifted, and sent boats to rescue us.

In Portland Harbor, destination of the paddle-steamer, I hired a cooper to seal Tom Coffin's remains in a rum-filled cask, which then accompanied us on the remainder of our sad journey. Jebediah had approved these arrangements with a nod of his heavy head, which lately seemed too large for his diminutive body to support. He sagged in his seat, chin down, staring at the hole in his world, and seemed, by my reckoning, to be well beyond fear.

He was, indeed, like a man already dead, and what have the dead to fear?

Alerted by my telegram, cousin Lucy kept vigil for us under the portico, wearing a black, hooded, full-length cloak that made her appear a stern and spectral figure. As our carriage came to a stop I saw her eyes register the newly made cask and then darken, as if she knew what it must contain. She raised a hand in silent greeting, a simple acknowledgment of shared sorrow, then turned and hurried into the house.

A moment later Barky emerged. With a gentleness derived of great strength he lifted Jebediah from his seat and cooed, "Young Jeb! Poor soul! You're home now, home with us that loves you."

My little friend did not respond, but he allowed the burly cook to carry him inside. After directing the men where to place the cask—it was taken to one of the sheds, to await more specific instructions—I joined Lucy in the kitchen, where a simple meal had been laid out.

"Shall I pour?" she asked, holding up a glazed teapot. When I nodded she filled a cup, leaving room for a generous portion of dark Jamaican rum, which she added without comment. I hadn't the heart to refuse, or to explain why that particular form of alcohol conjured such morbid thoughts. Out of politeness I downed the stuff like a dose of vile medicine, and was glad of the punishing burn it produced from throat to gullet.

Lucy then sat beside me and took my hands in hers. There was a look in her sad, lovely eyes that convinced me she wished to speak, but wanted me to prompt her.

"How are things here?" I asked, a quaver in my voice.

She sighed deeply, and then gathered herself. "Terrible, as you might imagine. Unbearable, really, but what choice do we have? We must bear it."

COFFINS 

"The brothers?" I asked. "How did they take it?"

Tears brimmed from her liquid blue eyes. Her voice was as soft as a caress, but infinitely sad. "When Benjamin and Nathaniel learned, it was as if they themselves had been struck dead. As if they became, in that moment, ghosts instead of men."

"Where are they now?" I asked, looking around the kitchen, which we had to ourselves.

"Ben has gone to tell his father. Nathaniel bides with his wife, at one of the rooming houses."

"Poor Benjamin," I said, mindful of the difficulty of imparting yet more bad tidings to the madman in the tower.

"Yes," Lucy breathed, squeezing my hands. "The only good news is that you have returned."

God help me, but my thoughts went to the last time her hands had touched mine, and the carnal heat that had coursed through my blood, and the icy chill that had followed. When I gave an involuntary shiver she drew her hands away and laid her palm upon my forehead. "You've taken ill," she said gravely. "I shouldn't wonder. With all you've been through. With all you've seen."

"Not ill, exactly," I said. "Sick at heart."

"Your telegram said only that Tom had perished and the ship gone down. How did such a thing happen?"

I'd wanted to spare her the specifics of our ordeal, but instead found myself spilling the tale and leaving nothing to the imagination. I even told her, God help me, how we'd had to saw through the broken bowsprit and pry poor Tom loose from his deadly perch. As if something in me wanted to punish her for not being there to see it with her own eyes, for not suffering exactly as the rest of us had suffered. But rather than shrink from the horror she pressed me for details, and I felt bound to comply, though it would surely ruin her sleep forever, as mine had been ruined.

When I came to the last, she placed her hands on her bosom and moaned as if she, too, had been penetrated by that great splinter of oak. Closing her eyes she wept and then suddenly collapsed upon the table. "So it is true what they say!" she gasped. "They are cursed, all of them!"

I begged her to tell me what she knew of this wretched curse. Little enough, she said, only what Jebediah had said, that night when he held the pistol to his head. "But why should the Coffins be accursed?" I asked. "What makes them think so?"

Lucy shook her pretty head as she wiped her tears 'way with my hankie. "I've heard Jeb allude to it in his darker moments," she said. "I assumed he meant he wished he'd never been born to such deformity. When he was a boy, you know, the others taunted him with that. As if his was the punishment for the sins of the family."

"Sins? What sins?"

Lucy gave me a curious look, as if startled by my naiveté. "Oh, the sin of success, I suppose. When a family gets too high above itself, there are plenty of volunteers eager to bring them down a peg."

"You speak of envy?"

"Envy isn't a strong enough word for what I mean. I don't know what word is. I take it you did not grow up in a small town?"

I shook my head. "I grew up in Boston, Hub of the Universe."

The jape brought a small smile to her lips. "Yes, I've heard it called that."

"I assure you, there's no lack of envy in Boston."

"Of course not. But the envy I speak of takes a different form in a small town. In Boston you think you know everyone, but what you really mean is you know everyone worth knowing. Everyone within your circle. In a village like White Harbor, remote from the city, relying upon itself, everyone really *does* know everyone else. They know each other intimately, in a way that city folk never do. They know each other's strengths and weaknesses. They know who said what to whom, and who did what to whom. They know each other's most shameful secrets, and they remember it all forever."

"You just ruined my postcard," I told her.

"What?"

"Nothing. Please go on."

"Remember that Cash Coffin was born in this village. No doubt he was a snot-nosed boy like all the other snot-nosed boys who race the streets, no better and no worse. But unlike the others, he grew up to be rich and powerful. Not only a shipmaster, which is a kind of royalty here, but the owner of a fleet of ships. So naturally there are those who thought him high above his station, who resented his success, his wealth. Some, I'm told, resented his five strong and perfect sons, destined to be ship captains like their father. Understand that Rebecca Coffin had five children, and all of them survived, and all of them were boys. Look around at the other family graveyards and you will see how many died in infancy. How many had one child perish for every one that survived."

"I know something of infant mortality," I reminded her softly.

Lucy looked startled, and her cheeks colored. "Of course you do. I'm sorry, Davis. I forget that your medical experience took you into the poor wards."

I shook off her apology, which was not required. "Why do you say that Rebecca Coffin had only five sons? Jebediah is the sixth son, is he not?"

Lucy nodded. "That's my point. Jeb was the sixth, after the first five were born perfect. And poor Rebecca died giving him birth. So there were those cruel enough to say Jeb was the curse upon the family. Proof that Cash Coffin didn't deserve his success. Proof of his sins."

It was hard, being forced to imagine what little Jebediah had endured. The cruel taunts from children his own age, and from adults who resented his father, or were merely offended by the very existence of a dwarf in their midst. His keen awareness of how others saw him, and how so many of them denied him his humanity, his manhood. How had he borne it? How had he become such a person as I first met in Harvard Yard, a man of courage, nobility, and unshakable conviction? There was only one answer: Jebby the dwarf had become Jebediah Coffin, Abolitionist, through the strength and support of his kind and generous brothers, who loved him for what he was, and what he would become. He was the sum of their wholes, and now with half of his family destroyed—by his own fault, he thought, for the temerity of existing—half of him was destroyed as well.

"It wasn't only the children and the ignorant adults," Lucy said. "There was Cornelius Remick."

"Who?" I asked. The name was familiar, but I was certain I did not know the man."

"Father Remick," Lucy said. "The Episcopal priest. I was told he presided over Rebecca Coffin's funeral, and that he was the first who alluded to Jebediah's deformity as just punishment."

"What?" I said, scarcely believing that a man of the cloth, a man of God, could inflict such cruelty on his own parishoners. "He said the family was cursed?"

"I don't know that Remick actually said that Jebediah was a curse upon the family. It may have been one of those priestly allusions, with quotes from the Scripture. All I know is that Cash stormed out of the church in the middle of the funeral and has never returned, and that shortly thereafter Remick was forced from his congregation and had to leave White Harbor. But no one who lived here has forgotten what the priest said, and they never let Jeb forget it, either."

"Does he still live?" I asked her. "This man Remick? Is he alive?"

"I've no idea," she said, "but there's someone who might know. The man who replaced him. Father Whipple."

"Then I shall speak with the good father," I said, getting to my feet.

And then, summoning my courage, I kissed her. A chaste kiss, but sweet.

## 2. The Good Father

It was unspeakably late when I approached the tidy building that served as the Episcopal rectory, located a few streets away from the church itself. The little house was precisely square, somewhat less than twenty feet on a side. The recent snow had collected into a glistening pile under the icicle-bound eaves. White smoke rose from a center chimney and a faint glow illuminated one of the small upstairs windows, so I assumed the inhabitant had not yet retired for the night. Not that a lack of candle would have prevented my fist from booming upon the storm door.

"Good Lord! Coming! Coming!"

The candle glow moved from upstairs to down, and soon enough the inner door creaked open and the storm shutter was unlatched.

"Father Whipple?"

"Yes, yes, who else? Get in, man, before the heat gets out!"

The priest, who I'd spoken to very briefly at little Casey's interment, was a moon-faced man of about fifty, with shoulder-length white hair and a neatly trimmed beard. Curled, Oriental slippers peeked out from beneath the hem of his floor-length sleeping gown. As he raised the candle to inspect me, I noticed bottle-thick spectacles affixed to his nose and held in place by means of a black ribbon. He peered at me with the faintly puzzled eyes of the badly nearsighted and asked, "Do I know you, sir? You do look familiar, but my eyes are weak."

"Davis Bentwood. I'm a friend of the Coffins."

"Yes, of course," he said. "You were at the infant's burial, were you not? Sad affair, very sad. Heard something of you from Griswold, later it was, after Sunday service, I think. Hmm? Yes, so it was."

"Excuse me?"

"Dr. Griswold. Member of the congregation. Mentioned a young scamp from away, 'poaching on his territory.' His words, not mine, couldn't care less. This way, Dr. Bentwood. To the heat, man, the heat!"

I followed the priest to the very center of his little domi-cile, where a Franklin wood stove had been installed in front of the bricked-up hearth. The cast-iron doors were closed, the draft was whistling, and the whole stove was pleasantly pink with warmth. Gratefully I joined my host, rubbing my badly chilled hands over the rising heat.

Father Whipple coughed, snorted, sniffled, cleared his throat, shuffled his slippers, and finally regarded me with a not-unfriendly gaze. "If you're here at this ungodly hour, I must assume the rumors are true. Another Coffin has met his Maker."

"I'm afraid so."

"And you wish me to preside at this funeral, too? Hmm?"

"Your service would be most welcome, of course, when it comes to that. But I came with another purpose, to ask if you know anything of your predecessor, Father Remick."

"Cornelius? Oh, indeed, I knew Cornelius quite well. He was a good man."

The air sighed out of me, and with it some of my resolve. "Do I take it Father Remick is deceased?"

Whipple stopped rubbing his hands over the stove and began tugging thoughtfully at his beard. "Five years. No, wait. More like six or seven. Died in his sleep, the lucky fellow."

I uttered an oath and then quickly apologized.

"Don't trouble yourself," he said, waving his hand as if the profane words were inconsequential puffs of smoke. "These walls have heard worse. I'm an old bachelor priest, but Father

Remick was not. Lived in this very house, small as it is, with a wife, five daughters, and his mother-in-law, who had a salty tongue and used it frequently." He paused from his recollection. "What did you want of Father Remick? Take a pew, Dr. Bentwood, and tell me all about it."

The man kindly offered me an upholstered chair. I slumped into it and buried my face in my hands, at a loss for how to explain that I was searching for an answer to a question that I couldn't even begin to formulate. The good father took a "pew" next to me, held his curiously slippered feet out to the glowing stove, and mused aloud. "Hmm. Let me think. Says he's a friend of the Coffins but wanted to see old Cornelius. Medical man, Boston accent. Hmm. There's a clue. Were you at school with young Jebediah, is that it?"

"Yes," I admitted.

"Hmm, hmm. Two and two together. So. First visit to our little village? Yes? I'd have known, I think, if you'd dropped anchor before. Tell me, Dr. Bentwood, are you sure you're not here about a proper funeral, speaking on behalf of the family, or of Jebediah? Because that wouldn't be a problem, despite that wicked old man's animus."

"Animus?"

"To this church, and to the late Father Remick in particular, and to me because I took his place. Never you mind, son, let bygones be bygones. We can organize a funeral mass at your convenience, if it would make the family rest easy, and when the ground thaws we'll see the poor Coffin boys buried proper, with every pomp and circumstance, not to worry."

"It isn't that," I said. "It has to do with why Remick left. Do you know anything of the circumstance? Can you relate it without, um, betraying a confidence?"

"Ah," he said, studying his slippers. "Hmm. Depends, I suppose."

"Depends on what?"

"On exactly what you want to know. I've no desire to go up against Cassius Coffin, after all these years. Ancient history."

"That's what I must know," I said urgently. "The ancient history. Specifically what Father Remick said at the funeral of Rebecca Coffin, Jebediah's mother."

"Ah," Whipple said, bobbing his head. "You know nothing of it, then?"

"Nothing. Only that whatever was said, it made the old man leave the church. I assume he was the one who drove your predecessor away."

Father Whipple nodded thoughtfully, studying my face as he might a map. "Oh, indeed he did. Quite right. Cash Coffin. A man of considerable influence. A man more interested, I might say, in burying the past than he was in burying his wife."

"Oh?" I asked eagerly. "What do you mean?"

"What do I mean? Let me get this right, my boy. Hmm, did I say 'boy'? You'll excuse me, Dr. Bentwood, for I'm an old man, old enough to be your father."

"I take no offense. What was this about not wanting to bury Rebecca Coffin?"

"Did I say that? Didn't mean it, if I did say so. You should know, if you're to understand what happened between the two men, that Rebecca Coffin was the bosom friend of Jessie Remick. Remick's wife Jessica. Hmm? See the picture? Rebecca Coffin was, they say, a lovely, generous lady. Never knew her myself, but I've no reason to doubt it. Much beloved in the village, for not getting too high above herself. They say she was on the point of convincing her husband to build a proper rectory for the church. Something with enough room to house the whole Remick clan in comfort. But then Rebecca died on the birthing bed and everything changed. The way I understand it, Jessie blamed Cassius for Becky's death, and she persuaded her husband to be of the same mind. Then he spoke his mind and Cash Coffin would have none of it. Didn't matter if everyone in the village knew, it wasn't to be spoken of, or alluded to."

"What wasn't to be spoken of?"

"Hmm? Ah? Why, where they'd got their money, of course."

"And where was that?"

"You don't know? Why, everyone knows that Cash Coffin made his fortune running slaves."

I gasped.

"Hmm. I don't suppose Jebediah would want to mention it, him being such a fervent abolitionist," Father Whipple mused, weaving his long elegant fingers through the scruff of his white beard. "For that matter I'm not certain how much your friend actually knows of the particulars—families have a way of smothering such unpleasant kittens. But his father wasn't the only sea captain made his pile in the African trade. Wasn't even the only one in this village, come to that. Many a Yankee fortune was made in the buying and selling of men."

This was hardly news to me, about the making of Yankee fortunes, but somehow I'd never considered that the Coffins might have been involved in the odious enterprise. It had never occurred to me that a slave trader would so generously finance his son's various abolitionist causes, to the point of having Frederick Douglass as an honored house guest. Was Mr. Douglass aware of the source of the family fortune? I wondered. Had I been the only one present at the Coffin house who couldn't appreciate the delicious triple irony of a former slave directing runaway slaves to safety in the home of a former slaver?

"If I remember correctly, and I think I do, Jessie Remick

said that Becky had for some time made it known to her husband that she wished him to quit the vile business. And her husband in turn blamed Cornelius for turning his wife against him, as he saw it, by preaching against the slavers and turning his congregation into a hotbed of abolitionism."

"And was it that?" I asked. "A hotbed of abolitionism?"

Father Whipple snorted and shook his head. "Hardly. Not by today's standards. But Captain Coffin couldn't abide it when any man dared disagree with him, especially in public. Also, let us not forget, that even back then transporting slaves from Africa was an illegal activity. So possibly Coffin felt that the abundant rumors put him in peril. Whatever was in his mind—and I don't pretend to know—he forbade his wife from seeing Jessie, and she in turn defied him and bared her heart to her dear friend."

"But what has this to do with Rebecca's death, or the funeral?" I asked.

The priest sighed. "I was told that a day or two before Rebecca gave birth, she came to Jessie in some torment. The two women closeted themselves and exchanged the usual confidences. And then Becky related some terrible secret having to do with her husband. Don't ask me what secret, exactly," he said, holding up his hand, "because I do not know. Jessie never said, not even to her husband, and she passed away some years ago, preceding Cornelius. All I know is that the subject was, in Jessie's words, 'unspeakable,' which explains, I suppose, her silence upon the subject."

"But it had to do with slaving?"

"I've always assumed so, but I can't be sure. Certainly Cornelius thought so. For that was the subject of the sermon that got him dismissed. 'The Curse of the Slave Trader.' That was the title. Old Corny was a direct sort of man, God love him. Didn't dilly-dally with words. And when Rebecca died, and the child with her, Father Remick saw it as a sign from God, a punishment like unto that of Job himself, and thundered so from his pulpit."

"Wait!" I said. "Did you say the child died? Jebediah didn't die!"

"No," Father Whipple agreed. "Jeb lived, but his brother died. His twin."

I don't know why the idea of twins should have stunned me so, but it did. Perhaps because of Jeb's precious twin brothers, Sam'n'Zeke, so recently and so horribly deceased. When the priest saw that I was at a loss, he rose from his chair and fetched us brandy from the cupboard. "I think the occasion warrants medication," he said with a smile, handing me a generous glass of the peachy-smelling stuff. "I see that you are shocked, but it is not so unusual that of two infants in the womb, one should be born flawless but dead, and the other deformed but alive."

"Jebediah's twin was not deformed?"

"According to the midwife, the baby was perfect in every way save that it had ceased thriving some weeks before labor commenced. Poor Rebecca gave birth to a tiny corpse. Not an unusual occurrence, but it was the first time a child of hers had not survived. A few minutes after they'd wrapped the dead infant in a shroud, Becky suffered the convulsion that killed her, and the result of that convulsion was to expel the infant that still lived, the twin no one had foreseen or expected."

"Jebediah. But as you say, the death of an infant is so common, why did Father Remick take it for a curse? Was it because the surviving twin was deformed?"

The priest lowered his empty glass. "No, it wasn't that. Or I should say it wasn't only that. It was what happened to the dead infant."

A thrum of excitement sat me upright and quivering. "Was it cold?" I said, feeling that an explanation, however unusual, was maddeningly close. "Was the dead twin unusually cold? As if mysteriously frozen? Was that it?"

Father Whipple was clearly baffled by my outburst. "Cold? Frozen? No. This is what happened: before the shroud was wrapped, the little corpse turned black. Before their eyes the perfectly formed white baby shriveled and turned black. As black as the souls that Cash Coffin traded for gold."

That so astonished me that I failed to hear the glass break when it dropped from my hands.

## 3. The Body in the Barrel

Long after midnight, when the moon was down, and the hour was black, and the stars were distant and cold, I returned to the Coffin house. I crept back like the guilt-ridden thief who wants to replace what can never be recovered. Namely the innocence with which I'd viewed my little friend and his exemplary family.

It had been a soul-killing night. Lucy had, unwittingly perhaps, canceled my mental postcard of a serene and pleasant White Harbor, and now a companionable, kindhearted priest had destroyed the nobility of the seafaring family I'd so admired. Fearless, self-reliant men whose courage and resolute behavior had, I thought, transcended the ordinary, and made each bell of their shiply watches chime as pure as the music of the Divine. Except that their very lives had been purchased with the lives of others, and so that each Coffin might thrive and prosper, a thousand men had been draped in chains, a thousand women raped and ruined, a thousand children whipped and starved.

It was enough to make a man retch, and I did so, spitting vile peach brandy onto the dull ice that glazed the granite steps under the portico. There it instantly froze, visible proof of my weakness. How could I not have known what the world had known? Was it mere innocence on my part, or willful ignorance? Why was I who had worshipped at the altar of the Rational and the Reasonable so unable to see the Evil right before my eyes? Emerson had seen the larger sin, the national disgrace, and he had denounced it in no uncertain terms. But I, who supposed himself attuned to the great man's insights, had been unable to recognize the obvious: that none of us can be innocent through ignorance, not when we dwell among evil-doers, and do nothing to stop them.

Do not suppose that my wretched state of mind made me think less of my friend Jebediah. It did not. For all that had happened, and everything I had learned, I could not help but admire a son who strove so valiantly to make amends for the sins of his father. That he did not confide his shame to me was easily forgivable, and in some sense eased my own mind, for it made me better understand his present torment. Jeb's whole life had been formed in the shadow of that terrible truth. His own dead twin, the soul with whom he'd shared his mother's womb, was proof of the Coffin corruption. If validation of sainthood is held to be the incorruptible body, then what did it say when an innocent, stillborn baby was putrefied to black-ness within moments of being delivered? No wonder Jebediah believed himself cursed. He *was* cursed. Cursed not by the doctrine of original sin, but by the willful evil perpetrated by those he loved.

But was it the punishment of a just God that cursed the Coffins? Were the recent tragedies a kind of biblical revenge, an Old Testament leveling of the scales? Or was there some other force at work? A greater evil, if such a thing could be imagined? But I did not have to imagine it. I had seen such improbabilities with my own eyes: a crypt defiled, a baby frozen solid in a warm room, a hanged man formed of light-ning, a prodigal son impossibly impaled on a splinter of oak. It was true that I had not actually observed Sam'n'Zeke cut in twain by the vengeful sawblade, but their fate was no less improbable, absent some sort of intervention by a force or presence invisible. A force or presence that could not be accounted for in the transcendental philosophy of Ralph Waldo Emerson, or Immanuel Kant, or the rational arithmetic of Descartes. And so I was left with only two possible explanations, two possible agents of the impossible: God or the devil. Who had brought such horror to this family, was it God or one of his fallen angels? And what did it have to do with "alchemy," that word shouted like a curse from the madman's tower?

Stumbling into the darkened hallway, my boots resounding on the oaken floor of that hollow place, my mind was, I am now convinced, unhinged by exhaustion, fear, and alcohol taken on a sour stomach. For I had formed a very fixed idea of what I must do to prove or disprove my thesis.

Tom Coffin's body must be taken from the cask and examined.

I did not sleep those last hours before daybreak, when I intended to rouse the world and put my plan into action. Sleep is impossible when your brain races like mine did, examining a thousand rational explanations and rejecting them all. It came down to this: I had to know if the body in the barrel was as blackened as Jebediah's twin had been, so long ago. Tom's remains had been placed in a hogshead cask of rum and if, despite that well-known preservative, his body was badly decayed, then I would take that as proof that my theory was correct: a force beyond human control or understanding was at work, destroying the Coffins one by one.

To this end I sent for the undertakers, Caswell by name. A father and son, both called Jasper. We were already acquainted, as they had supplied the tiny casket for the baby's burial. Like so many of their profession, the Jaspers looked the part. They were, father and son, pale and narrow and scarecrow thin, with melancholy, deep-set eyes. Jasper Caswell the elder drove the hearse wagon, which was drawn by a single, plodding, ancient horse whose hooves had been fitted with scuffed leather booties, the better to grip the ice. Upon arrival, Jasper the younger climbed down from his seat and with the utmost adolescent gravity held the old horse while his father shuffled to the door, brushing snowflakes from his black, swallow-tailed frock jacket. He bowed deeply, doffed his high beaver, and offered me condolences.

"We been waiting for the summons, having heard what happened to poor Master Tom," he added. "Terrible thing, when a man is taken in the prime of life."

"Yes," I said. "It was a terrible thing."

"I understand the Captain is feeling poorly?"

"Yes," I agreed. "He's greatly disturbed."

That was putting it mildly. According to Benjamin, bearer of the bad news, the old man had flown into a froth-mouthed rage, throwing everything but the cat at his eldest son, and then at whatever invisible thing it was that seemed to be abusing him. Yelling and eventually pleading with his unseen tormentor to stop laughing. When I asked Ben if he'd heard the laughter, he gave me a strange, appraising kind of look and finally said no, he had heard nothing of the kind, and didn't expect to, unless he, too, went mad. "What did you do?" I had asked him, to which he replied, "I prayed for him. I prayed for him and for me and for all of us—even you, Dr. Bentwood. I begged my father to join me in petitioning the Lord, but he said I was already dead and dead men needn't pray. That's what he does believe, too, in his madness, that all of his sons are dead. That I was a ghost come back to haunt him. Like he was all turned around about who had died and who had not."

I tried to speak comfortingly to Benjamin about the possibility of his father recovering his senses, but neither of us believed such a thing was now possible, and Ben trudged off to pray over Jebediah, in hopes of piercing the overwhelming gloom that kept the little man bedridden.

"So you'll be handling the arrangements on this one, too?" the elder undertaker asked, as his gray tongue wetted his chapped and colorless lips. "Still representing the family in their time of need?"

"Something like that," I said, somewhat sharply. "I'll see your fee is paid, if that's what you mean. As I did for the child's casket."

"Apologies, sir," he said, dropping his eyes. "I was only inquiring. Apologies most heartfelt." Undeterred, he took a deep breath and resumed. "I was only inquiring because a full-growed man is, of course, considerable more than an infant baby. For the handling of him and so on."

"Follow me to the carriage shed."

I was seething with fury by the time we managed to wrest the cask aboard the undertaker's wagon, with the help of such servants as could be found, and were willing to lend a hand. Mine was an inchoate form of anger, misdirected and all out of proportion to the offense. A muddled anger that had more to do with fear, I now think, than with any ill-considered phrases that issued from the hideous, saliva-specked mouth of Jasper Caswell the elder, who was thoroughly odious but sincerely did not mean to give offense. What terrified me so? I was terrified of what I might find in the cask, and what that meant to my orderly world, and to the philosophies that had thus far informed my life, given it shape and meaning. Why such furious anxiety should have been bound up in the idea of examining a body for signs of corruption I cannot now fathom, save that as it turned out, I was right to be terrified. Nothing I had learned or observed in the crudest autopsy theater could prepare me, or any man, for what I was about to discover.

J. Caswell & Son, Undertakers, was located in the lower end of the village, where the buildings were smaller, cruder, and more closely built together, as if proximity was necessary to keep them upright. A number of other trades prospered, more or less, in the same area. Carpentry shops, framing stalls, wheelwrights, gunsmiths, fabricators, and so on, many of them sharing buildings or spaces within. No doubt one of the cabinetmakers moonlighted for caskets, a number of which were on display in what Mr. Caswell called "the sample parlor," little more than four fly-specked walls and a pile of caskets set on sawhorses. They ranged from unfinished pine to varnished mahogany, but I was in no mood to make a selection or "set the price," in the undertaker's unctuous words.

"Do you have a workroom?" I demanded. "A place where we can lay out Mr. Coffin's body?"

"Yes, yes, course we do," he said, rubbing the knuckles of his pale hands. "But mostly, you understand, we tend to work from the home. That's how folks want it. We come to your house and do the necessary."

I glowered in a way that made both Jaspers retreat a step or two. "The 'necessary' can be accomplished right here!" I thundered. "The family must not be disturbed, is that understood?"

"Course it is, course it is. Only the back parlor, um, you might call, well, you might call it shabby."

"I might call it filthy and rat-infested, but that does not matter. Kindly take the cask into this 'back parlor,' wherever it is."

I had it right. Filthy and rat-infested fit the bill of particulars. The stench of flesh and sickness and grave rot I will not attempt to describe, save that I had never smelled worse, not even in the foul basements of the city hospitals. The cask was too heavy to be lifted by the three of us, but the younger Caswell was clever enough, as it turned out, and he engineered a way to winch our burden from the back of the wagon and set it square upon the floor. While his father stood by, rubbing his knuckles and muttering nervously, his son borrowed a mallet and pry bar from one of the adjoining establishments and set about breaking the seal on the lid.

Instantly the parlor filled with the fumes of rum, an odor

powerful but clean, and to my way of thinking it was an improvement. No stench of corruption rose from the cask, and this was reassuring.

"Take off your coat and help us," I demanded of the father.

"This is irregular, most irregular," he objected. "Not the way the Jasper Caswells do things, fetching bodies in rum barrels." But at a pleading glance from his beleaguered son he doffed his crusted black suit coat, rolled up his sleeves, and gingerly reached into the cask.

"On a count of three and heave, boy, are we agreed?"

"Yes, Father."

"Ready now. One, two, THREE AND HEAVE!"

As it turned out, the body was easily dislodged, for rigor had come and gone and poor Tom was pliant enough. First his head rose—still handsome in death—and then his once strong arms were gingerly unfolded by the grunting Jaspers. The dead man was still clothed in such garments as remained when he was removed from the bowsprit, blue woolen trousers and torn white cotton shirt, both now bearing stains of the preserving rum that ran in torrents as he was lifted free of the cask. As the two men shifted the cadaver, squeezing his horribly punctured chest for purchase, Tom's head fell back and the amber liquid gushed from the hole, and from his mouth, startling us all.

When the time came I grasped the ankles and with another count of three and heave we got the corpse upon the workbench.

"There!" said the elder Jasper. He stood back to admire his handiwork. "He looks quite fair, I'd say, for a gentleman three days gone or more. Fair about the face and head, I mean. That big hole in his chest, we can fill it with wax, if you like. New woolly togs from Eames the tailor and he'll shape up quite presentable, considering."

All of us were thoroughly drenched with rum, and a little

light-headed from the fumes, when the cadaver began to react with the air. I knew, of course, that soon after a body is removed from an alcohol solution the normal course of corruption may continue, particularly if the preservative hasn't fully penetrated. But then it hadn't been my intention to preserve the body for any longer than was necessary to facilitate a hygienic burial. My relief upon seeing the normal condition of the cadaver evaporated with the fumes, and with it any semblance of normality in the body itself, which began to change with an impossible rapidity.

"Father! What should I do?" the younger Jasper pleaded.

"You might stand back!" his father suggested.

Before our very eyes the cadaver was visibly swelling with the gases of decay. As the flesh filled and stretched it caused the limbs to move and twitch, in a disturbing mockery of life. No, it was not as if we saw Tom Coffin's ruined body come back to life. Ghastly as that might have been, the reality was much, much worse. There was nothing lively about the shuddering twitches of the corpse. Rather, we saw him getting deader by the second, his flesh putrefying and splitting apart, as if the normal, six-week process of corruption were being compressed into a few intolerable minutes. We watched in silent horror, made mute by terror and disbelief, as muscles and ligaments tightened, then relaxed, then unraveled from the bone. We saw the skin writhe as it sloughed away from liquefying organs, the whole running mess of it bubbling, foaming, blackening, yes, *blackening*, with flesh-rot and bone-mold and jellied excrescence. His eyeballs dissolved in their sockets and leaked like tears through his closed eyelids and ran down his now-black face. Fingernails ripened, exploding softly from the digits. His brain melted, spurted from ears, nose, mouth. And when, somehow, the calcifying ligaments pulled taut, wrenching the spine free of the flesh and sitting it bolt upright, Tom Coffin's jaw suddenly dropped away from Tom

Coffin's skull, and the scream that came from where his mouth had been, the scream that quivered the air and shattered the softened bones and dissolved the corpse into dust, that scream was mine.

# 4. Beneath the Paint

When I staggered from the undertaker's parlor I was a changed man, and not for the better. Everything I knew and believed had rotted away with the unnatural decay of Tom Coffin's remains. There was no rational explanation for what I had witnessed, no possible scientific theory. It made me see the world in a different way. Or rather it was as if I were suddenly looking through this world into another, as if the place I'd lived, worked, thought, and loved was nothing more than a trompe l'oeil, a clever, pleasant little illusion painted upon the horror that lurked just beneath it. I was unmoored, a soul loosed from the earth, and I did not soar, no, but plummeted into a feverish, waking nightmare.

For a time my senses became strangely enhanced. The drab, winter monochrome of a coastal village became vibrant with colors so bright and intense that my eyes ached. Signs and images seemed to sing or scream, as if color had a musical or vocal component. The cold, salty air carried a thousand piercing odors, some so fragrant I wept with physical pleasure, others so repulsive it made me choke on my own bile. The bloom of life, the stench of death, both intertwined, and so powerfully experienced that I thought my brain might boil away while I still lived.

Surely I was seen in this state, lurching like a drunken sailor through the narrow, winding streets of White Harbor, but I can't recall seeing another human being until at last I found myself once more at the Coffin house, scarcely comprehending how I got there. Barky the cook, observing my distress, urged me to lie down while he fetched a doctor. I threw off his gentle hands, reminded him that I was a doctor and would heal myself, whereupon I cackled like a madman and then fell to weeping.

"We are doomed," I told him. "All of us, doomed."

"Course we are," he agreed with a click of the tongue. "Every man must die. That's a given. But God made heaven for us, so we needn't despair. That's a given, too."

"Barky," I said, grasping his huge wrist and drawing him near. "Barky, what if there is no heaven?"

"There must be heaven," he squeaked. "It's in the Bible."

"What if there is no heaven?" I insisted. "What if hell exists all around us? All we have to do is scratch through the paint and there it is. Terrible things hiding behind the paint. Awful things. Waiting to leap out at us. Things that can cut men to pieces and freeze babies and shape themselves in lightning. It's true, Barky. I've seen it! Like the Captain sees it. Things behind the paint!"

"I wish you'd take this brandy, Dr. Bentwood."

"No! No brandy! It smells vile! Can't you smell it? Stinks like swamp fire! Get it away!"

"Easy now. I'll put the brandy aside, maybe you'll want it later."

"You must believe me, sir! I thought I knew what the world was, but the world you see is a trick of paint. An illusion. I thought there were rules, laws of physics. But there are no rules, there are no laws! Hell is right here!" I screamed, banging the table with my fists. "It waits beneath! Under the paint, Barky, under the paint!"

As I knew from our previous acquaintance, the huge man had the patience of a saint, and he somehow managed to restrain me without doing me any harm, or letting me harm myself. Like any nightmare the details are vague, but I think I was trying to scrape away my own skin to show him what was underneath. Then I must have fainted, because the next thing I remember is lying on my bed in my chamber, and Lucy holding a cool, moist cloth to my brow.

"Lucy," I muttered. "Your perfume. I can barely smell it."

"Not perfume," she murmured. "Rose water. It has, I'm told, a very light fragrance."

"Good, good. You smell lovely, really."

Then I slept.

By the next day I had recovered my composure, such as it was. Colors no longer blinded me. Odors no longer electrified my senses. I stopped raving and scratching at my skin. But what I confessed to Barky remained essentially true, as it does to this day. My recent experiences had convinced me that another world existed, an invisible world that might at any moment make itself known in the most horrifying way. For this was not the harmless sort of afterlife world described by spiritualists, where dead relatives milled about eager to communicate, or the cook's biblical heaven, but a place where demons dwelled among us, separated by the merest gossamer. Nothing else made sense. I had to believe it or go insane.

Fortunately I was clever enough to keep my own counsel. Captain Coffin had seen that world beneath, and for raving about it he'd been locked in a tower, or he'd locked himself in, which amounted to the same thing. I was determined that that not happen to me, even if I had to pretend to be the same supremely rational fellow who had first arrived in White Harbor. I told myself I must appear rational and reasonable, therefore I would act rational and reasonable, and if anyone asked what I'd been raving about I would feign loss of memory. Fever dreams, I would say, common delirium, pay no attention.

Anything but admit the truth. The new truth of the new Davis Bentwood.

The glimpse I'd seen was not enough to satisfy me. Not that I wished to return to that state. Far from it. But I wanted very much to know what, exactly, Cassius Coffin had done to scratch the paint, as it were. If I wanted to retain my sanity, and keep what was happening to the Coffins from happening to me, I must find out, and soon. One thing was certain: it had to be more than the grave sin of slavery, for if that was all it took, half the houses in the nation would be haunted.

"You look yourself again," Lucy said when I came down to breakfast, and found her eating alone. "I'm glad of that."

"Yes, yes," I said, fiddling with the pot of coffee. "I'm quite recovered, thank you. And I do apologize for frightening you last night."

Lucy smiled. "Oh, Davis, you did not frighten me. You were quite sweet, really. Why, you told me I smelled like roses and heaven."

"Did I? Oh, but you do, I'm sure."

She gave me a long, lingering look with her icicle-blue eyes, as if trying to read my secret thoughts. "I see that you're embarrassed. Please don't be. There's nothing unmanly about suffering a nervous disorder. You'd been through a terrifying experience aboard the schooner and you'd taken everything upon yourself, trying to help us. You were exhausted. You had to deal with the remains, and I'm sure that was awful. It's no wonder your mind decided to take a holiday."

I was astonished. "Is that what you think happened? My mind took a holiday?"

"What else?" She raised her eyebrows, as if waiting for me to disagree, or to supply an explanation of my own. Instead I accepted her description of what she perceived to be my breakdown, and then endeavored to change the subject.

"So. How do your cousins fare?" I asked, almost afraid to hear the answer.

"Well enough, considering. No, I do not tell the truth. This home lies under a pall," she said, with a gesture that seemed to describe the oppressive silence of the great house. "The Captain is mad again, they say, and Jebediah is not himself. Benjamin does nothing but pray, and Nathaniel frets for his wife."

"What other news is there?" I asked, indicating the newspaper she'd put down when I entered the dining room. "How goes it with the rest of the world?"

"More gloom, I'm afraid," she said with a sigh. "The train has been gathering speed and now, it seems, no one can jump off."

"More states have seceded?"

She nodded. "Nearly all those below the Mason Dixon line. And worse, they are spoiling to prove their independence, looking for any excuse to confront federal authorities. Which is something of a problem."

"How so?"

"Aside from postal workers, the only 'federals' located in this new Confederacy are a few soldiers stationed here and there, at long-established army bases. They're under orders not to fight unless attacked. They're certainly not attempting to enforce any federal laws. So if there's going to be war, the Southerners will have to start it."

We discussed the subject for a while, so as not to return to the gloomy prospects of the family, but I failed to summon any passion for argument, and so we found ourselves agreeing. Gradually the conversation diminished, and I was able to excuse myself by saying that I was obliged to check in on Jebediah and Captain Sweeney.

"You'll find poor Jeb in his chamber," Lucy informed me. "Captain Sweeney left here when you were en route to Nova Scotia."

"Really?" I asked, alarmed. "But where has he gone? Was

he well enough to travel?" I had no idea where the man might go. With his beautiful schooner destroyed, the salty fellow had, in effect, no home.

"He's boarding at the same house where Nathaniel and Sarah took rooms. My impression was that he's on the mend but not completely healed. He still had a terrible cough and could take no solid food."

"Why, then, did he leave, sick as he was?"

Lucy gave me the strangest look, as if I'd again lost my senses. "Why, I suppose he left because he could," she said. "Can you blame him?"

"Lucy!" I said. "Is it only obligation that keeps you here? You must not feel so. I'm sure Jeb would agree."

She shook her head. "I remain of my own free will. It is not obligation but friendship that keeps me. The Coffins are my friends as well as my relations. They took me in when I had no place else to turn. How can I leave them in their time of need? Surely you feel the same."

My heart warmed as I stared at this beautiful, valiant young woman. "Yes," I agreed, with all my heart. "We feel the same."

## 5. Another Kind of Dead

Mrs. Merriman's boardinghouse was a sturdy saltbox located a few blocks from the waterfront. Its narrow clapboards were painted a cheerful yellow, and each of the many small windows was fitted with a pair of black shutters. In the neatly apportioned front yard, small mounds in the snow revealed where beds of flowers would thrive, come spring. A cobbled walkway had been scraped and sanded all the way to the entrance. Despite my bleak cast of mind, I smiled approaching the door. There was something sunny and welcoming about the place, a personality that, alas, can't be ascribed to every boardinghouse, and it was obvious that Nathaniel and Captain Sweeney had chosen well.

I knew at once, upon entering the guest parlor, that the proprietress had a special fondness for cats. At least a dozen of the creatures lounged luxuriously upon stuffed cushions and braided rugs set out for that purpose. One very forward tom leaped down from an upholstered ottoman and began to writhe about my legs, purring like a little steam engine. A moment later Mrs. Merriman entered, saying, "Scat, Boozer! Leave the gentleman alone!"

If Boozer heard and understood, he gave no sign, but continued his joyous paroxysm undeterred. "I don't mind," I told the lady. "I like a cat about the house. For the mice, you know."

"Mice?" she tittered. "Mice know better than to venture here! There's a paucity of mice in these parts, believe you me."

The good lady was small and slightly plump, with her iron-gray hair up in a bun. She was dressed in the kind of pleated, fussily embroidered gown that was passé in Boston, but was now, no doubt, the height of fashion in White Harbor society. This being a small town, my introduction was a formality—Mrs. Merriman already knew who I was, and seemed to have a clear idea of what had brought me to the Coffin house.

"How is poor Cash faring?" she inquired. "All those handsome sons. What a terrible thing! He was so proud of those boys. We all were, come to that. A credit to the Harbor, every one."

We exchanged sympathetic remarks about the family, and I got the impression that Mrs. Merriman was sincerely fond of the Coffin brothers, if not exactly keen about their father, for whom she had respect but little apparent affection. "Have you come to consult with Sarah? If so I must tell you she is still greatly disturbed by any intrusion. Nathaniel has asked that visitors—and doctors—call at a later time."

"Has Dr. Griswold been treating her?"

Mrs. Merriman seemed uncomfortable with the question, as if afraid I'd be offended by another physician's proximity. "Dr. Griswold called once or twice," she said uneasily. "Nathaniel has requested that he not call again."

"I see."

"Is there nothing can be done for the poor soul?"

I shook my head. "Nothing a doctor can prescribe. In time she may return to herself."

"I will keep her in my prayers."

"I wanted to check on Sarah, of course, if only as a friend, but my main target is Captain Sweeney. I was told he's taken possession of a room."

That elicited a girlish laugh from my hostess. "Well spoke, Dr. Bentwood. That's exactly what he's done, the old rascal. I will bring you to him. And then I will flee out of range of his guns."

"Guns?" I asked, concerned, as she let me up the stairs.

There was a small woven rug on each tread, and almost as many cats to be avoided.

"Figure of speech, Doctor. Don't you fret. I doubt he'll do you any actual harm, beyond the usual tongue lashing. He's been in a fearsome bad mood since his precious schooner came to grief."

Black Jack Sweeney had been given a corner room, with low ceilings, a small but active fireplace, and a window that overlooked the harbor. I found him sitting in a high-backed chair, feet up on a stool. He was covered in one of Mrs. Merriman's crocheted shawls, and staring out the window with a dark, pensive expression. Upon spotting me with his one good eye he sucked on his long clay pipe and put a cloud of pungent smoke between us. "So you didn't go down with my ship," he said, sounding disappointed.

"I'm afraid I survived. May I visit?"

He scowled and pawed at the smoke. "Suit yourself. But I ain't taking none of your vile medicines, so don't even try me."

"I won't," I promised. "You seem better."

"Do I?" he leered. "You ain't much of a doctor, if you think that."

"I'm sure you're right. I'm not here as a doctor, Captain Sweeney. I'm here as a friend."

That gave him pause. "You consider yourself my friend, do you?" he said, scratching at the strap that held his shabby eye patch in place.

"I'd like us to be friends, yes. But I meant I'm here as a friend of the family."

He snorted grumpily. "I suppose you're that, I'll give you that much. How do they fare, then?"

"Not well," I said. "Not well at all."

"Jebediah?"

"Refusing visitors at the moment."

"Aye? He's a wise man, then."

"Mr. Barkham is doing his best, but Jeb won't eat. A little barley broth, that's all."

"That's bad," said Sweeney, with obvious concern. His gruffness was, I sensed, in part contrived, to mask whatever it was he truly felt.

"I'm sorry about your ship," I said. "I know how you loved her."

He swallowed and averted his eye. His voice, when he spoke, was husky with emotion. "Was me in charge of *Raven* she'd still be afloat. She'd be out there right now where I can see her," he said, pointing at the window.

"No," I said, disagreeing as gently as I knew how. "It wasn't Tom Coffin wrecked the schooner. I think you know that, even if you don't want to admit it."

"You do, eh?" he said pugnaciously. "You know a lot for a Boston fella."

Now or never, I said to myself, fire your broadside while he's dead in the water, unsuspecting.

"I know Cash Coffin was a slave trader," I said, bearing in. "And I know, or *think* I know, that something terrible happened, long ago. Something that still haunts the family. And I'm fairly certain you know more about it than I do."

"Eh?" he said uneasily. He sucked nervously upon the clay pipe, unaware that it had gone out. "What makes you think that?"

"Your name. Black Jack. You told me you got it while you were on the slave coast."

"Hmph. That's no secret," he said dismissively. "Everybody knows me knows that."

I pulled up a chair, blocking any chance of retreat. "I didn't come to inquire about your nickname. I came because the Coffins are being destroyed, one by one. Four dead in circumstances that defy rational explanation. I believe that something unnatural is happening, and I think you believe it, too.

Something frightened you enough to make you flee the house when you were too sick to leave under your own power."

That got him bolt upright in his chair, and made his single eye glitter with fury. "You came here to call me a coward?" he snarled, and raised a shaking, sea-gnarled fist.

"No, Captain Sweeney. Never would I say such a thing to a man like you. I came here to ask for your help, because I'm frightened, too. We're all frightened. Some, like Cash and Sarah and Jebediah, have been terrified out of their wits. Please help me. Please help them. I'm begging you, sir. I'll go down on my knees and beg if that's what it takes."

All at once the old tar's fury dissipated and his face crumpled and sagged. A tear ran from his one good eye and he hastily mopped it away with his sleeve. "You got me right, Doc," he croaked. "By the good Lord above, I swear I was so fearful I nearly wet my drawers. Wasn't nothing I could see, mind you. But something awful was in the room with me that night."

Sweeney then recounted, in his halting way, what happened the night his fever broke, the night *Raven* left the harbor without him. He awoke from a sound sleep and knew at once that he was in grave danger. There was, he said, a palpable presence in the room, and though it could not be seen he believed that it was sucking all the goodness from the air.

"I tried to open the window but it wouldn't rise. Then I made for the door, but it was like the air got thick or something, and I couldn't never reach that neither, no matter how I tried. So I commenced to hollering, but it was like the holler was dyin' in my throat, or got swallowed up somehow.

"Oh, I been in a tight spot or two in my time, and more than once I figured to meet my Maker. You sail the seas as long as I have, you're bound to come at a tight spot. I won't say death don't frighten me, but this was different."

I leaned closer. "Different? Different in what way?"

While Sweeney turned the question over in his mind, he filled his pipe bowl and got it fuming. "Hmm. Now that's a hard one, but let me try." He puffed some, and then grunted, using the pipe stem to make his point. "I had the feeling—no, no, it were a certainty—yes, sir, I knew in my bones that if I was to die in that room, with that thing so close, I wouldn't ever meet my Maker at all. I'd be dead in some other way. A kind of dead more terrifying and more horrible than regular dead." He paused and gave me a quizzical look. "Can you make sense of it?"

"No," I admitted. "But I know exactly what you mean."

"Do you? Then I'm sorry for you, Doc. It changes a man inside, to feel a thing like that. I ain't the same Black Jack Sweeney that sailed you into this harbor, and that's a fact."

"Nor am I the same man you delivered."

"What has happened to us, do you suppose?"

"I've no idea. Or nothing I can put into words. But I feel compelled to find out. I *must* find out, or be damned."

Captain Sweeney's gnarled hands still trembled, as if vibrating to that memory of fear. "I believe you're on the wrong tack, Doc. Whatever it is that preys upon Coffins, it can't have nothin' to do with how Cash made his pile. Too many years gone by for that."

"Perhaps," I said. "But does the word 'Monbasu' mean anything to you?"

The old tar visibly blanched, and gave me a look that couldn't have been more surprised if I'd pulled out a pistol and shot him. "Monbasu?" he gasped. "What's this got to do with that fella?"

Now it was my turn to be astonished. "Monbasu is someone you know? I thought it was a kind of curse. A word for devil."

"He were a slave trader," said Sweeney. "Then he was a slave himself, for a while. As rum a character as ever you wish to meet. He was a lot of things, some of 'em good and some of 'em bad, but he wasn't no devil when I knew him."

"And when was this?"

Sweeney's brow furrowed. "More than twenty years ago. Just before Cash give up the trade for good."

I nodded. "So Monbasu was a fellow slave trader. Was he French?"

Sweeney managed to laugh. "Was he French? No more'n I am. No, your Monbasu was an African sort of gentleman. He was black as your hat."

At that moment Mrs. Merriman threw open the door, put her hand to her heaving chest to catch her breath, and announced that Sarah Coffin had thrown herself into the harbor.

# 6. Another Kind of Sleep

It was not far to the harbor edge, and all of it downhill. I skid-ded most of the way on leather boot heels, which could find no purchase on the frosted cobblestones.

Although it was barely noon, the sun was but a small pale presence, a shy visitor to the leaden sky, and the air was cold enough to clot in your chest.

I calculated that the harbor waters could not be much above freezing. It is well known that flowing salt water can be colder by several degrees than frozen blocks of pond ice. One need not drown in such waters: simple immersion will likely result in death. As I ran and skidded my way downhill, I cursed myself for not insisting on a consultation with poor Sarah. Aware of her hysterical state, and of the possibility that she might seek to harm herself, I'd done nothing to help. The fact that her husband had forbidden visitors should not have deterred me. It was my duty as a physician to intercede, as Nathaniel was himself in a confused mental state, and there-fore not qualified to make such a crucial decision as to forgo all treatment.

Fool! Charlatan! Those were but two of the names I gave myself, on that headlong race to the harbor.

As it happened, Nathaniel Coffin had got there before me. I found him in shirtsleeves, racing back and forth along the waterfront, frantically searching the harbor waters for a sign of his wife. The most telling thing I saw was a pile of female clothing and undergarments discarded on the pier. That a woman of Sarah's modesty should strip herself naked indicated her desperate compulsion to destroy herself.

"Oh, God! Oh, God!" the poor man wailed, tearing at his beard. Then he cupped his hands around his mouth and shouted to the placid, freezing waters. "It is only me, darling! Only me! You can't be afraid of me!"

I attempted to steer Nathaniel away from the edge, fearful that he, too, might decide to end his misery. He was scarcely aware of me, and there was nothing I could do to deter his frantic, hopeless search, for like all the Coffins he had shoulders of oak and limbs of iron.

"I don't know what got into her so sudden," he muttered anxiously. "Like she didn't know me! Like I was someone that scared her! Why should my lovely Sarah be scared of me?"

I tried to reason with him, telling him we must get boats to drag the harbor, but he would not heed me. "Sarah!" he kept crying out. "Sarah, it's only me! Please come back!"

Apparently his wife had been relatively calm for the last day or so, which was why he had dismissed Dr. Griswold, whose visits only seemed to agitate her. The previous night she had slept soundly for the first time since the baby died, and Nathaniel was hopeful that she'd turned a corner. That morning they had prayed quietly together and then Nathaniel had read to her from a lady's magazine, articles about etiquette and ladylike deportment that seemed to soothe her by suggesting a world far removed from her present reality. Then, just before noon, he went down for a tray of Mrs. Merriman's luncheon sandwiches, convinced that his wife's appetite might return with her newfound composure. But when he entered the room, tray in hand, Sarah shrank from him with a look of horror. He asked her what was wrong. Her reply was devastating. "Where is Nathaniel?" she demanded, shaking with fear. "What have you done to my husband?" When he tried to embrace her she shoved him away with a strength he'd never imagined she possessed, and then fled the room, locking the door behind her. It took him less than a minute to break the door and follow, but in that one precious minute she'd flown headlong to the pier, torn off all her clothing, and vanished under the water.

"I turned the other way when I left the house," he said mournfully. "I supposed she was headed to the graveyard, to see the baby. Then I heard a splash and ran for the pier, fast as I could." He reached out to the pathetic pile of her discarded clothing but couldn't bring himself to touch it. He gave me a look of such beseeching misery it broke my heart. "Why'd she think I wasn't me?" he asked plaintively. "Why'd she think a thing like that?"

Before I could formulate an answer—not that I *had* an answer—something caught my eye. A patch of palest white upon the dark water. Nathaniel saw me react and instantly spotted the same object. "Sarah!" he cried, lunging for the handrail.

I tried to grab his legs and manhandle him to the ground, but he shed me effortlessly, and without hesitation leaped over the rail and dove headfirst into the icy harbor fully clothed, boots and all.

The black water closed over him like a shimmering curtain, and all was silent.

I sank back to my knees, convinced that Nathaniel would soon join his beloved wife in death, for her lifeless form floated facedown upon the waters, and betrayed no sign of life. The mere shock of plunging into water that cold—colder than ice, quite literally—was enough to render a man unconscious. I imagined his lungs filling, the weight of his heavy boots dragging him down, down. No pain, no anguish, no ability to struggle, only an overwhelming numbness as the nerves ceased to function.

A *splash!* shocked me out of my morbid reverie. There, thirty yards or more from the pier, Nathaniel had surfaced and was propelling himself forward with great, surging lunges of his powerful arms. Very soon he reached the floating body of his wife, locked his hands around her, and began to kick furiously back to the pier.

I, meantime, searched frantically for a boat or dinghy, but there was nothing nearby, and my only hope was to find some object I could extend out into the water, should Nathaniel falter. With that in mind I managed to wrench free a section of the hand railing and stood waiting anxiously.

"Here!" I cried. "This way! Quickly!"

Nathaniel heard me and veered to where I knelt. I held out the length of wood, and with it we managed to hold his wife up while he pulled himself into the braceworks under the pier. He was quite blue, but never once faltered. With one hand he pulled himself clear of the water, with the other he lifted poor Sarah. Her head lolled back, revealing lips as black as the water that had swallowed her, and when I took her weight into my own arms, pulling her up onto the pier, I could detect no life in her sleek, icy cold body.

With a soggy *thump!* Nathaniel levered himself onto the pier. Although he was shivering so violently his shirt buttons popped, his first thought was to cover Sarah with the garments she'd flung away. "She's so c-c-cold!" he stuttered. "We m-m-must warm her."

This, as it turned out, was very sensible, although at the time my concern was for Nathaniel, who was so obviously suffering from the ill effects of exposure. My first glimmer of hope was the discovery that Sarah's lungs were not filled with water. Indeed, her mouth appeared to have locked shut, as if the sudden shock of the unbearable cold had contracted the muscles of her jaw the moment she hit the water.

I searched frantically for a pulse, finding none, and then

realized that my own fingers were so cold as to be insensible. Shoving Nathaniel out of the way—actually, he moved willingly enough—I forced my ear to her chest and detected—was it possible, or was I imagining it?—one very faint thump that might have been a heartbeat.

"Quickly, man! Rub her arms and leg! Force the blood to move! No, don't worry about hurting her, just do it! Rub fast, man! Faster!" Meanwhile I flexed her limbs and prodded her abdomen, where the blood would naturally pool. When I felt a quivering under the icy skin of her belly, I again clamped my ear to her chest and yes, it was there, sluggish and slow.

Sarah's heart was beating. She was alive.

At the boardinghouse Mrs. Merriman brought heated bricks from the stove. These we wrapped in towels and laid upon Sarah's body. Nathaniel, who would see nothing done for himself until his wife was taken care of, urged me to cover her with blankets, but I was convinced we must keep moving her limbs to circulate and warm the blood, and I prevailed.

"Nathaniel! Look at me!" I commanded. When his eyes met mine I said, brooking no argument, "You must see to yourself, man. It will be no good saving Sarah if you expire from the cold."

The big man nodded dumbly, conceding the point. Without so much as a glance at our hostess, who quite properly averted her eyes, Nathaniel stripped off his clothing, wrapped himself in a wool blanket, and got as close to the wood stove as he could without setting himself on fire.

"Stay right there until you raise a sweat!" I called out. "Mrs. Merriman and I will see to your wife."

It was a near thing. A beating heart is not a guarantor of long-term survival in such cases. It is well known that the heart may beat for a time after the soul has left the body. During that wretched year when I made the hospital rounds, a man was carried in with most of his temple shot away in an argument over gambling debts. More than half his brain was destroyed and yet his heart continued to beat for three days. I very much feared that Sarah's revival was a similar exercise in futility, and when her eyes fluttered open I was speechless with relief.

"Cold," she said in a small, childish voice.

"You'll be warm soon," I said, and hastily covered her with a blanket.

Nathaniel overheard us and rushed to her side before I could warn him off. But rather than regard him with the horror that had driven her into the dark waters, she gazed at him blankly, as if she'd never seen him before.

"Sarah?" he whispered huskily, and then wept with joy.

"Sarah cold," she said.

It was there in her childlike voice, in her petulant, needy expression. The woman who had returned was not the wife and grieving mother who had thrown herself into the harbor, but a little girl who remembered nothing of her grief, or of the husband who loved her.

"Where's Poppa?"

"Poppa will be here soon," he said, shooting me a look that said Sarah's father was long gone from this earth.

"You're a funny man!" she said, and averted her face, almost playfully.

"It doesn't matter, darling," he said. "Only that you're alive."

I believed Nathaniel when he said that. It was enough for him that any part of his beloved wife had survived, even if it meant she did not remember him.

When I left to call on Captain Sweeney, they seemed to be making friends.

I found the door to his chamber open, as I'd left it. Captain

Sweeney had not stirred from his chair by the window. His hand lay in his lap, cradling his cold pipe, and his leathery, weather-beaten face was relaxed in sleep. Strangely, the sleep made him young again, and with the ragged eye patch he looked like a boy disguised as a pirate, exhausted after a children's party. Or maybe it was that Sarah had put me in mind of children, and the child who lives within each of us. In any event, I would not have disturbed such a profound and rejuvenating sleep had I not been desperate to learn more of his adventures in the slave trade, and what it might have to do with the present horrors.

"Jack?" I said, as gently as I knew how. "Captain Sweeney?"

Then I touched him and knew it was another kind of sleep.

# 7. The Goblins Inside

$A$ strange thing happens to a man when he is surrounded by death. He very quickly gets used to it. Death becomes for him the more natural state, and life the exception. That Nathaniel and his wife survived immersion into killing waters was a shock. That Captain Sweeney passed away in his chair was to be expected. Was he not ancient for a sailor, had he not been grievously ill? Was his heart not strained by sickness and fear and, I sensed, more than a little regret? Of course he died. Death was the norm. The miracle was that I'd managed to speak with him at all, although what little I learned was merely tantalizing. Monbasu was no devil or demon, he was simply a man in the same evil trade as Cash Coffin. Upon hearing the name, Sweeney had evidenced no particular fear—quite the reverse. *He's as rum a character as you ever wished to meet.* I was willing to wager that Captain Sweeney had much the same to say about numerous men from his colorful past. Monbasu was another, no more, no less.

Thus I comforted myself. The truth was, Black Jack Sweeney was such a lively, engaging sort of fellow that I would miss him greatly, though we'd been acquainted for only a short while. Mrs. Merriman, sensing my distress, kindly informed me not to trouble myself, that she'd handle the arrangements. It seems that Sweeney was an old friend, and had left a sum of money in her care that was more than sufficient to cover the cost of his burial. "Like all of the sailormen Jack was very superstitious," she told me. "It put his mind at ease to have planned for his own arrangements. He always told me that he'd probably die at sea, and be buried there, but just in case he made me his guardian in such matters."

This was a great relief, as I dreaded having any more contact with the Jasper Caswells, who as it happened were the only undertakers in the village. It was enough that they'd swept Tom Coffin's remains, such as they were, into a casket, and delivered it to the family crypt, and swore never to divulge what they'd witnessed.

"Had he family at all?" I asked.

Mrs. Merriman shook her steely gray head. "None living. Never took a wife, unless you count that schooner. How he loved that ship!"

With that she wept quietly. Our grief was somewhat tempered by the sight of his body in repose. It was obvious at a glance that Captain Sweeney had died at peace with himself, and with the life he'd lived, and for that I was grateful. Such a tranquil death had become a rarity in White Harbor, and was to become rarer still.

Jebediah asked for me that evening. I found him propped on his pillows, looking wan and disturbingly cadaverous. A number of sperm-oil lamps had been lit and placed around his chamber, adding to the funereal effect. The stench of illness, the dank odors of physical melancholia, overwhelmed the sweet perfume of the lamps.

"I hope you are feeling better," I said, feigning cheerfulness.

"No better, no worse," he responded morosely. "What does it matter?"

"But, Jebediah, old friend, surely—"

"Surely nothing," he said, cutting me off. "May we speak plainly, Davis? As friends?"

"Of course. But we always speak plainly, and as friends. That's why I'm here."

"Then you mustn't argue when I ask you to leave."

It was obvious that he wasn't jesting. "Jeb, if I've done something to offend you, please accept my—"

"Don't!" he said, grasping my hands and indicating that I sit on the bed beside him. "We've covered this ground before. My dear Davis, you don't have it in you to offend me, or anyone, I think. You are the least offensive man in the world, and the dearest to me, and that is why I insist that you leave this house and never look back."

"But, Jeb—"

"Hush now! Hush! Terrible things have happened. Terrible things! They will not cease until we are destroyed, and there is nothing you or anyone can do to stop it."

I decided the best tactic was to ignore his order to leave and keep him talking. That he remained in the grip of a profound melancholy, there was no doubt, but his mind was otherwise clear, and I had need of his memories, and his perceptions of the past.

"What do you know about how your father made his fortune?" I asked him gently, but bluntly. "Do you know anything at all?"

My little friend seemed to shrink even more inside himself, averting his eyes as if ashamed. "Of course I do," he said. "How could I live in this house, this village, without knowing? But I wished you never to know. I wished you to think well of us, Davis, but now, obviously, you've stumbled on the awful truth."

"Jebediah, listen to me." I took his chin in my hand and forced him to meet my eyes. "You are not to be blamed for whatever your father did in his youth. Original sin does not apply in this instance. The sin was neither original, nor was your father the first to commit it. In his favor, I know of no other man who made his fortune slave trading who then donated so much of it to the cause of banishing slavery from this earth."

"You don't understand," he said plaintively.

"Tell me then. What don't I understand?"

"My father doesn't finance abolitionists out of sincere belief. He gives to them out of fear."

I patted his hands. "Now we're getting somewhere. What exactly does he fear?"

Jebediah shrugged, and I saw how thin he'd become, and how his growing weakness made his large head wobble upon his frail shoulders. "I never knew until this all began. *This* is what he feared. That his family and his fortune would be destroyed."

"You spoke with him about this notion, this belief, that he had brought a curse upon you and your brothers?"

"No. Never. But I knew. Each time I went to him for funds for the cause he gave too eagerly. At no other time was he generous with his money. They used to say you needed a crowbar to pry a penny from Cash Coffin's hand, and they weren't exaggerating by much. And when he first invited abolitionists to the house, and encouraged me to hear them, I knew that he did not share their passion. Even as a child I knew that. Later I assumed it was shame that made him encourage me."

"You felt he was ashamed of you?"

"No, never that!" he said, almost eagerly. "The Captain was never ashamed of me, and that's why I still love him, despite the terrible things I suppose he must have done. No, what shamed him was that he believed his being a slaver had somehow made me a dwarf."

"The deformity is quite common," I insisted. "Dwarfs are born to the best of families, and to the worst. No one knows why."

"They say it is an affliction of the evil eye."

At first I was stunned to think that my educated friend might give credence to such ignorant superstitions, and that he had secretly harbored his fearful guilt for all these years. But then I saw that, given what had transpired, it was only natural that he seize upon any possible explanation for his wretched condition.

"Listen to me," I said, gently but firmly. "The notion of an 'evil eye' is an old wives tale. I take, as you know, the more enlightened view, and all of modern science supports me."

"Science? Bah."

"You may 'bah' all you like, but this is the age of reason, and reason tells me this: we don't know what causes physical deformities such as yours, but whatever may be the cause, it does not lie with you, or with anything like 'evil eyes,' or curses upon your family. Deformity is somehow an accident of the birth process, and is in that sense quite natural, even expected. It occurs in all life forms, not only human beings. Do we assume that a deformed calf is the result of some sin its parents committed? The very idea is ridiculous. So it is with human deformity. There is no possible connection to sin, or family curses, or the punishment of evil."

Jeb looked at me with grave curiosity. "Are you so certain?" he asked.

"Absolutely certain," I said with more confidence than I felt. "Now enough of that, do you hear? It solves nothing to keep blaming yourself for events beyond your control. We must get at this somehow. What really happened, long ago? Where did this all begin?"

"Before I was born, I suppose. Father sold his slave ships the day my mother died, or soon after. But he carried the weight of it always. I saw it each time he looked upon me."

"He never hinted what it might be?"

Jeb shook his head.

"Do you think he would tell me, if I asked?"

The thought made him cringe. "I suppose he might. But he might just as easily shoot you. You've seen his state of mind. He's capable of anything, Davis, you mustn't risk it."

"No," I agreed. "Not until I am better armed."

"Better armed?" The idea frightened him.

"With information," I assured him. "Surely there is some-one else who knows. Crew or business partner. It was a com-plicated enterprise, buying slaves and bringing them across the sea. He didn't do it alone. I think Captain Sweeney knew something of what happened, but the poor man expired before I had the chance to press him."

"Another victim," Jeb said with vicious self-loathing.

"No, I think not," I said, and described how I'd found the old tar in his chair, as peaceful as if asleep. That seemed to bring Jebediah a little relief, though hardly enough to lift his gloom.

As I was about to take my leave, Jeb propped himself up and asked, "Did darkness frighten you, when you were a child?"

"I suppose it must have. I don't remember."

"I used to put my pillow a certain way, and then the gob-lins under the bed couldn't harm me. Strange what children believe, isn't it? But I wasn't far off the mark. It isn't the gob-lins under the bed who can harm you. It's the goblins in here," he said, and thumped his chest.

## 8. A Light That Guides

Lucy found me in the parlor, drinking whiskey so that I might sleep. I was physically exhausted by the events of the long and arduous day, but my conversation with Jebediah had left me wide awake, in that state where the brain seems to twitch and the ears feel stuffed with cotton. I wasn't sure what my own thoughts were, other than that they disturbed me.

"May I join you?"

"Of course!" In leaping up I had to steady myself, which drew a sympathetic smile.

To my intense surprise, Lucy wore a tightly corseted gown of sky-blue satin, showing off her figure to the best advantage, as well as her startling eyes. The gown's bodice had been cut daringly low, and then discreetly laced in a way that left more to the imagination than was actually on display. The bottom of her skirts was widely belled with crinoline, to an extent that would have pleased the demimonde in Boston. Whiskey or no, I was more than a little nonplussed, as it seemed a costume more appropriate to a formal ball than a house in mourning.

"You think my dress improper?" she asked sharply. "I see the glint of disapproval in your eye."

"No, of course not," I stammered. "It's a lovely gown. Quite lovely."

"Pour me a glass of whiskey and I'll explain," she said.

Turning to cover my embarrassment—how easily she read me!—I did as she requested. A moment later she clinked her glass to mine and then leaned forward, so close I could feel the heat radiating from her bosom. Her complexion, normally of a porcelain paleness, had darkened somewhat, and that was worrisome, as it might indicate an oncoming fever or inflammation of the blood. "I've decided to defy death," she whispered in a husky, conspiratorial voice. "I conceived a notion that by wearing bright attire, I might lift the pall that hovers over us. A ridiculous idea, but there it is."

It wasn't only the whiskey in her glass, I realized. My beautiful companion had the distinctive scent of sherry on her breath. She was, not to put it crudely—for there was nothing crude about her behavior—halfway to being tipsy. It was alcohol, not fever, that darkened her complexion.

When I took her arm and guided her to the settee, she did not resist. She patted the cushion, indicating that I sit by her. "I won't bite," she promised.

I decided to drink no more of the whiskey, else I lose my composure. "My apologies, but you'll get no sensible conversation from me this evening," I told her. "My mind wanders."

"It's no wonder," she said sympathetically. "You are much put upon by circumstance. No matter what horrible thing happens in this house, or to this family, it falls to you. It hardly seems fair."

"Fairness doesn't enter," I said stiffly. "It is duty that compels us."

"Ah, yes. Duty. Mustn't forget the importance of duty, to God and country and Coffins. Why, you're blushing, Dr. Bentwood! I think I have made you angry."

"No," I protested weakly. "It's just that I'm exhausted. My mind is somewhat distracted."

"Of course it is, after rescuing poor Sarah."

"It was Nathaniel who rescued her," I corrected. "All I did was help restore circulation."

"Nevertheless, you continue to be our hero." She giggled, covered her mouth as she laughed outright. "Our knight! Our knight in shining armor."

"I'm pleased to amuse you, Miss Wattle."

Slowly she regained control of herself, and then begged my forgiveness. "Honestly, I did not mean to laugh. My compliment was sincere. But I've felt myself on the verge of hysteria these last few days, and with me it takes the form of laughter."

"Hysteria? But that is quite serious. I must prescribe a powder, or possibly a purgative." My concern was sincere, for up until now Lucy had never betrayed any evidence of nervous affliction.

"Powder?" she said, laughing dismissively. "Do you think you can cure what ails me with one of your powders? I thought you were a serious man, Dr. Bentwood, not a popinjay."

The insult caused me to stiffen, and though I did not otherwise respond, Lucy knew at once that she'd offended me. Her expression suddenly crumpled into despair.

"Oh, I've spoiled everything," she said, her voice breaking. "What a silly twit I am! I hate this dress. Hate it!" she cried, tearing at the lace on her sleeves. "I only wore it because poor Tom said he liked it. You've guessed, haven't you, that I loved him?"

"We were all of us fond of Tom."

"I didn't say 'fond,' I said 'love,' and I meant it. In all the ways a woman can mean it. I didn't care that he was my cousin, does that shock you?"

In fact it did shock me, but I demurred, not too convincingly.

"Of course he would have nothing to do with me," she said, sniffing in her misery. "In his eyes, I remained the little girl he remembered. But I can't help it. A woman can't choose who she loves, it isn't within our power. Oh, how I miss him!"

"There, there," I said, handing her my hankie.

"That he should have died so horribly. I can't bear it. And now you despise me."

I calmed her, as best I could, and swore that our misunderstanding was so small a thing as to be easily forgotten.

"Then you forgive me?" she asked plaintively, crumpling my handkerchief in her pale, perfect hands.

"I will forgive you under one condition," I said, moving to the writing desk and picking up a pen. "You must send to the druggist. Have him roused if necessary. He will prepare a solution of opiate. You will sleep and give your nerves a long rest. Agreed?"

"Agreed," she said with a sigh, lowering her eyes.

I handed her my scrawled prescription and went off to bed.

Despite my own agitation I fell asleep at once, without need of laudanum, and dreamed of poor Tom Coffin, alive and writhing upon the bowsprit. His mouth tried to form a word, but I could not make it out, and implored him to keep trying, convinced that if he spoke the word aloud, all our troubles would cease. I was clinging to the bowsprit, inching myself closer to him, hands slick with his blackening blood, when a bright light invaded the dream and woke me.

At first I groggily thought my chamber had been illuminated by starlight, for it had that quality. Cold and distant, and yet bright enough to read by, were I so inclined. Then my eyes registered the source of light and I became convinced that someone stood not far from the bed, holding a strange lantern.

It was no lantern. At least no earthly lantern. A ball of soft but brilliant light hovered near the end of my bed. All at once I became aware of a presence within the room, centered upon that glowing nimbus. A presence, but not a living presence, and perhaps not human at all, but a presence that hated me, and all living men. A hate so palpable that it crawled upon my skin and stifled the air in my lungs.

My heart thudded in terror, and yet I felt myself somehow removed from fear. Part of me, the rational core, wanted nothing more than to throw the blankets over my head and scream for the thing to go away, or myself to awaken from this horrible nightmare. And yet I knew then, as I know now, that I was not asleep, but as wide awake as a man has ever been.

Slowly the ball of light drifted away, toward the chamber door. No word was spoken, no audible command, but I understood what I must do, or it would stop my heart and suck away my soul.

I rose from my bed and followed.

The door opened of its own, and the strange, uncanny light pushed through, into the dark hallway. Out I went, wearing only my nightgown. Nothing stirred in the house, not a sound did I hear, not even my own naked feet padding on the icy floor. The light and the presence—they were one and the same somehow—drew me along on an invisible leash, helpless to resist.

I found myself at the base of a stairway, leading from the second floor to the third, to a rearward part of the house I had not before visited. The last thing I wanted to do was mount that stairway, but again the presence made me know that resistance was impossible. With each step upward my dread increased, until I thought my heart must cease beating. The presence was all around me now, painting my face with light. I was somehow within the terrible presence, this unimaginable *otherness*, but not yet part of it. That was the thing I feared most, that it would absorb me and I would be no more.

At the head of the stairs, another, smaller hallway, barely wider than my quivering shoulders. The very walls seemed to breathe, urging me on, a kind of deep vibration much lower than the lowest pedal of a cathedral organ, a sound beneath hearing, a sound of unbearable, unknowable, unstoppable dread.

I came—we came—to a small paneled door. As before, the door opened of its own, and then I was within a room that, by its musty odor, hadn't been entered in some time, for ages, perhaps. I could not see the walls—the light did not extend so far—but felt the room to be small, and understood from the stacked crates and boxes that it served as a storage place, a repository of things unused, or hidden away. A thick coating of dust lay over all, and a little of it rose, stirred by the hem of my nightgown.

I wanted to speak, to ask what was wanted of me, but no words issued. Words were not needed. The light, in answer, danced nimbly over the boxes and crates and came to hover over an ancient seaman's trunk, bound in leather and brass.

I went to it, guided by the light.

The old trunk was sealed with a massive padlock. I half expected a key to float before my eyes. Instead the padlock shattered with a cold *snap!* and fell away, kicking up another eddy of acrid dust.

There was no question of resisting, no possibility. I had been brought here to open the hasp and lift the lid, and I did so, fully expecting some ghoulish, undead thing to rise from the trunk. But the only thing that assaulted me was a distinct odor of salt air, as if the trunk had been sealed at sea, and the smell imprisoned.

Inside the trunk I found the ordinary instruments that might be cherished by a mariner. A sextant, lovingly wrapped in soft chamois. A brass telescope within a clever little deal-wood case. A weighty thing that, unwrapped, became a ship's chronometer. Another leather case contained a crude surgical kit, with huge curved needles that could have stitched a wounded sailor, or repaired a torn sail, perhaps both. And beneath these things, secreted in the very bottom of the trunk, a single volume bound in calfskin.

As I lifted the slender book from the trunk, the light glowed brighter. There being no imprint or clue upon the cover, I opened it and saw inscribed, in a neat plain hand, in blackest ink, the following words: "True log of the *Whippet*, 1837, C. Coffin, Master."

Once the book was safely in my possession, the strange light faded quickly, and the overpowering presence departed, leaving me alone and blind in that crypt of darkness for what seemed an eternity, until daylight, normal, ordinary daylight, blessed daylight! found me shivering and weeping in the dust.

# 9. The Alchemy

Night horrors rarely survive the blanching effect of the morning sun. The mind relinquishes its little fears, and a rational, scientific sort of man might convince himself that his hideous experience was nothing more than a waking, walking nightmare. True, I'd never been known to suffer from sleepwalking, but there was always a first time. This was a comforting thought, that I'd stumbled into that dusty little room while dreaming, and the invisible *otherness* that had so frightened me was nothing more than the invention of an exhausted mind.

Sleepwalking would explain my dislocation and my filthy nightgown, but how to explain the calfskin volume that I'd clutched to my chest? Was it a book I'd blindly seized in my dream, a book, for all I knew, of poetry or cooking receipts? With trembling hands I lifted the blank cover and saw that it was, indeed, exactly as I remembered, the "True log of the *Whippet*."

It was all true, every dread-filled, blood-soaked moment of it. Something had led me to a remote storage chamber, and to the ancient trunk, for a purpose. Within lay the secret of the Coffins and, I hoped—prayed!—a means to stop the horror.

I remained closeted in my chamber for all of that day, reading first by the wan winter light, and then by candle. Reading not only the lines and entries and the precise calculations of his commerce, but between the lines into the mind of a much younger Cash Coffin, owner and captain of the slave ship *Whippet*, who was engaged in the enterprise of extracting

what he called "black gold" from the western coasts of
Africa. . . .

\* \* \*

Editor's note: it was common practice for captains engaged in the "enterprise" of slaving to keep two logs, one for themselves and their investors,
another for the authorities, should the ship be boarded or seized. Whether
the "false log" of the slave ship *Whippet* still exists is unknown. This was
the only such log found with Dr. Bentwood's notebooks, and has been
inserted here to help clarify the narrative. All surviving entries are in the
same hand, and the common (and very frequent) abbreviations have been
rendered in full words, and with standard spelling, for ease of reading.

*True log of the Whippet, 1837*
*C. Coffin, Master*

April 3, Baltimore
Entered this day into an agreement with Mr. Birkead, of
Birkead & Pierce, for purchase of a vessel appropriate to the
enterprise. Birkead is a shifty sort of swell, even for a Balti-
morean, but when I present my requirements as "speed, wind-
liness, and beauty," he takes my measure and sees me right,
eventual. "Those are the qualities of a racehorse," says he, and
shoves a thimble of vile snuff up his poxy nose. When he's
done spewing, I tell him, "That's correct, sir, and I need a horse
that will win a race. She must drive to windward, as I'll have
great need for haste."

Mr. Sly Boots gives me the wink, and then we're off for a
tour of his shipyard. There are nine vessels available for immediate sale, and it amuses d——d Birkead to show me every
d——d tub, though he knows my requirements. I thought "go
along to get along" and keep my peace, and finally we "get
along" to the best of the fleet. Being a topsail clipper fresh off

the 'ways, and built for the trade. "Tight as a tick," says he, "tight as a Yankee captain, ha ha."

She is called *Whippet* by the man that drew her, who fancies racing dogs, not horses! Keel & frame are sawed white oak, planked with Southern pine heavy in sap, all new and sound and remarkable dry. Seams will likely open some under sail, and the bilge make water, but nothing worrisome. Paced off 110 feet on deck, 28 abeam. Two stout masts, Baltimore raked, and well stepped. Birkead sees I'm smitten with the look of her, and he's very droll for a Southerner. "I'll wager you like your women raked, too, Captain. Raked and fast, with a fine point of entry and a slippery stern. Am I on the mark?" I feel called upon to remark that I'm a married man, and that if he give me one more of his d——d winks, I'd take out his eye, and that cooled him off some. Then it was all business and we went at it hammer and tongs until I finally sounded his bottom, that be $2250 in gold for hull, masts, and yards, and then another $400 for hemp, halyards, rigging & canvas, to be rigged hasty.

I am much satisfied to have *Whippet* for under $3000, that I was ready to pay was d——d Birkead not so free with his talk of raked women and such.

Tomorrow I shall pick out a crew and slip mooring on the soonest tide. The enterprise is begun. Grant us Godspeed and I'll see Becky and the boys by September.

April 13
We are finally at sea. D—m all Maryland men for their lazy avarice! After much unnecessary delay, and having to cross many a filthy palm, *Whippet* is finally rigged, and the temporary rock ballast at last secured in the bilge. I'm well satisfied of my new crew. All six are lively, and able-bodied, and already grinning at the prospect of squandering their $10 in

the claptraps and rumholes of Havana. Those that last will be welcome on the next leg, for considerable more than $10.

I suspect we are all in high spirits to have d——d Baltimore below the horizon at last, and to find *Whippet* sailing as pretty as she looks. How she leaps with the wind abeam! We buried ten knots in a breeze, and that bodes well. She steers a little fat with the wind behind, but that may be remedied some by trim and a shift of ballast.

I'm much relieved. As always, the first run to sea in a new ship puts me in mind of my dear Becky and our boys. No other cause but their welfare would persuade me to risk such an enterprise as this! I will not sleep this night—never the first night at sea!—but amuse myself by calculation of the alchemy. Alchemy is my word for the secretive means of turning a $5000 bank draft into $50,000 in gold, in four or five months time. Here is my formula that has proved true for twelve such enterprises:

$5000 + 7000 nm* = $50,000

If all goes well, this will be my last enterprise, as I will have accrued sufficient capital to build me a splendid coastal fleet. I would have my boys at sea, as my father had me, but not so far from home, or for so long, nor engaged in this wretched trade.

---

*Editor's note: nm apparently refers to "nautical miles." Captain Coffin would anticipate covering approximately that distance for his "enterprise." His calculation of a five-thousand-dollar investment yielding fifty thousand dollars in profit is about average for a successful voyage at the height of the Caribbean slave trade in the 1830s, when the price-per-slave was driven higher by the risk of being seized by the West African Naval Squadron, which had been charged by Parliament with enforcing an embargo against the slave trade. The American government, which outlawed the importing of slaves in 1807, also stationed a small but feisty squadron off the Slave Coast to assist the British. The international embargo was enthusiastically enforced by the U.S. Navy, despite the fact that slavery was legal in the Southern states, an irony often noted in the abolitionist press.

I will pray for fair wind and a swift passage, and for the good health of my sweet Becky.

## May 2
We make Havana Harbor at last, after fighting squall and currents in the Florida Straits. Made port an hour before sunset, and will spend this night ashore at the Grandee, and have me a hot bath.

All is well!

## May 3
*Whippet* has been granted prime anchorage, very near to the main wharves of Havana Harbor, and that will be convenient for refitting, which is already under way.

I heard intelligence from others at the hotel, regarding the current state of affairs, and was assured the cane and tobacco plantations remain profitable in the extreme. Demand for field hands has kept the price up, and last year's high at auction is now average. This relieves any worry I might've had regarding the enterprise. It will not be unreasonable to expect $1000 per healthy buck.* No wonder that Havana Harbor stinks with ships built for the enterprise! Spit from the taffrail and you might hit a British frigate, a fat Dutch merchantman, and five cranky old Portagee tubs. Why, a dozen hulls lie rotting within

---

*A male slave employed as a field hand on a typical sugar cane plantation in Cuba or Brazil would be expected to "earn out" within six months. Survival rate in the field, where slaves were prey to rampant disease, averaged two years, by which time the exhausted slave had tripled his investment for the owner. Slaves employed as household servants typically survived much longer, but on average the population of field hands in Central and South America had to be replaced every two years, necessitating the smuggling of an estimated eleven million Africans to ports in the Western Hemisphere between 1498–1870. [Editor]

sight of *Whippet*, run up on the beach & abandoned once they been emptied of their cargo.

Disgraceful waste. Still, better to abandon than have a vessel seized by the d——d British blockade, and fines imposed. They take as proof of the enterprise any modification that includes grates, manacle posts, extra decks, and so on. Even the stench is enough to warrant seizure, and everyone knows it is impossible to eradicate *that* smell. Cheaper to abandon a ship than to risk the fines.

Such is the profit!

May 6

The enterprise, the enterprise, we all sing of the enterprise! I am back aboard *Whippet*, having spent three days on shore. The various debaucheries observed among my colleagues can't be fully confided, even here. They're a rum lot, and would spend every spare dollar in the claptraps, and upon clothing that would put the blush of shame on a peacock. What mudsill fools they are, smoking Havana nine-inchers as they strut along the wharves! What lies they tell, and what infernal habits! But, I admit, very cheerful company.

Still, these peacocks would do well to remember that the enterprise is a calculation, not an excuse for fantods and whorepox. A man must keep his wits about him, else the sharpies and the harpies'll strip him bare naked. Still, I do enjoy observing what my Becky calls "the human comedy," although she would blush to see what these particular players get up to when they're full of likker and free with money.

The only cash I care to spend is for the conversion of *Whippet*. Today the carpenters are tearing out bulkheads, and tomorrow will begin constructing an extra deck, with headroom sufficient for lying down. The smithy delivers two hundred iron manacles on the following day, or so he's pledged!

Manacles are dear this season, being one Spanish dollar each, installed, but the blacksmiths know we must have manacles, and so inflate their price.

I have also caused the forward hold to be converted for extra fresh water storage. Pumps to be rigged and the canvas hoses already purchased. This'll be an added expense, but I'm of the firm belief that fresh water is our second-most precious commodity. I know this from hard experience, on a previous enterprise, when tainted water ruined the alchemy and resulted in a fifty percent reduction in profit.*

## May 17

This dawn we departed wicked Havana with fifty tons of iron bar in ballast. Scuttlebutt among the peacocks is that iron bar now trades as good as gunpowder on the Slave Coast, for the making of Arab swords and muskets. Just to be sure, I put down a hundred and fifty barrels of powder. Gezo does love his gunpowder, that much I know.

Here's my calculation thus far:

| | |
|---|---|
| *Whippet*, converted for the enterprise | —-$3311. |
| Powder, Provisions & cash reserve | —-$1951. |
| | Total—-$5262. |

## May 27

A mere ten days at sea and we've logged near on two thousand miles! Never have I found winds so favorable on the eastward passage. This bodes well for the enterprise, and for the alchemy that makes it pay. *Whippet* performs as promised, and loves a headwind, though we've had precious few of those, but mostly sail abeam, well trimmed and "scooting."

---

*By this calculation it can be assumed that half of Captain Coffin's human cargo perished from dehydration.[Editor]

Lookouts have been posted at the mast head, with the promise of a five-dollar gold piece for whatever man first sights the blockade, be it a British warship or one of our own. Our tattered flag might be mistaken for Portagee—that is my intention—but will not fool them for long, as they're well aware that any Baltimore clipper in these waters is engaged in the enterprise. *Whippet* cannot "outgun" so we must "outrun."

Let them try and catch us!

June 14
Contrary winds. Many squalls. By my calculation we lie no more than 100 nm sou'west of Whydah. I pray that all is in readiness in Whydah, and the barracoons stocked full, so we can make a quick departure. How I pine for dearest Becky!

June 15
No sooner has the foul weather lifted than we're detected by the d—m blockade! *Whippet* was but thirty miles from the port of Whydah when ambushed by the light frigate *Stars & Bars*, under the command of a pup called Phineus Beale.

Lieutenant Beale is a clever d—l and saw us first, using the late hour and cover of darkness to his best advantage. He must've positioned his frigate in a bank of fog, furled sails, doused all lights, and waited upon us. *Whippet* ghosting prettily in light air, and myself on deck, standing by the helmsman. It was the creak of oars gave the sneaky d—ls away. I sounded the alarm by firing my flintlocks, but their launch was already alongside, and the U.S. Navy attempting to board. They had blacked their fizz with charcoal! I knew what they were, of course, but the blackened faces made it easy to treat 'em like African pirates, and rouse my own crew to villainy.

How the *Whippet* put the fear of G-d into the *Stars & Bars*! My best mate, Mr. Sweeney, leaped into the fray with a machete he'd got in Havana. Others beat chains, and we forced the d—ls back into their d——d launch in full retreat. Two of their number dropped into the water and swum to the launch, and I ceased firing the flintlocks, having hit no one. As *Whippet* swept along, they demanded we hove to and surrender for inspection, but I affected not to understand.

Our troubles were not done. While we were engaged repelling the boarders, Beale towed his frigate within range. Hailed us with his megaphone, the insolent pup! Thank G-d for the "rules of engagement." By law he couldn't fire into our hull, for fear of sinking us, and he dare not unload shrapnel to shred our sails, which is allowed, because his men were in the way. The winds were light but my crew was game, and got *Whippet* around right smart.

The race is on. Our ship is much the faster, but I dare not head directly into Whydah, as the frigate would surely summon reinforcements and blockade the port. And so we set westerly, away from Africa. I have ordered the men to crack on and run like we'd given up the enterprise.

This mayn't fool a clever d—l like Lieutenant Beale. Let him think what he likes. Once we've lost the b——ds I'll tack south for a hundred or so and come around to Whydah from there. With any luck, the blockade'll be engaged elsewhere by then.

Let Beale go north, where the wind takes him, or to h—l for all I care!

We have escaped their clutches and learned a hard lesson. A clever captain must never let down his guard, or trust to the lookouts, but at all times be vigilant. I must call upon experience & fortitude and see I'm never again at a disadvantage. But for the creak of their oar, they'd have seized us, and the enterprise ruined!

# 10. The King of Skulls

June 21, 1836

Made Whydah this night, undetected. No moon, and the sky as black as Africa. I've ordered the rig altered, and the masts unraked, so if that d—l Beale shows his wet nose, he'll not recognize *Whippet*. Our new name is *Lorca*. Painted in gold upon the stern board, and the Spanish flag flying high and proud.

When the sun rises I shall don my best blue frock coat, the one with the polished buttons, and call upon de Souza.*

June 22

Found Señor de Souza in fine fettle. And why would he not be, considering his vast estate, and all that he owns and commands? He has him a magnificent house, very like a Spanish castle in miniature, (though built of wood) with more than thirty rooms, and several lesser buildings, all surrounded by a formidable wall fixed with iron spikes. My host likes to joke that he should be called "Count de Souza" because he can count so many things he owns. By way of demonstrating, he ticks off five hundred bottles of prime French wine, three hundred slaves, and his own personal harem of ninety women. By them and others he brags he has fathered a hundred sons, and

---

*Francisco Feliz de Souza, the notorious and very wealthy Portuguese slave merchant. By royal decree of Gezo, King of Dahomey, de Souza controlled Whydah, and collected a tax on every slave dispatched from the port. [Editor]

doesn't bother to number the girls. As well as the "Count," he fancies himself the "African Casanova." You wouldn't know it to look on him, as he's a small and wizened man, with wrinkled skin the color of pale ash, and half his teeth gone.

Still, those teeth he's got bite sharp enough! In his official capacity de Souza makes to remind me that by setting foot upon the soil of his port, I am placed under the protection of Gezo, King of Dahomey, and that no American or British authority may touch my person or my ship so long as I remain. By the grin of his few yellow fangs he makes clear that he has the power of life and death in Whydah and is not hesitant to use it, though his pikes are headless at the moment.

We have us a splendid breakfast in his best room, presented on silver plate and chased goblets, served by his liveried slaves, who effect to speak the French language, and might, for all I know. They bring us quail eggs in casserole, thick slabs of Italian bacon, salt beef in sauce, some form of raisin pudding, and a light pastry the "Count" calls "Spanish bisket", dripping in dark honey. Wine, of course, and pitchers of native beer. The cunning fellow inquires of my family and seemed to remember me well enough, though our dealings have been modest, compared to some who trade here.

I assume that all is well, and the enterprise will soon advance into the bargaining stage. It isn't until the last crumb vanishes into his wet little mouth that de Souza confesses a "slight problem."

All six of his barracoons are empty! There's not a captive left in Whydah. A slave port with no slaves for sale!

"My dear captain," says he, having lighted his cheroot. "I have my usual sources in Aros, but Aros is presently at war, and all is turmoil. The war will produce more captives no doubt, so you must have patience."

Patience! If I wait for his little wars to end, it may be months, and this, as well he knows, is impossible. Yet I hold my tongue, knowing his mortal temper—de Souza has killed five unarmed men in "duels," some struck down in the back. He smiles sweet as a water snake, the old fraud, and says I'm free to try another port, one farther along the coast—he has heard there are slaves to be had in Sierra Leone. I make clear that Sierra Leone won't do. I been cheated there, once upon a time, and swore never to return, and might be hanged if I did.

"There is one other possibility," says he, "and I freely give you my permission to pursue it, if you so desire."

"And what does the Count suggest?" asks I.

"You might journey inland and treat with the king directly. I will collect my tax in any case, for each captive that leaves this port."

This I never tried, having always dealt with de Souza. King Gezo has a fearsome reputation for fits of pique and temper. It is well known that only three years back he had a hundred slaves beheaded because one of them stole a single cowrie shell. It is said that his palace is decorated with human skulls, as proof of his absolute power, and his willingness to use it. Few white men trade with him directly.

"My dear fellow, you've gone quite pale," says de Souza. "Have no fear of Gezo. He may be the King of Skulls, but they are all black skulls, and he always buys a man before he cuts off his head. I will tell you what I will do. I will lend you the use of my emissary. He will treat with Gezo, and if a head gets misplaced, it will be his head, not yours, ha! ha!"

De Souza has a price for this "favor," of course, which is five barrels of gunpowder. I agree without argument, and am to meet with his emissary on the morrow. He is called Monbasu.

June 23
Left *Whippet* in Sweeney's charge, with orders to fire the ship rather than let it be seized, and departed this day for Gezo's palace, in the company of de Souza's emissary.

I'm much surprised to find Monbasu most affable, and keenly intelligent, which is shocking in a nigger fellow. Must be because he's very high born, of the same clan as the king, and very rich in his person. Young Monbasu arrives at de Souza's gate in grand style, reclining in a slave-borne litter, accompanied by a retinue of armed warriors, which are slaves he owns himself. He wears brightly colored robes, a woven tunic of fine quality, and a peculiar little gold-braided hat upon his well-formed head. This hat, I am told, is a badge of his clan.

Monbasu is very quick to smile, and speaks English better than Señor de Souza. "Oh, yes, I am a man of many tongues," he says with a laugh. "In my mouth is a Portuguese tongue, a Spanish tongue, a French tongue, and a little Dutch tongue. And of course I have several tongues of the Dahomey tribes."

He has also a new gold tooth of which he's very proud. "Slaves will be no problem," he promises. "My cousin the king has many slaves, more than he can feed. Monbasu fix, you will see."

We travel in style and comfort, borne on litters, carried overland into the heart of Dahomey, greatest of the slave kingdoms. The curious bobbing rhythm of the litters is like a ship at sea, and some way comforting.

As we bob along, whisking away the flies that penetrate our cozy little compartment, Monbasu regales me with wondrous tales of his wit and cunning. Some of them may even be true.

June 25

We arrive this day at the palace of Gezo, King of Dahomey. I am much surprised by the quality. The way niggers exaggerate, I'd been expecting a thing more crude, a kind of African log cabin with a thatched roof, maybe. Instead I'm amazed by the royal splendor. Gezo's palace rivals that of some of the European kings. The walls are of various exotic woods rather than stone or marble, but inside each of the spacious chambers (there are more than one hundred) is encrusted with painted carvings, elaborate gold inlay, and woven mats and rugs of sublime distinction, from as far away as India. Indeed, the king has a great love of rugs, and collects them, as he collects human skulls.

I hoped to meet with the king directly, but Monbasu says such things can't be hurried at the palace. He counsels patience. First we must dine in the royal hall, then we must drink palm wine with the king's council of advisers, and then, perhaps, we will meet with Gezo himself, provided the king is in an expansive mood.

"While we wait you may avail yourself of the royal privilege," Monbasu suggests with a sly wink. When I ask what he means by royal privilege, he says a guest of the king may select as concubine one of the many female palace slaves, provided she is not part of Gezo's personal harem, which is, of course, forbidden.

"The king owns everyone in the palace who is not related to him by blood," he says, his gold tooth flashing. "Pick wisely and you will be a happy man."

Monbasu looks puzzled when I tell him his Yankee captain may be a sailor and a slaver, but he's also a married man, and so must decline his kind offer.

I'm in "Rome," but the thought of doing as the "Romans" do is disgusting. Share a bed with a nigger concubine? Makes my skin crawl to think on it. They are comely but very black. God would not allow it, even if base instinct might be inclined so.

There are no latches upon the door, but I've been left to my own privacy. If one of the comely royal maids should lean into my chamber and show me her black bosom, she will be admonished to leave! That I swear on this true log.

June 28

Three days and nights in the kingdom of Dahomey, and already I am beginning to feel that my world, the world I left behind, the world of *Whippet* and Becky and White Harbor, is but a pale dream.

How is such a thing possible, for a man of phlegmatic humors? For the first time, I understand how a white man might be seduced by the intoxicating darkness of Africa. No, I have not taken me a maid. In that I remain firm. But I have supped of the vitality here, that seems to be in the very air, an intensity and tumult of the senses, like the smoky, fragrant incense they burn.

I will make a list, and count the difference.

1. *Beautiful.* Much of Dahomey is beautiful beyond description, a beauty never seen by the likes of me, being a very feast for the eyes and senses.

2. *Ugly.* Much of Dahomey is as ugly as death itself. It is appalling, violent, and hideous beyond description.

The Beautiful and the Ugly, dwelling in the same place. Somehow the contrast has brought me to full awareness at all times, and makes it impossible to sleep.

The drums don't help, as it comes to sleeping. They are most always drumming about something. Monbasu has tried to explain the complications of the drumming, and what it means, but a Christian can't understand. The religion of Dahomey is some form of witchcraft, and each drum the voice of a different god. I seen what the drums do with my own eyes, which is drive the niggers into frenzy. Frenzy like an addle-brained man throwing a fit, except there are hundreds of 'em, dancing and worshipping. They kill chickens and smear the blood upon their persons, and blow powders in each other's faces, and then speak in the languages of their gods, that no one can make out, not even themselves.

Monbasu says the worshippers surrender their souls to the sorcerers who cast the spells and beat the drums and drink the blood of goats. I ask what is the attraction of such a religion, if it makes those who practice it give sorcerers the power of life and death over supplicants?

Monbasu is much amused. He's been drinking palm wine and though he don't join in the wicked dancing, I can tell he would like to, but for my presence. "Is your own religion so different?" he asks.

"Very different," says I, quite hot to make him understand. "Couldn't be more different. Christian priests don't have that mortal power, only God himself does."

"Oh, very different," Monbasu agrees. "Our sorcerers do not speak for god, they become gods. Much better, I think, to be a sorcerer than a priest, ha ha!"

He's too clever a cove by far to win me an argument on that or any subject. I find Monbasu much like the others of his clan, all very clever and cunning and friendly. We have met with Gezo's council, all of 'em Monbasu's blood relations, and dined with them most affably. After supping very well on roast goat and honey tubers, they ask if I want to see Gezo's Amazons. They use a Dahomey word for Amazon, but they mean the battalion of ebony-black warriors, all of 'em women, that has been trained with spear, sword, and shield. These Amazons they got are fiercely loyal to the king, who owns them every one, and are renowned in battle, and much feared. They're a strong bunch, some of 'em tall as men, and march around naked, but for their swords and shields. I am not too blushed to look upon them, because black nakedness is not the same as white nakedness. The color itself is a kind of clothing.

The king's Amazons have not a hair upon their private parts! I must ask Monbasu if they shave or pluck. He will know. But he's vanished somewhere into the palace grounds, leaving back a note that begs for my patience. "All is well," he writes, "all will be granted. Trust Monbasu."

The strange thing is, I do trust the fellow, as much as any of his race can be trusted. So I wait, and think pure thoughts of Becky and the boys.

My door has no latch. If the comely maids apply, I must be vigilant.

June 29
Disaster!

Monbasu has been arrested! Word comes that he violated the harem taboo, and his skull will soon decorate the royal dining hall. I'm fearful of being seized, too, for enjoying his company. The king's counselors, who are cousin to Monbasu (and to the king), tell me to be calm, and that I'm in no danger, but who can be believed, for surely Monbasu was betrayed by these very cousins? I'm told the forbidden assignation has long been suspected, and that the royal spies finally assembled the necessary evidence. It's no small thing, arresting a man of the king's own clan, but they've managed to extract a confession from the concubine herself, and now the thing is done. The female's name is Tambara, and I'm told she is a comely lass, but hardly worth it, as Gezo will no doubt have Monbasu's head, his new gold tooth, his many slaves, and everything he owns.

They have confined me to my chamber. It be a large room, lavishly decorated with rugs and billowing silk curtains, and a great feathered ceiling fan turned by unseen captives. And yet I take no comfort here. I've been betrayed, used by the wicked Monbasu as beard for his diddling intrigue! Surely the king will have me tortured for his pleasure and want my head, too, as warning for others of like inclination.

Tried writing to de Souza, to implore that he put in a good

word, but no one will take my letters, not for any bribe. My door is latched now, from the outside.

How I hate the drums. The drums pound inside my head like the cannon of a pursuing frigate! Stupid man, they beat, stupid man, stupid man. I pray for Becky, that she shall never know how her husband came to his end, for the stupidity of trusting a laughing nigger.

July 1
Should be midway across the Atlantic on this day. Instead I languish within this luxurious prison! They bring me ample food and palm wine (called "gin" locally) and keep suggesting that the "white captain" sample other delicacies. D—m the conspirators! Temptations of the flesh are nothing but a trap. Had I taken a comely maid for comfort, the cabal of blood cousins would surely have denounced me to their king. My refusal to give into the dark temptations has saved me thus far.

Last night I prayed (though I have no Bible), and in my prayers pledged that should I survive, the enterprise will be abandoned. Becky has long wanted me to give up the slave trade, and I've been partway inclined to please her, but now I am certain in my mind. Should I live, *Whippet* will be my last voyage as slaver.

[later]
Everything has changed!

At noon I'm summoned into the presence of Gezo, Skull King of Dahomey. The amazement begins at once. I'd expected to meet me a dim-witted tyrant, a blackish monkey man with bloody fangs. Instead I'm presented to a large, imposing fellow with mild, aristocratic manners. Gezo is at least six feet tall and remarkably fat, with many jowls, and piercing, gold-flecked brown eyes sunk deep into his face. His small, round mouth purses like that of a fish. My first thought—somewhat crazed by my anxiety—is that the King of Skulls resembles a great black codfish grown fat on a diet of herring. But there's nothing "fishy" about the king's manners, which are like any other king.

Gezo speaks many languages, none of 'em English, and he commands one of his advisers (a blood cousin) to act as translator, so that, as he soon says, "His Highness may address my guest and be understood." In that manner, with a translator keening out the words, the Yankee captain is welcomed to the Land of the Dahomey, also knows as Land of the King's Fathers. The Yankee captain has come with a favorable recommendation from Señor de Souza, and since Señor de Souza has helped make all of Dahomey rich, and all of Dahomey belongs to King Gezo, his recommendation counts for much. Lucky for me it counts for more than my association with the scoundrel Monbasu, since white men are assumed to be innocent of courtly intrigues.

In truth, Gezo explains, many of his clan had an association with the wretched Monbasu, but they've been forgiven for their poor judgment because they had the good sense to show loyalty by denouncing the foul viper, who not only violated the royal taboo, but may have had eyes on the throne itself.

The translator barely gets that out, about a conspiracy for the throne, when Gezo himself makes clear, by waving his hands, that the very idea is ridiculous. "Many scheme for my throne," he tells me, "none so far have succeeded. Look upon them, Yankee captain! Observe how their skulls are empty. Because only empty-headed fools intrigue against the great Gezo! And when they are, inevitably, denounced, their small, stupid brains are fed to the wild dogs!"

By some signal, the king has called for his skulls, and they are brought out in a great woven basket. Gezo paws through them, a thoughtful expression on his face, very like an old woman fingering apples, and culling the ones gone bad. He solemnly holds up skull after skull, poking his fat fingers in the eye sockets, and showing me where the brains have been taken out and the bone boiled clean. It's a very impressive collection, and serves to make me even more desirous of hanging on to my own stupid skull.

Gezo then commences to give out a lecture, all the while rubbing at certain skulls, as if for luck. "You have come here to treat with me for slaves," says he, prompting the translator. "Only last month the new English queen, who has no slaves, begged me yet again to outlaw the trade. Gezo refused! Why should the Father of Dahomey trade in palm oil when the lives and fortunes of his people depend on the selling of captives. The slave trade has been the ruling principle of my people. It is the source of their glory and wealth. Their songs celebrate their victories and the mother lulls her child to sleep with notes of triumph over an enemy reduced to slavery. Can I, by signing a treaty, change the sentiments of a whole people?"

I beg to remind him that I'm no Englishman, and pay no allegiance to English queens, new or otherwise, and he takes that as affirmation of his sovereignty, as I intended, and looks on me with approval.

Already, though, I've begun to have some pity for poor Monbasu, whose skull may soon join the others in that woven basket. To be the object of Gezo's wrath is surely the most horrible of fates, and all because the handsome young fool fancied a woman whose name the fat king can't seem to remember. How could he, as she's but one of three hundred wives?

At a sign from Gezo the offending pair are dragged before the throne. Monbasu and his lady love have been stripped naked and manacled about the neck and ankles, and linked by heavy iron chain. Monbasu's gold tooth has been extracted and presented to the king, who wears it on a fine golden thread around his plump neck. Both prisoners have been severely lashed, but that is not the worst. Each has had one eye put out, and the wound crudely cauterized. They must be in great pain, but betray no hint of it.

I'm put in mind of my mate, Black Jack Sweeney, whose eye was extracted for cheating a Senegalese slave merchant at cards. But at least Sweeney kept his head, and the two young lovers are about to lose theirs. They know it, too. It shows in their faces, which already seem to be calmly looking at the other side of death.

The executioner, a powerful eunuch equipped with a ceremonial sword, waddles forward and looks to the king for a sign.

I am determined not to flinch when the sword falls, as I must not betray sympathy for the sinners, but Gezo surprises me yet again. He surprises everyone in attendance, when, with a wave of his fat hand, he stays the executioner and turns to me.

"Yankee captain," says he, "what exactly is the fate of the captives you carry away? Are they treated like animals? Are they starved and beaten?"

I know better than to lie, and determine to speak the truth. "Oh, yes," I tell him. "A slave is treated like an animal because he is, for all purposes, an animal. Starvation and beating are, of course, useful methods to obtain obedience."

Gezo's little mouth makes a smile. "Are they whipped regularly?" he wants to know.

"Certain they are whipped. Regular whipping is common practice, particularly on the field hands."

"Are the women raped?" say he.

"If the female is attractive, or even if she is not, she will be made use of by factors, enforcers, and owners."

Gezo nods, very pleased with my answer. "Are the men emasculated?"

"Any male slave who shows the least sign of spirit is first beaten, and if that doesn't suffice, he is cut, the same as is done with horses and cattle, Your Highness."

"Ah, very good. And how long might a slave live?"

"In Cuba, where my cargo is destined, a slave who works the cane fields may live a year or two, or even three. Much depends on weather and pestilence."

"And such a field hand suffers until he dies?"

"Oh, yes, Your Highness, he suffers most horrible."

Gezo rattles a few of his empty skulls, and thinks over what I've told him. "Can a slave take a wife?" he asks slyly.

"No. Marriage between slaves is forbidden. The Cuban grandees discourage any lingering association between males and female slaves, believing it can only lead to trouble, and because a slave with wife and child will fight for them."

"Ah, very wise. And may a slave keep his own name?"

"No, Your Highness. It's easier for a slave owner to name them himself, as he would a dog or a horse."

Gezo nods, and I must suppose that nothing I said was unknown to him, as he is well acquainted with slavers and slavery. What he says next surprises me yet again. "Does the Yankee captain know that Gezo is himself the son of a slave?"

This unexpected confession makes me fearful. Have I offended the Skull King somehow? But no, he merely wants to relate the peculiar circumstances of his ancestry. It seems his mother was sold into the harem of the previous king, and through her beauty and intelligence impressed that king, who made her his queen. Then, alas, she fell out of favor and was sold and transported to Brazil.

"When Gezo became king," he says, "he put out a search for his mother, offering a great reward, but nothing was found. If a famous queen can vanish so absolutely, imagine the fate of a mere concubine, ha ha!"

That "ha ha" put a chill down my spine, and not because I

think the fellow is actually amused by his mother's disappearance. It is the laugh of a man capable of anything, the laugh of a man who smiles gently while he fingers the skulls of those who have offended him.

Gezo seems pleased by the effect he's had on the assembly, and on me, and calls for the prisoners to be brought closer to the Yankee captain for inspection. Guards grab them by the ears and hold their heads up. Even with his one good eye, Monbasu will not look at me, out of shame and what little remains of his pride. The woman, not surprisingly, is beyond fright, or pain, and something awful oozes from her vacant eye socket.

"Would a male slave with one eye be employed as a house servant?" Gezo wants to know.

"No, Your Highness, very unlikely. If he is young and strong he will certainly be used in the cane fields."

"Would a female with only one eye find a place in a fine house and live a long, comfortable life?"

"No, Your Highness. Female house slaves are used as maids or concubines, and tend to be comely, so as not to offend the owner, his wife, or their many guests."

Gezo grins. "What would they do with a one-eyed wretch like this, Yankee captain? Would they send her to the cane fields and let the men use her?"

"Yes, Your Highness, very likely."

This "Yankee captain" has only a little schooling, but I am no man's fool, and pretty certain where the king has been leading this strange conversation. Indeed, I have helped him lead it there, for my own purposes, and so am not surprised when he pronounces his final judgment.

"Gezo, King of Dahomey, Father of his People, has decided to let this worthless wretch and his worthless whore keep their heads, because losing one's head is, after all, quite painless. Over in an instant, ha ha! Gezo's revenge will be much sweeter and more satisfying if the offenders suffer most horrible for a year or two. Therefore, if the Yankee captain agrees, Gezo will sell him Monbasu and the woman for a trifle, a few cowrie shells, which is all they are worth. Will the Yankee captain do the Skull King this favor?"

I glance at Monbasu, but he will not meet my eyes. "It would be my honor to serve Your Highness in this matter."

"They must suffer!" Gezo insists. "Make certain they suffer, and I will sell you all the slaves you desire."

"Oh, they will suffer, Your Highness. Be sure of that. All slaves suffer. It is their fate, in your religion as in mine."

# 11. Madness

July 4, 1837

All is well. *Whippet* lies in port, loaded with cargo, ready to depart on a favorable tide. In the end King Gezo was in no mood to bargain, and sold me 180 of his best slaves, for a price lower than had I purchased from de Souza directly. As to the "Count," he demanded three more barrels of gunpowder, and the remainder of the iron bar as compensation for his supposed efforts to keep the American patrol at bay. I suspect he lies, that the *Stars & Bars* has not been sighted, but I do not argue. My ledger is even, the tally matches, and I have my cargo for the price anticipated. With any luck I shall never see Señor de Souza, or Dahomey, again.

As I write, Monbasu and his lady love are chained to the slave deck stanchions, along with the rest of the captives. Monbasu's behavior has been somewhat strange. During the fifty-mile march to the coast, I attempted to engage the young man in conversation, but he refused to respond. At first I was puzzled, and then I understood. He fears that Gezo will change his mind if he thinks the Yankee captain had taken pity on him, and so would as soon be treated cruelly.

He is much changed, and his spirit broken.

July 5
Got clear of Whydah without incident. No sign of d——d Beale. Once land is down and the ship trimmed, I have Monbasu brought up on deck. The iron collar remains about his

neck. The chain fixed to the collar is held by Sweeney, who remarks that once he had a pet monkey that was better-looking, and didn't need to be leashed. I order Sweeney to go about his business.

For Monbasu I've a proposition. In exchange for his freedom he must act as factor of the slave deck, keeping calm among the captives. My plan is to have us a passage uninterrupted by outbreaks of panic, which can be time-consuming and expensive, due to loss of life.

At first he assumes the Yankee captain is playing a cruel trick. Why would a man free a valuable slave, legally obtained? Monbasu owned many slaves, and never freed any of them, says he. But he's soon persuaded of my sincerity in this matter, and by the time the iron collar is struck from his neck, Monbasu has miraculously recovered his poise, and his previous confident bearing. He even has the gall to ask if I'll give him a legal manumission. "With papers, a man of experience can find a position as an overseer. Monbasu can't go back to Dahomey, so he must make a new life for himself. A legal manumission will make all things possible."

The man has nerve! Blinded and beaten and robbed of all he owns, and yet still he dreams! And he talks like a Philadelphia lawyer.

I agree to give him such a letter upon safe arrival in Havana.

July 29
We are becalmed, and worse, set back by contrary currents! Delay is to be expected on the western passage but still it makes me rage against the air and sea, for every extra hour at sea is an hour away from White Harbor, and Becky and my boys.

The one bright spot is my bargain with Monbasu. With him in charge there's been not a peep from the slave deck. The captives are terrified of Monbasu and believe that he, like his cousin the king, is a great sorcerer, a god of the drums and a drinker of blood. That he managed to free himself from captivity they take as proof of his great power. Such a man is to be dreaded and obeyed.

Strange though it may seem, Monbasu shuns his former lady love, and does her no special favors. After a few pathetic attempts, Tambara has ceased trying to reach the man who brought her to such misery. She knows she is a slave like the others, a commodity to be sold, nothing more. There she lies in her chains. But for the missing eye, she's still strikingly beautiful. But what has her beauty brought her, but misery, and a short future?

Will this shunning continue once we have reached Cuba? He's a cunning one, and it's possible Monbasu may eventually purchase her, and make her his wife. With the damage done, she'll fetch no more than $300 at the Havana market, and he is clever enough to accumulate such a sum, if he so desires.

August 2
Disaster! We are no longer becalmed, but worse has happened. The extra water hold is contaminated. My hygienic efforts have backfired. Each day I had the slave deck hosed clean of filth, and flushed into the bilge, where it was then pumped out. But somehow the tainted bilge water has leaked into the water hold, and many of the captives have contracted an intestinal illness. The stench is overpowering. Something must be done or the cargo will be lost, and with it the profit of the enterprise!

I have ordered that the water hold be sealed. Consumption of foul water will only make it worse. Fortunately there's a reserve of fresh water, sealed casks I put aside for just such a contingency. By my reckoning, a prudent rationing will keep crew and cargo alive until we reach Havana.

I have set out in my ledger an exacting reckoning of how the water will be apportioned. Crew to get sufficient water to keep up their strength and keep the ship sailing proper. The slaves will get them a single pint a day, which is just enough to keep them alive.

Rations to be strictly monitored and enforced, making no exceptions for the infirm!

In the ledger I've listed Monbasu as a member of the crew, and eligible for the larger portion, as his power on the slave deck must not be diminished.

August 7

The weather is "cruelsome hot." Many of the captives still suffer from cruel dyspepsia and cramping of the bowels, but by and large they been improved somewhat. None complain of thirst, out of fear they'll have no ration at all. I credit Monbasu for keeping order, and myself for having the foresight to free the man, in exchange for his cooperation.

Tambara, his former lady love, is among those who have recovered. Indeed, she looks healthier than the rest.

August 8

Something has gone wrong with Monbasu! The cook reported that the African was seen down on his knees, licking salt from the deck. When asked to explain himself, he began raving in a foreign tongue, and the cook retreated, afraid for his life.

I seek out Monbasu and find him on the slave deck. It is instantly apparent that he has been preaching to the captives, who are becoming more and more agitated! The stronger ones shake their chains and beat on the deck in rhythm, like drums.

When I demand to know what he's saying to the captives, Monbasu refuses to translate. "Go away, white man," he tells me. His eye glitters strangely and spittle flies from his mouth. "The black gods are busy," he says, and rudely turns his back on me.

Such insolence cannot be tolerated on board ship. I've ordered the slave deck sealed, and Monbasu with it, d—m him. He has gone quite mad, and soon enough I discover the cause of his madness. He has secretly been giving his entire ration of water to Tambara, and has been driven insane by thirst!

August 9

The madness does not end. Monbasu has been agitating the captives for many hours. The beat of chains does not abate, but thunders from the slave deck, a wild thrashing of the chains, terrifying the crew. They know of a ship overrun by slaves, and all the whites hacked to death, and they want their captain to make it stop.

I know what must be done, and it must be done quickly, before the captives rip their chains from the stanchions. I order that Monbasu be taken from the slave deck, and then bound and gagged.

Sweeney makes the suggestion that it would be easier and safer if the mad nigger be shot where he stands, but I cannot answer for how the captives might react, if Monbasu is suddenly killed in their presence. No, the thing to do is throw a net over him. And finally, at the end of the day, the deed is done. With great difficulty, the madman is netted, seized, and removed.

At first the captives are very agitated, moaning and so on, but with their black god defeated the drumming of the chains gradually lessens, and there is silence, blessed silence, from the slave deck.

The worst may be over.

August 10

I am wrong, and it may yet cost me the ship! Just before dawn Sweeney wakes me and reports that in the night the prisoner broke his restraints, violently overpowered his captors, and is assumed to be at large somewhere on the ship.

I have unlocked the munitions and armed myself, and will go out looking for trouble and expecting to find it.

[later]

Much has happened, and little of it good. Seeking Monbasu, I go first to the slave deck. He is not there, but Tambara is, draped in her chains. Despite the extra ration of water she's been getting, she now looks close to dying, as if her lover's madness has burned away her desire to live. Still, she may be of use, and so I remove her chain from the stanchion and try to coax her from the slave deck.

Fearful of my intentions, she fights like a rabid dog, biting me upon the leg most fiercely. I finally drag her up to the main deck. There I call for Monbasu, and make it clear that the wretch must show himself, or the girl will be cast over the rail, into the sea, and eaten by the sharks that trail every slave ship.

One hand wrapped in her chains, the other clutching my flintlock pistol, I wait upon the madman. I'm alone on deck because my d——d superstitious crew have barricaded themselves in their wardroom, convinced that Monbasu has the magic to overpower them all. How else could the African live without water, if he does not have magic? Such tripe fevers my brain into the worst of tempers and makes me rage against the cowardly crew, and against Monbasu. Again and again I threaten to throw Tambara over the side, shouting, "Show yourself! Show yourself or she dies! I swear it!"

Monbasu does show himself, eventual. His appearance is shocking in the extreme. He's smeared with blood and his nappy, unkempt hair is matted with filth. He seems outward calm, except for his eyes, where the madness dwells. "You must turn the ship around," he tells me, as if ordering a subordinate. "The black gods have spoken. You will take us to Senegal. In Senegal I will be made king, and Tambara will be my queen."

Madness.

The madman strolls closer, careless of my pistol, or maybe he thinks bullets can't touch him. He carries no obvious weapon, although I can't guess what he might conceal under his blood-spattered tunic. Oddly, Monbasu pays no heed to Tambara in her chains. How can a man bring himself to this, maddened with thirst so that his lady love might live, how can a man do such things and then refuse to look upon her? There is something cunning in it, I suspect. A kind of feint to draw my attention elsewhere, as a mother bird will feign a broken wing to distract a predator from the nest.

Yes, that must be it! Monbasu knows exactly what he's doing, he's been feigning indifference from the beginning, from the moment he was dragged before Gezo, and all the while he's been using subterfuge and diversion to make sure that his precious Tambara survives.

The cunning madman strolls within an arm's length, and when a smile transforms his face from madness to cunning, I drop Tambara's chains and shove the pistol under his chin, shouting, "Gotcha! You scheming black bastard!" and prepare myself for a struggle.

Before either of us can make a move, there comes a wild cry and a splash. Tambara has gathered up her chains, scampered up the bulwarks, and thrown herself into the sea!

Monbasu cries out and flies to the rail, calling her name most piteously as he searches the oily seas. But the chains are like an anchor, dragging her down quick, and there is no hope. While he's wailing and rending his own clothes, begging for

Tambara, I take my chance and smash his head with the pistol butt, and knock him senseless.

Presently we get him chained to the deck. I know what must be done.

August 11

There are only two possible outcomes when a man foments rebellion aboard a ship, any ship. Either he succeeds, and takes command, or he is hung. There are no exceptions for love or madness, how can there be? Order must be maintained. The law of the sea demands it, and the crew demands it. These matters are best handled as they happened, with a man strung up as soon as he's in custody.

So why have I delayed these last twelve hours? It is as if I don't know my own mind. While the crew frets and complains, I make me up two lists.

Why he must be hung:
1. For preaching rebellion.
2. For mutiny.
3. For assaulting a white man.
4. To prevent further bloodshed.
5. To please the crew, who demand it.

Why he should not be hung:
1. He was not right in his mind.

Try as I might, there is only the one reason not to hang, and it don't balance. Meantime the prisoner does nothing to help his case, and never once pleads for pity or begs for his life. Instead, Monbasu, bound to the foredeck by shackles attached to each of his limbs, flat on his back and forced to look up into the masts and shrouds where his life will end, instead of begging for his own life he begs for the lives of his people on the slave deck. "You are thinking, Yankee captain, that these poor peasants cannot be my people. How is that possible, when they are not of the same clan, not even of the same tribe? I will tell you how it is possible. Because the black gods have spoken to me, they have spoken through me, and I am their instrument."

To appease the black gods he confesses that his people would not have been taken from the land of their fathers had it not been for him, for Monbasu, whose entire life and fortune had been devoted to the taking of captives and the buying and selling of slaves, and he asks the Yankee captain, his good friend, his boon companion, surely I will find it in my heart to set his people free.

"Hang me, but set my people free. I know I must die, and I go willingly, to the place at the river where Tambara waits. She has found her eye in the shallow waters and she waits for me. Hurry. Kill me, please, so that I may go to her. But give me your word as a man that you will set my people free."

I know what I must do, but can't find the will, and beg the crew indulge their captain.

Ship becalmed, and her captain, also.

August 12
The wind decides. Not long after dawn a fair wind rises strong from the east and it must be done; it must be done and the sails set, to take advantage of the fair wind.

Monbasu is unshackled from the foredeck. His hands are bound behind his back. A halyard is noosed around his neck. The crew waits, mighty anxious, smelling the wind, eager to haul away and be done with this troublesome, dangerous man. Let him go to his damned black heaven, why does their captain hesitate?

Before the clever slipknot on the noose tightens, Monbasu

looks me in the eyes and says, "Speak to me as a man. Will you swear to set my people free?"

"No," I tell him. I can't lie to a man about to die.

Monbasu lowers his head for a moment, and when he looks up he seems to be wearing the face of another man, which gives me a chill. Then he curses me.

"You will be cursed," he growls, in a voice unlike his own. "You will be cursed and your sons will be cursed and the womb of your wife will be cursed, until there are sons no more, and everything and everyone you ever loved will perish from the earth!"

I will hear no more of this blasphemy. At my command the mad nigger is hauled up and hung by his neck. After a few minutes his struggles cease, but even before he has been cut down and his body thrown to the trailing sharks, the topsails are set, and *Whippet* tightens her shrouds, bound for the Havana.

The enterprise is saved.

\* \* \*

Editor's note: This concludes the daily entries in "The true log of the *Whippet*. The remainder of the voyage, which must have taken at least ten days, is not remarked upon. In an appendix, damaged by stains that appear to be blood, Coffin tallies his expenses against the price his captives fetched at auction, and indicates that *Whippet* has been sold to an unnamed Dutchman. By his tallies, Cash Coffin has his profit.

No further mention is made of Monbasu, or the curse he uttered before hanging.

# IV

## BLACK MAGIC

*The sorcerers of Dahomey have the power to change shape, and to visit the living even after they are dead. White men think they are immune to their power, because the Dahomey gods are black. This is a mistake.*

FRANCISCO FELIZ DE SOUZA

# 1. Why the Sea Isn't to Blame

I closed the "True log of the *Whippet*" with a heavy heart, convinced that although I might have discovered the source of the curse, and the reason, still I had learned nothing to change the present course of events. The part of my mind that clung to the rational, and begged to divine some logic that might explain the horrors of the previous weeks, could find no reason to ease my fears.

I slept, but sleep brought no relief.

Benjamin woke me not long after dawn, and begged my pardon for intruding at so early an hour. A large and powerfully built man, he had lately lost weight, and the flesh hung loose upon his bones. His beard was streaked white, and his eyes seemed to have been pressed deep into his head, as if by savage thumbs into a lump of damp, gray clay. He was dressed, as always, in a slightly shabby black sack suit, a ready-made cotton shirt, and Hessian boots.

"The Captain wishes to see you."

"Ah. Does he know who I am?" I asked.

"More or less," he said uncertainly. "He believes you to be a friend of Jeb's, and a fellow abolitionist."

"I am both, the one more than the other."

Benjamin nodded curtly. "There's, um, something else you should know. He's somehow formed the impression that your true name is Emerson."

I sighed, heaved myself from the bed, and washed my face in the warm basin Benjamin had kindly supplied. "How is Nathaniel faring?"

The eldest and quite possibly the proudest of Cash Coffin's surviving sons, Benjamin was obviously at his wit's end. At the mention of his brother, he sank onto a chair by the basin, looking, to my physician's eye, very near the point of complete collapse from nervous exhaustion. "Nathaniel," he said. "Poor Nathaniel. He believes Sarah will soon recover her wits, and remember that he is her husband. Is that likely, do you think?"

"Truly, I don't know what to think."

"I will pray for her."

I asked that he pray for all of us, and meant it. I no longer had faith in prayer, but Benjamin obviously did, and besides, what harm could it do? "I'll visit the Captain, of course," I assured him. "Is he still armed, by the way?"

Benjamin looked greatly embarrassed as he nodded. "I tried to persuade him to give me that old flintlock pistol. He prefers to keep it." The big man hesitated, and looked at his hands. "You are not obliged to visit the tower, Dr. Bentwood. No one will think the less of you for refusing."

"Thank you, Benjamin. Allow me to dress myself, and I will attend him. But for you, I really must insist on bed rest. Immediately. Even if you can't sleep, you are to lie down with your eyes closed, is that agreed?"

"You are very kind, Doctor," he said, with a tentative smile. "I will attempt to obey."

"See that you do," I said, trying to sound confident and cheerful. "Please don't worry yourself about me and the Captain. We're old friends."

Tucking the logbook into my jacket, I left him there, sighing and staring at his hands, as if deciding whether or not to fold them in prayer.

Since my last visit to the tower, Captain Coffin had lost his only grandchild and another son, not to mention a fine ship, and I did not expect to find that his mental facilities had improved in my absence. I reflected ruefully that the best his logbook could do me now was to stop a bullet, if he had it in mind to shoot me, or mistook me for one of the black devils that haunted him. For that matter, my own facilities had hardly improved, having lost my place in this world and glimpsed the horror beyond. There was nothing in Emerson to help me, or in the Bible of my youth, and I felt empty at my core, as if something vital had been sucked out of me.

The Captain might be armed with his pistol, but this time I was armed with a better understanding of what to expect. If the narrow stairs of the tower seemed to mire my feet in dread, it was not so powerful a sensation as when the presence had invaded my room. Indeed, to my relief the presence or force that had compelled me to search for the logbook was altogether absent from the tower. What dread I felt was the dread any man might feel, at the prospect of confronting a grief-stricken, guilt-ridden madman.

Was it possible that the presence, having revealed the logbook, was done with us all?

With that happy thought I turned the final corner and came at last to the top of the tower. Rather than knock—what if the old man reacted by firing through the door panels?—I stood back a ways and announced myself. "Captain Coffin! This is Emerson! I believe you wanted to see me, sir!"

Nothing could have astonished me more than what happened next. The door eased open, and Cash Coffin presented himself. But a different Cash than I'd met previously. This one had his hair carefully washed and combed, and his white beard had been neatly trimmed, and his face scrubbed. He was dressed in a finely tailored black suit of densely woven wool, waistcoat and frock jacket both, and his knee-high seaman's boots had been polished to a gleam. A black cravat showed under clean, starched white collar of his boiled shirt. But the greatest surprise was his eyes: his eyes were as tired and deeply sunk as Benjamin's, but there was no gleam of lunacy apparent. To all outward appearance, his sanity had been recovered.

The old man studied me from the doorway, sniffed with his hawkish nose, and then grunted. "You're Jeb's friend, Dr. Bentwood. But if you'd prefer to be called Emerson, I'll oblige."

I stammered, and felt the heat rise in my cheeks. "No, no. Davis Bentwood at your service, Captain. May I come in?"

He bowed slightly and made a gesture of formal welcome. I formed the impression that the spiffy, go-to-meeting togs and the sartorial improvements were for my benefit, as if to correct any wrong conclusions I might have drawn from our previous encounter. "Scat there, Charley!" he barked, and his enormous, green-eyed coon cat vacated his chair and limped away with great dignity, taking up a position near the stove, where it endeavored to ignore us completely. The bandages on the animal's hindquarters were smaller, boding well for its recovery. I reminded myself that the Captain had shot the cat, which he loved, and that although his sanity had apparently returned, it might leave him again without warning.

The tower room was filled with daylight that warmed the floorboards under my feet, and eased me somewhat. The fist of nervous tension in my mind relaxed, and I was able to look about me with something like equanimity, or acceptance. All of White Harbor fell away below the windows, the snow-dusted roofs of the village, and harbor beyond, and the visibility was such that distant islands seemed to hover slightly above the flat, black waters of the placid sea. A man might float here, serene as the eye of God, and paint such pictures in his mind, that transcendence would be as easy as drawing a breath. But make no mistake, I no longer believed that such a state was possible, certainly not in this house, and I took the calmness of the moment to be nothing more than a cruel illusion that might at any time be snatched away.

I stood gazing out those windows, lost in such contemplations, while my host prepared coffee on his little ship's stove.

"What do you see?" the Captain asked companionably, as he set out the cups and poured.

"I see as beautiful a village as ever existed. I see a rich, prosperous town of sea captains and merchants. I see ships in the harbor, and boats of all sizes."

"What else?"

I looked again. What was the old man getting at? "The sea?" I guessed.

"Right, the sea. Calm today, but not always calm."

"I suppose not."

"Calm today, but sometimes it rages and storms." He favored me with such a frank look that I knew he wasn't talking about the sea conditions, but his own. "Sea can't help it when it storms," he said, studying me over his cup. He'd given me the better chair and taken the three-legged stool, the very one where he'd forced me to strip and shiver for the duration of our previous encounter. "Ain't the sea that makes the storm, it's the wind that drives it. Can't see the wind but you know when it's there. Wind makes the waves, but the sea gets blamed."

"I never thought of it that way."

"Make sense to you, does it?"

"I think it does."

He nodded to himself, satisfied. "Never know when the wind'll kick up. But when it does, remember the sea can't help it."

"I'll remember."

"Jebediah says yer a good 'un. Ben, too. Says they couldn't cope with all our terrible sorrows, but for you helping out."

"I don't feel that I've helped all that much, sir. There's not a lot a man can do when the, ah, when the wind comes up, as you say."

Coffin smoothed his beard as he digested my reply. He nodded to himself again and then said, "I'm pleased we understand each other so well, Dr. Bentwood. As you know, I don't hold much with doctors or priests, as a general rule, but you're the exception."

"Thank you, sir."

He grunted and finished his coffee. "So," he said. "What did you think of it?"

"Excuse me, sir? I don't follow."

"My logbook. You've got it under your coat, I assume you've read it."

In hot embarrassment I looked down, and sure enough a corner of the calfskin volume protruded from under my waistcoat. I tried to say something, but the words caught in my throat. I'd meant to return it to him, if the situation warranted, but hadn't meant to reveal the book in so underhanded a fashion. The Captain made a gesture that meant I was not to trouble myself, that he understood how the thing had come to be there. "I expect you was led to it," he said. "Is that how it happened?"

"Um, yes, sir."

"Felt you couldn't resist, did you?"

I nodded.

"You couldn't," he said. "No more'n the sea can resist the wind. But we already agreed about that. I want you to know," he said, pointing at the book under my coat, "there ain't nothin' in there I'm ashamed of. Ain't saying I don't regret it happened, but shame don't enter into it. I tried to do the best I could by him, up 'til the very end. Had I tried to free them poor, miserable captives, my crew'd've hung me from the same yardarm, and that's a fact. Then when I come back home

I kept tryin' to make amends. Gave heaps of honest money to them who asked, for the cause. Gave money to black men, too. You ask Jebediah, he'll tell you I did."

"He told me so himself."

"See? What else could a man do to make amends for a situation that was never his fault in the first place? You think if *Whippet* hadn't touched in Whydah the slaves would have been freed? Never happen. Them blacks was currency, like money, and nobody throws money away, or doesn't pick it up when they find it lyin' in the street."

"I suppose not," I said uneasily, not wanting to rile him further.

"Then you suppose right! Listen here, Dr. Bentwood, you may have read what I wrote, but you ain't seen what I seen in all my travels. Men have been buying and selling each other since before they invented money, and they'll still be doing it after money is forgotten, one way or another. We may end the practice here in this country, and I hope we do, but that don't mean it will end in Cuba or Brazil or anywhere else where there's gain to be made by it. China? Why every Chinaman's a slave, except he's a Mandarin. India? What about India? You think the British don't own the Indians, every blamed one of 'em? Course they do, and use 'em most cruelly, too! A Georgia plantation, the worst you can imagine, it don't have nothing on the East India Company, when it comes to owning folk."

"I never thought of it quite that way."

"Why would you? You ain't in the business. But the point is, Cassius Coffin ain't in the business, either. Not for years and years. So why's it rise up at me now, after all this time?"

"I've no idea," I said, in all sincerity.

Cash leaned forward, speaking in a low, conspiratorial tone. "Tell you why, boy. Because he's a right cruel bastard. Crueler than ever I was, for all I did. Since my mind cleared I been thinking on it, thinking heavy, and here's what I know for certain. This ain't no struggle of good and evil, like you might find in the Bible. It's only evil. That's all he's got left, the evil part of him."

"You speak of the African, Monbasu?"

"Who else?"

"I thought, you know, the drums, the black gods—"

"It's him!" he said fiercely, reaching out to grasp me by the wrist, with a strength that belied his age. "He's the wind, see? He makes it happen."

His agitation was such that I feared his reason would soon be lost again, but there was nothing I could say to calm him. It was all I could do to free myself from his iron grasp. Finally he seemed to regain control and stood up, biding me to do the same. "See how calm it is, the sea? It isn't only wind that makes it move, or storms that can wreck us. There's a thing they know in the Pacific, those island folk, where a great wave rises out of a sea as calm as that. Out of nowhere, mind. No warning at all. One minute you're there, the next you've been washed away by a wave so huge a man can't hold it in his mind, how a thing like that would look. We never know, exactly, because them that have seen it aren't alive to tell the tale. But we know it happens because we see what it leaves behind. Do you follow, Dr. Bentwood?"

"I think so," I said, uncertainly, moving toward the door, and escape.

"We've seen the storm and felt the wind," he said. "But the worst is still to come."

"Good day, Captain. I'm wanted below."

"Nothing we can do," he said, bending to feed his little stove. "A great wave is coming to wash us all away."

When I looked back the green-eyed cat was staring at me.

## 2. The Rattle of Chains

To clear my head I went out into the village and walked about aimlessly, filling my lungs with crisp winter air that was redolent of ice and salt and the cold harbor waters. The Captain's logbook remained under my waistcoat, next to my heavy heart. Despite my protestations, I had come to believe as he did, that a vengeful presence emanated from the house, a presence able to make itself felt wherever a Coffin might be, and through some incomprehensible agency, wreck havoc and destruction on his progeny. But whether it be a force strictly of evil, as the Captain so fervently believed, was less certain in my mind.

Monbasu may have been flawed, as all men are flawed—he, like Cash, was a slave trader profiting in human misery—but it did not necessarily follow that the ruthless punishment of a great sin is itself a great evil. One does not equate with the other. To suppose that the punishment of sin is evil is to suppose that God is evil, and that was a distance I wasn't willing to travel. Better to believe that God did not exist than that He was in equal parts Good and Evil. Was the God of the Old Testament practicing evil when he sought revenge upon the sinners, destroying Sodom? Was it evil of God to torment poor Job to test his faith? To believe so is to believe we Christians worship Evil in the guise of Goodness, that Satan impersonates God and makes fools of all humanity. Were such a thing true, a man of conscience could not continue to live in the world but must, by his own hand, depart.

The thought of ending my life by violent means brought

me up short, and returned me to my surroundings. I was somewhere in the neighborhood of the tradesmen who catered to the seafaring families of White Harbor. From nearby came the hammering of tongs upon iron, and the hot smell of a forge. A smell not unlike the hot stink of a gun barrel, after the charge has been fired. Fired into the grateful, overwrought brain. How reasonable that sounded! Why had I stopped Jebediah when he sought surcease of sorrow? Did I not, in my secret heart, seek the same end?

I found myself much shaken to have such thoughts careening through my mind. Never, even in the lowest moments of my life, had I contemplated suicide, and yet somehow my philosophical musings had led me to a place where suicide seemed a rational act of conscience. It was as if something outside of me had insinuated the darkest and most dangerous ideas into my addled brain. Satan impersonating God? It was a thought so corrosive that it might unseat reason, and leave me gibbering upon the cold and windswept streets.

I determined to hurry back to the Coffin house, and face whatever demon might dwell there, for it could be no more terrifying than the easy contemplation of self destruction.

The familiar crunch of white oyster shells under my boots was oddly comforting, but what drew my attention was an elegant, German-style landau drawn up to the front entrance. The carriage was painted a deep enamel black, with modest but tasteful filigree in gold, and drawn by a pair of handsome white horses. There was a large trunk lashed to the roof, neatly covered with a fitted tarpaulin. A liveried coachman stood by, tending the horses, who snorted quietly in the cold air. Obviously a coach-for-hire that had come some distance, but I'd heard nothing of any expected visitors.

Hurrying into the parlor I found Lucy deep in conversation with a short, matronly woman who looked strangely familiar. As if I had seen her plump, pleasing face, framed by the long curling ringlets of her white hair, staring out at me from a famous painting. Both women looked up at me with startled expressions, for I'd entered at a rush, expecting some emergency, or, at the least, the arrival of more bad news. Lucy was, as usual, in her solemn mourning dress, black from hem to ruffled neck, her thick hair restrained and made properly modest by black silk ribbons. Her companion was very well turned out in an exquisitely tailored, high-collared blue dress a few shades darker than her keenly intelligent eyes. Her sleeves were puffed, and as round and plump as the rest of her. As a gesture of sympathy for the household, the stranger had affixed an identical black silk ribbon to the fashionably wide brim of the cabriolet bonnet she carried in her lap.

Both women stood up. Lucy's normally pale complexion was slightly blushed, as if by excitement or stimulation. "Dr. Bentwood," she said. "May I present my dear friend Mrs. Stanton."

It was not, then, a visage made familiar in a famous painting, but a face engraved for a thousand newspapers and magazines. Elizabeth Cady Stanton, the radical proponent of suffrage for women, the much reviled mother of seven children who had challenged the very idea of the sanctity of marriage, her own marriage not excepted, and been attacked from pulpits all over America, and the world. Lately she'd put aside her lifelong ambition to secure voting rights for the gentler sex to campaign as a full-time abolitionist, which was indeed how she'd first entered public life.

Women's rights had never, I confess, been one of my particular enthusiasms, but then I'd never had much enthusiasm for any of the various reform movements that periodically swept the nation, whether it be temperance, abolition, vegetarianism, or universal suffrage. I was not opposed to the notion that women should have rights of property—a right

now gained through the efforts of Mrs. Stanton and her followers—nor was I among those who believed the Republic
would be destroyed by women getting the franchise. But I had
never bothered to attend a female rally or convention, any
more than I would have attended an abolitionist rally, had I
not be dragged to one by Jebediah. My interests were mainly
philosophical, academic, and utterly selfish.

Still, one could not read of Elizabeth Cady Stanton's
remarkable accomplishments without feeling admiration. As a
young mother married to a roving abolitionist, she had conceived the idea that the legal rights accorded to all men should
be expanded not only to Negro males, but to all women as
well. In 1848 she'd had the audacity to rewrite the Declaration of Independence, and make it say that "all men and all
women are created equal," calling it her "Declaration of Rights
And Sentiments." At the same convention she then proposed
the most shocking resolution of all, that women should be
given the vote. The scandal was enormous. Over the intervening years the idea had become less shocking, if not less contro-
versial, but at the time even the most ardent campaigner for
women's rights, Lucretia Mott, would not support her, for fear
that demanding suffrage would make women appear ridiculous. Many ministers and abolitionists still considered Mrs.
Stanton's demands ridiculous, but I did not, even if I'd never
stirred myself to actively support them. Indeed, to be in her
presence for more than a moment was to know she was anything but ridiculous. She was formidable in her small, rotund
person, and in the way her almost violently blue eyes seemed
to command attention.

"Very pleased," Mrs. Stanton remarked as I took her hand.
"Lucy tells me you are a sensible person. I'm hoping to find
you so."

"Oh, indeed?" I replied uncertainly.

"I have been attempting to persuade her to depart from

this very charming village and act as my secretary, a role she once filled most admirably."

"Oh, please, Elizabeth, you must let me—" Lucy began, and was cut off by a gesture from her friend.

"I have been on the lecture circuit these last few weeks, and in Portland heard disturbing news of the situation here," she explained, leveling her intensely bright eyes at me. "Madness, mysterious deaths, and so on. I felt compelled to visit in person, and see if I might convince her to leave."

"I see," I said, somewhat disingenuously, for Mrs. Stanton's intentions were not at all clear to me.

The suffragist bade me sit down and then turned in her chair and faced me resolutely, ignoring her young friend's now obvious embarrassment. "Lucy left my employ to care for her ailing father. This was commendable. But I've since learned that having been left more or less destitute, she's placed herself in an even more desperate circumstance."

Lucy protested indignantly. "Really, Elizabeth, how can you speak of me as if I'm not in the room?"

"Hush, child. You know I have your best interests in mind. Dr. Bentwood, please dissuade me. Convince me that I'm mistaken, and that Miss Wattle is not in danger."

"Well," I began, at a loss.

"Convince me this unfortunate family is not in the grip of madness," she went on, as unstoppable as a steam locomotive. "Convince me that my friend—and you are my friend, Lucy— that my dear friend may not suffer the same awful fate as so many of her blood relations."

I took a deep breath and steeled myself, for I knew Lucy would oppose me in what I was about to say. "I cannot in good conscience attempt to dissuade you, Mrs. Stanton."

"Call me Elizabeth, please," she said primly. "Continue."

"Actually, I share your concern. I'm convinced that all who stay in this house are in danger, if not of death, than of self-destructive madness. But I'm equally convinced that Lucy will not abandon her cousins because she believes that duty compels her to stay. We had occasion to discuss the subject, and she made herself very clear."

"I see. Thank you, Dr. Bentwood." She turned to Lucy. "Do you see, child? I am not alone. Surely no one here would prevent your leaving."

"No one but myself," said Lucy, her eyes brimming with tears. "Oh, Elizabeth, I do appreciate your concern, but this is the only family I have left in the world, and were I to abandon them in their hour of need, I couldn't live with myself."

The suffragist sighed. "I know something of family obligation, and will not press you further. But my offer stands. If you should ever have occasion or need to leave, there is a place for you, so long as I live—and I intend to live a very long time! Now dry your tears, dear, and we shall visit a little."

Barky brought in a tray of hot tea and scones, and Mrs. Stanton regaled us with tales of her recent speaking engagements, very charmingly told, for she loved to laugh and had a quick, sharp sense of humor. "A sourpuss parson in Portland became very distressed by my statement that only war would settle the question," she said. "So distressed, indeed, that after heaping insults upon me he fell from his pulpit and fractured his ankle. I could not help myself, and remarked that he'd not have been injured if his foot hadn't been so firmly stuck in his mouth. I'm afraid I made an enemy, which is regretful, but still, if you could have seen the man's face! As if he'd been biting lemons, and the lemon bit back! May I take it, Dr. Bentwood, that you are in sympathy with abolition?"

"I am. Though like your unfortunate parson, I hate the idea of war."

"We all hate the idea of war, sir, but war must come!" she responded, her fine voice rising. "The secessionists have made that very clear in these last few weeks. They shall deny and defy until the end of time, or the end of their repulsive Confederacy. We must oblige them in that."

In the light of midafternoon the parlor was warm and pleasant, and it did not seem credible that any threat dwelled in the house, or among the family. I knew better, but it was a relief to pretend otherwise, and to hear intelligence from someone outside the small world of our troubles. Mrs. Stanton spoke movingly of the abolitionist cause, and of her recent differences with her long-time associate, Susan Anthony, who was greatly distressed that Mrs. Stanton had given up on the suffrage movement. "I can't make the dear woman understand that I have not given up on getting us the vote, I've only deferred my desires until the even more terrible problem of slavery is resolved. Once the issue is settled, I'll climb back on my horse and ride it to victory. Unfortunately poor Susan is of the belief that if we suspend the cause now, suffrage will not come in our lifetime. I cannot persuade her otherwise, and so she has retired to her farm to wait out the war."

"You speak as if war is inevitable," I said.

"And so it is. I expect hostilities to begin in the next few months, possibly sooner. The Union army will put a quick end to that foolishness, and having won the war, Lincoln will have no choice but to emancipate the slaves and grant them voting rights. That done, how can he give the vote to the black men and not to women? He cannot. It must be so. It will be so."

Her steely confidence was almost as shocking as her belief that emancipated slaves be allowed to vote. I supported the idea of abolition, but surely the notion of granting suffrage to uneducated Negroes was unwise? Not at all, she countered, hundreds of thousands of ignorant white men made their marks on ballots each election day. In New York, for instance, half the voting population was staggering drunk upon entering the polling place. Would I deny to a sober if illiterate Negro the privilege granted to a drunken and illiterate white man? On what basis did I defend such a proposition?

In the face of one of the great thinkers and debaters of the day, I found myself quite speechless and utterly unable to defend what was, in truth, a merely instinctive reaction to her radical propositions. In any event, I did not seek debate, but only polite discussion, and so meekly surrendered before I, too, found myself fallen from the pulpit.

"Have you seen Frederick Douglass recently?" Lucy wanted to know. "He stopped by and entertained us with his violin."

Mrs. Stanton sighed again. "There is a difficulty there, I am sorry to say. The situation is that we sometimes share a stage or podium, but our personal conversations never stray beyond the weather. His connection to Miss Assing is most unfortunate. It is not so much that I disapprove, but my own call for legalizing divorce puts me in an awkward position, as Douglass will not divorce his wife. I fear it will end in disgrace and disaster."

"For Douglass?" I asked.

She shook her head briskly, making her curls jump. "For Miss Assing. Douglass is too great a man to be much reduced by a marital scandal. In any event, men are forgiven for their urges. It is women who must wear the scarlet letter."

I could not disagree, though I thought the Douglass-Assing scandal had more to do with racial taboos than infidelity. Having dispensed with her fellow abolitionists, I asked Mrs. Stanton what she knew of Lincoln's disposition. She snorted and said, "I suppose his disposition is that of a man who finds he must either cut off one of his own limbs, or die. He has no belly for making war, that's obvious, no great enthusiasm for using the army. But very soon he will have no choice but to use it, and when that happens I think we'll be well served by Mr. Lincoln. He is a politician and therefore shares the bloodlines of ferret, weasel, wolf, and serpent. They all must do, or they can't be elected. So 'Honest Abe' will lie and feint and bite and slither on his belly when it serves his purpose, and that facility will also serve in prosecuting a war."

When the time came for her to go—she was expected at a rally in Waldoboro that evening—Mrs. Stanton embraced Lucy, patted her back, and said, "Child, if ever you need shelter from the storm, look to me. Is that understood?"

"Understood," said Lucy.

The famous suffragist shook my hand briskly, and left us without a backward glance.

Mrs. Stanton was not gone but a quarter hour when Barky cried out from the kitchen. With his ruined voice, it was really no more than an excited squeak, but still it started me running to help.

I found him on his hands and knees, where he'd been scrubbing at the floorboards with a pair of holystones, to make the floor as clean and smooth as the deck of a ship. His great round face had gone quite pale, and his small, lively eyes squinted in fear. "Did you hear?" he asked in his high-pitched voice, and pointed at the floor.

"Hear what?" Lucy asked, gliding into the kitchen behind me, with considerably more grace than I'd been able to muster.

"A noise," he squeaked. "Like a thump. Coming from below."

I crouched upon the damp floor and touched my hand to the boards. Exactly as I did so, there came a distinct *thump*, seemingly from directly beneath my feet.

"Felt that, didja?" Barky asked with concern, as if fearful that the strange *thump* might have originated in his mind alone.

"Does the cellar extend under the kitchen?" I asked him.

"Oh, yes," he said. "Under the whole of the house. The Captain's a great one for wanting a good foundation. Dug it down to ledge, they did, and built up with slabs of quarried granite."

I stood up and dried my hands on a handkerchief. "Someone must be down there. One of the brothers, possibly."

"Not Jeb, he ain't left his bed."

"Benjamin or Nathaniel?"

Barky considered the question. "Ben ain't never liked the cellar much. Says the damp gets in his bones, and everybody knows cellar damp is worse'n ship damp. And Nathaniel bides with his wife, at Merriman's boardinghouse."

There was another, louder *thump* from beneath our feet, and something that sounded like muffled voices.

"Fetch a lantern," Lucy suggested, and marched resolutely for the cellar door, situated in an alcove off the kitchen.

"Stand back, missy," Barky suggested, when he arrived with lantern in hand.

He was about to thumb the latch on the door when Benjamin appeared in the hallway, demanding to know what was going on. When I explained that noises had been heard, coming from below, he shot a stern glance at Lucy. "Have you anything to tell us, cousin? Has your friend left us with more runaways?"

I instantly understood that he was referring to Mrs. Stanton, and to his suspicion that she, like Mr. Douglass, had come to visit while shepherding fugitive slaves along the underground railroad.

Lucy took a breath and met his stern gaze. "If so, she told me nothing of it," she said firmly.

Benjamin nodded, satisfied. "They know this place," he said. "Could be a stray, I suppose. Crack the hatch, Mr. Barkham, and let us shed some light on our 'visitors.' "

Immediately the door was open, voices came up from the

stairwell. I took them to be Negro voices, speaking one of the African tongues, for it was not a language familiar to me. "There," said Benjamin with some satisfaction. "Strays. Lucy, you stay behind. We'll see to their needs."

"Nonsense. A woman's kindness may be needed."

Seeing that she would not be dissuaded, Benjamin shrugged his big shoulders as if to say, *let it be on your head*. With the door open, and the musty smell of the cellar air rising to greet us, Barky led the way, holding high the lantern. We were about halfway down the stairs when there came a distinct *crack!* of a lash on flesh, and a stifled moan of pain.

"What evil is this?" Benjamin exclaimed.

Behind me Lucy caught her breath. Suddenly the stairwell began to vibrate with the sound of chains smashing rhythmically against a wooden surface. Foul smells rose up from below. The stinging, highly unpleasant odors of unwashed human beings confined in a small, hot space.

"How can this be?" Lucy cried out, grasping my arm as she nearly lost balance on the stairs.

Meanwhile Benjamin was bulling ahead, having taken the lantern from the cook's reluctant hand. He had the attitude of a man who must move swiftly or be frozen by fear, and the fear emanating from the cellar was palpable, as strong and nauseating as the eye-watering stench of human waste.

I begged that Lucy leave us at once, but she would not, and linking her hand firmly to my own, bade me follow Benjamin into the black depths of the stairwell, into the gloomy, Stygian darkness of the cellar itself.

The smashing rhythm of the chains was like that of drums. African drums, I supposed, never having heard any. I tried to imagine the previous group of fugitives—meek and frightened—having the rude audacity to raise such a din, and could not. They had moved like silent shadows, fearful of discovery, and the only thing that had disturbed their furtive silence was the cry of a newborn baby. What kind of fugitives were we about to encounter, then, who announced themselves so purposefully? And why, having freed themselves from their masters, had they kept their chains?

I confess that I wasn't thinking clearly, or I might have had some intuition as to what we would find in that terrible black cellar. As it was, the sensations came too fast for me to reason properly. The noise, the smells, the chanting voices, it was all too much for my poor, addled mind to comprehend. It wasn't until Benjamin got to the bottom of the stairs and pivoted around, using the lantern to illuminate the darkness, that I got an inkling of the true reality—if truth or reality can be said to factor into the inexplicable phenomenon we all experienced.

I say "inexplicable" because the cellar was empty. Completely empty save for ourselves. Though Benjamin bravely carried his light to every corner, searching for the source of the deafening noise, we found not another human being in that place. And still the frantic cacophony carried on around us—the smashing of chains, the moaning of prisoners, the haranguing of the one most powerful voice, and the responding chant from his followers or supplicants. A phantom voice raised in high dudgeon, calling, I could only suppose, the gods of the drums, seeking vengeance.

It was exactly as if the slave deck of the *Whippet* had somehow sent forth an echo from the past, or from hell itself, and whose angry voice could it be but that of Monbasu, exhorting his fellow captives to revolt? Had I not been in the company of others, I might have supposed these horrible sounds to be a figment of my overwrought imagination, but we all heard it as clearly as if we, too, were chained upon the slave deck.

Poor Benjamin seemed to take it the worse, as if the manifestation was a blasphemy against his own God, and he raised his voice, trying to shout down the pagan chants. Lumbering about with his lantern swinging, as if determined to give the shadows substance.

"Be gone from this house!" he shouted, as fearsome as any Old Testament prophet. "Leave us alone! In the name of God, get thee out!"

Whether his exhortations had any effect I cannot say, but within five or ten minutes of our entering the cellar, the chanting slowly began to fade, growing ever more distant, as if the foul ship was drawing away from us through the intervening years, carrying the plaintive moans across the unseen waters. The last we heard was a distinctly feminine whimper, the last gasp of an unbearable life drowning in pain and misery, and then silence.

Only the stench of human degradation remained when we wearily mounted the cellar stairs, and bolted the door behind us. We stood there in the hallway, in the welcome stillness of the great house, and could not bear to look upon one another, as if we had witnessed something too shameful to acknowledge.

As, indeed, I believe we had.

## 3. What They Did to Witches

That evening, after a cold supper at which we all picked glumly at our portions, appetites ruined by foreboding, Lucy and Benjamin whispered among themselves, and then left the house without explanation. I assumed it must concern poor Sarah, but less than a half hour later they returned in the company of Father Whipple, the kindly Episcopal priest. He was delighted to see me again, and straightway wrung my hands with such enthusiasm that his spectacles went askew, which had the effect of making him look like he was about to tip over.

"Father Whipple has agreed to help us if he can," Benjamin informed me, somewhat shyly, as if he thought I would disapprove.

"Whatever's expected," said the priest agreeably, as Lucy took his shabby greatcoat and hung it up to dry. "We'll keep this on the hush though, will we?" he said sotto voce. "Mustn't upset the old boy, hmm?"

Benjamin quietly assured him that Captain Coffin had not left his tower room in weeks, and would not be likely to do so even if he knew a priest was present. Then, he added, "Bless you, Father. It was fine of you to come, considering how you and your kind have been abused in this house."

Whipple waved away his concern as we drew up seats not far from the parlor stove. "Piffle. Didn't take it personally, hmm? Your father had his reasons."

"Father is a great man," said Benjamin, somewhat stiffly. "But in this he's been a great fool. Why should the word of

God be forbidden in this house, just because a priest once insulted him?"

Whipple looked alarmed. "Forbidden? The word of God? But surely you have prayed, Ben?"

"He's done little else but pray, these last weeks," Lucy said primly, casting a glance my way, for confirmation.

Benjamin hung his head, quite miserable. "I keep praying, Father, but the presence I spoke of, it pays no heed, but comes and goes on its own evil whim. I'm a weak vessel."

Whipple patted his arm, attempting to console him. "Nonsense! Weak vessel, what rot! A Coffin, weak? Unheard of. Nothing weak about you, Ben, but that we're all of us weak in the eyes of God. All humans are, in that respect, hmm? I'm certainly no exception."

"Then tonight you must be strong, Father," said Lucy, making clear she expected no less.

"Yes, my dear, I'll try. With the Lord's help."

"There is evil in this house, and you must cast it out," she said, staring at me as if daring me to disagree.

Whipple gulped, his watery eyes magnified by the odd spectacles tied to his head with a black ribbon. "Only our Savior has the power to cast out evil, Miss Wattle. I explained that when you came to find me. All we can do, as true believers, is ask for the Lord's help."

"Yes, so you said," said Lucy, in her argumentative way. "But isn't there something in the Bible about casting out devils? What good is a priest if he can't cast out devils?"

"Lucy!" said Benjamin, highly insulted on Whipple's behalf.

"No, that's all right," said the priest gently. "Go on," he encouraged her.

"The Pilgrims cast out devils, didn't they?"

"They were Puritans," Whipple patiently explained. "They believed that every flaw of human nature was the result of demonic possession. But we live in the Age of Enlightenment, Miss Wattle. We have come to understand that we're all flawed creatures, and the fault is within us, not the devil."

"He doesn't understand," said Lucy in despair, to her cousin and me. "How could he? Tell him, Davis, tell him what happens in this house!"

I hesitated. How much did Benjamin know of his father's hidden past? Could he, as a devout, God-fearing Christian, accept the idea of another, darker god having dominion over his own father, and his father's children? It was contrary to everything he understood and believed, to all that he held dear, to the very shape of the world he carried within. And yet I, too, believed the time had come for plain words about all that had happened, even if it grieved Benjamin to hear it.

"Father Whipple, do you consider me a rational sort of man?" I began.

"Oh, most certainly," he responded, very eagerly.

"A man of science and the modern philosophies?"

"From what I know of you, yes, indeed."

"Would you be surprised if I confessed that as of a month ago, I did not believe in devils or ghosts, and lacked what you would call faith?"

He chuckled. "I'm not one for ghosts or devils myself. But what do you mean, you lacked faith? Do you mean belief in our Lord?"

"Not exactly that," I said, hedging a trifle. "Let us say I had more faith in Emerson, who teaches that we all have God within us. And that if we seek the God within, we may achieve a state of transcendence."

"Hmph!" said Whipple. "Can't say I've ever understood what that Emerson fellow was always going on about. Sounds a bit like having visions, hmm? Saints wandering in the wilderness and so on."

"But you take my meaning, that I was not in the least

superstitious? That I abhorred the very idea of otherworldly manifestations, or spiritualism?"

"I'll so accept," Whipple said, looking around the room and smiling at our little gathering. "Let us all stipulate, 'Dr. Bentwood is not given to superstition.' "

"Then you may be surprised to learn that I now believe this family to be haunted by an evil presence that seeks revenge upon Cash Coffin and all of his descendants. I say this by direct observation and experience. A few hours ago we all heard it. And only last night I felt it move me."

Lucy gasped in astonishment and covered her mouth with her hand. "Oh, Davis, you, too?"

Benjamin also groaned, and buried his face in his hands. "We have all felt it, Father. An invisible thing that sucks the life from your soul."

"Ben!" Whipple cried with concern. "Poor lad!"

"I live in dread that I will die in its presence," said Benjamin, his voice thick with weeping. "It steals into my dreams. It steals my faith away. You must help us, Father, please! Bring God back into this house, and cast the devil out!"

Then, for a time, all was silent, as Lucy comforted her cousin in his misery. Father Whipple was busily leafing through his Bible, but it was obvious that he was becoming exasperated. He looked to me for commiseration. "The Roman church had a rite that was used for casting devils out of souls possessed, but it has fallen out of use in the last century. From what I understand, their so-called exorcism was little more than an excuse to persecute the Jews for an imperfect conversion to Christianity, during the Spanish Inquisition. It's what they used on witches, too, when they wanted to drown or hang them. I'm not familiar with any Episcopal rite that's applicable."

"It isn't that we're possessed, Father. Or not exactly that. More that the evil presence wishes to do harm. And has done great harm."

Lucy was growing more and more impatient with the gentle, well-intentioned priest. "Father Whipple, do you believe in good?"

"Of course I do, my dear. If I believe in God, and I do, then I must believe in his goodness."

"Do you believe in evil?"

"Evil exists. There can be no doubt."

"And do you believe that good will triumph over evil?"

Whipple took her questions most seriously. The last he gave some thought to before replying. "In the end, child, yes I do. I believe that the goodness of our Lord will prevail."

"Then please, Father, look in your Bible and find a way to say so!"

That prompted more hurried leafing through the book in question, until at last Whipple settled on a page and put his finger to a line. Clearing his throat, and pitching his reedy baritone to be heard throughout the room, if not the house, he began. "Oh, magnify the Lord with me, and let us exalt his name together, I sought the Lord and he heard me and delivered me from all my fears. The angel of the Lord encampeth round about them that fear him, and delivereth them. Depart from evil and do good, for the eyes of the Lord are upon the righteous, and his ears are open unto their cry."

"Amen," Benjamin uttered with a whimper. And then, gathering courage, a little louder, "O Lord, amen! Deliver us from evil!"

"More, Father," Lucy urged him, her eyes darting fearfully to the dark corners of the parlor. "Keep going, for the love of God!"

"Yes, hmm." He cleared his throat, and began reciting from memory, only occasionally consulting the text. "God is our refuge and strength, a very present help in trouble. Therefore we shall not fear, though the earth be removed, and though the mountains be carried into the midst of the sea." A sudden chill stole into the room. The priest looked about him with mild concern, and then seemed relieved that the stove had gone out, as if that explained it. "The heathen, um, the heathen raged," he continued, "the kingdoms were moved: He uttered His voice, the earth melted. The Lord of hosts is with us, the God of Jacob is our refuge. Lord, bless us and bless this house, Lord God deliver us from evil."

The air began to move, lifting the hairs on the back of my neck. The lamps dimmed, and now it was Lucy who whimpered, and begged that Whipple not be distracted, but continue with his good agency. But the poor fellow could not help being distracted when the wind stole into a closed room and billowed his robes, snatching the brightness from the sperm-oil lamps and guttering the candles. It was not so dark that I could not see the light of recognition in his eyes, that our minds were not, as he must have supposed, addled by grief. The presence was with us, and all around us, and it seemed to be focusing its malevolence upon the priest.

"The Lord is my shepherd," Father Whipple said, as bravely as he knew how. "I shall not want. He maketh me to lie down in green pastures, he leadeth me beside the still waters."

At that moment the floor beneath our feet began to vibrate, very like a platform does as the train approaches. Lucy screamed, but the sound of it somehow died in the air, muffled strangely, as if the presence in the room had the power to stifle our very utterances. I could see Whipple's mouth opening wide, as if he was shouting into a full-blown gale, but I could barely make out the words of that familiar psalm. "He restoreth my soul!" the priest recited, struggling to remain upright as something pushed him backward, flattening his robes around his spindly legs. His spectacles flew off, leaving him blinking and half-blind. "He leadeth me in the paths of righteousness for his name's sake."

At that very moment the Bible leaped from his hands and smacked up against the ceiling, where it remained, as if glued.

But the brave fellow didn't need a Bible, he knew the psalm by heart, as we all did. Lucy, who clung to Benjamin—his eyes rolled in fear, and all of him trembled, even his beard—Lucy implored me with her eyes that we must join Whipple, and recite together. "Yea, though I walk through the valley of the shadow of death, I will fear no evil! For thou art with me!" we shouted together, feeling our words muffled and compressed, and hearing ourselves as if from a great distance. "Thy rod and thy staff shall comfort me! Thou preparest a table before me in the presence of mine enemies!" Beneath us the floor rumbled, and furniture began to slowly spin about the room. A low growling came from the snuffed out stove, as if a savage beast crouched within. The tin chimney rattled and shrieked. Father Whipple was leaning forward, hands clutching at his flapping robes, as if struggling to make his way in a nor'east gale that only he felt. "Louder!" Lucy shouted, but we could barely hear ourselves, though our throats were raw with the strain of trying to make ourselves heard. "Thou anointest my head with oil! My cup runneth over! Surely goodness and mercy shall follow me all the days of my life! I will dwell in the house of the Lord forever!"

The priest's struggling feet suddenly lost traction, and he was flung backward, his black robes rippling in an unnatural way, as a hideous snake might writhe beneath sheets. Poor Whipple, who had come out of the goodness of his heart, to offer us the comfort of his religion, poor Father Whipple was flung rapidly backward until he collided with the thick, black velvet curtains that covered the window, dark mourning curtains that seemed to swallow him up and spit him out as he was expelled from the house, and cast through the shattered window glass and the broken mullions with a scream that was much, much louder than all of our prayers.

## 4. Making the Beast

By the time I found the village doctor's house, it was past nine o'clock in the evening and Griswold had to be roused from his bed. To say that he received me with ill temper is putting it mildly, for the furious little man was obviously loath to find himself in my presence. In his mind I'd not only displaced him as the Coffin family physician, but my conduct regarding the death of the infant Casey was questionable, possibly suspicious. And then I dared to bang upon his door, many hours after sunset, raving about a wounded man who had, in all probability, been assaulted by none other than myself. It's no wonder that his first words were a threat to send for the constable.

"By all means, do so," I told him. "But not before you attend Father Whipple," and with that I dragged the semiconscious victim into the small room that served as Griswold's surgery, where I laid him on the examination bench. "I think he's concussed. He was struck a terrible blow on the head when he went through the window."

"Through the window! You threw a priest through the window!"

"Not I."

"If not you, then it must have been that scoundrel Coffin!" the doctor cried, but already he was directing his attention to his groaning patient. "That crazy old fool should be locked up!"

"He is locked up," I informed him. "I must leave, they've need of me at the house."

"Wait, you son of a bitch! How dare you!" he cried, reaching out to snag my trouser leg, and hold me.

Truth be told. I was more shocked by his intemperate language than by him grabbing me. "Calm yourself, Griswold. When Father Whipple regains his senses he can tell you exactly what transpired. I doubt you'll believe him, but that's not my concern. Terrible things have happened, and I must return."

"Terrible things? What terrible things?"

"Things beyond your understanding. Do you want to come round to the Coffin house, and find out for yourself?"

That put the fear into him. He let go of me, muttering about what cheeky devils those Boston doctors were, and I fled while I had the chance, flinging the surgery door shut behind me.

Outside I ran through the darkness, boots crunching on the new-fallen snow, knife points of cold air in my wheezing lungs. I'd hated to abandon my friends, but the priest had had obvious need of medical attention, and I was in no state to provide it, nor was it safe, obviously, to bring him back into the house. Lucy had urged me to take him to Griswold, and come back as quickly as I could, and I intended to make good on my promise.

By the time I made it to the top of the hill, and saw my destination before me, the weaker part of my conscience was suggesting how sensible it would be to turn around and take a room for the night with the widow Merriman. Had I not risked enough already? Surely the bonds of friendship no longer required my presence. It was not as if I'd been of any real assistance, nor was it within my power to lift the curse, or interrupt the cruel process of destruction. Jebediah himself had begged me to leave, had he not? Seize your chance, Davis, and retreat with your tail between your legs, or it may be you who is flung out a window, or impaled on a splinter of wood, or driven mad.

In the end my conscience, cowardly though it might be, would not let me abandon my friends to the strange forces unleashed within the house. And so I trudged the rest of the way up the hill, keenly aware of the tower looming over me, of its jagged, starlit shadow on the snow, and the darkened windows that look as empty as the eyes of the dead.

I had expected to find the house in a state of dark melancholy, given what had happened to the priest. But scarcely had I entered when Jebediah himself emerged from the library, his face ablaze with excitement as he waved a sheet of paper.

"The day has come!" he announced. "Come, you must join the celebration! You must propose a toast! We must all propose toasts!"

My first reaction was to suppose that my small friend had joined his father, and crossed over into the land of the mad. What else could have caused him to rise from his bed? But he soon allayed my fears. It seemed that intelligence had just been received, by telegraph and fast rider: the Southern militia had finally fired upon the federal forces they'd quarantined at Fort Sumter, and war would be declared tomorrow.

The impromptu celebration had been convened around a stout bottle of champagne long cached for this day, and set out on the very desk where Cash Coffin had drawn so many checks for the cause.

"Raise your glass, my friends!" Jebediah implored us. Us being myself and Lucy, whose uneasiness somehow prevented her from making eye contact with me, as if, I could only suppose, she did not wish to discuss the impossible events that had resulted in Father Whipple's expulsion from the parlor.

Dutifully, we raised our glasses. Jebediah beamed. "In

three months—six at the most—the rebel army will surrender," he declared. "Their sham government will be soundly defeated, and their slaves set free!"

In truth, I was not moved. Whatever events might be taking place far to the south were eclipsed by the present danger. But Jebediah was deaf to anything but the happy prospect of the war he had so eagerly anticipated. He didn't want to hear about poor Father Whipple's ordeal, or why, after boarding up the shattered window, Benjamin had taken to his bed. The troubles of the Coffin family were, he avowed, of little consequence, now that the tide of history had at last begun to turn, and its waters soon to run red in battle.

"Think of it, Davis! Think of it, dear Lucy! Is it not wonderful? We will arm the fugitive slaves. They can take revenge against their masters, earning freedom by the same means as our white countrymen did, at the point of a bayonet! Freedom must be written in blood, never forget that!"

It soon became obvious, alas, that my little friend had been roused from his languorous state by more than champagne and cause for celebration. Jebediah was raving. His eyes had taken on a peculiar glassy hue, as if he were looking not upon a meager audience of two, but a throng of thousands cheering his cause, and himself. In his haste to dress, his coat jacket was buttoned askew. He'd also neglected to put on his boots or stockings, and his twisted, hair-tufted little feet poked out from under his trouser legs in a way that might have been comical under more benign circumstances. Oblivious to his own appearance, or our reactions to it, he strutted around his father's library, gesturing grandly with the champagne bottle and hoisting his cup to the imagined multitudes, as if the shelves held not volumes of books, but people. "Heed the call to arms! Countrymen, do your duty! Will you let this nation be torn asunder, and all we have gained be lost, so that a few rich plantation owners can keep their pound of flesh? Arise! Grab your muskets and follow me!" and so on.

Both Lucy and I attempted to soothe him into a more placid state, but he would not be calmed. "What do I care what happens to me? I have lived to see this day! That is enough! That's life enough for any man! Our cause is just and we have prevailed! The chains will be broken! See, Davis, do you see? Lucy! You can see, can't you? We will march together, all of us, and carry the banner! Let Lincoln step aside, and Douglass replace him! YES! Let Frederick Douglass appoint me Secretary of War, and I'll show those so-called Southern gentlemen what happens to traitors! They'll fear Jebediah Coffin like they fear the devil himself! More! More champagne!"

Jeb's forehead was so hot with excitement that Lucy brought in a handful of snow, and I made an ice poultice for his fevered brow. He took it as vastly amusing, our concern for his physical well-being. "What does it matter now, what happens to me or my family?" he crowed. "You can't cool the heat of revenge, or keep down the black masses. No! We sinners are doomed. Soon there'll be coffins aplenty and no more Coffins to fill 'em, isn't that a great joke? Go on, Lucy, laugh, you're so lovely when you laugh!"

Eventually the champagne took its toll on his small body, which was in mass no larger than a child, and as easily overcome. After ranting for nearly an hour, finally his mind slowed and his speech began to slur. When at last he collapsed with a groan, I summoned Barky and we were able to carry poor little Jeb upstairs to his chamber and put him to bed, still muttering of war, glorious war, and of coffins to be filled. He roused himself enough to mutter, "Why do you weep, Davis? I lived to see my dream come true. No man can ask for more," and then his head lolled back on his feather pillow and he began to snore.

In the hallway outside the chamber, Barky touched me on the elbow and inquired, in a squeaky whisper, "Is there nothing can be done for him or the rest?"

"Nothing I know of," I said. "We've tried medicine. We've tried prayer. Nothing avails."

"But we must have hope, Doc, mustn't we?" he asked plaintively, looking back at Jeb's door.

On the subject of hope I no longer had an opinion, and left Barky with his candle, hovering outside of Jebediah's chamber in case he was needed.

Downstairs I nearly collided with Lucy, who was coming from a closet with a straw broom in hand.

"Don't trouble with the mess," I begged her. "Tomorrow we'll hire someone to tidy up."

That made her trill a sarcastic laugh at my expense. "Tidy up? I doubt you'll find a charwoman willing to stand on her head and 'tidy up' the ceilings."

She bade me follow her into the parlor and look up where she pointed. There, still firmly affixed to the ceiling like a leather-bound spider, was Father Whipple's Bible. A trickle of icy water ran through my veins and raised the small hairs on the back of my neck. Impossible, but there it was, in defiance of the laws of nature and gravity. The sight of it filled me with dread and fear, but Lucy's reaction was quite the opposite. She raged at the thing as she strove to dislodge it with her upended broom. "How dare you! How dare you mock us with the book of God! Davis, tell it to let go!"

"Let me try," I said, taking the broom from her hands. It took more courage than I possessed to stand on a sturdy chair and poke at the unholy Bible, but I did it anyway. Mostly because I was deeply afraid that Lucy's intemperate rage would summon the awful presence back into the room, and perhaps into us.

I mashed and poked and pried, but the priest's book would not relinquish its limpetlike hold on the ceiling. Trembling with my effort, and with the fear it inflamed, I got down from my perch and admitted defeat.

"Never mind," said Lucy, turning her back on the scene. "We shall ignore its impudence. Let it have the damned Bible."

"Lucy!" I hissed.

"Oh, shut up, sir, and pour me a drink. A very strong drink."

Shocked and not a little hurt by her tongue-lashing, and disturbed by the change in her nature, I complied and went to the sideboard for the whiskey. Considering what we'd been through, strong whiskey was doubtless appropriate, if only as medication to dull the nerves. Turning with the drinks in my hand, I heard a distinct *plop!* and a delighted cry from my beautiful companion.

"There!" she said, picking the Bible up from the floor. "Ignore the thing and it goes away!"

"I wish it were that simple," I said, handing her the glass.

She covered the Bible with a cast-iron bookend, lest it seek to rise, and turned to me with a look of triumph as she lifted the glass to her lips. "To our health, Dr. Bentwood."

"To our health."

"Come sit with me. The air has a chill and we daren't build a fire in that wretched stove."

No, quite true, the wretched stove had its chimney pipes askew, and the parlor was, indeed, quite cool, though I hadn't noticed it before, heated up as I was by my efforts to dislodge the wretched book—no, never the wretched book, the Bible was not at fault—why had the term "wretched book" come so easily into my mind? Ah, the stove, yes, a confabulation of an exhausted mind. . . .

Thus were my thoughts addled, as I placed myself next to Lucy on the damask fainting couch. Smiling brazenly, she snuggled somewhat closer than was comfortable and placed a hand upon my knee. "You think me bold? Tonight I am quite bold. I don't care a fig what anyone might think."

"Lucy, we—"

"Shhh!" She placed a finger upon my lips. "Bide with me for a while."

Humming a tune I did not recognize, she laid her head on my shoulder. Truly I do not know what made my senses swirl the more, the whiskey or her perfume. Not only perfume, but the scent of herself, as fragrant as any blossom. "What does your Mr. Emerson have to say about love, Dr. Bentwood?" she whispered in a sultry way. "Any wisdom worth repeating? No, don't speak—think of it and I will sense your thoughts. For I do believe such intimacy is possible, when two minds think alike."

It was not difficult to remain silent, as my thoughts were incoherent; mere sensations rather than deliberative thinking, really, and centered upon the precise place where her hand touched so delicately upon my knee. If she sensed the flush that must have turned my face quite pink, she was not offended and leaned, if anything, a little closer. So close I could hear her swallow as she hungrily consumed the whiskey. "Another," she purred, raising her empty glass. "I want more, Dr. Bentwood."

It took all of my will to disengage, and rise from the fainting couch. All of my will to take a deep breath and shake my head and try to regain control of my intense desire; a desire that might lead, I feared, to an act that would compromise my beautiful young companion's virtue. And surely, for all of her sultry talk, and the light play of her fingertips, she could not wish herself compromised. Surely not. We would have, I decided, one more small whiskey, as requested, and this time I would resist sitting so close.

But when I turned, holding out her glass, Lucy had risen from the couch. Her eyes flickered strangely, as if she was about to faint, but before I could react, the moment of weakness passed, and the eyes that looked upon me suddenly smoldered knowingly, as if she really was able to see into my mind, and discern the animal lust within. Her voice was husky, and had a deliberate, insinuating intonation I'd never heard her use before. Almost, it seemed, as if another spoke with her voice.

"Look at me," she commanded, her eyes never leaving mine.

"I am," I responded with a thick tongue.

"No," she insisted. "I mean really look at me." And with that she reached down, grasped the hem of her gown and her ruffled crinoline petticoats, and lifted all to the height of her waist, exposing her naked body to my astonished eyes.

I knew I must look away, but I could not. Surely this was not my Lucy, exposing her pale hips like a woman of the streets, but an aspect of the presence that possessed her; indeed, that possessed us both. The presence had stolen upon us quietly, seductively, insinuating itself into our mutual desire, inflaming our animal passions in the most foul way imaginable. I found myself trapped within a small, dim corner of my own mind, able to share the view through my own eyes, but unable to restrain my own actions. No matter what my conscience might declare, I must look upon her well-formed legs and the enticing shadow that lay between them, limbs that had the soft glimmer of the palest marble in the flickering light of the sperm-oil lamps.

It was not Lucy's voice, but the voice of a brazen succubus that came from her swollen mouth. "Come, sir, let us make the beast," and then she pressed her nakedness against me, and found my lips with her lips. Her fingers deftly peeled away the intervening clothing and in a moment we were joined and thrusting.

There is a place in Cambridge, notorious among the undergraduates, where slatterns fornicate standing up against a piss-stained brick wall, for whatever coins they might receive. No slattern there was ever more bold than Lucy Wattle, or rather the presence that had taken possession of her body that night. We writhed and panted, grunted and pawed each other like animals in rut. She ripped the lace from her bosom and placed my hands there to feel the heat that radiated from her tender flesh. We spoke not in words, but in spasms of carnality, as desperate as if we were drowning in desire.

When I felt I must stop or die of exquisite pleasure, she snarled and bit my shoulder and held me within her. Twice she cried out "Tom!" as if I had been displaced by her dead cousin, but even that did not deter me. Our thrusts became violent and painful, and yet we could not stop, dared not stop, as if stopping would bring death, or something worse than death. Once I saw a flicker of the real Lucy trapped within her eyes, and I wanted to weep with humiliation. Instead I took her from behind, howling like a dog, snapping and spitting and rubbing my face on her back.

That was how Barky the cook found us when he rushed into the parlor, crying, "Please, Dr. Bentwood, it's the Captain. He needs help!" The words were out before he saw us with half our clothing ripped away, madly coupled, and still we did not stop.

I managed to cry out, "Help us, please!" but he did not understand my meaning, how could he? And then when Lucy rose on her haunches and hissed, unfurling her long black serpent tongue to lick him, he dropped his candle and fled from the room; indeed, he fled from the house.

## 5. Revelations

We were both torn and bleeding when Nathaniel Coffin finally put an end to it by dashing us with a bucket of cold water, as if we were a pair of dogs trapped in coitus, which was not far from the truth. The shock brought us back to our senses. Lucy, soaking wet and sobbing with shame, crawled out from under me and tried to cover herself with her soiled petticoats. "Don't cry, cousin, I care not what you do," Nathaniel said, his voice as cold as the water he'd flung upon us. He turned to me with something like restrained contempt. "The Captain is trapped in the tower, Dr. Bentwood, and Jebediah has gone to help him. I fear for them both."

He'd been summoned by Barky, who'd run to the boardinghouse to rouse him. Having done so, the brave cook had then gone to plead again with Benjamin, who thus far had refused to leave his chamber, no matter how Barky begged him, or what dire scenes he painted. I learned that much from the grim-faced Nathaniel as he led me to the tower staircase.

"What you saw back there," I stammered, hurrying along as I set my clothing right, or as right as it could be made, considering. "It wasn't what you think. We were made to do that. Forced against our will."

"I care not," he repeated sharply. At the stairwell door he raised his lamp to see my face and asked, very sternly, "What do you know of this tower curse?"

"Only that it comes from the black gods." I told him. "From the mouth of a slave your father killed, many years ago."

"My father? Kill a slave? Are you mad?"

"Believe what you like," I said. "But we must get your father and Jebediah out of the tower." I was well aware that the presence could make itself known anywhere, if need be, in sawmills and schooners, a hundred miles hence, but it seemed especially powerful within the house. Our only recourse was to remove Captain Coffin from this place, against his will if necessary.

What I did not then share with Nathaniel was my idea that Cash's surviving sons should be separated from their father by as great a distance as possible. The malevolence seemed to flow through him as it was directed toward them, a kind of evil electrical current conducted from father to son, with fatal results for the latter. Send Jebediah off to California, say, and Benjamin to Brazil, and Nathaniel to the Far East, and the presence might be constrained to work its harm on Cash Coffin, and leave his sons alone.

I now believe the idea, born of desperation, had no merit whatsoever, but that night it was fixed in my mind like a shining beacon that pierced a fog of fearful uncertainty. What Barky had forlornly called "hope" came to me in the form of a scheme for the family's survival, even if the patriarch must perish for his sins. Get them out of the tower, out of the house, out of their father's past, their father's life, that was my plan. So intent was I to save my dear friend Jebediah from what seemed an inevitable fate that I was able to overcome the paralyzing shame of what had happened in the parlor. Nathaniel's contempt and Barky's revulsion mattered not—for the present all that mattered was Jeb's salvation.

Strangely enough we heard nothing of the commotion in the tower until Nathaniel opened the door to the stairwell. Then the air suddenly rushed past us, making an unnatural wind that whined and whistled eerily up into the tower. "There, that's him!" said Nathaniel, cocking an ear. "Jeb!" he shouted. "Are you there?" but the only answer was another moan more pitiful than the first.

"Hold on, brother, I'm coming!" Nathaniel cried, taking the steps three at a time while I struggled to keep up.

As it turned out, Jeb was not so near as he'd sounded. We were almost to the second landing before we found him huddled in a corner, shivering in terror, his eyes rolling in his head. My little friend had on nothing but his cotton nightgown, and even in the quivering light of our lamps, it was instantly obvious that he'd soiled himself. "In my chest," he muttered, gasping. "Inside my chest!"

Afraid that his heart might have failed from fright, I put my ear to his chest and heard a reassuring thump. His pulse was very high, of course, but the beat was strong, and betrayed none of the fluttery, hispy gurgles associated with heart failure.

I was gradually made to understand that Jebediah believed something had reached into his chest and squeezed his heart like an overripe peach. That would explain the soiled nightgown, and his pitiful state of fear.

"Will he live?" Nathaniel begged to know, with a concern at least as great as my own.

"We must get him away from this place. As far away as we can, do you understand?"

He nodded. "What about my father?"

I shook my head. "Too dangerous. There's nothing can be done for him."

"What?" Nathaniel demanded angrily. "You'd leave him here?"

"Do what you must," I urged him. "I'll see to Jeb."

At that moment the Captain cried out from the top of the tower, a terrified wail of unbearable anguish that set my teeth on edge. The cry struck Nathaniel like the crack of a whip, driving him up the stairs. A courageous man, considering what he had seen and experienced in the last weeks. Having lost his infant child and the affections of his wife, he was determined not to lose his father, even if it cost his life, or his sanity.

Much to my surprise, Jebediah seemed to understand what had just transpired. "Stop him, Davis!" he begged me. "It wants him. It wants our Nate, don't you see?"

I tried to ignore his imprecations and, taking him up in my arms, began to work my way down the stairwell. My mistake was in underestimating his strength. In stature Jebediah might be no larger than a child, but his strength was equal to my own, and he easily loosed himself from my grasp and at once began to crawl up the stairs, seeking his brother.

I tried to persuade him to flee, but he adamantly refused. "I would not die a coward!" he said with a fierceness that could not be doubted. As if to goad us into action, Nathaniel's shriek echoed down through the stairwell. "No! God help me, no!" he screamed in panic. Then a high keening: "Help me! Please help me!"

My heart sank, and with it all my hopes, for his brother's cry meant that Jebediah would not be deterred, or persuaded from the tower. My own dread was such that my knees felt weirdly unhinged, but what could I do? It was not a question of courage—I had none—but of shame. I'd been shamed in the parlor with Lucy, and could not bear the thought of another shameful act.

I took Jebediah's hand in my own and helped him mount the stairs, saying, "Here, friend, I am with you," and so upward we struggled, as if eager to face our doom.

We were halfway to the next landing when the walls began to drum. Each *boom!* loud enough to make us jump. I stumbled, bumping my shoulder against the wall, and felt an insistent, pulsing rhythm that made my head whirl and my mouth go dry. A crazy phrase began to run through my mind: *the drums are gods, the gods are drums, the drums are gods, the gods are drums* as if the drumming itself was capable of inducing insanity by altering the rhythms of the mind.

*the drums are gods, the gods are drums, the drums are gods, the gods are drums*

"Don't listen!" I cautioned Jeb. "Don't touch the walls!"

Whereupon the drumming increased in volume and intensity, until the air itself began to pound. The lamp's flame jumped with each beat, and that in turn made the shadows twitch with the repeating rhythm. This was the sound of madness. It must have been, because I knew what the drums were saying.

*the drums are gods, the gods are drums, the drums are gods, the gods are drums* chanting, beating, pulsing into the bone marrow.

"Davis!" Jeb whispered hoarsely. "The runner!"

The steps were covered with a rug or runner tacked to each tread. Blood oozed from under the runner, squishy and sticky under my boots. Poor Jeb was in agony, trying to scuff the blood away, but only smearing more upon his twisted little feet. "Ahhh!" he cried in panic. "Get it off me! Off! Off!"

Nathaniel cried out again, and that brought my friend to his senses. We hurried up the stairwell, drawn by the scream, trying to ignore the hideous sensation of stepping on the blood-swollen rug, unable to sustain our shudders of revulsion. And all the while the lamp flickered in rhythm, the shadows twitched, the walls pulsed, the air condensed, expanded, condensed as the drums kept chanting *the drums are gods, the gods are drums, the drums are gods, the gods are drums* in strings of repeating rhythms that entwined, overlapped, writhed like the black snake tongue that had protruded from Lucy's blood-red lips *the drums are gods, the gods are drums, the drums are gods, the gods are drums* the entire structure of the tower booming, shaking, booming with the drums; the horrible, maddening drums.

We found Nathaniel on the last landing before the top, his screams still echoing as we made the turn. Which made no sense, as he was sprawled insensible on the floor, with a gash above his left eye that had been bleeding for several minutes, at the very least. I helped him sit up and pressed a hankie to the wound, which did not appear to be serious. "Tell them to stop," he implored me. And when I asked "who," he said, "The awful drums."

*the drums are gods, the gods are drums, the drums are gods, the gods are drums* on and on, never ceasing, always changing, weaving and unweaving, writhing and doubling back upon itself.

"Nathaniel! Look at me!" I said, holding the lamp, so I could see that his eyes still functioned, the lack being a sure sign of concussion or worse. "What happened?"

He shrugged, muttering, "I don't know. Something came out of the dark, just as the drumming started. That's all I remember."

"So it wasn't you screaming for help?"

Nathaniel shook his head.

"But I recognized your voice," said Jeb.

"Father called out, not me. We must go to him," and then to me. "We must!"

I knew then that the Captain could not be left behind, even if he put us in peril. "Trust nothing," I warned them. "We must stick together. We will link hands, find the Captain, and then all of us will leave together, is that agreed? Nathaniel?"

"Agreed."

We each took one of Jebediah's hands and, holding our lamps aloft, advanced to the top of the stairwell, as the treads pulsed and bled beneath us *the drums are gods, the gods are drums, the drums are gods, the gods are drums*, never ceasing.

The Captain's door was wide open, which I did not take as a good sign. We stepped through the door and all at once the drumming ceased and the blessed silence nearly made me weep with gratitude. Indeed, it was unnaturally peaceful within Captain Coffin's solitary chamber, so much so that I at first assumed he had fled the place, or left by some other means of egress.

Nathaniel and I raised our lamps with considerable trepidation, only to discover that the old man was sound asleep on his couch. The coon cat lay curled on his chest, wide-eyed as he protected his master. "Scat," said Nathaniel, but the great beast took offense and rose up, perched on its bandaged hindquarters, ready to spar.

The disturbance awakened Cash Coffin, and the old man sat up groggily, stroking the cat that clung to his lap. "Nate? Jeb? What has happened?" he asked, as if expecting the worst.

His two sons assured him that all was as well as could be expected, considering, but that he must come with us, down out of the tower, before the drumming resumed and tore the walls to pieces. "Drumming?" he said. "What drumming?"

"You must have heard, or felt it, even in your sleep," I said.

"I know what drums are, sir, and I heard none."

A strange thought struck me, and I went back through the doorway. Sure enough *the drums are gods, the gods are drums, the drums are gods, the gods are drums* and then once again the blessed silence as I returned to the sanctuary of the Captain's chamber.

"Father, did you not call for help?" Jeb asked him.

"I did not."

"We've been tricked," I said. "It wants you here. It wants the sons together with the father."

"What should we do?" Nathaniel asked, with real fear in his voice.

"Leave at once," I said. "Captain Coffin, if you wish to join us, please come along. But I believe Nathaniel and Jeb are in great danger if they stay."

The old man was shaking his head even before I got the words out. "It waits for me below," he said. "If I leave this room, I won't survive the hour."

Nathaniel was now gazing at me with palpable distrust. "Why does the doctor want us to leave, hey? Think on that, Jebediah. Wants us to leave the safety of Father's chamber. Why's he want us out there with the drums?"

Jebediah looked even more stricken, and begged his brother not to distrust me, after all I'd done for all concerned. In response Nathaniel rose to his full height and shoved his lamp nearer to my face, as if checking for signs of deception. "Didn't do nothing for Sarah, did he, until it was too late, and then what he saved was half a child, not my wife."

"What are you saying, Nate?"

"Laid his hands upon her, he did. Maybe that's what made her simple, not the drowning. When did drowning ever make a person simple, hey? Drown and you die. There's never an in-between, except when Dr. Bentwood lays his hands upon you."

The physician in me was wondering if the blow on the head had precipitated Nathaniel's irrational rage—the effect was not uncommon—but the more sensible man knew enough to draw back, out of range of his powerful fists.

"Answer me, Doctor," he demanded, advancing. "Tell us your true name. Is it Bentwood? Emerson? Or is it some other impersonation? More like Beelzebub!"

I was at the point of making a stand, and having to defend myself, when the floor of the tower shuddered violently beneath us, and the whole structure began to sway perilously, as if forced by a strong wind—and yet there was no wind.

"It comes!" cried Captain Coffin.

While the others clung to whatever they could grab hold of, I crawled to the doorway and pulled myself through the opening, out into the stairwell. The terrible noise of the drums was nearly overpowered by the cracking and splitting of timbers. Spikes and nails wrenched free with shrieks that were nearly human. Treads exploded from the stairs as the entire framework of the tower twisted under the pressure of imminent collapse.

We must get out or be crushed. There was no longer any need to persuade my companions; they could see with their own eyes that the tower could not long survive. In the panic of confusion Captain Coffin became somewhat addled, crying, "We are wrecked! All hands to the boats!" and barreled out the door with his cat cradled protectively in his arms, as if diving into a stormy sea. He was not entirely delusional, because he recognized the stairwell for what it was, and cautioned his sons to avoid the missing treads, and cling to the walls as we descended.

"Stick together, boys," he urged them. "Remember who you are, and where you came from."

Cash hadn't the physical stature of his full-grown sons, but he possessed a remarkable strength for a man his age. I saw him lift a heavy, broken support beam with one hand, and shove it to the side, clearing the way down to the landing.

Behind us the glass of the tower windows shattered, and the air from below began to rush up the stairwell, seeking escape. The wind seemed to dampen or carry away the pounding of the drums, and very gradually it subsided, until it was nothing more than a vibration under our feet, or felt in the hands where we clung to the walls, finding our way down.

Both Nathaniel and I had managed to retain our lamps, but even so we had to feel our way, not trusting the ever-shifting shadows, which often obscured gaps in the stairway. Our progress was torturously slow, and the tower continued to slowly disintegrate around us, twisting and swaying as if struggling to unnail itself.

The Captain stopped us, raising his head to sniff the air. "There's a fog coming," he announced.

I assumed this was due to his addled state, that he was confusing the tower's wooded interior with the ship cabins where'd he'd spent most of his life. And then I, too, got a whiff of the sea, or rather of the seaweedy smells of the harbor, and a moment later there it was, wafting through the broken rafters and beams, rising up the stairwell like smoke.

Fog. Thick fog. Fog that could not be penetrated by our lamps. Fog so dense I could not make out Jebediah, though I had him by the hand.

I heard Cash Coffin say, "It thinks the fog will make us afraid, and stop us moving. Never mind the fog, we know the way down. Fog's no worse than the dark, if you trust your compass."

"What do we have for weapons, Father?" I heard Nathaniel hiss, his voice made strange by the clinging mist.

"My old flintlock pistol, the very one that clubbed him to the deck," the old man said with a kind of fierce pride.

"Pass it to me, Father, and I shall lead the way."

I heard a fumbling, and then a grunt of satisfaction from Nathaniel, and was relieved to know the Captain was at last disarmed. Doubtless bullets would not be effective against our invisible adversary, since you cannot shoot what you cannot see, but now at least the old man could not wound one of us, or himself. I did wonder, though, if the ancient weapon might have some power to repel the presence, and if it was the old pistol and not the tower chamber that had thus far kept Cassius Coffin safe from his adversary.

Small comfort in the fog, in the dark, with a building collapsing all around us, and the very steps beneath our feet sliding away like pats of butter on a hot fry pan. With every passing moment my terror increased, and my eyes began to invent nightmare shapes in the fog. There a face, there a coiled snake, there a chasm that did not, could not exist, and yet it frightened me all the more.

I waved my lamp, wielding it before me, desperately trying to penetrate the mist. I could not help but think of the fog that had clung to *Raven*, in that hour before the schooner was destroyed, and Tom Coffin so hideously impaled. Truly, so excited was my imagination, and so palpable my fear, that it would not have surprised me if a ship had suddenly loomed before us, though we were a thousand yards or more from the harbor. The fog made anything seem possible. Let your mind invent whatever fed its fear, and the fog would give it shape.

It was all I could do to keep from screaming. Jebediah must have felt my growing desperation, because he gave my hand a reassuring squeeze and said, "It can't be far." I could feel his hand, hear his voice, but for all I could see, he had ceased to exist. Was I the same to him, a phantom connected by touch? I wondered if this was what it was like to be a ghost, haunting a world you could not see, and which could not see you.

On the step below, not a foot away, I heard the old man grunt. "I hear a strange thing," he said, and sure enough a new sound had insinuated itself into the confusion of noises as the tower struggled to tear itself apart. Between the shrieking of the nails and the creak of the timbers there came a low animal growling.

Once I heard an African lion, caged for the circus, and turned to see it eyeing me balefully, the growl catching in its mighty throat. It was an old lion, suffering from the mange, and no doubt in pain, but it let me know that but for the cage I'd have been its meat. I was ten years old, or thereabouts, and pretty fearless for my age, but that lion frightened me, and I ran from the circus all the way home, imagining that it might escape and follow me, bounding over the brick and cobbled streets of Beacon Hill, hungry for boy.

This was not a lion's growl, exactly, but something like it, with a similar guttural power. Whatever it was, it seemed to be coming from not far below us, just around the next turn of the stairs, and I froze on the creaking steps, not wanting to advance, not willing to retreat.

"It's a trick," I heard Jebediah say. "It doesn't want us to leave the tower. We must ignore it and go forward."

The growl purred louder, as if in anticipation. Hungry for us. I would sooner have walked into a hail of bullets than go forward, toward that angry animal growl, but above me the timbers were collapsing. The entire structure settled to one side, pressing me against the wall, while under my feet the stair rafters shifted and sagged.

"Hurry!" Nathaniel urged us, and so we stumbled down, feeling with our feet.

I very nearly lost my grip on Jeb's hand, my own was so slick with cold sweat. Our urgency was such that I was unaware until much later that my face had been slashed by exposed nails, or perhaps a splinter of snapping wood. There was blood in the air, I knew that much, and I was terrified that the scent of it was drawing the growling closer. A growling so large and powerful that it shivered its way into my chest, and made it hurt to breathe.

"Look!"

A glow approached from below, dipping and swaying as if trying to find us in the fog. Not a single glow, but two, it seemed, twin orbs searching for the source of fresh-cut blood. Slowly a shadow condensed around the orbs of light, and the black beast took shape. The orbs were eyes, yellow and terrible, and the shape was neither man nor animal, but something of each, and hideous, like the beast of Revelation, come at last to proclaim the end of days.

The growl became a thunderous voice: "AND HE CRIED MIGHTILY WITH A STRONG VOICE, SAYING, BABYLON THE GREAT IS FALLEN, AND IS BECOME THE

INHABITATION OF DEVILS, AND THE HOLD OF
EVERY FOUL SPIRIT, AND A CAGE OF EVERY
UNCLEAN AND HATEFUL BIRD. FOR ALL NATIONS
HAVE DRUNK THE WINE OF THE WRATH OF FORNI-
CATION, AND THE KINGS OF THE EARTH HAVE COM-
MITTED FORNICATION WITH HER, AND THE
MERCHANTS OF THE EARTH ARE WAXED RICH
THROUGH THE ABUNDANCE OF HER DELICACIES.
LET THEM SLAY EACH OTHER, ALL OF THEM, AND
CHOKE ON THE BLOOD OF THEIR TONGUES, LET
THEM ALL DIE FOR A THOUSAND GENERATIONS,
UNTIL THE DUST OF THEIR DUST IS FORGOTTEN."

It coiled then, as if readying itself to spring. A black, mis-
shapen monstrosity with glowing eyes and a growling, sul-
furous voice that became a great roaring of wind, driving the
mist before it, mounting the buckled stairway with an inhuman agility.

I heard Nathaniel cry out: "Back! Let us pass!"

With a roar it leaped for him. A hot spark flashed, the pistol roared back, and the roar became a scream of pain, a whelp
that sounded almost human. Indeed, it was human, for as the
mist suddenly cleared, sucked upward by the wind, we saw
Benjamin collapsed on the stairway, an oil lantern in one hand,
and his Bible clutched to his breast. The bullet had pierced the
Bible, then torn a great, sputtering hole in his throat, and his
life bled away in but a few moments, with each beat of his
dying heart.

I rushed to his side, but there was nothing to be done. He
tried to speak, choked weakly, and then the spark of life
departed.

Nathaniel gently pried the lantern from his brother's hand
and stood up, holding it out. "Father, I have killed him," he
said, in a small and terrible voice. "I've killed poor Ben, who
came to save us."

"You thought he was the beast," said the old man. "We all did. It tricked us."

"I can't bear it," said Nathaniel, looking away from us. "I won't bear it."

With that he lifted the lantern above his head and emptied the reservoir of oil upon himself, soaking his beard and shirt. A blue flame ran down his arm and in an instant the oil ignited.

"No!" Jebediah screamed.

I lurched to grab him, thinking I might muffle the flames with my coat, but he deliberately took one step back and plunged through a gap in the steps, falling out of reach. He lay in the rubble below with his head and shoulders on fire, and did nothing to save himself as his face began to melt away.

It was all I could do to seize Jeb by his nightgown and haul him back from the edge as he clawed and cried and watched his brother burning.

The horror was not done with us. As the smoke rose in black billows from beneath the broken staircase, as the splintered timbers caught flame, and the fire commenced to take hold of the building, the old man suddenly clutched his throat and fell to his knees, his eyes rolling upward. His body convulsed and a wet gargling scream issued from his mouth.

Beside him his great green-eyed cat howled piteously, tail and hair erect.

"Davis! Do something!"

I let go of Jebediah and threw myself on the old man, trying to pry loose his hands. But the convulsions had locked his fingers in place, in a death grip around his own throat. As I desperately pried, fighting to get a purchase, his eyes bulged horribly and his lips curled back in an awful grin. A lump of flesh shot from his mouth, followed by a great black clot, and I knew then that Cassius Coffin had bitten off his tongue, and was choking on his own blood.

*Let them choke on the blood of their tongues, let them all die for a thousand generations, until the dust of their dust is forgotten.* With a *whoosh*! his hair caught fire, and before I could back away his flesh began to swell and blacken, splitting open to reveal the white bones of his skull. And yet something of him still lived, enough to comprehend what was happening, and to suffer. As his flesh was destroyed, his living eyes continued to look at me, and I saw in them an awareness that was unbearable, but nevertheless must be borne. He knew everything that had happened and everything that was to come. He knew what had been taken from him: all he had made himself, all he had bequested to his sons, and their sons, all had been destroyed, and he would carry that knowledge to the grave and beyond, forever and ever. Death would bring no relief, but the misery of eternity.

Cash Coffin had written down the curse in his own hand, in the true log of his slave ship, then waited anxiously for years, until at last it came to pass: *You will be cursed and your sons will be cursed and the womb of your wife will be cursed, until there are sons no more, and everything and everyone you ever loved will perish from the earth.*

I knew of the curse, and believed it inescapable, but duty compelled me to do whatever I could to save the last of the Coffins, and myself. And so I picked up my little friend, who was as soiled and bloody and helpless as a newborn child, and ran straight into the flames.

# Epilogue

*July 2, 1863*

There is little more to tell. We are encamped here on a field near Gettysburg, in Pennsylvania, among the companies of the Army of the Potomac, readying ourselves for war. The reader—if ever there is to be a reader—will know that I survived the great fire that consumed the Coffin house, and was later spread by evil, spark-insinuating wind to the houses and buildings below, leaping from wood-shingled roof to wood-shingled roof, until all of White Harbor was set aflame, and its final, beautiful agony reflected in the cold waters that lapped the shore. The slow but relentless progress of the conflagration was such that all the inhabitants of the village escaped the flames, except those already lost in the tower.

I first carried Jebediah outside and rolled us both in the snow, to damp the flames that had singed us. Then I ran back inside only to discover that Barky had already escorted Miss Lucy to safety, which was a great relief, and then returned again to rescue what he could of our belongings before being forced out by the heat and smoke.

When I later found Lucy on the road, hurrying away, she was wearing a black, fur-lined cloak, and had the Captain's enormous, green-eyed cat cradled in her arms. I begged her forgiveness for my shameful carnal acts, and promised to marry her, if she would have me. At first she would not meet my eyes, and then when I implored her to respond, she confessed she would rather throw herself into the fire than marry a monster like me, and if she found herself with child she would have it torn from her womb—never, never would she bring forth a child of our unholy union.

To my utter despair, I found that I could not disagree. "What will you do? How will you live?" When she would not at first respond, I suggested that she might seek out Mrs. Stanton, and secure a place with her.

"Mrs. Stanton is an admirable woman, but she is not family," Lucy said, as if appalled by my ignorance, or quite possibly by my very existence, which she now found so offensive. She vowed to abide with Sarah, who now had need of a companion and caretaker. "We shall live as spinsters, simple Sarah and I. The children will call us witches, and taunt us. But we will sit on our porch as the world goes by, and laugh at the folly of men." With that she walked away and passed out of my life forever.

As to myself, there is little of further interest. I joined with my old friend Colonel Chamberlain, and have followed him dutifully, sawing off whatever shattered limbs they bring me, always expecting to find one of Jebediah's young Harvard Yard tormentors under my knife. If that happens it must be soon, for I am convinced a bullet waits for me in the fight about to commence.

Jebediah disagrees, or rather the one who speaks in his place disagrees. "You will live to be an old, old man," he says, knowing how much I dread the thought. "You will die alone, far from the field of glory, and your only friend will be Monbasu. You will come to love me, and to love yourself."

Then he laughs and laughs.

The little man has followed me into the army, acting as my assistant, although the men say he is more like my familiar, and try to keep their distance from the "mad dwarf." For this I cannot blame them. The presence who dwells within my old friend, and has done since the night of the fire, speaks in many languages, Spanish, Portuguese, French, Dutch, and the several dialects of Dahomey, and his laughter is more cruel and cutting than any of my instruments. It amuses him to act as my slave, and fetch my cocoa, and pick the vermin from my bedroll. He calls me master, but we both know who the real master is, and who the slave.

Tomorrow a great battle begins, a battle that may decide the war, and our little band of soldiers must defend a bluff against rebel forces that are certain to overrun us. Colonel Chamberlain believes that our fate is already decided, and that he himself is sure to be killed, but he will not be dissuaded from his duty. Nor I from mine. For I know now that the whole nation is cursed, and we must cleanse ourselves with the blood of the righteous. Only then may our chains be broken and our souls set free.

Only then will the horror end.

*Captain Davis Bentwood,*
*Surgeon, 20th Maine, V Corps*
*Army of the Potomac*

# AFTERWORD BY THE EDITOR

There is no record of a Captain Bentwood being killed in action while with the 20th Maine. Premonition of death was common among Civil War soldiers, and many who were haunted by such premonitions survived, or like the heroic Joshua Chamberlain, "died of their wounds" at an advanced age. Chamberlain was a former schoolteacher whose brilliant strategic maneuvers at Little Round Top turned the tide at Gettysburg, and secured a victory that was the first death knell of the Confederacy. Although at the time of the battle Chamberlain sincerely believed he would never survive the war, he did, and went on to be governor of Maine, and lived to be eighty-five years old, much honored and beloved. What his relationship to Davis Bentwood might have been remains unknown, although there is a curious entry in the governor's daily journal of 1871, noting that Governor Chamberlain made an official visit to the village of White Harbor, recently rebuilt, to cut the ribbon at a new sardine cannery. "Governor had tea with his old friend Dr. B. and his dwarf, and spoke of Africa." That is all.

Whether or not this was Davis Bentwood, or if he was at that date still accompanied by Jebediah Coffin, or how long they both may have survived, is unknown at this time.

*Rodman Philbrick*
*Kittery, Maine*